CW00832147

BLOOD

SWORN & DEFIED

DUET

MARIA LUIS

THE BLOOD DUET

Sworn & Defied

MARIA LUIS

Alkmini Books, LLC

For those who take cover in the darkness, the shadows will always keep you safe.

A Note on Tarot

Though Tarot is written into the very heart of Lincoln and Avery's story, I want to stress that there is no one way to interpret the cards nor is there a universal deck.

Avery reads from Thoth (the major difference being the use of the term "Disks" instead of "Pentacles") because it's the deck that my mother used to teach me Tarot. However, in formatting the Blood Duet omnibus, I opted for a more generalized deck. What lies ahead is an interactive reading experience that I hope you'll enjoy!

And, in case you're in need of a simplified breakdown of Tarot before diving into *Sworn*, don't worry—I've got you covered.

Understanding Tarot in Thirty Seconds or Less

Major Arcana: While no one card holds ultimate power, anything included under Major Arcana certainly packs a big punch. These cards reflect major shifts in your life, long-term, and often symbolize events that are completely out of your control.

Minor Arcana: Each suit includes what my mother fondly refers to as "royalty" cards (i.e., Knight, Page, Queen, etc). Overall, Minor Arcana symbolizes events that are actually in your control to change or influence. If Major Arcana shows you the big picture, Minor Arcana represents the day to day events impacting your life.

The Four Suits:

Wands: This suit is all about action, invention, and energy.

Swords: These group of cards indicate mental challenges, both the strength and weakness of your own mind but also of those around you.

Cups: Love, of course. More specifically, Cup cards reflect your emotions, intuition, and relationships.

Disks/Pentacles: These cards are most often associated with work, finances, and wealth.

A Reversed Card should be interpreted as the opposite or even the negative meaning of the card. If a card is upside down, be sure to take note—a plot twist may be ahead.

SWORN

MARIA LUIS

I bow to no man.

The words are tattooed on my skin, just as they're branded on my heart.

But I never planned for Sergeant Lincoln Asher, a man as deceptive as he is cold. His dominance sets my teeth on edge . . . and my body on fire. He won't stop until I'm his, but I'm not his to take.

My secrets bind me—and blind me.

I live in the shadows of New Orleans. Hidden and protected in the underworld I call home. I know who I am.

I vow never to kneel before a man...

Save one.

And he will be my downfall.

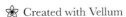

To Panic! At The Disco:
Thank you for the amazing-ness that is Don't Threaten Me With A Good Time. I'm pretty sure the Blood Duet wouldn't have been written without this song - to date, I've listened to it 867 times, which means…2,887 minutes later, it only seemed right that this book be dedicated to you, since you've (technically) been along for the journey anyway. No song could have been a better fit for Lincoln & Avery.

Good job, honey.

NINE OF SWORDS

Prologue

AVERY

The death was not mine to see.

The tremble in my knees told me that.

The slick sweat on my palms told me that.

The—

Heavy boots moved along the corridor, echoing against the hardwood flooring, and I sank to the ground, behind a wall, away and out of sight. My arms locked around my shins, my crooked nose buried between my bent knees.

Don't breathe. Don't breathe. Don't—

"Where is she?"

That voice.

It was sickening the way that I found a measure of calm in hearing him speak. Sickening because he'd given the order to have Momma murdered—calm because his voice had been the center of my world since I'd entered preschool. Helping me into my school uniform, reminding me to brush my teeth at night, pouring me a bowl of cereal in the morning when Momma slept in too late, the vodka bottle cradled to her chest like a newborn babe.

He killed her, and he'll kill you too.

3

He would. I knew he would.

I lifted my face from the safety of my jean-clad knees and surveyed my familiar surroundings.

"How the *fuck* do you not know where she is?"

"She cracked open the window in her bedroom," said an unfamiliar male voice. "What the fuck did you want me to do? Follow her out and drag her back in here? Or finish off the job you wanted from me and kill your wife?"

Breathe, breathebreathebreathe.

I'd come back for Momma after the man had locked my door. I'd heard her screams. I'd heard her pain. I'd been halfway across the front lawn, already circling to the other side of the house to another entrance, when I'd heard the gunshot that drove me to my knees and pulled the vomit from my body.

"Find her."

"Is she worth all this? You've done her mother in. You that much of a sick bastard that you want your thirteen-year-old stepdaughter dead for shit that—"

The sound of flesh hitting the wall sounded like the pistol used against Momma.

Loud.

Startling.

Furious.

"If I *wanted* your fucking opinion, I'd ask for it. You hear me?"

There was no fight, no struggle.

Only the harsh sound of my breath quickening against my interlaced fingers, and then the soft, dangerous laugh of a man who welcomed death. "You gonna kill me, too, Jay? You going to use the same gun on me that I used on your wife? You gonna fuck me up because I let your precious stepdaughter slip away?"

Nothing.

Nothing.

Nothing.

And then the blinding crack of a pistol erupted like thunder across a hot New Orleans summer day.

I felt that inferno.

I felt the heat and the rage and the fear of the unnamed man who hadn't chased me, even though I'd spotted his silhouette in my bedroom window.

This time, I didn't throw up.

I scrambled to my feet, using the opportunity of the man's death and my stepfather's distraction to make my escape from the only home I'd ever known. I ran. And I ran.

And I didn't stop until the soles of my bare feet were scraped raw from the cement, and there were no thoughts left of Momma, or my stepfather, or the man who'd let me live.

There was nothingness—a black void that swept over me and sucked me down into the abyss.

It wasn't until the sun peaked out over the horizon the following morning that I realized I'd found harbor just outside the iron gates of Lafayette Cemetery #1 on Washington Avenue.

I'd entered my own slice of purgatory, just like Mrs. Holland had taught us about in religion class last week. But this time, I had no indulgences of my own to buy my way into heaven.

I had nothing.

I had no one.

And I suspected that if I wanted to live another day, I had to *become* no one.

THE MOON

MAJOR ARCANA

ONE

Avery

TWELVE YEARS LATER

I n the bowel of New Orleans, I was the gatekeeper to the no-longer living.

The woman seated across from me leaned in, elbow resting on my rickety fold-up table. One manicured finger tapped the Death card, little puffs of smoke curling from her mouth as she sucked on a Marlboro Red like it was something a whole lot dirtier.

"I'm gonna die, aren't I?" Her cheeks hollowed out around the cigarette as she spoke. "This right here? Skeleton can't be any good, Miss Washington, can't be any damn good."

Tarot was an art I'd picked up from the other readers in Jackson Square years earlier. For me, it was a means to an end. I lacked the Sight that my peers possessed in spades. I lacked their ability to look at a card and see a tangled web of lust, lies, and love—I saw the cards' illustrations, knew their meanings from years of study, and wasn't opposed to taking a little creative liberty.

The better the reading, the higher the tip, which nicely

padded the conservative fee I charged to encourage people to come to my table as opposed to one of the others.

In other words, survival of the fittest.

"No, ma'am," I purred in a throaty voice, "not death."

Her shoulders sagged with relief.

"Not always, anyway." Her eyes went wide and, hiding a victorious grin, I shuffled the Thoth deck and selected another card from its midst. "The Death card symbolizes regrowth, a new change. The shedding of the old and the gradual shift into the new." Turning the fresh card onto its back, settling it next to Death, I offered a genuine smile. "Lust, ma'am. Are you newly single?"

The woman's mouth dropped open, her cigarette dangling. Even within the shadows of the towering St. Louis Cathedral, there was no mistaking her pink cheeks and rapid blinking. "Divorced." She plucked the Red from her mouth and stomped it out on the cobblestones beside my table. "How'd you know that?"

Because I've seen you before.

Not *her*, obviously, but women like her. Men, too. They all carried that faraway gaze—some more cynical than others—that spoke to the man-made hell called marriage. A trap society whispered that you needed, that you should crave above all else.

I didn't crave marriage.

Hell, I barely craved men at all—living on the streets for most of my teenage years meant that my breasts had been pawed at by disgusting assholes, my ass grabbed, and I'd been told one too many times that I was such a pretty girl and wouldn't I look so damn good on my knees?

I'd be dead before I ever got on my knees for a man.

I hummed a sound of faux excitement in my throat, stroking a finger along the crisp edge of Lust. "The cards, ma'am. You've clearly come to N'Orleans for something new. You wish to get lost, and yes"—I pointed to the first card I'd selected, the Queen of Disks—"you're prepared to spend some money on what you want. Disks represent external items. Material possessions, money, that sort of thing. But I would caution you against leaning too heavily into lust."

Her eyes tracked the motion of my hands as I packed the cards against one palm and set them all down. "I want to be wanted." Her hushed tone hardly concealed her wistfulness. "I want to *feel* again."

"Don't we all?"

At that, she blinked and pulled back, arms locking around her belly. Her chin tipped to the right, her gaze flicking to the line of Tarot readers bordering the square. It was a Saturday night, which meant money. Lots of it, if we did our job correctly—and clearly, I'd failed to live up to expectation.

She wanted the lies, the promise that she'd meet her "one and only" during her time in New Orleans. She just plain old *wanted*, and either I played the game and walked away with cash in my pocket or I went back to my apartment and stressed over making rent this month.

Put aside the guilt and tell her what she wants to hear.

Do it, Avery, just do it.

Self-hatred settled like soured milk in my stomach, as did the heavy reminder that I was no one. I had no family and few friends. I left little trace of my existence, save for the sight of my face as I strolled through the French Quarter. Runners like me were a dime a dozen in New Orleans, but even knowing that didn't erase my bitterness for what could have been.

Avery Washington was just one alias I'd chosen in the last twelve years. I'd been Samantha Lovelace for most of my teens—a naïve little idiot who placed her trust in all the wrong people. Ruby Matheson during the year that I'd turned twenty—a little more jaded, but no less of an idiot.

It took me awhile to realize that people sought to protect their own interests, and no one gave a damn about mine.

I'd become Avery Washington ever since I'd caught sight of a suspicious-looking man following me home one night, sing-songing my name like he wouldn't mind taking me into a dark alley and abusing my body for his pleasure. He'd been a stranger who stalked the readers in the square before being arrested on an assault charge. Even after the cuffs were locked around his wrists, I'd been terrified to walk the shadowed streets alone. But there'd been no one to protect me then just as there was no one to protect me now.

A name change did only so much.

Ice skittered up my spine, and the self-hatred slipped away.

I met the woman's eyes, ignoring the flash of hope in their depths. "You'll meet him." Her soft gasp bounced off my steel heart. "You'll meet him exactly as you envision, and you'll be *wanted*, ma'am, just as you dream." With hardened resolve, I tapped the Queen of Disks card once more. "But love will continue to elude you if you focus on the material things. Seek more than just the external, and you'll discover the man who waits for you."

"But where will I *find* him?"

It was with a sense of good timing that the bells of St. Louis Cathedral chimed on the hour. Midnight.

"Church. You'll meet him at church."

The woman's lips peeled back in a grimace, revealing crowded front teeth. "I don't *go* to church."

"If you want to meet this man, you will."

She didn't like that, I could tell. But aside from casting

a quick glance at the imposing structure behind her, she didn't fight back. Her fingers dipped into her purse, scrounging around for what I hoped was my tip.

A crinkled dollar bill fluttered to the table.

Clearly, I shouldn't have taken inspiration from my surroundings.

"Have a good night."

She didn't return the sentiment, only drew up her jacket and hunched her shoulders as she skirted around the other readers. I watched as she gave a little jump when a homeless man sat up on a wrought-iron bench and stuck out a tin can in her direction.

I didn't need to hear her to know that she'd responded with something offensive.

The man reared back, can to his chest, his expression lost to the moonless night sky, and I felt the familiar stirring of anger.

I had been that man, begging for a dime, a sandwich, a scrap of hope.

My knees cracked as I stood, my flimsy lawn chair teetering on its hind legs before I settled a hand on the dirty fabric and righted it again.

Don't. Don't go over there and get in someone else's business.

The woman's voice carried on the upwind breeze: "Don't *touch* me, asshole."

Yeah, there was no way I could let that slide. It was one thing to ignore the man, to step around him and lift your chin and pretend he didn't exist.

Another thing entirely to make eye contact and act like a dick.

"Avery."

Involuntarily, my shoulders twitched at the sound of my name coming off the lips of my regular neighbor, Tabitha. Didn't matter that I'd been "Avery" for three years now, sometimes I still didn't answer when called. *You aren't Laurel anymore, just remember that.*

Easier said than done.

"You might want to go home."

"Why?" I met Tabby's gaze. "You hear something?"

She touched her chest, right over her permit, and then pointed in the same direction my client had taken.

The woman had moved on from the homeless man and had stopped to talk to a different guy. The flickering gas lamps did nothing to hide his imposing physique—tall, broad, narrow waist. He stood like a soldier or a cop or *anyone*, really, that I did not want on my radar.

With one hand latched onto his arm, the woman turned back and . . . pointed. At *me*.

Oh, shit.

"Get out of here, Ave."

Yeah, Tabby didn't have to tell me twice.

That was sort of the thing about operating a Tarot card stand illegally on Jackson Square. I wouldn't recommend the no-permit stint, but hey, I'd managed to do well enough for the last few years.

The pin of my fake badge stuck me in the breast as I jerked my chair closed and shoved the table's accessories into my backpack. Candle (unlit), Tarot cards, crystals, pendulum. The backpack's zipper sounded unnaturally loud when it jammed, and I tugged, and—*screw it.*

I slung the strap over one shoulder.

Grabbed the chair by one pointy leg.

Made a hasty swipe of the plush-velvet tablecloth and tossed the heavy fabric over my arm.

Time to go.

Implausible as it was, the air seemed to thicken as he stepped up behind me like some sort of crazy scene out of a horror movie.

A masculine hand landed on my shoulder, fingers broad and strong.

I didn't scream—I'm *not* a screamer.

But all words stuck in my throat, and then there was nothing but the sound of his baritone drawl.

"Going somewhere?"

TEN OF SWORDS

TWO

Lincoln

She looked like she'd seen a ghost.

Then again, she'd spotted me—and I was as close to dead as a man with a pulse could be.

"Going somewhere?"

Her shoulder tensed under my hand, and I pulled back. I was a heartless bastard, but even I didn't get my rocks off on frightening the vulnerable. And this girl . . . I lowered my gaze to her trim form. She was thin, almost too thin, though her loose-fitting skirt and the equally billowy shirt didn't do her any favors.

If she had even the slightest hint of curves under all that fabric, I couldn't tell worth a damn.

"In a hurry?"

Fingers turning white as she clutched the strap of her backpack, she faced me. Full-on. Eyes on my face, unwavering, chin tipped up at an angle.

Fuck. Me.

Her body might be lost to the tent of her clothes, but her face was another story. Gorgeous, despite the drawn lines of her dark brows and her pursed, angry mouth. That mouth of hers was fantasy material—full and pink and lush, the sort men spent their nights jerking off to in the hope that, one day, they'd wake up and have it wrapped around their cock.

From the way her hazel eyes flashed, I'd venture a guess and say *that* particular fantasy was nothing but a pipe dream.

"I have an appointment."

Her throaty voice jerked my eyes back down to her mouth. Jesus, but the sound was like velvet. Tempting. Sexy. Haunting. The perfect melody to hear after a night of back-clawing, hard sex.

Shaking myself from the vivid reverie, I focused on the anger. Her anger. I'd long ago learned to live with my own. "You have an appointment at midnight?" I'd been a cop long enough to recognize even the best bull-shitters. "Really."

Hazel eyes narrowed on me, her mouth flat-lining another degree. "You going to arrest me?"

Something about the way she'd ID'ed me, even with a nondescript jacket drawn over my Class B's, made me feel as though she'd had her fair of run-ins with the NOPD in the past. To say nothing of the fact that her jaded attitude mirrored my own.

Slipping my hands into the front pockets of my navy-blue, department-issued slacks, I cocked my head toward the other vendors. "There've been a few calls about harassment lately. Juveniles, mostly." I paused, waiting for her to cut me some slack. One second passed, and then the moment bled into another. On my third breath, I demolished the silence, like a roach beneath my shoe, and spoke: "Wanted to do a quick walk-through of the square before heading home for the night. Make sure no one was having any trouble."

Not even a hint of a relieved smile softened her expression.

I didn't blame her for the suspicion. Hell, there wasn't a single soul on this planet that I trusted not to stab me in the back the moment I looked away. It came with the territory of living double lives—of playing two sides of the same coin, always fully aware that one wrong move could end with my throat slit and my body tossed into the swamp.

It was the reality of my life.

At thirty-four, I knew nothing else.

When the woman turned, dismissing me, I withdrew my wallet from my back pocket. Flipped it open and removed my police identification card like that would help me earn some street cred with her. "Sergeant Lincoln Asher." I held out the ID, the back of my hand accidentally grazing her breast.

Or where her breast *ought* to be, but again, her tent-like shirt concealed everything.

It *didn't* conceal the way her jaw worked tightly, though. Nor the hard swallow that slid down the length of her neck before she snapped, "I don't care who you are."

No, she clearly didn't.

The feeling wasn't mutual. And that was . . . unusual, really fucking unusual.

The ID went back into my wallet, and the wallet back into my pocket. "You been reading cards for a while?"

"If you're going to arrest me, Sergeant, just do it."

"I'm not going to arrest you." Although maybe there was a reason why I should. *No one* put up a fuss like this woman had in the span of five minutes unless she'd done something bad and more than a little illegal. "So," I said, drawing out the *O*, "you read."

As if resigned to her fate, she dropped her backpack

onto the crooked table and then let the chair clatter to her feet. A piece of paper fell from the unzipped backpack. Dark as the evening was, there was no mistaking the scribbles across the page.

"Are you trying to ask me if I'm a fraud?" she demanded.

I couldn't tear my gaze from the leaflet. Instinct had me itching to reach for it, to hold it up to the scant light from the reproduction gas lamps and see what the hell she'd written down so furiously that her words didn't even stay on the correct lines. "I don't know. Are you?"

"No."

"All right then."

She shifted, her elbow knocking into the backpack. More papers floated out, along with two worn-down candles.

"Shit," she cursed, the word leaving on a breathy sigh.

Curiosity may have killed the cat, but I figured I had at least another two lives left in me—and no way would this slip of a woman have the chance to steal one.

"Let me get that for you." *Yeah, just play the gentleman card like you give a shit.* I didn't, and maybe tomorrow I'd wake up and wonder why I'd pushed this woman's buttons. Maybe tomorrow I'd remind myself that I wasn't in a position to wonder about this woman's jaded air or her pink, fuckable lips, or the way she looked at me as though she *knew* that I was no good.

That my heart was as cold and impenetrable as the cobblestones we stood on.

Right now, though, I didn't think.

I bent, my knees popping from years of excruciating labor, and I snagged the papers straight from her grip. Like the asshole I was, I lifted them well above her head so that

I could read the words scrawled in perfectly imperfect chicken-scratch.

What in the—

I flipped to the next page.

To the next.

And to the next.

"You a stalker, ma'am?" I kept my voice cool, easy.

"I'm not . . ." A growl escaped her lips, and she made a hasty swipe at my hand. Fuck that. My hold on the leaflets went iron-tight as she blew out a frustrated breath. "I'm not a stalker."

"Then why"—I curled the stack in one fist, dipping my chin to meet her eyes—"do you have notes on at least five of my officers?"

The blood drained from her face, and this time when she swallowed, I knew she tasted fear. "I don't . . ." Her tongue swiped out in a nervous gesture, touching the cushion of her bottom lip. "It's not just police officers."

"No?"

"No, I-I—" Eyes slamming shut, she counted to ten, if the way her mouth silently formed the numbers was any indication. Then she looked at me again, and I felt lust spear me, unwanted and misplaced because while I'd done some fucked-up shit in my life, I still had boundaries. Screwing a woman who noticed the minute details was not in my future. Ever.

Visibly swallowing, she finally ground out, "I watch people, okay? It's a-a *thing* for me."

"Like a voyeur."

"What? *No.*" She pointed at the papers, and then reached into her backpack for her tarot cards. Holding them up with a little wiggle, she muttered, "I take notes, all right? On the people who visit my table and have me read their cards. *Only* ever on them."

Adrenaline grasped my lungs, heaving a deep breath from my chest. I needed to stop the trajectory of my thoughts. Hell, I needed to walk away and go the fuck home. It'd been a long night. Long and unforgiving, and not because of the shift I'd pulled for the NOPD.

For everything else.

Everything else I wasn't allowed to say, and everything else I would never repeat to another human soul.

The deck clasped tight in her hands drew my attention. "You never tell anyone what you hear?"

Uncomfortable silence stretched between us before her throaty voice answered, "It's for me. I . . . I analyze patterns in what's told to me."

She was a shit liar, but she could keep those secrets of hers to herself.

"Read me."

"Excuse me?"

"My cards." I lifted my gaze to her face. Shock resided in those hazel eyes of hers, as did blatant distrust. She was right not to trust me—that was a fact. I cleared my throat. "Read my cards."

"Absolutely not."

Lifting a brow, I murmured, "Scared?"

"Of *you*?" Disbelief coated her tone like thick honey.

"You see anyone else standing here?" At her silence, I folded my arms over my chest. "Read my cards . . . unless maybe you *are* nervous, just a little bit."

Her teeth worked her bottom lip, and I wouldn't be surprised if she broke the skin. "You don't scare me."

"Don't I?" I tested her words, taking a step toward her and breeching her space. But she surprised me—for all the lip-nibbling and the stammering, she didn't budge and she sure as hell didn't retreat. Defiance radiated from every inch of her.

It was more of a turn-on than I'd like to admit. Worse, it made me curious. Who had broken her spirit so badly that her armor was as thick as my own? I didn't have the answer, but the longer she stood there, with her hands balled into fists and her eyes narrowed into slits, the more I wanted to dredge the truth from her lips.

No matter that it wasn't any of my business.

"No one scares me," she said.

Another lie, but I wouldn't press her on it.

I only studied her, allowing my silence to bait her into giving in. *Patience, man, have patience.*

Three . . .

Two . . .

One—

"*Fine.*" With a hard glare, she slipped the cards from their velvet pouch and shuffled them with sharp motions. "Two cards. Your past and your future."

"What about my present?"

The shuffling slowed, then stalled completely. "It doesn't matter. In a moment, this will be your past too."

I wanted to tell her that she looked too damn young to be spouting out that sort of wisdom. But was she really that young? It was too dark to tell, her features lost to the shadows, and she didn't give me the opportunity to give it another thought.

She cut the deck, wrists moving fluidly. Selected a card from the middle and held it up, allowing the sparse moonlight to reveal the image. I wrangled in the urge to snag it from her grasp and hurry up the process.

"Ruin."

My chin jerked back. "Excuse me?"

"Ruin," she reiterated, voice soft but unyielding, "it's the Ten of Swords."

"I have no idea what that means."

Her teeth audibly clacked together. "I'm aware, Sergeant. Ruin—it's a card in the Minor Arcana." She flicked her nail against the card, and then turned it toward me. In the slight shadows, all that remained visible was the color red and what looked to be a sword with a myriad of other, smaller swords piercing the largest one. "It represents a period of endless fighting, a struggle that you can't win."

This was a bad idea.

Maybe she was a fraud—in that moment, I hoped it was true. I hoped that she'd lied to every single person who had ever sat at her table here in Jackson Square because I refused to believe that everything I had worked toward in the last thirty-four years had been for nothing.

My fingers sank into my dark hair, my palm following the curve of my skull to where I'd been branded like cattle years ago.

Hazel eyes met mine. "With no hope, your past has led to your destruction."

I opened my mouth to speak. Or maybe I only thought that I did.

There were no words—only blood. The blood I had spilled and the blood that I had given. Not for the first time in my life, I felt dirty, rotten, all the way to my soul. And *hopeless*, like there was no end to the struggle and to the pain and to the goddamn detachment I forced upon myself so that I could do what I needed to do and not consider the consequences of my actions.

"Interested in your future?" she asked apathetically, already swiping another card from the deck.

No, I wanted to yell. If Ruin was my past, then there was no telling what the hell my—

"Death." She turned the card around to show me. "Your future is Death."

And as I stood there woodenly, my fucking brain trying to wrap around the reality of my existence, she gathered her belongings and swept off into the night.

Leaving me alone.

As I'd always been.

THE HERMIT

MAJOR ARCANA

THREE

Avery

I'd lied to Sergeant Lincoln Asher.

Oh, not about the cards I'd picked for him. Not exactly, anyway.

But I'd allowed him to believe that he was doomed, past and future, that there was no hope left for him to believe in. If anything, the Death card marked a turning point in his future, where something inherently good, no doubt, waited just around the bend.

Except he'd made me feel uncomfortable. He was too rugged, too forward, too in-your-face masculine, and in a split-second decision, I'd sought to force his weight off the proverbial seesaw and set my queen directly in front of his king. *Checkmate.*

Curiosity led me to pull yet another card for him on my way back to my apartment.

His present.

Cruelty.

Whenever I felt the sharp blades of long-standing hate seep into my bones, I pulled out my deck and chose a card. And *always* the card was Cruelty—in other words, the constant analyzing and deciphering which inevitably ended in nothingness.

Tabitha once explained the card to a client as a person lost in a maze. No matter how many times you peered over the uncut hedges, no matter how many times you retraced your steps, all of your work always led you to . . . nothing.

Cruelty was a mind-game, so it made sense that I'd been pulling the same card now for four years. Before that, even, if you counted the number of times one of the readers in the square rolled out a spread for me—long before I'd ever picked up a deck myself.

But why would Sergeant Asher play mind-games?

With a glance over my shoulder at the empty street, my fingers stole under my too-big shirt for the key I'd hooked onto a chain around my neck. The French Quarter may have been my home for the last twelve years, but I wasn't ignorant to its many ghosts, those of fictitious rumors and others which were firmly rooted in reality.

Too much went unseen in New Orleans for me to ever feel truly safe.

Keying the antique door open, I slipped inside the multi-apartment, nineteenth-century building and locked everything up behind me. I lived in what New Orleans' legend called the Sultan's Palace, a home of alleged brutality and death and chopped-up human parts.

No part of the tall tale was true, and the only reason I'd agreed to live here, at the corner of Dauphine and Orleans, was because the rent was cheap and the landlord didn't ask questions.

Lugging my belongings up to the third floor without an elevator was annoying but habit at this point. My fold-up chairs bounced against the outside of my leg, and my backpack hung low on my shoulder. The table had been left behind—hopefully it'd be there tomorrow morning.

Would Sergeant Asher come back then?

I hoped not.

He'd been . . . I didn't know, really. Harsh, maybe? His face certainly had been. Even though I had pretty much no sex drive, I could recognize a good-looking guy when I saw one.

Lincoln Asher wasn't good-looking, not in the classical sense. Thick dark hair, as black as the Mississippi River at night, had been swept to the side. His nose, like mine, had clearly been broken at some point. Full lips that didn't tug up into a smile, not even once. A series of jagged scars that cut across the profile of the right side of his face.

The prettiest thing about him had been the color of his eyes—an icy blue that was an exact match to the underside of every porch ceiling in the city. Haint blue, it was called. A color that homeowners bought by the gallon to paint their porches with, so birds wouldn't nest, thinking it was the sky. Legend had it, however, that the custom was rooted in Voodoo—where porch ceilings were painted blue, the color of water, so that spirits couldn't trespass into the home.

In Sergeant Asher's eyes, I'd seen nothing but the ghosts of his past.

The man was dangerous, self-destruction in wait, and I couldn't lie and say that I wasn't exactly the same.

Didn't mean we needed to step off the edge together, though.

"That you, Avery?"

I closed the apartment door with my elbow, still juggling everything in my arms. "Yeah, Katie, it's me."

Our apartment was miniscule, a whopping five-hundred-square-feet. You'd think we lived in Manhattan and not in New Orleans, but after three years, it was home. We had a single bedroom that belonged to Katie, a galley-style kitchen, a narrow bathroom, and a living room that seconded as a bedroom for me.

The apartment was in Katie's name, and she paid an extra hundred bucks on the rent each month. I would have given her the bedroom anyway—she often invited certain guests over, and the thought of walking in on naked asses and naked cocks and naked everything else didn't appeal to me.

Leave me to my pull-out couch and I was perfectly fine.

"How was the square?" she asked, coming into the living room from her bedroom. Dressed in shorts and an extra-large T-shirt, Katie's blond hair was a tangled mess on the top of her head. At my raised brows, she wiggled her own and hooked a thumb over one shoulder. *Company*, she mouthed, which said it all.

Guess I'd be making use of my headphones again tonight.

"It was fine. Had my fair share of people." I set all my stuff down behind the couch, so that they wouldn't be an eyesore for our *guest*. "A few regulars. Nothing too crazy."

Liar.

All right, so maybe I was itching to sit on the couch and record my night. I hadn't lied about that to the sergeant—I really did pay close attention to everyone who sat at my table. For the first few years after my mother's death, I'd done nothing but hide from my own shadow. A teenage girl in New Orleans, alone, was never a good idea. Slowly, as the initial fear had dissipated, everything came back to Jay Foley, my stepfather.

Now the current mayor of New Orleans.

So, I watched and I waited. Like tonight, no one could resist having their cards read for long. I'd told the fortunes of lawyers and firefighters, of school teachers and strippers. I harbored the information away from all the pertinent people, always pushing the telling questions and patiently teasing out the answers from the darkest parts of their souls.

They all had secrets to hide, and I was particularly adept at uncovering their fears.

"Nobody bothered you, right?" Katie asked, leaning one shoulder against the door to her bedroom. "You know I worry."

Katie and I had met at the strip club a few years back. I'd gone with a client who promised me a good time after I'd finished his tarot reading, and I'd been desperate enough for human interaction that I'd agreed to go with him. Three hours later, my "date" had decided to wine and dine a tourist from Montana, and I'd drank one too many cocktails at the bar. Katie had lent me extra clothes when I'd puked all over myself, and she'd listened when I confessed that there had to be something wrong with me: no matter how many times I tried to let a man touch me, I couldn't.

"You a lesbian?" she'd asked after sipping on the salted rim of a margarita. "That's cool."

"I'm not a lesbian. I'm just like . . ." No words fit. How did I explain that what I wanted and needed were two different things? I needed men as a gender to stay far away from me, and, yet, I still *wanted* a man to get me off. Not that my brain ever turned off long enough for that to happen. "I'm me," I'd finally muttered pathetically.

Or rather, I was no one.

A figment of mashed identities, hoping to survive yet another day.

"I was good all night," I told Katie, refusing to meet her eye. If she caught onto the fact that I'd had a run-in with the sergeant, she'd never let it go. "Is that"—I lowered my voice—"George in there?"

Katie's mouth lifted in a wicked grin. "George *and* Tyler."

I laughed, not even scandalized by her overt sexuality. Just because I was messed up in the head didn't mean my roommate deserved to live the abstinent life right along with me. "Get it, girl."

"I already have, and I plan to do so again. I keep trying to convince them to, *you know*."

"Fight swords?"

Her blue eyes lit with humor. "Hell, I wish. At this point I'm just hoping for a damn kiss between the two of them. It's not every day you get two hot military dudes in your bed at once."

I stepped behind my makeshift closet curtain and drew it closed. Stripped off my work clothes—too-large items I'd found at the thrift shop—and pulled on a pair of leggings and a comfy sweater. "Something tells me that you're going to have your way by the end of the night."

Katie's voice turned hopeful. "You pull a card for me?"

"The deck is in my backpack." I pushed the curtain to the side. "But I can, if you want."

Biting her lip, she glanced back at her bedroom door. "I think I might live the spontaneous life tonight."

"Live your best life," I teased, dropping onto the sofa. "Promise them double penetration if they swap spit."

Katie's bark of laughter echoed in the living room. With a shake of her head, she leaned forward over the back of the couch and wrapped her arms around me for a hug. "Every time I think you can't surprise me, you do, Avery. I just know you're a kinky bitch under all those don't-touch-me vibes."

Kinky probably wasn't the best word for me—could virgins be kinky?

According to books like *Fifty Shades of Grey*, yeah. According to my reality, I'd give it a hard hell-no.

I couldn't lower my guard long enough for a man to kiss me, never mind take out his dick and put it inside me. A romantic visual, I know, but I didn't have a romantic bone in my body.

Katie kissed the top of my head like I was a younger sister, which I guess I was. She was thirty-one to my twenty-five, and she was one of those suffocating affectionate people who believed hugs ought to be arm-delivered at least ten times a day.

In my ear, she whispered, "You'll meet the right guy for you, Aves. And I have a sneaking suspicion he'll be just as kinky as you."

Rolling my eyes, I shooed her away with my hands. She skipped back, a tinkling laugh emerging from her lips, before she swung the bedroom door open and announced, "All right, boys, who's up for a little D-P, huh?"

The door clicked shut behind her, and I drew in a deep breath. Katie didn't know my history, aside from the basics: I had no family; I'd dropped out of school at the age of thirteen; and I'd spent a large portion of my teenage years bouncing from one homeless shelter to another after Momma was murdered and I was left on my own.

Small as it was, this apartment in the Sultan's Palace was my most luxurious accommodation yet.

To the left of the couch was a small file cabinet, and I keyed open the top lock and removed a black binder, settling it on my thighs. Because of the whole no-school thing—teachers and administration asked too many questions—reading wasn't a pastime of mine. Still, a few years back I'd been riffling through the plastic baskets at the French Quarter Market, when I'd discovered a tiny picture frame with a quote that might as well have struck me dead:

If you want to shine, New Orleans will let you thrive. But if you want to hide who you really are, the city will keep your secrets too.

The words had kicked around in my head for days after, taking root deep in my heart and spreading like wildfire.

New Orleans had hidden me; it had harbored me. And now, it gave me the opportunity to discover the truth.

I slipped the binder open, traced the tiny, wooden picture frame I'd squirreled away into my pocket all those years ago, and then flipped past all of my notes.

Lawyers and firefighters, school teachers and strippers.

Whoever brought up Mayor Jay Foley, no matter if the information was told to me in a positive or negative light, went in the binder. His was a name on the tip of everyone's tongues these days, now that he was up for reelection.

The man tonight had said nothing about my stepfather, and yet for some reason I wanted to remember the cards I'd picked for him. Ruin. Death.

Cruelty.

I wrote it all down, recalling those blue eyes of his and the hard clench of his jaw. My pen scratched against the paper, my crappy penmanship drifting across the page and skipping out of the printed lines.

Sometimes, in life, you couldn't remain within the confines.

I worried about that. I worried that I'd lived in the shadows of New Orleans for too long and that I would never have all of my answers unless I took that next step. My palms grew sweaty at the thought. I had the courage to watch Foley from afar, picking up information here and there that could ruin him forever.

Whether I had the courage to do more than cling to the shadows—my safety net—remained to be seen.

My eyes fell shut, and I shoved aside the binder. Grabbing the throw blanket off the back of the coach, I wrapped it around my shoulders and stepped out onto our small balcony—another perk to living in the Quarter.

Three stories below, Dauphine Street was dimly lit. A group of tourists meandered down the way, arms wrapped around each other's shoulders, green Hand Grenade drinks clasped in tight fists.

"Gimme that! I need more."

"You always need more . . . in *bed*."

Their conversation floated up to the balcony, mingling with the jazz and rap music from Bourbon Street, one block over.

That could have been me.

Living life, hanging out with friends without having to constantly look over my shoulder. Maybe, twelve years after Momma's death, I should start thinking that Jay Foley had forgotten all about me, about his stepdaughter who'd escaped while he killed another man.

Under any other circumstances, I'd believe that it was all in my head and that I'd grown paranoid over the years.

But then I'd hear him on the radio or see him on TV. I'd listen as he fed the public lies and pretended that my mother had died of cancer, out of the public eye, and *not* with a single bullet straight to the back of her head, execution-style. I'd listen as he spun a tale of a touching scene with Momma surrounded by loved ones as she passed and not, as events had actually played out, alone in her dining room while her husband watched the blood soak the antique rug beneath her body. I'd listen as he pretended that *I* had been so distraught over my momma's death that I'd spiraled into a depression and taken to inflicting self-harm.

"Laurel was a sweet, sweet girl, but there was nothing anyone could do to save her," he'd told the media. "I doubt she even realized what taking too many pills might do to her sweet, little body."

He'd effectively killed me without pulling the literal trigger.

And then he'd held a funeral, leveraging a body that was not mine into the Foley family tomb in St. Louis Cemetery #1 on Washington Avenue . . . exactly where I'd ended up, feet bleeding, a year earlier.

In that moment, at the age of fourteen, Laurel Peyton had ceased to exist.

A cry ripped through the night, high-pitched and keening, and the blanket fell from my shoulders to my feet.

Not Momma. It wasn't Momma.

Another cry, followed by deep, masculine grunting.

Right, Katie orgasming.

Not Momma dying.

Sometimes it was hard to tell the difference.

THE MAGICIAN

MAJOR ARCANA

S ergeant Lincoln Asher was back.
It was Sunday night, cold and windy, and most of the other readers had already packed up for the evening.

You should have too.

Yeah, clearly, I'd missed the memo.

Dressed in navy-blue slacks, just like last night, and the same jacket over his baby-blue NOPD uniform shirt, he covered the short distance between Pirate's Alley, nestled alongside St. Louis Cathedral, and my table. Without a word, he pulled out the chair opposite mine and dropped his big body onto it.

The chair's legs squealed under the sudden onslaught of his muscular frame and then quieted, as though understanding that the sergeant was not a man to piss off.

Which was possibly the only reason that I opened my mouth and attempted to do just that: "Still alive?"

His full lips didn't twitch at my snarky jab. "Don't sound so disappointed."

"Trust me, I'm not."

Blue eyes zeroed in on my face. "You're not disappointed that I'm alive?"

My brain pin-wheeled, trying to unravel the riddle of his words. "What? No. I meant that of course I'm disappointed."

"Of course." He drew out his wallet from his jacket and pulled money from the cash pocket. A crisp hundred-dollar bill winked at me just before he pinned Benjamin Franklin to the table with his palm.

"What is that?"

"What's it look like?"

Unease settled in my limbs, as did a ball of disgust. Familiar memories of unknown hands, groping my body awake, boiled deep, and I purposely cut eye contact with him to drink some of my hot chocolate. "I'm not sucking your dick, Sergeant."

Briefly, so briefly I wondered if I'd imagined it, his mouth tightened with displeasure. "Did I ask you to suck my dick?"

My gaze dropped to the money.

"I want you to read my cards," he growled, "the way you did for that woman yesterday."

"You mean, you want me to tell you what you want to hear?" I leaned forward, catching the flash of his blue eyes. "Let me tell you something." I tapped the corner of the Benjamin Franklin, making sure not to touch his hand. "You could put five-hundred bucks on this table, and I *still* wouldn't suck your dick."

That did it.

His features hardened, and my breath caught. Yesterday, he'd been relatively easygoing, halfway engaging. Right now, there was nothing easy about Lincoln Asher. *Callous* was the first word to come to mind. *Cruel* was the next, as though he was a man so deep in hell that he'd not seen sunlight in years.

"If you were any other woman, I'd test that theory of yours."

My back straightened at the punishing note in his voice. "What the hell does that mean?"

"It means that everyone has a price, and I've got no doubt that yours is lower than most." He matched my pose, leaning in, twining Benjamin between his index and middle fingers like the most enticing bite of candy I'd ever seen. "It means," he went on, voice low, "that I followed you home last night and I saw where you lived. I've been in those apartments before, and it's no secret that your living situation isn't exactly high-society living. Five hundred bucks would go a long way for you."

I . . . I—

There was something obviously wrong with me. My fingers trembled and my knees locked together and my breathing sounded erratic even to my own ears, and I was . . . aroused. For the first time in my life, I was turned on, and it figured that after a childhood like mine, a stalker would be the thing to harden my nipples and make me want to set my hand between my legs.

Arrogant prick.

My hands moved over the Thoth deck, shuffling mindlessly.

Put him in his place.

"I carry a gun."

I stifled a groan. Of all the things to threaten a police officer with, *that* was my choice of weapon?

Asher's dark brows lifted. "You ever fire it?"

"Yes." *No.* I had, however, made use of my taser on multiple occasions when the situation called for it.

"At what?"

A hard swallow stuck in my throat. "Wouldn't you like to know?"

His husky laughter rang loud in my ears. "You're a shit liar."

"I wasn't lying."

"Yeah, sure you weren't."

"Do you want me to read your cards or not?"

He fell silent, and for a moment there was nothing but the distant sounds of laughter and screams from Bourbon, mingled with the quiet murmur of Tabby weaving a story of lust and love to her client. I took the reprieve to study him in a way that I hadn't last night—I didn't need to have the Sight to know that Lincoln Asher was a dark, restless soul. His sins were apparent in the jagged scars on his cheek, as well as a split in his bottom lip.

The cold weather, maybe, but more likely that he'd taken a fist to the face recently.

Dropping my gaze to his hands, I noted his bruised knuckles with a silent whistle of appreciation. I had no doubt that Sergeant Lincoln Asher had returned the punch tenfold—aside from the break in his bottom lip, his harsh face was otherwise untouched.

Except for the scars, of course.

Blue eyes seared me when I met his gaze, and those icy depths were as turbulent as the waters swirling in the Mississippi River. "I want to know my future," he said roughly. "My past . . ." An equally rough laugh reverberated in his chest, the sound so devoid of emotion that it might as well have been a gust of wind without a storm. "I don't give a fuck about my past."

I slipped a card from the deck, setting it facedown on the table. "You can't run from the past." I knew that for a fact—on the rare occasions when I tried to let go of the hate, a trip of fate always had me right back at the start again, staring at Jay Foley's face on some screen and remembering that he'd ripped my world straight from under my feet.

I pulled two more cards and settled them on top of the first—the stack of three would represent the sergeant's heart.

If he even had one.

Card by card I laid out the rest of the spread, all the while wondering why a man like Asher would be so utterly consumed with something so fanciful as tarot readings. Then again, it was human nature to crave the unknown, to be titillated by the notion that with the flick of a wrist and the flash of a card, your destiny could be revealed.

Setting the deck aside, I drew my heavy jacket deeper over my shoulders to ward off the late-night chill. "I can't read your future without acknowledging the past." With my index finger, I gently tapped a selection of cards on the left half of the spread. "You'll find that your reading is uneven, unexplained, and whatever answers you seek will have a bottomless pit." At his silence, I added, "But I can read to you what's in your heart, what it desires most above everything else. Maybe that, combined with your future, will make up for ignoring the rest."

TEN OF WANDS

FIVE

Lincoln

I dipped my chin toward the spread she'd laid out. "That's fine," I said, like my heart actually factored into the equation—as though it had factored into *any* equation during the last thirty-four years. I agreed to what she said as though I gave a fuck about what a set of cards might tell me.

Despite my initial reaction to her reading last night, I firmly believed that free will triumphed over destiny or the fates or whatever the hell people were calling it nowadays. My actions had direct consequences, and on the flip of a dime, I could find myself in a very different situation than I had ten minutes earlier.

The cards weren't why I was here tonight.

No, I was here because of *her*, this unnamed woman who lived in one of the largest homes in the Quarter, though its (alleged) tortured past meant that no one gave a shit that the stories of murdered sultans and flayed human body parts were nothing more than rumored fabrications regurgitated for every tourist who wandered past on a tour.

This woman intrigued me, with the way she'd hugged

the shadows last night, as though unnerved that somebody might be watching.

I'd watched, but like I'd told her, I'd done so to ensure she made it home safe.

Because you suddenly have a heart?

Yeah, not quite. Or rather, not at all. I'd left that son of a bitch behind in my first foster-home stint. I had no use for it, not then and not now either, which was further proof that this hazel-eyed girl had somehow ground herself under my skin.

There was no tangible reason for my sudden fascination with her, but here I was, ready to pay her to tell me my fortune . . . simply because I'd wanted another chance to talk with her.

Silently, I watched as she flipped over the first card— my "heart's innermost desires," she'd said—and sat back in her chair, a little frown tugging down her lips. She adjusted her jacket again, drawing it closed over her chest even though two buttons were missing.

"Odd," she murmured.

I leaned in, chair creaking beneath me, and stole a glance at the card half-hidden under her hand. Red fiery flames peaked out from behind what looked like arrows. "How so?"

"Oppression." With a slight shake of her head, she smoothed her fingers over the card. "It's the Ten of Wands, and—"

"What?"

"Nothing, it's just that I get this card frequently. Always in this exact spot, too."

"Coincidence." Dropping my elbows to the table, I nodded to the cards laid out before us. "It's like Murphy's Law. If you really think that everything that can go wrong will go wrong, it probably will. You're looking for those idiosyncrasies that indicate you've called it all out correctly —that your life is in the shitter." I tapped the card, just to the side of her hand. "Same goes here. If you're looking for similarities, they'll appear."

Hazel eyes blinked up at me, and in that moment, I could have sworn she'd taken a read on my rotten soul.

"In the cards, oppression represents a separation from the spirit." Again, she drew the jacket tighter, like the bite of the night wind sank deep into her bones. "It's as though your moral compass has disappeared in favor of cruel force. You don't recognize yourself anymore, your needs or your desires—you're blinded to whatever drives you, a slave to an ulterior motive that destroys everything else in its path."

Jesus.

This time it was my turn to tug on the sleeves of my jacket—for a different reason entirely. She hid from the cold, and I hid from the chance that she might notice the blood stains on the cuffs of my shirt.

The familiar grip of guilt weighted my limbs. All of it —every death, every fight—all led to one goal. So I guess she was right; I had become oppressed by my own motives, no matter how dirty and vengeful they were.

My phone vibrated in my pocket, and with a raised finger to ask her to wait, I slipped it out from my pants and checked the incoming message from an unknown 504 area code number: *Is it done?*

The blood had been washed from my hands, if not from my clothes, so yeah, it'd been finished. *10-4*, I typed back and then hit SEND.

A second later, a single word greeted me on the screen: *Good.*

My dead heart gave a rare, pitiful thump, which I ignored. Emotion could get you killed in my line of work.

It could end you in a heartbeat, strip away your life in a second.

"Something important?" she asked, drawing my attention back to her face.

I shook my head. "Just work."

Her hazel eyes never left my face. "You like working for the NOPD, then?"

My life would be easier if I'd only ever clocked in for the police department. But the NOPD wasn't responsible for the scars on my face, the split in my lip, the blood on my clothes. I cleared my throat. "I like putting the bad guys in jail."

The look she leveled on me spoke volumes. "I'll be honest, and I might be wrong here, but crime seems just as rampant as it's always been."

Her words only piqued my curiosity. "How old are you?"

"Do you want me to read your cards or not?"

I didn't give a damn about the cards, especially when her selection seemed to only reflect gloom and doom. Ruin. Death. Oppression. Not a hint of rainbows or unicorns in sight. "Do you get a kick out of telling tourists that their lives are about to take a morbid turn?"

Her shoulders lifted with a casual shrug. "It's life. I'm not telling anyone anything they don't already know."

"Tell me your name."

At my abrupt switch in topic, her eyes narrowed and her teeth sank into her bottom lip with a sharp indrawn breath. "Why do you want to know it?"

Because I . . . well, fuck, what could I say? That from the moment I'd walked up to her, I'd felt some sort of unexplainable pull, like we were tethered to the same string . . . just at opposite ends? That beyond the random need I had to strip her of her clothes and to see her eyes darken with lust, I recognized a little of myself in her?

I'd made a life out of lying and thieving.

I'd dug myself out of hell only to realize that I'd never be able to shake off the embers.

That the darkness which ran through my blood, as cliché as the saying goes, never calmed or fled, but for a reason I couldn't pinpoint, I felt as though this girl could take it. She could handle my shadows, if not the pure darkness.

Never had I craved someone more.

"It's Avery." My gaze jerked up to her face, and she tilted her chin up defiantly, daring me to question her. "My name is Avery Washington."

I rolled her name over my tongue silently; imagined whispering it against her neck as I plunged into her body; recited it two more times with the fantasy of her on her knees, her lips closing around my cock.

She was a shit liar.

To anyone else, her defiantly raised chin and the challenge in her eyes would have left them feeling as though she'd uttered the truth. But I read liars for a living—hell, *I* was a liar, and I recognized the twitches in her façade for what they were.

I settled back, observing the way she pressed her feminine fingers to the base of her neck and swallowed. "You from N'Orleans?" I asked, wondering if she'd lie about that too.

She met my gaze head-on. "Born and raised."

"Same here."

She didn't roll her eyes but I had the feeling that she wanted to. "I figured."

"Yeah?"

With a short nod, Avery flipped the cards over on the

table. "You may meet a lot of different people, Sergeant, but so do I. Everything about you screams this city, starting with the jaded twinkle in your eye."

I laughed hard at that, the sound entirely foreign and rusty to my ears. I never smiled. I never laughed. But, damn it if she didn't make me want to start practicing. "A jaded twinkle?"

Shifting in her chair, Avery muttered something beneath her breath. Then, louder, "It's the color blue of your eyes."

Heat spiked south of my belt at her admission. When I spoke, there was no mistaking the husk in my voice. "Did you spend last night thinking about the color of my eyes, Avery?"

"*What*? Absolutely not."

I stretched out one arm, making no effort to conceal the way I set my hand next to hers. Tan to pale, large against small. She was tiny compared to me, and even that was enticing. My thumb crossed over her pinky, and I stifled a satisfied purr when she flexed her hand . . . and kept her hand right next to mine. "I'd be all too happy—"

"Avery." Jerking toward the sound of the unknown voice, I noticed that the reader one table over had stood up and crossed over to stand beside Avery. The stranger's eyes zeroed in on me, unwavering. "I'm going to pack everything up for the night and I suggest that you do the same."

Her hand slipped away.

"You're right," Avery said, her tone more tepid than I'd heard from her yet. She spared me a quick glance. "It's late, Sergeant Asher, and it's obvious that you haven't come back tonight to learn about your future."

Apparently, she'd sussed me out just as I'd done to her.

I rose from my chair and folded it. "It's obvious," I

drawled, using her words, "that you don't care for the bullshit."

"I don't."

Succinct as her tone was, I spotted a blush crest her cheeks. "Then, no bullshit." When she set her backpack on the table to unzip, I closed in, stepping up close so that she was forced to look up at me. Only when we locked eyes did I speak in a tone low enough that the words were clearly intended only for her and not for her friend. "I spent last night wondering about that smart mouth of yours—how you'll taste or what noises you might make when I drive you to come on my tongue."

I waited, not moving, for her to reply.

She didn't disappoint.

Her tongue swiped out along her plush lower lip. "I don't date."

"No one said anything about dating."

White teeth bit her lip, and those hazel eyes of hers flashed fire and unmistakable want. "I don't fuck."

That word coming off her lips was like a calling card to my dick. She might not *fuck* now but she would, dirty and raw and so damn good that she'd carve her territory into my back with her nails. "If you don't," I drawled, "that just means you haven't done it right."

Her jaw snapped shut, molars cracking together. Her cheeks burned red. "I wouldn't . . ." She swallowed, then ducked her head to continue packing up. "You couldn't handle someone like me, Sergeant—"

"Lincoln."

"What?"

"Call me Lincoln," I repeated, fully aware of the fact that I wanted Avery Washington like nothing I'd ever wanted in my life—outside of one thing. "Lincoln," I said again, "not sergeant."

"As I was saying, *Asher*"—the challenge in her eyes lit my own to see her flat on her back with that same damn fire goading me on—"you couldn't handle me. You think you could, but you can't. Now, if you'll excuse me, I have places to be." She shrugged into her backpack and then bundled up the chairs under one arm. The table, she glared at, and then stepped away. "Don't follow me tonight or I'll call the cops on you."

Her threat stole more rusty laughter from me. "I'm sure my guys will enjoy the chance to cuff me."

"Someone has to," she said, "and it will never be me."

With that, she turned away and ducked down Pirate's Alley. The shadows of St. Louis Cathedral enclosed her within their depths like a physical door being clamped shut behind her.

Locking me out.

"Stay away from her, Sergeant Asher."

I glanced over at Avery's friend, refusing to show her even an ounce of the desire Avery sparked within me. Inclining my head in a short nod, I stepped back. "Have a good night, ma'am."

"I've heard about you, you know—we all have."

"My condolences."

She approached, and it was in that moment that I spotted the tattoo on her right temple. It was small and round, like a stamp made for deceit. She'd been marked by the devil himself. "You kill without guilt, destroy lives without impunity. You act"—she dropped her voice to a rough pitch—"like you are the executioner and the jury, all in the name of what? Money? Conceit?"

If money were a motivator, I would have moved far from New Orleans years ago. But I didn't owe this woman a damn thing, and so I gave her a small salute and then turned on my heel.

She could hate me for what I'd done—I didn't care one way or the other—but the tattoo on her face was a direct indication that she was no better than me—even if she'd left that life behind. She'd fucked; I'd killed. At the end of the day, when the result was exactly the same, we were equals.

I knew that for a fact; I'd been marked with that same tattoo the day I'd turned sixteen.

JUSTICE

XI

MAJOR ARCANA
reversed

Between my legs, my core pulsed.

It sounded ridiculous, *so* ridiculous, and yet as I stepped up to the register at my local corner store, it was all I could think about.

Damn you, Asher.

The cash drawer clanged shut. "Just the bottle of wine tonight, Avery?"

When you went to the same corner store five days per week for odds and ends—for *years*—you tended to build up a camaraderie with the staff. "Just the wine, Pete." Feeling my cheeks redden, I adjusted my backpack. I'd dropped everything else off at home before deciding that wine was in order because I couldn't, no matter how hard I tried, pretend that Asher hadn't flipped the script on me. "Just been a long day."

Pete, one half of the duo who owned and operated Flambeaux, nodded and passed over my change. "Try running a twenty-four-hour convenience store, baby." His tone was dry, but the smile on his face remained open and friendly. "You ever decide to quit with the cards, Salvatore and I could use an extra hand."

Pete and his husband, Sal, had been trying to recruit me for years now. Back when I'd been a teenager, I'd considered it. Discounts on food, two bosses who were so damn kind it was almost unreal—and it didn't hurt that they both knew I was a runner, and thus put up with the name changes without even a blink of the eye. But always the fear lingered that one of my stepfather's cronies would wander in and I'd be screwed.

Or that Pete and his husband would discover my real identity.

Jackson Square lent me its shadows and tourists; Flambeaux could ruin everything with its fluorescent lights and steady stream of French Quarter residents.

"You push a hard bargain," I murmured, dropping my wallet into my backpack and pressing the merlot bottle to my chest. "If I had any good sense . . ."

The bell over the front door chimed with a newcomer, and Pete called out a hello. To me, he said, "If you had any good sense you'd ditch the tarot gig or at least take up with one of the local fortune-reading businesses in the area. Sal and I worry about you out there. People are idiots."

I offered the wine up in silent salute. "People are *definitely* idiots."

Pete slowly shook his head, even as he let out a sigh in clear disappointment. "Stick to Bourbon on your walk home, baby girl. Text me when you get there."

Twenty-five years old or not, I'd still be a kid in Pete's eyes until I was wrinkled and gray. After a quick hug goodbye, I stepped outside with the wine in hand. I didn't drink often because I hated losing control over my body, but tonight . . . I briefly squeezed my eyes shut.

Tonight, I'd discovered my first taste of lust and, honestly, I wasn't a fan.

Once upon a time, in a far, far away land, when I'd first found myself alone and scared, I'd pictured my savior. Chalk it up to a youth spent devouring Disney films, but I'd absolutely imagined my Prince Charming as the requisite blond with the blue eyes and the tall physique—to say nothing of the fact that he'd be sweet and gentlemanly and oh-so-handsome.

If it was a test to see if he measured up to a girl's youthful dreams, Lincoln Asher failed on every front— aside from his Haint blue eyes.

Maybe he's the sort of man you crave now.

I wouldn't know.

From the first time I'd awoken on my cot at the home- less shelter to find a strange man's hand between my legs, I'd refused to entertain even the possibility of dating or fucking.

Until now. Until Lincoln Asher had given me a glimpse of what he could offer to ensure that I came screaming the way Katie had last night.

Kicking a stray glass bottle out of my way, I strolled down quiet St. Phillip Street toward Bourbon. On either side of me, nineteenth-century properties sprung up like vibrantly hued doll houses. At this time of day, their cheery vibe took a backseat for a more haunting quality. Sparse lights lined the street, and up ahead a group of teenagers formed a tight circle, their voices pitching loudly into the still night.

"Look how pretty she is," one guy drawled, his voice a little garbled since his back was to me. "Her hair is so shiny."

"So shiny," his buddy echoed. He slung an arm around

his friend's shoulders, leaning forward as though to inspect something on the ground.

I waited for the bark of a dog or a mewl of a feral cat. On more than a few occasions, I'd taken strays in. While the Quarter's stray cat population numbers in the hundreds, dogs weren't that far behind in numbers. My apartment building allowed animals, and I'd registered Katie and myself with the local LSPCA as a foster home for animals.

Maybe it was a downfall of mine, but I couldn't bear to see a living creature relegated to the streets. It just wasn't in me.

My pace hastened as I approached the group, fingers tight around the wine bottle because you never really knew. But if they were messing with a stray, then there wasn't a chance in hell I'd let them carry on and hurt the poor thing.

"Hey."

No one turned at my greeting.

"Hey!"

The two closest whipped around, their faces cast in shadows. Now that I was close, I noted that they were college-aged. Bigger bodies, broader shoulders. Worry pierced me, and I shoved it aside recklessly.

"What the fuck do you want?" the one with brown hair snapped.

Don't be Laurel. Don't cower. Don't run.

"I thought I heard y'all messing with a dog. Came to see if maybe you'd like for me to take her off your hands."

Good, that was good.

"You hear that?" He punched his red-headed friend in the arm. "This chick wants to take the dog off our hands."

Red hitched a laugh that reminded me of dark alleyways and lost souls. "If only we had a collar for her."

"Right? A collar and a leash"—he looked to me, chin dipping as his gaze no doubt skimmed down my body— "so we could let you take her home."

Were all college boys idiots? These ones had clearly wandered down here from Uptown, near the universities. Their preppy clothes screamed *privilege*. If the street were more lit, I had no doubt that I'd spot red eyes and haggard features. Boys like them came down to the Quarter for their latest fix, which generally came in the form of little white lines of powder.

"Don't need a leash or a collar." Swinging my backpack to my front, I made sure to keep my eyes on the idiots as I unzipped the bag and searched for the spare leash I always kept on hand, just in case. The wine bottle I tucked under my left armpit. "Let me take the dog and you can go back to the bars."

Red laughed again. "What do you say, boys? Should we give her the dog?"

He stepped to the side and my stomach bottomed out.

In the center of their circle was a girl on her knees. Jeans torn, shirt ripped, hair a tangled mess down the length of her back. She hugged herself around the middle as though she'd never know kindness from another human being again, and I didn't have to look at her face to know that the whimper of sorrow echoing in my ears belonged to her.

Mother. Fuckers.

"Step away from her." All too familiar memories clouded my vision and I thrust them away. "Step the fuck back from her."

Another whimper, this one so keening that she actually sounded like an abused pup.

"How about we take you, too?" Red's grasping hands

found my backpack and tugged me forward in a hard pull. *Don't cower. Don't run. Don't be Laurel.*

I fell to my knees beside the girl, my shoulder crashing into hers.

Shoving his face close, Red's breath wafted over my face like a harbinger of death by cigarettes and booze. "How about we take that leash out of your hands and tie you up? How about that, boys?" He glanced away at his friends, teeth shining off-white as he grinned. "You think we should walk her down Bourbon like the bitch she—"

The wine bottle shattered over his head.

Silence pervaded our circle, aside from the girl's crying, as Red dropped to the cracked sidewalk with a heavy *thump*.

And then everyone shifted into motion.

"Jesus fucking Christ!"

"Get the bitch!"

They launched toward me as my hands peeled open my backpack in frantic motions, diving for the taser I always kept hidden in the front pocket. Only problem was, the electric-prongs were a one-shot only type of deal. And while I had my gun in the bag, too, I'd lied to Sergeant Asher about something else.

I'd never fired it, not a single time.

Pete had given it to me a few years back for safety. We'd always talked about going to the range, but life had gotten busy for him. Which meant that I owned a gun I didn't even know how to use, aside from a general knowledge to pull the trigger and hope for the best.

Fan-flipping-tastic.

Large hands went to my shoulders, dragging me away from my backpack, away from my gun, away from the girl who needed saving. Her wide eyes followed me as I let my body go lax, the backs of my legs scraping raw along the unforgiving cement.

Don't fight. Wait.

I held onto my breath until my captor released me with the order to "get down, bitch."

I was a great order-follower when I wanted to be.

I leaned back against the sidewalk just as he said, then wrapped my hand around the base of my taser where I'd quickly stashed it in my jacket pocket.

He didn't see it coming.

I aimed the taser at his crotch.

Pulled the trigger.

The two electrode prongs released, zooming straight for ground zero, and I curled and rolled to the side to avoid his massive body landing on mine.

Satisfaction flared at the sight of him cupping his dick, eyes rolling to the back of his head.

"Asshole," I ground out before hopping to my feet, not a little wearily. There were three more of them and only one of me, and as bad as I was at math, the odds were certainly not in my favor.

The sound of bone crunching had me whirling around to see Lincoln Asher grab Brown Hair by the shirt collar and deliver a punch straight to his face. Another crack, this time the man's nose splintering. Blood burst like a fountain, which didn't stop Asher. He reeled back and clocked the guy yet again, his knuckles glistening under the dim lighting.

My stomach heaved.

Don't think about blood and Momma and death. Focus, focus, focus.

Scuffling shoes across the cement teased me back to reality, and I turned just in time to see one of the guys come at me from the side. He went for my hair, chubby fingers grasping at the long strands, ugly words crossing his lips. I jabbed my taser into his rib cage, thankful for the stun-gun feature when his brows lifted in shock and he mumbled something incoherent under his breath.

He stumbled, one foot crossing over the other like a drunken sailor, hand outreached for the stucco wall of the house beside us. His fingers barely grazed it before he went down, hard.

Thank God.

"Done this before?"

I wouldn't have thought I'd find Asher's raspy voice comforting, but I suppose that was before I'd been jumped by four boys who thought their dicks were the equivalent to a unicorn's horn.

Asher had the last guy on the ground, belly flat on the sidewalk, as he handcuffed the guy's hands behind his back.

"Not a single time," I muttered, then turned my attention to the girl. At the sound of my shoes crunching over gravel, her shoulders visibly jerked. I knelt beside her, careful to leave space between us so she didn't feel threatened. "Are you okay?"

Her bottom lip quivered and she ducked her head. "I-I . . ."

I understood her fear. I'd breathed it, I'd been reborn to it.

Like she was a terrified colt, I parked my butt on the cement and settled my hands on my knees so she could keep watch on where they were at all times. With a tilt of my chin, I said, "That's Sergeant Asher. He's with the New Orleans Police Department, and I can guarantee you're safe with him." Hadn't he said that he found no thrill in pursuing those who couldn't protect themselves? "My name is Avery."

She swallowed and then gave a little nod. "Casey. Thank you . . . thank you for stepping in."

It hurt to know that she'd expected me to walk on by, even when I'd thought she was a dog. It indicated that others had; they'd put down their heads and continued on with their night even as she'd been assaulted.

Shrugging out of my jacket, I held it out to her. "Take this."

"You'll be cold."

I offered her a small smile. "I've dealt with worse. Take it."

When she did, Asher stepped forward, his face menacing and dark and unholy—but he'd saved Casey and me both. "Ma'am, you'll need to go to the district station over on Royal." As if sensing the girl's hesitation, he put up his hands, palms facing out. "I know you don't want to. I know it's going to be hard to explain what happened and relive it, but a statement from you will ensure these guys go to jail, you hear me?"

"I hear you."

Asher gave a clipped nod. "Good. Now, you can wait until backup arrives, so they can transport these guys to lockup and I can take you—it might be a minute. Or maybe Avery wouldn't mind walking you over to the station. Your choice."

What? *No.*

In no universe was it a good idea for me to bring Casey to the Eighth District Police Station—not because I didn't care to see her safely there. I did, really. But bringing her would be like walking into the lion's den.

I swallowed thickly as youthful fears set in like prongs latching onto my skin.

It would be just my luck to run into someone who recognized me.

Red emitted a groan as he tried to roll onto his back and then realized his bound hands limited his mobility. "Uncuff me, man," he groaned. "Fuck me."

Asher shot him a look of disdain. "You're not anyone's type, kid. But your wish might be granted with where you're going."

Casey's eyes went wide, and she shuffled behind me. "Can we go?" she whispered. "I don't want . . ." She licked her lips, clearly nervous. "I don't want to stay here."

It was on the tip of my tongue to tell her no.

I tried but the words wouldn't come. With a sigh, I grabbed my backpack by the strap and hooked it over my right shoulder. My taser went into the front pocket of my bag, just in case.

"Thank you." Casey wrapped her arms around her middle. "Just . . . thank you."

Her quiet praise didn't sit well with me. It felt too much like a spotlight, bright and without a single place to hide. I averted my gaze from the gratitude lining her bruised features. "Don't worry about it. Let's go."

I didn't make it two steps past Asher before his large hand clamped down on my forearm, stilling my escape. He'd touched me twice tonight; the first, a simple brushing of our fingers, had stolen my breath. This time, my heart thudded in my chest with something that felt a lot like anticipation.

"Have a problem, Sergeant?" I kept my tone light, slightly wry, but I worried he could detect what I so wanted to hide. Interest, in him. It was incredibly inconvenient.

His thumb stroked my arm. "Don't leave the station without me."

"Is that a request or an order?"

I felt his breath by my ear, rustling the strands of my hair. "An order, Miss Washington." His thumb continued its up and down strokes, sending sparks of *something* throughout my body. "You good at obeying?"

There was no mistaking the way his voice dropped an octave. This man was not one for bullshit, as he'd told me, and so I wouldn't give him any in return.

With a little tug, I pulled free of his grasp and flashed him a grin. "Not in the least. Obeying has never been one of my strong suits."

"Start learning," he growled in what I had to assume was the tone he took with the men and women in his unit. "I'll see you at the station. Don't make me chase you."

The words had the opposite effect on me than what he'd probably hoped.

They didn't inspire fear.

No, they inspired lust.

Sergeant Lincoln Asher could chase me all he wanted, but unless I let him, he'd never catch me.

SEVEN OF SWORDS

SEVEN

Avery

T he back of my neck prickled with anticipation as I waited on Asher by the eighth district precinct. It would be all too easy to blame the goosebumps flaring to life on my skin on the cool, wrought-iron fence against my back. A lot easier than admitting the truth, which was—

"You followed a command, Miss Washington. I'm impressed."

My gaze cut to his powerful form striding toward me from Royal Street. The dim street lights allowed the darkness to hug him, casting shadows across his face. His left hand rested on the butt of the gun on his hip, and I swallowed that inconvenient anticipation all over again. Pushed it as far down as it would go until it'd been strangled into nonexistence.

I didn't have time for men, not even ones who looked like, or exuded the confidence that Lincoln Asher did.

Tilting my chin, I allowed my crossed arms to fall to my sides as I pushed away from the fence. "I thought I'd show you how it's done, considering you followed me when I specifically told you not to."

Nothing in his stoic expression hinted at humor, but I had the impression that he was laughing at me. "We can pretend that's what went down."

"Pretend?" My nose wrinkled as I kept my eyes on his face. He stopped less than a foot away, looming large in front of me. His close proximity forced me to tip my head back to maintain eye contact. Lincoln Asher was a big man —a lot bigger than me.

"Pretend," he confirmed evenly. "I was on my way home for the night when my radio went off with a 103-F." He cupped my elbow and, for a half-second, I was convinced he was about to pull me into his embrace. My mind raced with the possibilities, shifting through them each individually—would he kiss me? Did he want to? Hell, did *I* want him to?

Then his words actually penetrated the thick fog of that unwanted anticipation, and I blinked at the unfamiliar term. "103-F?"

"A fight."

Asher didn't pull me into a hug. Instead, he backed me up, using his much larger frame to intimidate me into stepping backward, toward the pale-yellow district station that looked a lot more like an elegant English mansion than a home base for cops.

My feet followed his lead, regardless of the fact that I had no plans to step back inside the building with him. "So what, you thought you'd come and rescue me?" My voice stuck in my throat, and I forced a rough cough to clear it. "You're assuming I needed your help."

Blue eyes flashed in my direction. "You're assuming that I even knew it was you."

Good point.

Embarrassment slithered like vines around my legs, dragging my pace to a slow crawl.

He mimicked my pause, his heavy combat boots grinding to a halt, his wide shoulders turning so that we were chest to chest. Or, more accurately, chin to chest. His fingers fluttered up my arm, coasting over my right shoulder. Landing directly on that sensitive place where my neck and shoulder met. Stealing my breath and infusing my head with wild, foreign fantasies that were as alien to me as the man invading my space.

"I had no idea it was you, but the moment I did . . ." His thumb arched upward, sweeping under the jut of my jaw in a gesture that was both erotic and possessive. "I don't get angry, Avery. I never lose my cool. And then I saw you hit the pavement, and I was ready to unload my clip into any fucker who touched you. *No one* touches you or they answer to me."

At my swallow, I felt the imprint of his thumb like a stamp on my neck. "You hardly know me."

His blue eyes fell to my lips. "No, I don't. Not yet, but I will."

With that mysterious comment, he stepped back, and the sudden space was like I'd been relieved from a vacuum. My lungs seized air in one, two, three quick breaths. Desperate to change the conversation, I averted my face and watched a group of tourists stumble down Royal with green Hand Grenade bottles clutched in their hands.

"You want me to give a statement, don't you?" I asked, my gaze locked on the tipsy tourists. "That's why you asked me to stick around?"

"In part."

"And the other part?"

It happened then, just the smallest uptick of his mouth. It was hardly a smile. Hardly worth noting at all, really. But still, I felt it all the way down to my toes. Felt it all the more when Asher tucked a hand against the small of my back and murmured, "Don't ask questions when you aren't ready for the answers."

Did I want to push for more?

Pushing meant admitting to this unwanted attraction, an attraction like I'd never felt before.

But pushing also meant gaining something in return— information, for one. Lincoln Asher carried himself like he held the weight of the world on his shoulders. It seemed unlikely that he could get to where he was now within the NOPD without learning a thing or two about the city's ring of politicians. I wanted access to those secrets. I needed access to that information.

I craved, after all these years, to set aside my thirst for revenge and live my life without glancing over my shoulder every other moment.

More than anything, I wanted to know the reason why my stepfather had my mother murdered in cold blood. A former oil tycoon like him, Foley had swept her death under the rug with hand-rolled cash to all the right people, I had no doubt about that. And that wasn't even covering the fact that he'd wanted me dead, too.

Mentally shaking loose the memories, I indicated the station with my hand. "Should we go in? I'd rather not spend my entire night on the front steps."

My abrupt change of heart earned me a hard, unrelenting once-over.

Asher didn't say a word as he spun on his heel and took the steps two at a time. I followed at a brisk pace, head held high. It was time for me to stop hiding in the shadows, however terrifying the prospect.

Pulse racing as we entered the marble-floored foyer, I glanced around the brightly lit room. Receptionist desk to my right. A hallway extending away from the lobby, leading to god-knows-where.

"Follow me."

At the sharp note in Asher's voice, I drew my jacket tight around my shoulders.

This is what I'd wanted all these years—an in. A chance to learn more about my stepfather. An opportunity to do more than just passively collect information from those who sat at my table to have their tarot cards read.

Not that I expected the mayor of New Orleans to be strolling around a police precinct on a Sunday night, but the mere possibility had me stretching on my toes and craning my neck, just in case.

"This is us," Asher murmured as he paused by a wooden door to our right. He palmed it open and ushered me inside with a hand to the center of my back. Desks were haphazardly arranged throughout the room. Some had computers on them. Others were bare, save for stacks of papers. A lone officer sat on the far end of the room, shoulders slouched as he stared at the computer screen before him. Asher indicated to a desk to our left, and he settled his hand on the worn wood. "Take a seat here. I need to grab something first, and then we'll get this over with."

I met his gaze. "Not even a little scared that I'll take off?"

Asher glanced at the other officer, and then retrained his attention on me. "You aren't going anywhere."

"You're cocky."

"No," he said with another one of his barely-there smirks, "I'm just confident that you're craving something else entirely from me, and I plan to deliver until you're weak in the knees and sprawled across my lap." The grin that widened his mouth was all male satisfaction. "Get comfortable."

The expanse of his back winked at me as he slipped through the open door and out into the hall.

It took a whopping two seconds for the bravado to un-pinch from my features.

I dropped inelegantly to the rolling desk chair, my knees—true to form—trembling way too hard to keep me upright or my dignity intact. Lincoln Asher was . . . he was —I skipped my sweaty palms across my thighs and drew in a sharp breath.

He was trouble with a capital T.

Trouble for my piece of mind, for my aims, for my body. Even now, I couldn't forget the way his hand had felt curled around my neck. The rapid tattoo of my heart rate had yet to slow, and as I sat there, there was only one lingering thought: *I wanted more*.

I was twenty-five, a virgin, and the only man who'd ever kissed me had taken that desire from me with a disturbing thrust of his tongue in my mouth and his fingers yanking painfully on my hair. I'd sworn then that I would never give another man the opportunity to take what wasn't his.

I bowed to no one.

And yet, in the span of two days, Asher had thrown everything I wanted to believe about myself out the window—and he'd done it all with nothing more than the timbre of his voice, the rawness in his blue eyes, and a touch that was impossibly seductive.

"Stop," I muttered beneath my breath.

Here I was sitting at his desk, and instead of making use of my time, I was acting like a lovesick idiot. *Get your mind back in the game*.

Casting a quick glance at the other officer, whose

head was bobbing as though he'd passed out at his desk, I drew my attention back to Asher's workspace. Papers were stacked orderly in manila folders. Post-it sticky notes lined the right edge of the desk—across them all, he'd scrawled phone numbers and names of people I didn't know.

As quietly as possible, I tried each desk drawer.

The bottom one was filled with nothing but excess computer paper and empty envelopes.

The chair across the room screeched back when I tugged on the second drawer's handle, and I dropped my hand like I'd personally picked up a ball of flames. Clutched the lip of the desk as though I hadn't just been snooping.

"You good?" the officer asked, strolling toward me. He had bloated features and an equally round gut. Something told me he rarely worked the streets anymore. He nodded toward his desk. "Can't believe I fell asleep."

My fingers dug into the wood. "I noticed." I forced a casual smile. *Act normal.* "Long shift?"

His mouth melted into a grimace. "Didn't even realize I slept straight through the end of it."

"Ouch."

"Yeah." He cocked his head to the side. "You Asher's girl?"

"What?"

"You dating Asher? He doesn't bring anyone in here, ever. Straight to the interview rooms for civilians." He paused and let his dark eyes rove over my face. "It's protocol. Not bringing non-personnel in here, I mean."

Palms turning slick, I shifted in the rolling chair. My heels dug into the ground, and I pulled myself forward. Hands moving forward, glossing under the desk until . . . My index finger brushed against cool metal. It felt like a latch, and one trace of it with my fingers proved that accurate. But it wasn't—no, there was no way.

"Ma'am?"

My spine stiffened with the effort to not jolt at the sound of the officer's voice. "We're, umm . . ." *Think!* "We're old friends. We go way back." *To, like, yesterday.* I pushed down on the latch and sent up a silent prayer that I hadn't just doomed myself. "I'm not his girl."

Dark eyes didn't move from my face. "Then why did he say he was about to put you over his lap?"

The second drawer, the one I'd wanted to open earlier, popped open. It extended no farther than an inch, maybe two, but holy crap, this was the moment. I tore my eyes away from the drawer and tried to look normal.

Act normal.

My heart, meanwhile, thundered in my chest like a stampede of elephants dancing on already-fractured ice.

"It's an old joke," I told the officer with a smooth smile. The same smile I used on my customers in Jackson Square. "Ash—*Lincoln,* he's had a crush on me for years."

The guy's nose wrinkled as he shifted his gaze downward, over the top half of my body—which was all that was visible to him above the desk. "How old are you?"

Clearly, not old enough. "Thirty." I lied, smiling wider, toothier, faker. "I've got a baby face. It's the curse of all women in my family."

His answer was nothing more than an incomprehensible mumble.

"What was that?" I itched to pop open the drawer fully. Patience was both my strongest suit and my biggest weakness. I was complicated like that. "I'm sorry, I didn't catch what you said."

Digging into his back pocket, he pulled out his wallet and flipped it open. Five steps brought him to the far corner of the desk, and then he was palming a rectangular white card and sliding it over to me.

I picked it up, turned it over, and stared at the name printed in small, block font across the back: DT. SAMUEL LOCKAR. "Thank you?"

"In case you need anything." He rapped his knuckles against the desk. "Lying won't get you anywhere, miss."

It was a struggle to swallow the sudden lump in my throat. "I didn't lie." Twenty-five to thirty was more like a dramatization, if anything.

"Yeah." The detective didn't sound like he believed me. "Let's put it this way. Asher's known to like 'em younger. Just think about that before you keep up y'all's . . . friendship."

Lockar didn't give me a chance to say anything else. He swept out of the office, gently shutting the door behind him. Leaving my breath somewhere over the Mississippi River because it surely wasn't with me right now.

What in the hell did he mean? Asher liked them *younger*?

I caught my wide-eyed expression in the black screen of the desktop computer. There was no way Lockar could mean . . . . I lifted my hand to trace my reflection in the screen. No way. I hadn't gotten that sort of vibe from Asher at all.

And what do you really know about men?

Fuck.

I turned sharply from the computer and got down to business. This was not an opportunity I was going to lose out on. Snapping open the drawer, I gave the interior a cursory glance. Restaurant menus littered the space. I dove in a hand, shuffling through the folded pamphlets.

At the sound of a door slamming shut, my shoulders twitched and I held still.

My lungs seized a fistful of air I didn't dare let out, and when three seconds passed with no one waltzing into *this* office, I went back to work.

There had to be something.

Why have a locked drawer if all you kept inside were takeout menus?

On a whim, I tried the other drawers again. They all popped open without trouble, which meant . . . Option Number Two it was, then. No way would a man like Lincoln Asher waste a drawer with a lock. I refused to believe it.

I shoved the menus aside, and if it weren't for the fact that I was searching hard, I never would have noticed it.

Pressed up against the outer edge of the drawer, its cardboard backing facing me, a small, thin notepad caught my eye.

Among restaurant menus and receipts, it stuck out like a jaguar in an aquarium.

I flipped it over.

Names were scrawled down half its length, taking up perhaps four or five lines of the white-lined paper. There was no header at the top. Nothing to signify who these people were or why Asher had taken the time to document them all, and then shove it to where it wouldn't be noticed. I skimmed the names, one by one, my heart hammering in my chest at the mere possibility that Asher might push open the door and catch me.

Josef Banterelli.

Ba-dump.

Micah Welsh.

Ba-dump.

Tom Townsend.

Ba-dump.

Zak Benson.

Ba-dump.

A familiar name on the last line stopped me cold.

Tabitha Thibadeaux.

And then, with a pained whine of dry hinges, the door swung open.

FOUR OF PENTACLES

A sher kicked the door shut with his heel.

Under his right arm, he carried a set of folders—all of which he dropped on the desk, just beside my elbow. "Sorry you had to wait," he said. "I had to pick up Casey's report, and then one of my guys had a question." He glanced up from the folders, in my direction. "You'd think they've never gone through Academy with some of the shit they like to bring to me."

My smile was tight, and I was surprised I could even hear him over the persistent ringing in my ears. The metal rings of his notebook stabbed me in the butt as I shifted uncomfortably in the office chair. Was sitting on the notebook particularly savvy? Not even a little bit. But there'd been little time to do anything else, even unzip my backpack and thrust the notebook inside.

"I always thought that there are no stupid questions."

Taking the seat opposite mine, Asher flipped open the top file. "There are stupid questions. The only people who say there aren't have got too much heart."

An interesting response.

I hummed a little in my throat, deliberating on my answer. There was no mistaking the way his blue eyes flashed hot at the noise, nor the way his fingers tightened around the pen he'd picked up in his left hand. Did I affect him the same way he did to me? I made the noise again, just to test him, and Asher didn't disappoint. His gaze dropped to my mouth, his jaw visibly tightening as though he wanted nothing more than to throw the desk against the wall and sit me on his lap.

The look on Asher's face . . . it was of a man restrained. My thighs clenched together at the realization, and I pinched my knee beneath the desk to break the spell of desire heating my core and curling my toes. It wasn't why I was here.

Liar.

"Are you suggesting that you don't have a heart?" I finally asked, leaning forward to prop my elbows on the desk. The notebook's spiral rings went flat under my weight. *Aw, crap.* Swallowing, I added, "You don't strike me as the cliché type, Sergeant."

He cleared his throat. "Cliché?"

"Yeah." I mimicked him, clearing my throat and dropping my voice by at least an octave. "Hello, I'm Lincoln Asher and you know what's different about me? I'm heartless." I watched his lips twitch, barely skimming the surface of a true smile but coming pretty damn close. "Fun fact," I said in my normal pitch, "the only people who go around saying they're lacking a heart are generally the folks who have actually got *too* much of one, but don't want people to know they're an inner softie."

"You got stats to back you up on this theory?" He set the pen down and met my gaze head-on. "Or are you just theorizin'?"

I offered a smile. "I've lived in the Quarter for over ten years. I know my fair share of heartless assholes."

"And I don't fit the mold?" He sounded pleasantly intrigued by the prospect. "And here I've been thinking all these years that I'm king of the heartless assholes around here. I'm a little ticked off that someone took my crown."

His response made me choke out a surprised laugh. "Was that a joke?"

"What?" Dark brows rose high on his forehead. "Heartless assholes can't be funny?"

"Not the king."

"Ah," Asher murmured, "but we've already agreed that I've been dethroned."

He sure fit the mold for dethroned royalty. Messy hair, bright blue eyes that shone like topaz gems, and those scars that carved the side of his face. Something in his tone intrigued me more than even the scar. Leaning back in my chair, I gave him a slow once-over. "Looking at you, I'd be inclined to think of you as less like a king and more like the king's executioner."

If I weren't studying him so acutely, I would have missed it—the smallest flare of his nostrils and the slight pull of his mouth into a harder, more uncompromising line.

Interesting.

Asher dropped his gaze to the folders before him. "Let's get this done."

For the next twenty or so minutes, he put me through the test.

Where were you walking when you stumbled upon the assault? Back to my apartment.

Did you utilize your stun gun before or after the perpetrator laid hands on you? After.

Did you recognize any of the perps as someone you may have had contact with before tonight? No, they were complete strangers.

With each new question, my hands grew damp and my stomach roiled at the memories. Memories of a younger me, a more innocent me—of groping hands and rickety beds that squeaked under heavy weights.

I'd always been resourceful, even at the age of thirteen when I'd found myself living on the streets with nowhere to go. And there's something to be said about open-ended possibilities.

At any time, I could have filched a ticket for the Mega-Bus, Destination Unknown.

I used to sit by the bus stop, over on Elysian Fields and North Claiborne, with a fried chicken-wing restaurant at my back and concrete all around me. I used to walk there from the French Quarter, at least two miles there and back, and watch people come and go with their colorful suitcases and their laughter catching in the humid, Southern air. At any time, I could have snuck onboard. By the time anyone realized there was a stowaway, like some ruffian-kid out of an old-time movie, we would have been halfway to Alabama or maybe Texas or even Arkansas, depending on which MegaBus I took.

I never did get on that bus.

I never could leave this city, which has gifted me more bad memories than good.

"We're all set."

Hands clenched together in my lap, I put voice to the question burning on my tongue. "Do you like what you do?"

Asher's face gave nothing away, as was the norm for him, I was beginning to see. "Excuse me?"

I nodded to him, and he'd have to be a fool not to realize that I was talking about the noticeable scars across his cheek. He bore his wounds for all to see; mine were secreted away in my heart. But for him, he could leave this job and do something else. I couldn't leave being *me*, no matter how many new names I adopted.

"Do you like being a cop? That's a better way to put it."

Like a veil unraveled by a string, Asher's blue eyes flicked away. "I've been on the job for over a decade."

I'd wondered about his age. Aside from the faint lines that appeared by his eyes when he (rarely) smiled, Lincoln Asher could have been anywhere from mid-twenties to early-forties. But, as a cop, it made sense that he'd blend in.

I've been on the job for over a decade—I turned the words over in my head, pulling them apart and quickly dissecting them. "All right, Mr. Vague." I waggled my brows, teasing him. "You do realize that's not an answer, right? Being on the job and *liking* the job are two completely different things."

Dropping a forearm to the desk, he leaned in. "Reverse the tables. Do you like reading cards out on the Square?"

I could give him the lie or I could give him some semblance of the truth and hope for a smidgeon of it in return. I went for the latter: "It pays the bills." *And gets me much-needed information.* "But, no, it's not a long-term career for me. You won't see me out there in thirty years still catering to folks who refuse to see what's directly in front of them already."

Nothing in Asher's face registered shock, but instinctually, I got the feeling he hadn't expected for me to pull the blunt act. His fingers drummed a monotonous beat on the desk. "Working for the NOPD keeps me focused," he said after a long pause. "If I had the opportunity to do something else, I'd honestly be lost."

"I would be a veterinarian."

Dammit.

Asher's left brow arched high at my unintended confession. "You can't now?"

Not without a high school or a vet degree. Not with a fake name. Not when your stepfather still liked to wax on about his poor dead wife and the stepdaughter who'd turned up dead after killing herself.

"Nah," I murmured, my tone casually dismissive. And then I spun the lie I'd repeated to myself for years now: "It would be fun, but it's hard work. I'm much more suited to reading cards. I can go down to the square whenever I want. There are no rules, no high expectations."

For a moment, he said nothing and the air seemed to shrivel in the silence. Then, "We're all set here . . . unless you've got a question for me about the report?"

My toes curled in my shoes. Right.

"No questions." I hastily stood, then, remembering the spiral-bound notebook on the chair, collapsed back down. "Actually, I have one." My fingers snaked under my butt as Asher watched me from across the desk, his expression all but reading, *Get to it already*. "I'm a little hungry. Maybe it's the adrenaline calming down, I don't know."

Slowly, a smile pulled at his firm mouth. "Are you asking me out to dinner?"

It seems that I am.

Snagging my backpack strap, I drew the bag between my legs and made a show of ducking my head, feigning a bashfulness that wasn't at all me, and drew the zipper tags apart. "Maybe I am." Right butt cheek lifted ever-so-slightly, I pulled the notebook from its place and inched it to home base. Slowly. Slowly. *Slowwwllyyyy*. "It's a little late for dinner but maybe some beignets?" I lifted my chin to peer at him from behind the curtain of my dark hair. "Café du Monde is *so* romantic at this time of night."

For the first time in my life, I fluttered my lashes.

Asher sat back in his chair, his crisp uniform shirt pulling tight across his broad chest. Under the office lights, his NOPD sergeant's badge shined like a beacon of trustworthiness.

The notebook currently dropping into my backpack said otherwise.

Because now that I'd had time to think about it, I recognized the two top names from a recent spread in *The Times-Picayune*. The obituary section, in particular.

Both Josef Banterelli and Micah Welsh were dead.

Slit throats.

Bodies bobbing in the Mississippi River in the early morning hours.

"Beignets it is." Asher flashed me a quick, almost-missed-it grin. "Why don't you wait for me in the hallway? I'll wrap this up and then we can go."

"You got it." I saluted him with fake confidence and hightailed it to the door. The moment I burst free, I pressed my back against the neighboring wall and filled my lungs with oxygen.

It was just a notebook. Nothing more. And yet I felt as though I'd stolen contraband from a drug lord.

Maybe that's because Asher sort of looks *like a drug lord.*

Albeit a sexy one.

With the visual of his shiny fleur-de-lis NOPD badge in the forefront of my mind, I tightened my hold on the strap of my backpack and waited for him to emerge from the office.

A casual sharing of powdered donuts had never hurt anyone, and no matter how touristy the restaurant, Café du Monde had been a local favorite of mine since I was a young girl. Before Momma was brutally murdered and my life upended for reasons I still didn't know.

"Ready to go?"

Like I'd been caught with drugs myself, my butt cheeks clenched together, and my heart went into triple-time as Asher stepped out and then slid the door closed behind him.

"Yup!" The way I popped my *P* was not suspicious at all . . . *not*. I stifled an awkward laugh and tried again. "I'm starved."

Better, that was better.

"For beignets?" He settled a hand on the small of my back, directing me toward a door at the end of the hall with a red-neon EXIT sign posted above it. "I'll be sure to get us two orders."

One shove of his free hand against the steel and we were back out in the Quarter again, music blasting from nearby nightclubs, a hot and humid breeze tangling my hair and whipping it across my face.

I reached up to tug the strands back behind my ears, only Asher beat me to it.

Big, masculine hands framed my face and if I'd been concerned about breathing regularly beforehand, it was nothing compared to now. My lips parted as though on someone else's command and my hair seemed to glue itself to the cushion of my bottom lip.

Asher's hands didn't move, but his blue gaze roved over my face.

Lust.

I wasn't so much of a novice that I didn't recognize the emotion swirling in his eyes, nor the way his body stiffened even as he hunched his shoulders . . . to get closer to my height? It was tough to tell.

"What are you doing?"

Such a stupid question but it formed anyway and found life in the space between us.

"I'm starved," he said, the pads of his thumbs brushing over my jawline with an achingly soft touch. I barely had time to register the fact that it might be the softest caress I'd ever known—at least from my cognitive, adult years— before Asher added, "And not for beignets."

My back collided with the police precinct behind me, my backpack squishing audibly at the abrupt contact, as Asher slid his hands from my face down the length of my arms to where he captured my wrists. He lifted them, and I swore my breathing grew more uneven the higher they were drawn.

Up.

Up.

Up.

Above my head they went, until my wrists were criss-crossed, and he had one hand holding them in place.

Sharply, I inhaled through my nose. I was back in that place again, torn between lifting my knee and nailing him in the balls for manhandling me like I was some throw-away toy and—my eyes squeezed shut at the truth— wanting to see where this led.

My hands jerked at the realization, and Asher only readjusted his grip and dropped his other hand to my collarbone, his fingers teasing at the collar of my shirt.

"What are you doing?" This time when I repeated the question, there was no denying that I sounded like I'd run for miles.

Naturally, Asher sounded completely composed when his firm lips parted to confess, "Kissing you."

This is where you knee him right in the dick. Go on. Do it. Heel up, leg lifted, knee primed in position.

I didn't do any of that.

As if my body had decided to operate on instinct alone, my hips angled to better cradle his weight against my body.

It was a total betrayal—I didn't hook up with men and I definitely never gave them the time of day, but Lincoln Asher wasn't like most men.

He was a police sergeant, which meant I had to obey him in some capacity . . . right? Since he was an enforcer of the law, it only made sense that if he set a new rule, it was my duty as an upstanding citizen of New Orleans to see it through to the end.

Sometimes, it felt criminally good to lie to myself.

I tossed my hair back, careful not to smash my head on the stucco behind me. "If you're so hungry," I drawled, trying to gauge the thoughts glittering in his inscrutable blue eyes, "then why haven't you broken your fast yet?"

His grin was lightning-quick.

It was there and then it was gone, and yet I felt warm from its second-long presence anyway.

His grip retightened on my wrists, his gaze never veering from mine. "Oh, I will," he said, his low baritone brimming with silent conviction, "but I think I'll start here first . . ." His fingers tugged at my shirt collar, exposing my neck.

Asher took full advantage.

He lowered his head, kept me pinned to the wall with one hand, and dragged his mouth along my skin.

I trembled under his touch—my limbs, my lips, my damn toes all shaking.

My eyes fell shut and for the first time in my life, I allowed myself to feel.

His broad chest moving against mine as he inhaled deeply.

The soft puffs of air against my skin, with every exhalation, as he gently bit down on my earlobe.

The rough callouses on his palm as they rubbed against my restrained wrists.

Nothing about Lincoln Asher was soft—except, perhaps, for his tongue.

And nothing about my locked position should have been a turn-on, but it was. Oh, it *was*, and when a moan broke free from between my clamped teeth, it was only to hear Asher chuckle softly, like he'd just been given entry to the one place which had always been off-limits.

His lips landed on the underside of my jaw, and I gasped at the contradiction of his roughly-stubbled cheeks as they grated and marked the soft skin of my face.

Another kiss, this one to my cheek.

And then yet another, this one to the corner of my mouth.

It was going to happen.

My fingers curled in expectation and my heart kicked into overdrive and I had a split-moment decision to make: angle my head to receive the kiss or meet him halfway?

I cursed my inexperience.

I cursed my childhood obsession with TV shows that focused more on wildlife in the Rockies than kissing.

I cursed myself for spending hours in the club, waiting while Katie tended the bar, and only imagining what it might be like to be in any pair of feminine shoes while a man worked me into a kissing frenzy.

In the end, I opted for the classic face tilt seen in every rom-com movie ever. Romantic. Unassuming. Patient.

"Open your eyes," came his low order, "I want you to know who's kissing you."

My blinking didn't coincide with a kiss.

Not even a peck.

Instead, a phone's ringtone sliced through the air, angry and loud. Asher's hand fell from my wrists as he stepped back, already reaching into the pocket of his uniform slacks. "Fuck," he ground out, his face a mask I couldn't decipher as he glanced at the name blinking across his screen. "I've got to take this."

"Okay." It was better this way, I told myself. Kissing Sergeant Lincoln Asher was wrong on so many different levels, starting with the fact that he was well-appointed within the NOPD, in a way that made me uncomfortable —and ending with the fact that I didn't particularly *like* him.

Liar.

I shoved the little voice out a window and slammed the proverbial glass shut.

In a voice that I prayed sounded one-hundred percent unaffected, I murmured, "Don't worry, I got it."

The phone kept on with its incessant ringing.

"Avery, just wait a damn second. Don't—"

I ducked past him, head down. "I'm going to head out." With a wave of my hand, I gestured at his phone. "Have fun with that."

Vibrant cursing was all I heard as I hustled away, getting lost in the crowds of the French Quarter.

This was for the best. Kissing Asher—kissing a *cop*— would be a disaster of epic proportions. Like the city's politicians, half of the police force in New Orleans were as crooked as they came.

New Orleans has been corrupt since 1718, Jay used to joke while we sat at the dinner table. *It's all this city knows.*

My mother would laugh, a gentle sound that always soothed me.

My stepfather would smirk.

And now, as I wound my way through throngs of people on Bourbon, my blood ran cold.

I could want Asher until the end of my days, but unless I could determine that his connections with Tabitha and the two dead men were nothing more than a coincidence, it was best that I kept far, far away from the brooding sergeant.

Something told me that that would be easier said than done.

And when I snicked my lock closed after entering the Sultan's Palace ten minutes later, I peered out the peep-hole, just in case I wasn't truly alone.

MAJOR ARCANA

"Take a seat, Sergeant."

What remained of my erection died at the sight of my lieutenant's *I-eat-small-children-for-breakfast* expression when I knocked on his office door. Stefan Delery had always been a ruthless motherfucker—I'd halfway convinced myself over the years that he'd been born with a stick shoved up his ass, and everyone in the district knew better than to piss the man off.

Everyone except for me.

I lowered myself in the chair opposite his, keeping my feet evenly planted on the tiled floor as I settled in for what was indubitably going to be an ass-chewing. "I'm surprised to see you here this late at night, L-T." I kept my tone passive when I added, "It's got to be way past your bedtime."

Nothing in the man's face twitched, not even his mustache.

"How long have we known each other, Asher?"

His question came like an unexpected left hook to the face when you're prepared for a right fist. Refusing to show my surprise, I murmured, "Are we counting the first time we met, when we were so obliterated that we rode the streetcar Uptown and back to the Quarter four times before we realized we were on a fast track to nowhere?"

Delery stared at me, his green eyes unblinking.

Christ, this wasn't going to go well.

Scrubbing a palm over my mouth, I let out a pent-up breath. "You were my sergeant when I was first assigned out in the East. Ten years ago."

"First night you were there a car blew up."

Despite the years since, the memories of licking flames and torched steel teasing at my combat boots, as I rounded the explosion, still hadn't been erased.

Feeling as though I'd just swallowed the fumes from the roasting engine, I said, "You told me to find the perp."

"And you did." Lines fanned out from Delery's eyes, as much of a smile as he'd ever given since his wife had passed two years earlier. "You were that crazy fucker running into the flames with no gear on but your damn duty belt, not a worry about your safety."

The silver lining about having nothing to live for was that taking a risk wasn't terrifying. I had no one at home to return to, no kids to tuck into bed or a wife to press into my side as we fell asleep after a long day.

I'd been alone since birth, an unwanted child who'd been dropped in foster care at an early age.

I dropped my elbows to my knees. "Where are you going with this, Stefan?" We'd known each other for years, had worked side-by-side through some of the roughest cases of the last decade in this city. "I know you didn't ask me to come in here past midnight so we could shoot the shit about the good old days."

"You've always been a good cop because you're fearless, Ash. You're levelheaded. That's the *exact* reason I put in a request to have you transferred here when you passed the sergeant's test three years ago." Delery leaned in, forearm on the desk, his closed-off expression unraveling into twitching mustaches, grinding teeth, and narrowed eyes. "I wanted that calm motherfucker who ran into the flames and then didn't lose his goddamn *shit* when he caught the perp."

Pressure built in my chest.

I needed to stay calm. Hell, I needed fresh air. The office suddenly felt stifling, even though I'd been in here dozens of times over the last three years since my transfer from New Orleans East to the French Quarter.

Hands balling into fists on my thighs, I kept the top half of my body, waist-up, completely nonchalant. I wouldn't react. I wouldn't lose my cool. I wouldn't—

Delery did none of the above.

"You chose the wrong asshole to throw a fist at tonight," he snapped, voice rising with furor. "The wrong fucking asshole." With one hand, he shoved at a stack of manila folders off the desk, sending them soaring to the floor.

The papers scattered like confetti.

"Did you read my report? Those *kids* publicly assaulted two females tonight. I got physical. It happens, and I wrote it up as a use-of-force." It was damn hard not to yell or demand understanding, but that wouldn't help me. Not when Delery was out for blood. *My* blood, that much was clear. "Maybe I should have stepped aside. Let two innocent girls become victims just because I hadn't stayed in my place."

"You chose the son of Pershing University's president for your little showdown."

Just like that, every argument died on my tongue.
Every. Last. One.

"Marcus Hampton called his daddy as soon as the guys on the platoon brought him and his buddies to lockup, and no one—and I do mean *no one*—stood a chance once Joshua Hampton got involved."

I knew "Big" Hampton from assignments I'd worked at Pershing's football stadium as a rookie. Tall guy, a real bastard. He had his toes dipped in all of New Orleans' muddy waters, particularly those that made his coffers heavier and the women on his arm more attractive. In the years since he'd taken office, no one dared challenge the president of Pershing University.

And he'd never liked me much, not after his second wife had flirted with the "hot cop" right in front of him.

Sometimes New Orleans was really just too small.

I met Delery's gaze. "Big Hampton know it was me?"

All I was given in response was a slow nod that might as well have said *you're screwed*.

Raking my fingers through my hair, I slouched down in the chair and brought my fingers up to undo the top button of my Class B's. "What a fuckin' night." Which was, of course, the understatement of the century.

Delery matched my posture and did me one even better: he unpinned his badge from his chest and dropped it on the desk. My gaze latched onto the gold as it spun in a half-circle before falling flat on its back.

Symbolism if I'd ever seen one.

"He's already had words with Harlonne." At Delery's mention of our police chief, I barely held back a cringe. "Big Hampton wants you out of the force, Asher. No one touches his son, least of all a dirty cop. His words, not mine."

I was a dirtier cop than most, but no one knew that.

No one but Joshua Hampton, who now wanted my head on a platter.

It was assuredly *not* a great day to be me.

"So that's that, then?" I laughed, and even to my own ears, it sounded bitter. Angry. I had every right to be. I'd invested *years* into the NOPD, into the politics of New Orleans, into—

I cut those thoughts short, clenching my fists on my knees and tipping my head back to stare at the popcorn-raised ceiling. If it weren't Hampton holding the reins, there wouldn't be an issue. But there were three men you didn't cross in this city:

Joshua "Big" Hampton.

Jay Foley.

Jason Ambideaux.

I had the luxury of being on the shit list of two of the three "J's" that ran ship here.

"I talked with Harlonne an hour ago," Delery said, his voice low as though he worried someone might overhear him, "and we're not going to get rid of your sorry ass."

Relief sank into my limbs. "Thanks, L-T. Christ, it's been a hell of a—"

The lieutenant's mustache twitched as he averted his gaze. "Unfortunately, we've got to keep up appearances. Which means that we're cutting you a D-1. You're suspended, effective now."

Suspended? Back snapping straight, I dropped a fist to the desk and leaned in. "For how long? A week? Two weeks?"

Green eyes swiveled to meet mine. "For as long as it takes for Big Hampton to calm the hell down, *Sergeant*. We don't want to lose you—you're too damn good—and the men here respect you. But there's some shit we just can't get around and there's some people we don't need breathing down our necks, you hear me?" Like a mirror image, Delery brought a balled hand down on the desk.

"Hampton is one of those people, as we both know. So, you're going to sit your ass out until shit gets quiet again, and when it looks like you aren't about to be ripped a new asshole because you touched the man's kid, we'll welcome you back with open arms and a bouquet of flowers."

"Can we skip the flowers and go straight for the beer, at least?"

Delery's eyes crinkled again. "That'll have to be approved by Harlonne." Once again, his face turned somber when he rapped his knuckles on the desk. "Give me your badge and your gun, Ash. Let's get this over with."

Fifteen minutes later, my feet hit the concrete steps outside of the district station, and I might as well have been stripped naked.

No badge.

No police ID.

No department-issued .40 on my hip.

For the next however long, I wasn't Sergeant Lincoln Asher.

Just Lincoln Asher, and nothing about my suspension was a good thing.

No, I was just fucked.

EIGHT OF CUPS

TEN

"**Y**ou need a life."

My fingers froze on the computer keyboard at the sound of Katie's voice. Minimizing the internet tab so that Katie couldn't scope out anything over my shoulder, I twisted on the couch to face her. "I have a life."

"Let me amend that," she said, coming around the edge of the couch to take the opposite side. She sprawled out, legs tangled on the middle cushions, and nabbed a pillow to hold to her chest. "Ahem. You need to get *laid*."

Like she'd pulled him out of thin air, my mind immediately brought forth a visual of Lincoln Asher. Warming at just the thought of him, I closed the laptop and set it on the coffee table. When Katie wanted to have a discussion, there was no stopping her. It seemed futile to pretend otherwise.

And, honestly, maybe I did need to talk to her—to *someone*—about what I felt for Asher. Which was lust, nothing more, nothing less. Just plain and simple lust.

As though sensing my indecision, Katie grinned. "My boys are willing to take care of you."

If I'd been drinking something, I would have come up spluttering. As it was, I choked on thin air and gave myself a little shake. "I'm not—" More coughing. *Wonderful.* Nothing said "virgin" more than being unable to even have a conversation about sex. Clearing my throat, I tried again. "That's great, but I'm, uh, not having sex with George and Tyler."

Katie snagged her lower lip with her teeth. "What about George and Matt?"

I blinked. "What happened to Tyler?" Swinging my gaze to Katie's bedroom, I tacked on, "Tyler was balls' deep a week ago."

"Yeahhh, about that." My roommate shrugged, then flicked away imaginary lint from her shoulder. "Turns out that he didn't really like being *balls' deep* when another guy was dick deep, if you know what I mean."

Really, I shouldn't laugh. I *shouldn't* but the laughter bubbled up anyway. "You're kidding, right? Tyler bailed because you wanted him to participate instead of just jerking off in the corner like a voyeur?"

"I guess being that close to another dick made him feel uncomfortable."

I stared at her, hard. "You met him at a gay club, Katie, while he was back on leave. The man was oiled up and grinding on dicks when you waltzed in there."

"Okay! Fine, fine." She rolled her eyes, pillow going over her face. "Turns out that he wanted *me* to watch them together and let's be honest . . . I can be self-centered when it comes to sex. I wanted to be the center of attention and watching them fuck each other wasn't my idea of a good time."

"And the truth comes out!" I saluted her, one finger to my temple. "So, Tyler's off the table."

"Well, he's off the table for *me*." The pillow flung to the side as she sat up, a grimace pulling at her features. "But that doesn't mean he's off the table for you, so long as you've got another guy there with you. One word and Tyler will be hard and waiting."

But would he be as hard as Asher?

I blushed at the thought, then cursed myself for blushing in the first place. I'd felt the hard imprint of his erection against my belly, so what? It didn't mean anything. Plus, there was the whole I-shouldn't-be-looking-at-a-cop factor to consider.

One wrong move and he could out me completely, and then where would I be?

Possibly dead.

Probably dead.

Involuntarily, my gaze flicked to the closed laptop on the table again—a refurbished one that didn't have all the latest bells and whistles but certainly did the trick. I had no reason to suspect that Asher was the person who'd killed Josef Banterelli and Micah Welsh, but after following paper trails all night . . . Well, I wouldn't be surprised if he knew who'd been behind their ill-timed deaths.

And that was something I needed to discover quickly because if that list had any commonalities, then I needed to ensure Tabby was far, far away from here before her turn came around.

Maybe seeing Asher wouldn't be such a bad idea . . .

"You've got that face again."

Careful not to show my ace, I offered an easy grin. "*That* face? Last I was aware, I only had one of them."

From the way Katie studied me, it was clear she didn't believe me.

"Don't even play that game," she said, tossing back her hair and snuggling deeper into the couch cushions, pillow once again clamped to her chest. "I've known you long enough to know when you're up to something, Ave. Hell, I might be the *only* person who knows you well enough to figure out when you're up to no good."

I shifted on the couch, uncomfortable under her acute assessment. "I promise that I'm up to only good." Flashing her a wink, I prayed that she'd let the matter drop. Talking about sex I could handle, but whenever Katie hooked her claws into me, demanding that I open up and spill my heart out, it generally meant for a few awkward days after.

It wasn't that I didn't trust her.

Of every person I'd met since my mother's death, Katie was perhaps the *only* person I trusted.

But even that trust went only so far.

All it would take is one slip-up from her at the club to the wrong patron and I'd be on the run. *Again.* I'd spent years looking over my shoulder, terrified that if I made the wrong move, I'd find myself at my stepfather's mercy. And, this time, there wouldn't be a merciful, faceless man to let me escape into the night.

Katie stared at me, then announced, "I need wine." Jumping up from the couch, she headed for our kitchenette. "You want wine?"

I wanted to research the two murders and hopefully connect the dots to Tabby. Still, Katie wasn't just my roommate, she was my best friend. I wouldn't take it for granted, now or ever.

Folding my legs beneath me, I propped an arm on the back of the couch. "Do we have any chardonnay left?"

Katie pulled open the fridge and a wine bottle emerged two seconds later. "We're skipping glasses tonight." Bottle in hand, she twisted off the top and tossed it on the kitchen counter before moving back to the couch, where she collapsed with absolutely no grace. "To girls' night," she said, lifting the bottle high.

"To girls' night," I echoed, gripping the chardonnay bottle by the neck when she passed it over after taking a pull from its mouth. The chilled wine slipped down my throat, and I tried to ignore Katie's unwavering stare. I passed the bottle back over to her. "So, everything going okay at work late——"

"I went through your files."

My heart flexed. Nerves. Fear. And, yes, beneath all the panic, anger.

I pressed my trembling hands to my lap and did my best to control that same tremble in my voice when I spoke. "Those files don't belong to you." I didn't succeed. My voice quivered, as did my entire body. "That wasn't . . . they aren't . . . you can't just go through people's belongings because you feel like it, Katie. T-that's *bullshit*."

She chugged the wine like a professional, then clasped the bottle between her knees. "It's not bullshit, *Avery*."

Every limb, muscle, tendon, went rigid at the way she uttered my name. There was nothing in the filing cabinet that could discriminate me—or that mentioned Laurel Peyton anywhere—but, still, worry cramped in my belly. *What if she knew?* I didn't even have the opportunity to open my mouth before she plowed on, all accusing fingers and narrowed eyes.

"It's not *bullshit*. We've been living together for years and I know close to nothing about you. *Nothing*. You've never had sex. You didn't drink liquor until you were twenty-one like some good girl from God-knows-where. You're twenty-five. *That's* what I know."

Desperation clawed at me, a silent urging for me to pack my things and get the hell out of dodge. Where I would go, I had no idea. Maybe it was time that I had no destination. That I left New Orleans.

And years of careful research would be washed down the drain, not to mention that if I left, there was a good chance Tabby could end up just like Josef and Micah. I couldn't even stomach the possibility.

Not that I had any idea of how to worm my way out of this showdown with my roommate.

A deep breath did nothing to calm my jitters. "Listen, Katie, I—"

"I'm over the lying," Katie marched on. "Do you realize just how much you owe me? I mean, yeah, you pay your own way and never ask for even a dime. But this rental property? It's in my name. Same with all of our utilities. I like you, Avery. I'm a girl who operates on gut instinct, and I've always liked you. But I can't—" She shoved her fingers through her hair. Drew in an uneven, shuddering breath. "I could kick you out right now. I could tell you to pack your bags and you'd be shit out of luck within the court of law."

It was definitely time for wine.

I reached forward, fingers ready to grasp the bottle, when it was snatched up and away.

My fingers caught nothing but air.

"You scared me last week, Ave, with those guys attacking you." Katie shook her head, and it was then that I saw the misery in her green eyes. She looked . . . well, she looked horrible. Exhausted.

"Kat—"

Another shake of her head, this one sharper than the last. "No, I need to . . . I need to get this out. You know that I don't have anyone. My parents are divorced; they remarried with so many more kids that I doubt remember who I even am. I moved to New Orleans with some idiotic idea that I'd find myself, and that, you know . . . my uncle might want to take pity on his brother's wayward daughter." Her lips curled in a bitter smile. "I found a stripper pole instead, so we all know how *that* worked out. I tarnished the family name, through and through. *Anyway,* what I'm trying to say is, just like I'm all you've got, you're all *I've* got. And right now, something could happen to you and you don't even have a real ID."

A startled laugh leapt to my lips. "That's what this all boils down to? Me having a fake ID?"

Katie tossed her pillow at my face, and I swatted it out of the way before it made contact. "You know what I mean," she muttered, "you're like this . . . this *shadow* or something. I don't know."

Strangely enough, that's how I felt. Like this city had kept my secrets, and I'd been sheltered ever since.

Until now.

I couldn't reveal everything to Katie, no matter how much I wanted to unload my burdens. There was still so much I didn't understand . . . so much that eluded me. So much that she simply couldn't know.

I dug my elbows into my knees, back hunched. *Say something.* It was either that or lose her completely, and the latter wasn't an option. "I've lived in N'Orleans my entire life." Ugh, not a great opener but it'd have to do. Lips parting, I tried to find the words that would unruffle Katie's feathers while still protecting my own. My gaze went to the laptop again, and this time I didn't look away.

"Someone murdered my mother," I finally said, only to hear Katie's shocked gasp. I didn't stop, in fear that her sympathies would derail me. "I was young and I don't remember much." The lie came out easily, even if I could still hear the *boom!* of the pistol now as it fired. My shoulders curled more, so much so that I nearly hugged my legs.

Just as I had that night when I'd buried my face into my bent knees. Nausea gripped my insides, and I forced myself to continue. "I ran, back then."

From between her fingers, my roommate whispered, "You saw her die?"

The blood, yes. Her body, no. "I heard it." *Continued to hear it.* "I was a scared little girl who was even more frightened by who could hurt me. What I'm trying to say is, the fake ID and all that . . . the underworld of New Orleans doesn't stop at the clubs on Bourbon. You know that. Runners like me, there are hundreds of us. Thousands, maybe. I swear to you, I'm exactly where I need to be."

"But you don't want to . . ." Biting down on the pad of her thumb, her gaze jumped from my face to the wine bottle to the stray couch cushions. "You really don't mind the anonymity? The constant hiding? What if . . . what if you ever want to get married? You'll never tell your spouse that you're actually someone else?"

It didn't seem worth the trouble to tell her that marriage wasn't in the cards for me.

Marrying someone meant trusting them to put you first, and I was highly skeptical of *anyone* putting me first—especially a man. Lightly, I ran my fingers over my sweatpants, over my inner left knee, tracing the spot where words were inked into my skin as a reminder: *I bow to no man*.

A lesson Jay Foley ensured I would never forget.

When I smiled, it seemed to creak across my face. "I figure I'll cross that bridge when I get to it."

As though I'd passed some sort of test, she handed me the wine.

I'd told her close to nothing, and even that felt like information overload.

Katie was bright colors and loud music.

I was darkness and silence.

She'd figure it out one day, and I could only swear to myself now that when shit finally hit the fan with Jay Foley after all these years, my best friend would be nowhere to be found. She'd be safe. And far, far away.

"Love you, Ave," she whispered, reaching out to squeeze my arm. "I'm sorry I went through your things."

"Don't worry about it." I returned the squeeze. "And love you too."

I thought of the files and notebooks I'd stashed in our unused cupboard above the refrigerator, files that included every ounce of information I'd accumulated over the years about my stepfather, along with any mention of my mother's death and my faked one in the newspapers.

Self-disgust clung to me.

I was good at hiding. Even better at deception.

And Katie would never know that the documents she'd found were nothing but decoys.

I brought the wine bottle to my mouth and took a large sip. I didn't deserve a friend like Katie, but that wasn't something I didn't already know.

You couldn't deserve a relationship when it was founded on a lie, and Katie, my roommate, my friend, my step-cousin, would never forgive me if she learned the truth.

Of that I had no doubt.

IV

THE EMPEROR

MAJOR ARCANA

ELEVEN

Lincoln

G rowing up, I'd been the kid who skipped school and then skipped detention right after that on principle alone. No doubt about it, I'd been a little shit.

But there'd been one day in the ninth grade where I'd managed to keep my ass in class long enough to learn something. English literature. Ms. Mackenzie. She'd been the real reason I'd stuck around, and it was her that I had to thank for discovering *Dante's Inferno* and his nine circles of hell.

No one else had found the book intriguing, but to me, it'd felt like I'd found a bible of sorts. Or, at least, a bible for the permanently fallen.

Ms. Mackenzie had thought it funny to test us all, just a little pop quiz to determine in which circle of hell we'd find ourselves. A personality quiz of epic proportions.

The girls giggled into their palms.

The other guys sat forward because, yeah, death and destruction was their thing after playing endless rounds of video games after school.

And me . . . I'd worked down the eraser of my pencil to the nub as I filled out the multiple-choice options. Determined to evaluate my fate by a scaling system some dude had created centuries before I was even conceived.

Pencils down, Ms. Mackenzie asked that we stand when our "circle" was called upon after she read out the answers. The overall average determined which circle we would have found ourselves in had we existed in the book.

One by one, she read out the questions and which answers correlated with which circle.

One by one, everyone stood.

And, one by one, I'd noted that my peers rose in clusters, with most falling into Lust or Limbo, that halfway, in-between spot where you descended no lower but weren't allowed to enter Paradise.

Not me.

Question after question, I climbed to my feet to find myself in a new circle of hell.

Lust.

Greed.

Treachery.

Violence.

Anger.

Ms. Mackenzie paused, pencil eraser against her cheek, to stare at me when it was all said and done. "Looks like you're well-traveled, Lincoln," she said with wide, pretty blue eyes.

The me at fourteen years old had nothing on me at thirty-four, twenty years later, and as I entered my house a week after my implemented suspension, there was no denying that I was on the verge of revisiting every damn one of Dante's circles all over again.

The bastard sitting at my kitchen table, drinking my

Scotch straight from the bottle, would have it no other way.

I snapped the door shut behind me and flicked the dead bolt into place, not that it had done me any good tonight. Dropping my mail onto the entryway table, I schooled my features into the blank mask that had served me well for years.

Almost as well as the .19 tucked into the waistband of my jeans and the second one attached to the concealed ankle holster on my right leg. I'd been safer as a cop than I was now as a civilian, and the irony of that wasn't lost on me as I took an empty seat at the kitchen table, my back to the refrigerator.

Damn bastard had already taken the seat that kept his back to the wall, and I scraped my chair across the tile so that I had a clearer view of every possible entry into the kitchen.

"Don't trust me, Lincoln?"

I bristled at that sly, familiar tone. "Last time we were in the same room, you aimed your nine-millimeter at my thigh and fired. Twice."

Jason Ambideaux, New Orleans's most infamous real estate mogul, chuckled into my bottle of Scotch. "Ever hear of the saying, 'let bygones be bygones?'"

It took every last ounce of self-control I possessed not to pull out my gun and unload a clip into the man's head. *Breathe*, I warned myself, fingers digging into my thighs. "Should I remind you that you left me to bleed out?" *And that maybe I'd like to return the favor, finally.*

With his slicked-back hair, dyed black to hide the grays, and the sharp business suit he wore like a second skin, Ambideaux was the physical embodiment of the power he'd wielded over New Orleans for the last twenty years. He was the bane of every competitor's existence, and those who didn't acquiesce gallantly to his established rein eventually found themselves face-down in the swamps of the Atchafalaya Basin two hours outside of New Orleans.

My sixteenth birthday had been commemorated with my first Basin run, at Ambideaux's command.

On the way back to New Orleans, I'd pulled over on the I-10 and vomited until there was nothing left but me dry-heaving on the side of the highway as the clock struck midnight like some fucked up fairy tale. If Cinderella had been given a gun instead of some glass slippers, she wouldn't have lasted an hour in my life.

At Ambideaux's silence to my question, I filled it in for him, my temper close to snapping. "Nothing to say?" More silence, each passing second more grating on my nerves than the last.

And then, finally, the bastard spoke: "The scars are worse than they told me."

It was the wrong thing to say.

The Scotch bottle shattering on the tile coincided with the mouth of my .19 connecting with Ambideaux's forehead. The force drove his skull into the wall with a sickening thud, and it was there, in the deepest recesses of my soul, that whispered for me to pull the trigger.

Revenge delivered swiftly was never as satisfying, but, goddammit, it would feel *good*.

"You don't have the balls, son," Ambideaux said, voice as even as if he'd been discussing a play by play of the weather and not staring down the barrel of a pistol, "put down the gun."

I put the gun down all right—dragging it down the center of his face, over the slope of his straight, aristocratic nose, until it settled against the pulse beating at his neck like some sort of hickey of death. Only when Ambideaux's right eyebrow twitched tellingly did I growl, "It wasn't enough for you to just let me die, was it?" The mouth of the .19 dug in a little more, my finger resting on the trigger guard. "Nah, you had me driven out to the Atchafalaya and tossed in as fuckin' gator meat like the rest of them."

I met his dark eyes. Felt the way he struggled to swallow with my gun jammed against his throat. The grin that spread across my face was one born of vengeance. "What was it you told me right before you pulled the trigger? Oh, yeah." I leaned in, breath coasting across his face, finger lifting off the trigger guard. "I won't think any less of you when you piss your—"

Arms clamped around my throat, squeezing off my oxygen supply, dragging me backward.

Pft! Pft!

Splintering glass echoed in my ears as my gun went off before being torn from my hands. Vision swirling, I gasped for breath and let instinct take over, driving an elbow into the body behind me. My attacker was big, but I was bigger, and I dug in my heels and wrapped my hands around his forearms, fully prepared to flip the asshole right over my shoulder and put the .19 at my ankle to good use.

There was always a benefit to being a walking artillery.

With my full weight, I arched my back to get momentum and then snapped my body forward like a slingshot, thighs clenching, knees tight, core flexing. I felt my attacker's feet come off the floor behind me as I assumed his full weight, and I buckled down, tightening my muscles, ready to—

Cold metal to my forehead stilled the fight in me, and I glanced up, past the barrel of my own weapon, to Ambideaux. His slicked-back hair was disheveled, his pristine suit rumpled, his expression ambivalent.

"You done?"

A sneer caught in my throat, even as gravity dropped

the bastard on my back, back onto my kitchen floor. Not even a second passed before he'd readjusted his grip, massive arms binding me once again.

Ambideaux twisted away, setting the Glock on the table, out of my reach. "Sit his ass down and make sure he can't move."

Ambideaux's lackey shoved me into the chair I'd just vacated, then snapped handcuffs around my wrists, the *click-click-click* of metal sliding into place a completely unmistakable sound. "Benefits to breaking and entering a cop's house," he grunted brusquely, "you made this way too easy for me." He drew up another chair and positioned it behind me. A half-second later, familiar cold metal touched the back of my skull. "We're all set, boss."

My fingers flexed in the restraints.

Ambideaux planted his ass on the edge of the table, arms crossed over his chest. "You're still a hothead, Lincoln." He shook his head with a low laugh, like I hadn't just been seconds away from ending his life. "Once a hothead, always a hothead. Damn, but I wish I'd been there when you punched Little Hampton. Would have made my year."

Grinning at my expense, he added, "Actually, you would have made my life a hell of a lot easier if you'd just" —he mimicked slicing his throat open—"finished off the deed."

When I opened my mouth to speak, the pressure point at the back of my skull increased. Narrowing my eyes, I gave that pressure right back, leaning my weight into that gun, challenging the owner to get on with it and shoot me.

After a moment, the pressure slackened, and my chest hitched with minute relief.

"I'm going to assume you didn't bust in here to remi-nisce about the good old times *or* talk about how much you want Hampton's kid dead." I eyed the gun on the table, then redirected my attention back to my old boss. "So why don't we cut to the chase and get this over with? Fill in the blank for me. You're here because of . . ."

"Impatient still, too." Ambideaux's mouth quirked up in a humorless grin. "It's like the last twelve years haven't existed, wouldn't you say?"

I bit the inside of my cheek to keep from mouthing off. I wasn't a hothead, not in the way he remembered. "Just answer the question, Jason. You're here . . . *why?*"

"I heard about your suspension."

Just like that, my heart threatened to leap out of my chest. I yanked forward, caught back by the handcuffs, and then grit my teeth. "It's not happening."

Ambideaux sank to his haunches before me, and then the gun at my head angled forward, leaving me no choice but to dip my chin and keep my eyes on the real estate mogul. If he were closer, I'd drive my foot into his chest hard enough to send him sailing backward.

But Jason Ambideaux hadn't spent years working toward being one of the three most feared men in New Orleans without learning a thing or two. He squatted just out of reach, one hand on his knee, the other on his inner thigh as he watched me.

"A deal is a deal, son," he murmured, looking not even a little remorseful about playing puppeteer with my life. My mother's life. "We agreed that for however long you were on the job, I'd leave you alone, but you've never been good at stepping back from playing hero." His dark eyes roved over my face. "Tell me, did you feel like a champ to know that you saved that poor girl from being raped? Or perhaps the other one, too . . . the one a colleague of mine spotted you with outside of the station last week?"

My vision flashed red, my chest heaving with labored breathing as the implication behind his words hit me.

He grinned wolfishly. "Ah, you're just figuring it out. Good, that's good." He tapped his knee as though debating on giving up information. "In case you're still concerned, Casey's doing quite well. I believe she opted for a gift card in exchange for her troubles, but I had something more sentimental in mind."

Sentimental, my ass. Visions of the poor girl sinking into the Atchafalaya Basin etched across my retina, and it was like I was sixteen all over again, feeling the urge to retch after tossing my first dead body into the swampy marshlands. My scars prickled with memories better left forgotten, and I swallowed the bile rising in my throat.

"You've always been such a saint, Lincoln," Ambideaux said in a contemptuous tone, "but you can't save them all."

Between clenched teeth, I ground out, "I won't help you. Put a bullet in the back of my head if it'll make you feel better, I don't give a shit."

"And leave your mother as she is? No, I don't think so." Knees popping as he stood, Ambideaux picked up the Glock and stared at it, his gaze almost wistful. "A deal is a deal, Sergeant, and you've already paid in blood. I agreed to leave you be for as long as you remained with the NOPD, but it seems that you've recently been suspended."

There was no end to the hatred that thrived in my veins. It pulsed, and, like poison, spread through me like an infection. "You fucking bastard," I spat, "you organized all of this. You really think you can—"

The pistol came out of nowhere, but holy hell, I felt it.

My head whipped to the side as the barrel made contact with my scarred cheek. The metallic taste of blood spurted in my mouth, pain erupting in my tongue as the impact forced me to bite down.

And all the while, the gun at my skull never wavered. If anything, the pressure increased, forcing me to look down completely, chin to my chest.

Like I was bowing to Ambideaux, no matter the fact that I was still slouched on the chair, hands handcuffed behind my back.

The longer I sat there, the drowsier I became. It wasn't my first concussion and I knew the symptoms well.

Stay awake. You need to stay awake.

It'd be easy to surrender to the darkness, to slip into the abyss and ride out the numbness of my existence until everything went black. Permanently.

Ambideaux had other plans.

His fingers sank into my hair, pulling my head up. I blinked and then blinked again, but no matter how many times my lids fell shut and opened again, he remained a hazy mirage that wouldn't sharpen.

"This is how it's going to work, son," he said, voice chipper for the first time since I'd walked in to find him drinking my Scotch. "I've got a little list that I need you to take care of for me. Knowing you, you'll get it squared away for me before you're back to work. And if you're not" —his fingers tightened their grip on my hair and I swallowed a hiss—"I'll just make sure your suspension ends up being just a little longer. How's that sound?"

He let me go and set the Glock on the table again, only to ferret around in his suit jacket. He revealed a spiral-bound notebook that he tossed at my feet. "Two are already done, which means that all that's left are three Basin runs . . . once you've taken care of business, of course."

My gaze latched onto the compact notebook, my

stomach turning at the sight of the familiar names. Two dead—Josef Banterelli and Micah Welsh. I hadn't seen them in years, but I'd still felt a pang of remorse over old times' sake when I'd heard about their deaths on the news. It was on the tip of my tongue to ask why Ambideaux had chosen the Mississippi River as their final resting ground, but the momentary concern was swept away under the frustration bubbling under my skin.

Twelve years. I'd spent *twelve* years putting this shit with Ambideaux behind me, and even if I'd done runs recently for a few people, *nothing* had ever been as bad as what Jason enjoyed tasking his "employees" with.

"I should point out that if you're hoping to get out of this, I've left an identical one of those notepads in your desk at the station." Grinning widely, Ambideaux straightened his suit and turned for the door. "And as we all know, *Sergeant*, you aren't allowed to set foot on NOPD property for the length of your suspension or risk being permanently terminated. What a predicament you've found yourself in, wouldn't you say? At the risk of working for *me* permanently, I suggest you take care of what I've given you. Your mother will thank you, I'm sure."

The door swung open and Ambideaux strolled out, whistling like a damn lunatic.

Another ten minutes passed before the bastard at my back stepped away and flashed me a gold key that he set on the table—on the *other* side of the table—before following his boss out.

Leaving me alone to my past that was, once again, my present and my foreseeable future.

The sinner.

The executioner.

The man who belonged in every circle of hell.

ACE of WANDS

MINOR ARCANA

He was here.

Surprise snapped my back straight, twining up my legs as my feet ground to a halt by the bar, sending my cocktail up, up, up, until the straw fit between my teeth and I'd guzzled half a Hurricane.

"You going to slow down there, girl?" Katie asked from behind the bar. Unlike mine, my roommate's shirt was tugged down low to show off the goods to the patrons, and with every shake of the cocktail mixer, her breasts shook almost as much for the crowd.

Meanwhile, I looked like a nun in comparison—jeans paired with ankle-high boots, topped off with an oversized sweater that did nothing for my figure. All that I was missing was the chastity belt and we could call it a day. My lack of sex appeal had never bothered me, and it hadn't bothered me as I'd waltzed out of the Sultan's Palace and walked the three blocks to the club with Katie.

Now it bothered me.

Because of *him*, I wanted to tie my sweater up around my ribcage and prove that I could be just as enticing as the

121

women gyrating on the bar tops. Him—Lincoln Asher. New Orleans police sergeant. Arrogant asshole. Almost-kisser of women up against brick buildings when they weren't expecting it and were hardly prepared to get in on the whole *kiss him back* bit.

To say nothing of his ill-timed phone call.

My cheeks flamed at the memory, and even though it'd been only a little over a week since then, I could still feel the grain of the brick scraping against the backs of my arms, as well as the constant, on-loop realization that Asher had smelled acutely like aftershave and hot male.

I finished the Hurricane and set it on the bar. "I'm good," I told Katie, ignoring the way she eyed me skeptically with a once-over.

She'd wanted me to come tonight and live a little. *You need to pick up a guy, Avery*, she'd said, fluffing her hair in the mirror as we got ready. *An orgasm will un-crankify you.*

I hadn't come tonight with the plan to find myself an orgasm, but I hadn't expected to find Asher here either. And if there was ever a man who looked like he whipped up orgasms for a living, it was him.

It was now or never. I'd managed twenty-five years without feeling an attraction for a man, and if I didn't hop on the opportunity now, there was a good chance I'd go another twenty-five years without feeling this all-consuming need again.

You never cared about orgasms before you met him.

I thrust the thought away, burying it deep, as I waved off Katie's concern. "I'm good! All good. You go do your thing."

Tossing a garnish into a margarita, she shoved it at a patron and took his card. "You sure?" she asked me, turning for the cash register along the back of the bar.

"You hardly ever drink. Hold on, let me get you some water."

"Katie."

Over the din of the crowd and the DJ playing a song from the latest Top 100, she cut me a look and then gave a self-deprecating roll of her eyes. "Okay, yeah, I'm mama-bearing right now. I'll chill."

Wanting to perk her up, I said, "I can't find myself an orgasm in this crowd if you're hovering."

The guy to my left winked at me and then grabbed his junk. "I know where you can find one."

I smiled sweetly. "I'd rather eat nails."

Face contorting with displeasure, he snatched his drink off the bar and disappeared into the crowd, only for Katie to place a plastic cup of water in front of me a second later. "Guess he wasn't the one?" she asked, right brow arched high.

Not even a little.

"I've got someone else in mind."

Her left brow rose to meet the right, but a guy hollering at the other end of the bar cut her response short. With a *behave-yourself* finger wave in my direction, she grabbed a rag off the counter and slung it over one shoulder before hightailing it down to the customer.

I waited, giving her a moment to get lost in the frenzy of a weekend night in the French Quarter, and then I craned my neck, seeking another glimpse of the man determined to drive me insane.

The only man I could envision between my legs.

Fingers grazed my left hand, shockingly warm in comparison to the ice-cold cocktail I'd just sipped, and I pulled away from the unfamiliar touch.

I didn't get far.

A strong hand wrapped around my wrist, stalling my

flight, and then it was *his* voice that I heard next to my ear, rustling the strands of my hair, enflaming me as though my body operated on his command.

"Goin' somewhere?"

It was the same question he'd asked when we'd first met in Jackson Square. The same gravel-pitched voice. This time, unlike the last, I was in no mood to run away.

I wanted what he'd offered me in a dark alley against the police precinct a week ago. I wanted what I hadn't been bold enough to take then—pleasure, sex, the mutual understanding that it was a one-time deal only.

Simple. Uncomplicated.

Perfect.

And, yes, maybe curiosity still lingered as to why he'd had that notebook in his desk drawer. The one with Tabby's name on it . . . along with the names of two dead men. Getting up, close, and personal with Asher killed two birds with one stone.

Though right now the only bird I wanted to know more about was why, of all people, *he* was the one to flip my proverbial switch.

He stood so close that my shoulder grazed his chest when I turned toward him. My gaze lifted from his black, ribbed sweater, past the thick column of his throat to his rugged face. Under the bar's florescent lighting, the jagged scars across his cheek might as well have been a calling card for DANGER AHEAD.

My entire life had been spent sequestered in the shadows, and I didn't know what it said about me that I was willing to step into that danger now, to hell with the consequences.

"Following me again?" I asked boldly.

"I was already here."

He said it casually, with absolute conviction, and I was

suddenly thankful for the shadows, which hid my flush. Flirting wasn't my forte, and it figured that I couldn't even manage a decent conversation starter with him.

Of course, he'd been here. I'd spotted him along the back corner, seated at a table with someone I didn't recognize, minutes after I'd entered the club and taken a seat at the bar. I should have turned around then. Walked out. Gone home.

Instead, I'd downed a Hurricane for fortitude and waited for Asher to notice me in return.

Now, his hand skimmed my forearm, my bicep, not stopping until his palm settled on my neck, his thumb brushing the sensitive skin of the underside of my jaw. Goosebumps flared to life on my arms as I buried a swallow, worried that he might sense my spiking nerves. A guy like him—if he caught even a scent of my inexperience— would move on to the next girl in seconds.

I forced myself to meet his gaze casually, like my body wasn't turning into liquid fire at the barest hint of his touch.

"You're nuzzling my hand like you're regretting us stoppin' the other night, Avery."

Shock filtered down my spine, jerking my shoulders at the truth. I *was* nuzzling his hand. Shamelessly, too. Briefly, my eyes squeezed shut. If I hadn't seen him tonight, if he hadn't appeared here as though my dreams had sketched his muscular build into reality, I wouldn't have sought him out.

It's officially *now or never*.

With feigned confidence and a rapidly beating heart, I pressed my palm to his abdomen. Even through the fabric of his sweater, it was impossible to ignore the hard ridges of his muscles and the way they flexed with every breath he pulled into his lungs. I counted those inhalations like they were my own, and nearly gave into the little devil on my shoulder, which whispered for me to push his shirt up and touch him, skin to skin.

As I all but petted him, his blue eyes never veered from my face. If I were weaker, I'd let the intensity of his stare get to my head—let myself think more of this moment than what the facts bluntly told me.

And the facts were simple: tonight was about lust only, nothing more.

I shifted my hand upward, needing to level out the playing field. "Your heart is beating fast, Sergeant," I murmured, loud enough to be heard over the crowd. "Don't tell me you're nervous."

Mouth firming into a thin line, his hand locked around my wrist again. "Don't twist this into something that it's not. I don't get nervous."

I lifted my brows. "Because you're such a stoic cop?"

"Because I don't do commitment."

"Perfect," I said with a small nod, "I'm not looking for that either." Jerking my chin toward the front door, which sat beyond a sea of grinding couples, I added, "Should we go?"

His grip tightened. "What changed your mind?"

He had changed my mind. With my back to the police station and his big hands on my body, something in me had cracked. Broken free. Like a drug, I was hooked on the feeling of liberation already, and Asher had only given me a small taste of what might come after submitting to the pleasure he wielded. Refusing to show him that he held the upper hand in our little dynamic, I shot back, "Why do your scars look like they've been busted back open?"

Lincoln Asher responded exactly as I expected him to —a careful mask that concealed every trace of emotion. No twisted lips, no narrowed eyes, no steam that billowed out of his nostrils like a cartoon caricature from my youth. No, Asher was stone silent, his rugged face appearing only more tormented with its new pinkish tint to the old, flattened scars.

Old intersecting with the new. If I thought he'd tell me what had gone down, I would have pushed harder.

As it was, he eliminated the remaining distance between us, forcing me to tilt my head back or cut eye contact and cede this round to him.

"If we leave, I'm going to fuck you," he murmured, all games tossed to the side. "Do you get that? There's no third chances. You either agree or you go find someone else to play this cat-and-mouse chase."

I was grateful that my hand was on *his* heart and not the other way around. Mine thundered in my chest with ridiculous fervor. "I'm not running away . . . Does that answer your question?"

In a million years, I never could have anticipated the way he lifted my hand and pressed his mouth to the soft skin of my inner wrist. Heat, scorched heat—it licked at my feet as Asher's blue gaze zeroed in on my face, his mouth hovering a hair's breadth over my wrist. "Your pulse is beating fast, Avery," he said, voice low, a wicked glint in his eyes, "don't tell me you're nervous."

A gasp lodged in my throat as he caught my fingers with his and turned to wind through the crowd, never severing our connection. Throngs of people pushed inward, forcing me to squeeze through or be left behind.

But Asher never released me.

His shoulders were wide, his back broad, his waist trim, and the only thought on repeat in my head was, *This is about to happen*.

Katie would be so proud, and I was . . . at odds even in my own head.

I wasn't ready, not fully prepared for stripping my control and handing over the reins, the power, to a man I hardly knew, but I couldn't say no. Couldn't walk away. He did this to me. Twisted all my emotions inside out and set me on fire with nothing but the rough way he uttered my name.

The air outside was humid, thick, and my hands immediately turned clammy.

I'm not nervous, I reminded myself as we cut to the right, around a group of people mingling outside, smoking cigarettes.

I've got this, I told myself as Asher tugged me down the next street, onto St. Phillip.

Act confident, I ordered myself as my back gently hit the wall of a building and all I saw was Asher.

"Hands on the brick," came his low command.

He's recreating the other night.

I sucked in as much air as my lungs would allow and then set my hands against the building. The brick scraped my palms and my fingers curled in, mimicking the way my toes did the same in my shoes.

Asher leaned into me, lending me his weight, eliminating any chance for my escape into the night. The scent of his aftershave tickled my nose, and I fought the urge to tuck my nose into the crook of his neck and smell him.

"What next?" I whispered, though I tried damn hard to sound unaffected.

Blue eyes met mine, startling me with the heat that I saw there. His face was uncompromising in its firm lines and scars, but his gaze . . . *oh God*, for the first time I wondered if a mistake was knocking on my door. He looked at me like I was the first meal he'd been given after years of starvation. It was carnal, the way his gaze devoured me. Needy. Raw. And when his chest brushed mine as he inhaled, every ounce of heat in those startling blue eyes of his made me feel like I'd been stumbling through life just to get to this moment with him.

This man was dangerous, wicked, and as though my brain had been usurped by someone else, I heard the words trip off my tongue: "Don't make me wait, Sergeant."

Like a candle being snuffed out, the intensity in his gaze wavered, flickering, before sparking back to life again with a ferociousness that had me inching back . . . but there was nowhere to go and nowhere to escape.

"Don't make threats you can't keep," he warned.

"How do you know I won't keep them?"

His hands landed on mine to drag them up until they were on either side of my head. Pinned.

"For tonight," he growled, "you belong to me. Do you understand?"

And then his mouth was on mine, and I could only summon one word, even if it existed only in my head: *yes*.

TWO OF CUPS
reversed

THIRTEEN

Avery

Asher claimed my mouth as though he was starved for something only I could give him.

Blood surged in my head, clouding my vision, and I slammed my eyes shut against everything but the feel of him. The heat of his big body, the way his belt buckle was like a brand against my sweater-covered stomach. One masculine hand released mine to coast down my body, following the swell of my breasts to stop at the dip of my waist.

And all the while, he kissed me. It wasn't gentle and it wasn't soft and even though this was the first kiss I'd ever given a man willingly, I refused to ask Asher to slow down. To take it easy on me.

To—

A gasp broke free from my chest as he nudged my chin to the side, his lips coming to nip the skin just below my jawline. My hand, the one still locked by his to the wall, flexed forward, seeking the softness of his hair.

Asher readjusted his grip, hand splayed over my wrist. I might as well have been chained, I had no slack.

"Until I say otherwise," he rumbled against my neck, "you're going to have to take it." He soothed the bite with a swipe of his tongue, making my pulse skyrocket and my heels come off the cement as I strained closer. "Can you do that, Avery?"

All I saw were the backs of my eyelids when I half-gasped out, "Anyone ever tell you that you're a pompous asshole?"

Another nip from him, another gasp from me, and then a roughly uttered, "I'm a cop. Never had anyone call me a sweetheart before while on the job."

If I weren't so turned on, I would have laughed. As it was, I could hardly think straight. "Devil's more like it," I said, moving into complete shameless territory when I tilted my head a little more in a silently encouraged, *I-want-more-of-that.*

Asher, asshole that he was, either didn't recognize the request or decided to play dumb because his weight lifted from mine. "I prefer sinner, actually." He tangled our fingers together and, before I could even plan for what he'd had up his sleeve, he spun me around, chest to the wall. "But I'm willing to play whatever role you want me to tonight."

My chest heaved at my new position, the backs of my hands cushioning my cheek from the brick.

You're going to have to take it.

His words rang loud in my head, and there was no doubt about it: I was in trouble.

Because Asher's gruffness, the domineering way he put me where he wanted me, didn't make me want to run and never look back.

Not even a little.

Instead I arched my back, seeking his touch. I twisted my upper body, my left ear taking the place of my cheek on my hands as I looked for him over my shoulder. He was there, less than a foot away, and for a moment, I did nothing but study him.

In every other one of our interactions, he'd been dressed in his NOPD uniform. The dark slacks. The jacket over the crisp button-down shirt with the shiny, gold badge pinned to his breast pocket—so respectable. Honorable. An upstanding citizen of the first order.

Tonight, he looked like the devil I'd claimed him to be, and it was an intoxicating contradiction.

Dark jeans, the even darker sweater with the sleeves rolled up to his elbows.

But it wasn't the clothes that had my heart racing, nor even his powerful body.

No, it was the wild look in his blue gaze. With the shadows splicing across his face, his features were drawn tight, almost savage in the way he watched me. Drawing in a steadying breath, I licked my lips and wondered if the darkness in me had found its echo in him.

"Don't make me call you an asshole again for making me wait," I whispered, then mentally cursed myself for coming just short of begging him.

If he reacted with a smile to my hot retort, I couldn't make it out as I turned back to the wall.

I did, however, hear the clip of his heavy boot hit the cement. One step. Two steps. And then he was there behind me, hands coming to rest on the building, bracketing me within his embrace. "You going to let me take you right here?" he drawled softly. "Is that what you want?" With one hand, he gently swept my dark hair over one shoulder, and then—oh God—he fisted the strands and everything in me snapped with instant awareness.

Fight or flight.

Not me.

Letting instinct overrule all rational thought, I ground my ass backward, right into his crotch, just like every couple in the nightclub we'd left twenty minutes ago. I was rewarded for my boldness—his guttural groan echoed in my ear, his hand clamping down on my hip to still . . . no, no, he wasn't even stopping me. If anything, he crowded me further, eliminating whatever distance remained between us. Shielding me from the street.

My heart was a torpedo in my chest, a torpedo with no destination in sight.

Like I was hurtling forward as opposed to standing still; like my skin was on fire though I'd pulled on my sweater earlier this evening to ward off the chilly, nighttime breeze from the Mississippi River; like if I wasn't careful, I'd let Asher take what I'd given no other man, right here on an empty, semi-dark street with music blaring from Bourbon not some three-hundred feet away.

I wasn't this woman. I'd *never* been this woman.

I was more likely to whip out my taser and stun the hell out of a dude for stepping too close, but here I was. My ass driving back into Asher's very obvious hard-on. My fingers digging into the ridges of nineteenth-century brick. My core tightening as though Asher was already inside me when he'd done nothing but steal my breath with a kiss.

To put it simply, I was screwed.

Maybe literally.

At the sensation of the waistband of my jeans loosening, it hit me that Asher had popped the button on the sly. "You're playing with fire, Avery." I couldn't hear the teeth of the zipper coming undone over the strands of jazz, but my brain filled in the blanks with acute precision. "You have three seconds to tell me that you don't want this. You hear me? Nod yes."

Like I'd already told him twice before now, following orders wasn't exactly my thing.

I snagged him by the wrist, and, sucking in hot air, went for gold—namely, his hand down my pants.

Thank God for oversized sweaters.

Asher cursed violently under his breath, his fingers *so* tantalizing close to where I wanted them. "You're off your fucking rocker," he bit out, and then he shifted to bind me to him with his left hand, although if he pulled any harder, we'd become one.

"I figured I'd speed up the process," I said, then fell into a small pause. "Unless you were just trying to scare me, and you never planned to follow through on your whole *I'm-going-to-own-you* speech."

Maybe it was my imagination, but I swore I could feel the thud of his heart beat against my back.

"I planned to follow through." The words came out sounding both tortured and arrogant. Typical man.

I swallowed my remaining nerves and gave him a taste of his own *arrogant-I'm-a-badass-cop* medicine. "I'm losing faith with every second."

A beat passed and then another, and then *I* was the one sounding tortured as the pad of his finger collided with my clit. *Oh, God*. My knees quivered when he pressed down, sensations spiraling through me, and I shifted my head so I could bite down on the outer part of my hand. Music might be blasting but I needed to keep quiet; I needed to be inconspicuous. And, yeah, I knew how ridiculous that sounded, considering the fact that I had Lincoln Asher's hand down my pants. In public.

My thoughts scattered completely when he rubbed that finger in tight, little circles. Slowly. He did it so slowly that there was no denying that he wanted to make me pay for wrestling control of our hookup from him. Faster, I needed him to move faster, and even though I'd never felt sensations like this before, I instinctually knew that the languid pace he'd set would only get me so far.

Standing on my toes and shoving my hips back into his hard-on did the trick.

Those languid circles sped up, just enough that I couldn't keep quiet. I needed air, and I loosened my jaw as I turned my head—only to have a masculine hand clamp down over my mouth.

"Stay quiet," Asher muttered by my ear, and I could hear it, how that tortured note deepened the pitch of his voice. Another finger landed on my clit to join the first, and those tight little circles grew in pressure and speed. "Unless you want to be caught, stay quiet."

I'd be quiet when I was dead, which might happen soon, I was so wound up.

My belly caved in when I inhaled sharply through my nose. This time, I nodded the "yes" he'd wanted earlier.

His hand fell away from my mouth, and though his touch hadn't been rough, I imagined the way my lipstick must now be smeared, my chin and cheeks painted a blush pink from my makeup.

"More," I whispered, sounding drugged, forehead pressed to the back of my hand, "more. Please."

My jeans were tugged down, far enough that Asher snaked his hand farther between my legs, and then I *did* die.

One broad finger sank into me, and I disobeyed once again by releasing a small whimper. It wasn't at all the experienced front I'd wanted to portray.

"Jesus, fuck," Asher muttered almost incoherently, "you're so tight."

I felt tight. No, I felt like I was being cleaved in two.

My chest ached, though it was nothing in comparison

to the way my hips now curled away from Asher—fight or flight. My confidence waned, my boldness slithering off into the dark, and all I could do was breathe through the stinging happening between my legs and hope that Asher didn't notice—

"Avery."

Cold. He sounded so very, very cold.

My eyes squeezed shut. *Dammit. Dammit, dammit, dammit.* "Please, don't."

"Don't what?" His finger left me, trailing up past the sensitive nub he'd worked like a magician, to rest at the waistband of my jeans. "Don't mention how fucking tight you are? That you cried out in pain?" His hand left me completely. "Tell me the truth."

It was in my very nature to defy, but I couldn't do so now, not in front of him.

And I'd be damned if I drew out this conversation any longer than it had to be. He wanted the truth? Then he'd get it, and there was no point in mincing words.

Pulling up my jeans, I glanced over my shoulder to meet his gaze. The blues of his irises looked nearly black, but there was no mistaking the fury lingering there.

I was right—he was the devil personified.

But I wanted him anyway.

Swallowing past the lump in my throat, I broke my silence and prepared for the worst.

"I'm a virgin."

III

THE EMPRESS

MAJOR ARCANA

FOURTEEN

Lincoln

A virgin.

It wasn't a word that existed in my vocabulary and hadn't been since I was twelve years old and fondling a girl from the grade above me in her daddy's fancy office. It was the one and only time I'd ever set foot in a house as nice as that, and the only memory I had of the experience was coming in my hand while the girl's great-grandfather glared down at me from his portrait above the gold-leaf mantle.

Nothing about that orgasm was particularly spectacular, aside from the fact that it was my first, post-virginity-loss.

Shrewdly, I slid my gaze down Avery's frame.

She'd appeared at the club tonight like an angel designed by my imagination. One minute I'd been seated with Josiah Templeton, a colleague who'd heard about my suspension from the NOPD and wanted to "talk it out," and in the next I'd been at her side, Templeton summarily dismissed.

From the moment I'd spotted her in Jackson Square,

I'd craved her. But right now, when I felt raw to the core after being thrust back into a life that was as familiar as the gun I always kept holstered on me, desperation demanded that I take her. Avery made me feel alive. With her smart mouth and her expressive hazel eyes and the way she watched me like she didn't know if it was in her best interest to put her stun gun to use or climb on my lap . . . I felt more alive in her presence than I had in my entire life.

And for the length of time that it took for me to have her coming all over my cock as I drove her to the brink, I could pretend, at least, that I wasn't a man leashed to death.

On the heels of that thought came another: "Your ID says you're twenty-five."

She didn't shirk under my stare. If anything, her chin shot up in that increasingly familiar way of hers and her shoulders squared off like she expected a fight. And that, *that* was the reason I'd thought of nothing but her since we met. I wanted that fire underneath me, above me, giving as good as I gave to her.

"I am," she said, her hands at her side, fingers lax. "I have my own reasons for keeping my hymen."

Her lips quirked, and I got the impression she was waiting for my reaction. But I'd spent years battling my emotions into submission, and I'd be damned if I paraded them before her now.

Softly, I drawled, "And let me guess—those reasons aren't going to be shared with me?"

If possible, her chin kicked up another notch. Any more and she'd be nose to the sky. "They won't be," she confirmed with narrowed eyes.

Avery Washington was a challenge wrapped up in temptation, and against my better judgment, I stepped forward. She surprised the hell out of me by meeting me halfway, her face lifting so that the sparse moonlight high-lighted the bridge of her nose and the high crests of her cheeks.

"Are you scared?" she teased, one hand lifting to tug playfully on the front of my sweater. With her other hand, she held her index finger and thumb close together, millimeters apart. "Maybe just a *little* terrified that you'll get attached to me after you take my virginity?"

The thought alone shouldn't turn me on. It shouldn't, but there was no denying how my cock leapt to attention at the mere thought of having her crying out my name and no one else's. Possessing Avery when no one else had ever had the chance . . . Christ, there was nothing I wanted more than to mark her as my own. A kiss to her neck, another to her inner thigh. I'd make it so damn hard for her to even *look* at another man without remembering me claiming every inch of her.

My voice sounded like gravel when I ground out, "You're assuming that I still want to fuck you."

Her fingers danced from my shirt down to my belt buckle and then pressed the heel of her hand against the crown of my cock.

A curse sprang from my lips at the same time she said, "*Some* part of you still wants to fuck me, and I vote that we let him do the talking."

I caught her wrist, angling her hand so that it rested vertically alongside my hard-on. "You're playing with fire." Fuck, *I* was playing with fire just considering this at all. I wanted what she offered readily, her hazel eyes burning with desire as she stared up at me. I wanted to forget the hell I'd reentered the moment I'd walked into my apartment to find Ambideaux sitting at my kitchen table.

But, hell, she was a virgin, and there was something inherently wrong about taking that from her. I didn't deserve what she offered, and yet I couldn't imagine walking away.

Letting her give that innocent part of herself to someone else . . .

No shot in hell.

"Do you get that?" I demanded harshly. "You do this with me and there aren't roses waiting for you on the other end of tonight. It's fucking," I said, "and there won't be a damn romantic thing about it."

The heel of her hand inched over to drag along the base of my dick, and, *holy hell*, but my body grew taut. Strained. Heat trailed along my spine, and I thanked God for self-control when she whispered, "Maybe I want to be burned."

For my entire life, I'd straddled the fence. Saint. Sinner. I lived and thrived in the murky area in between, always cautious to keep looking forward.

One glance back and I'd end up dead with a gun trained between my eyes—a real possibility now that Ambideaux had waltzed back into my life and demanded his due . . . in blood.

I stared down at Avery, and squashed caution beneath the toe of my steel-toed boot. She was twenty-five, an adult, and if she wanted a good, dirty fucking, then I was more than happy to deliver. She'd regret it later on if she ever attempted to peel back my layers of police uniforms and badges.

That man—the man I'd been from the age of sixteen when I stole my first life—would turn her stomach. Right now, I was badge-less, anyway. More sinner than saint.

But there wasn't a single inch of me that could turn down the chance to go up in flames with the woman currently determined to light the matchsticks.

It was her decision to push. It was my decision to take.

"Bring me back to your place," I told her.

Flashing me a brief smile, her remaining nerves only evident in her hazel eyes, she turned on her heel without another word. I followed behind her, watching her six, feeling the noose of damnation tightening around my neck.

Say no.

Turn back now.

Don't take what doesn't belong to you.

I didn't say no.

I didn't turn back to the club.

In my life, I'd only ever taken what didn't belong to me, and Avery was no different.

We didn't speak as we cut through the darkened French Quarter streets, over from St. Phillip and onto Dauphine. But the increased distance quieted the music from Bourbon, and I craved the noise—to both swallow my thoughts and demolish my guilt.

Avery kept pace ahead of me, and by the time we stood on her front steps five minutes later, she only twisted around to say one thing: "Just so you know, in case you're having any doubts, I want this."

Whether she said it for herself or for me, it didn't matter.

The door creaked open and Avery gestured for me to step inside first. The front parlor was dark, not a single bulb lighting the space.

"Third floor," Avery told me, her hand grazing mine as she slipped around me once again. "No elevator."

Our shoes echoed off the stairwell as we wound our way up, my gaze on her full ass, her face tilted up.

Thirteen more steps and we were at her front door.

Ten more seconds and she slid the key into the lock and pushed it wide open.

Three more deep breaths before it closed and I was on her again, like a savage born of the wilderness. Her mouth parted beneath mine, a feminine moan slipping between us, her hands finding purchase on my shoulders.

She wanted the devil, and that's exactly what I'd give her.

"Bedroom," I grunted, my hands going to her tight ass so I could lift her up into my arms. She weighed close to nothing and if she wasn't holding onto that hymen of hers after all these years, I would have torn off her jeans and fucked her against her front door.

Her teeth nipped at my lower lip. "Right behind you."

I spun around, my gaze searching the shadowed room for the door. I caught sight of the sofa, the blankets, the pillows. The sheet used as a curtain just beyond the couch. Something told me that Avery didn't live here alone, and that the bedroom wasn't where she tucked into bed each night but rather on the couch.

I wouldn't embarrass her by bringing it up, though, and I carried her into the bedroom that wasn't hers and then set her down on the queen-sized bed that wasn't hers either.

She lifted up onto her elbows to watch me at the foot of the bed. "Condoms are in the nightstand," she said, nodding her chin in the general direction.

I kicked off my shoes, then pulled my sweater over my head. "We don't need one of them yet." Undoing my belt buckle, I popped the button of my jeans and then leaned forward to strip off her boots. "Get rid of your shirt, Avery."

Hazel eyes blinked back at me before she jumped into motion, her sweater sailing across the room and her arms looping behind her to pop open the clasp of her bra. The black satin slipped down her shoulders, revealing sun-kissed breasts and dark, rosy nipples.

My cock strained at my jeans, and I ignored the bastard, choosing instead to appreciate the sight of Avery almost naked. Fucking gorgeous. Her dark hair, her flushed cheeks, the tantalizing glimpse of her tits.

On my hands and knees, I moved toward her. Straddled her. Pressed her hands to the mattress on either side of her head. Lowered myself and caught one perfect nipple in my mouth, swirling my tongue around the tip until it pebbled, and Avery whimpered loudly.

Asshole that I was, I devoured those sounds and relished how her nails bit into my knuckles as I restrained her. Asshole that I was, I imagined that the sounds she made were for my ears only—and that they'd never be heard by another man.

Asshole that I was, I gave one last swipe of my tongue against her nipple and then shifted upward to capture those moans completely. Absorbed the way her chest reverberated with them, her pleasure so acute, so vibrant, that I felt like an addict and dove back in for seconds.

I stripped off her bra, hooking it by the middle and tossing it over my shoulder. Her chest heaved with uneven breaths, her one freed hand sinking into my hair. Her nails raked down my skull until she was palming my neck in silent encouragement for me to keep going.

Laughter climbed my throat at her show of dominance.

I allowed her to have her moment, sucking on her flesh, keeping my gaze on her face.

And then I reestablished that I was king in this bed, in this room, in this so-called Sultan's Palace.

My hands flipped her over and she released a small shriek. "Asher!"

"Lincoln," I corrected. I urged her to lift her hips, then freed the button of her jeans all over again. Tugged the denim down the length of her legs. Repeated it all with her matching black underwear. "When I make you come so hard you lose your voice, 'Lincoln' is going to be the very last thing you say."

"Asshole," I heard her mutter, but she betrayed her defiance by spreading her knees.

Goddamn, she was a sight. Tight, round ass made perfect for the fit of my hands, a slender back that arched as her knees turned outward and her toes curled into the rumpled sheets.

"The very one," I replied hoarsely.

I palmed her ass, then pushed her all the way onto her knees. It wasn't in my nature to take it slow, and at the sight of her wet core, temptation rose to thrust into her now, hard, until her moans could be heard in the apartments on the first floor.

Keep your jeans on.

It'd be her only saving grace.

But I did give in to the temptation to discover how she tasted. With one hand to her lower back so that she was arched and ready for me, I nipped one ass cheek, relishing in the twitch of her hips, and then moved south until I inhaled the very scent of her.

"Don't forget," I murmured casually, my heart thumping almost violently in my chest, "it's Lincoln."

The first swipe of my tongue against her pussy was met with a keening cry that echoed in my ears like a personal trophy. And I sought out to hear it again and again and again. I circled her clit with my tongue, alternating between hard and soft, languid strokes, changing the pace frequently enough to keep her on her toes.

"Asshole," she whimpered, and I sensed her gripping the sheets.

"Lincoln," I told her, and then drove my tongue into her sweet heat. I wrapped my arm around her right leg, keeping her locked to me, and then rubbed the sensitive hood of her pussy with my finger as I devoured the very center of her. She tasted like heaven and sin wrapped up in a package that I worried I'd never tire of.

With my fingers and my tongue, I worked her into a frenzy until her ass drove backward, seeking more from me, and I gave her what she wanted. My palm connected with one ass cheek.

"*Oh!*"

"Lincoln," I reminded, and then soothed the sting with the flat of my hand. It was all too easy to feel the affect it had on her—her legs trembled and her pussy quivered and either I took her now or I'd be the one coming in my pants.

The latter wasn't an option.

I left her there, my fingers heading south to yank off my jeans. I'd be damned if I ever admitted to it, but there was no denying the tremor in my hands as I pulled open the nightstand drawer and snagged a condom from the already opened box.

Definitely not her room or her bed, and I fucking hated it that I was about to take her here anyway.

The alternative, however, was to stop and call this whole thing off, and I'd take the gun between my eyes from Ambideaux before I agreed to that.

Rolling the condom down my length, I turned back to the bed to see Avery watching me, her bottom lip caught between her teeth.

"It's going to hurt."

I looked down at my cock, which had never, not once, been described as small. "It might."

"This is where you tell me you'll be a gentleman and take it easy on me."

I'd never be that man for her—a man who knew softness and kindness—and she'd known that when she'd all but begged me to take her virginity anyway. Kneeling on the bed, I said, "You should have picked someone else."

A small smile lifted her lips. "I'll remember that for next time."

Next time.

A time that wouldn't belong to me. An orgasm that wouldn't be mine.

"Sit on the edge of the bed." My harsh command was met with a slow blink, like she was cataloguing the words and trying to make sense of them. Then, she moved into position, right in front of me.

I lifted her legs and settled them over mine, grabbing my cock so that I could run the crown through her wetness. She moaned, and I bit back a groan. "You get one more chance to tell me to stop."

Avery leaned forward and gripped my dick in her hand, positioning me against her entrance. "Stop talking, would you . . . *Lincoln*?"

Christ.

I sank into her just as she leaned back, doing my best to go slow, to not make her regret giving me her virginity, no matter what she said.

I couldn't go slow.

My back tightened and my balls drew up, and at the sight of Avery tipping back her head, her neck exposed, her tits on full-display, I lost all semblance of control.

Every. Last. Bit.

"I'm sorry," I whispered, to us both, just before I thrust in deep and claimed her. *Mine.*

A curse leapt to my mouth. Fuck. She was so tight. Fuck. She was wet, so wet and I was on the verge of losing my damn mind. *Fuck*, I thought, as she pushed down and swirled her hips, urging me on.

My hands gripped her hips as I angled for a better fit, a deeper reach. Each pump of my hips pulled a moan from her lips. I made it my goddamn mission to hear that sound again, and when she arched her back and gripped the sheets, moaning like she'd never felt better, I did it all over again.

My skin grew tight and the fact that I was already about to come was like a damn death wish—I wouldn't, not until she came first.

My hand left her hip to circle her clit, applying pressure, keeping my angle all the same.

"Asher," she cried out at the first hint of pressure, "I can't. I don't know if . . . Oh, my God, I can't—"

"It's Lincoln," I muttered, then drew her left knee up, up, up, so that it grazed her chin, "and you can."

I dominated her that way, owning every part of her, exposing her pussy completely, so that with every glance down, I saw the tight way she enveloped my cock. And when she came all over me, it was exactly how I'd hoped.

A flush spread across her chest and her lips parted and her hands left the sheets to grip my biceps instead.

I wasn't far behind. I pinned her other knee upward, plunging in deep with every thrust. And, holy fuck, I burst apart almost instantaneously—a growl ripping from my chest, my gaze hooked on her gorgeous face, my hips losing all semblance of an even rhythm.

I never lost control.

Until her.

I collapsed on top of her, then rolled us to the side.

She sprawled halfway across my chest, then tapped me right over the heart. "Avery," she murmured, half out of breath.

I blinked, surprise momentarily infiltrating the pleasure. "What?"

"When you come, you needed to say my name."

I skimmed my gaze over her, taking in her hesitant smile with the realization that I was totally fucked. I was hooked, line and sinker, and that wasn't a good thing—for me or for her. Not when there wasn't a damn thing that could come of this, of us.

"I'll remember that for our second round."

She nodded shortly. "You do that." A small pause. "And Lincoln?"

Pleasure smacked me straight in the chest at hearing her say my name. "Yeah?"

"I like it when your dick does the talking. He's a whole lot better at communicating than you."

FOUR OF CUPS

reversed

FIFTEEN

Avery

"Do you find it weird living in a place that tourists gawk at daily?" Asher asked as he sat on the edge of the bed, tugging his jeans up his thighs with masculine grace.

And I . . . well, to be completely honest, I wasn't sure that I was ready for him to leave. It wasn't that I wanted him to stay, necessarily, but, okay, yeah, I wanted him to stay. *Dammit*, that was not part of the plan.

With Katie's sheets tucked against my chest, I watched him pull the denim of his jeans over his butt.

"Avery?"

Startling, my gaze leapt to his face. "Sorry?"

In that familiar way of his, nothing in his expression changed . . . except that, this time, his blue eyes crinkled. Just enough for me to know that he wasn't completely composed of stone.

His fingers slipping the button of his jeans through the matching hole, he said, "I asked if you find it weird to live in a notorious house like this one."

Oh. Right.

153

I shook my head, both to get my brain back in the game and also in answer to his question. "There's nothing but rumors to it. The sultan being buried alive in the courtyard? Fake." Holding up my hand, I tucked my index finger down. "The vengeful brother murdering the members of the sultan's harem and leaving the bodies strewn about the house? Also fake." Another finger went down. "The blood seeping down the front steps the morning after a horrible storm?" I shrugged. "I don't know. That part could be true. New Orleans has always been a violent city, even if it has nothing to do with some sort of bizarre mutilation scene in this mansion."

He stared at me, hands still on his waistband, and his silence spawned more word vomit from me: "People will always believe the story that aligns with their best interests. It's why people come to see me in Jackson Square—they're seeking validation for what they already believe to be true."

"So, the cards . . ."

I cocked my head, considering him. "What about them?"

"They aren't real?"

The more time he spent away from the bed, the more I found it necessary to get some damn clothes on my body. "Sure, they're *real*," I said, scooting my butt to the edge so I could peer over the side in search of my shirt. Or my underwear. Anything, really, would do at this point. "But like anything else, the cards represent what we make of them. I could pull the same three for you and someone else, but their meanings would change immediately. No two readings are the same."

Spotting my sweater beneath the window, I let out a relieved breath and slipped from the bed. *Be bold. Be confident.* Much easier said than done when I ditched the sheet and scooped up my sweater off the floor, naked as the day I was born.

"Is that ink?"

My sweatshirt was over my head when Asher voiced the question. Fabric masking my vision, I only heard the *pop! pop!* of his knees and then felt the trace of his finger along the inner line of my own knee. The left one.

I stepped back on instinct alone, not wanting him to have the time to read the words, and I went tumbling to the floor as my foot caught on a stray object. My arms pinwheeled, a curse leaving my lips, as I went down.

"Got you," came Asher's deep, rumbly voice, his bulky arms circling my thighs. The stubble on his cheeks scratched my thighs, and the warmth of his clothed body was like a furnace to my naked one. The moan that worked its way up my throat had nothing to do with my acute embarrassment for tripping and everything to do with the man who'd caught me.

I was accustomed to taking care of myself, and as I popped my head through the neck hole of my sweater, I vowed to get over this idiotic crush before it swallowed me whole.

That was, until my surroundings blinked back into focus and I found Asher staring at the words tattooed into my skin.

"Don't," I muttered, pulling on my leg.

He didn't let me go. Hand flexing around my thigh, he held me in place. "You bow to no man, huh?" His tone gave nothing away, his thumb idly brushing over the calligraphy. "You get this done recently?"

Two years ago, on the ten-year anniversary of my mother's death—not that I would ever divulge that sort of information.

I bow to no man, the script read in neat lettering. I'd gone to a place called Inked on Bourbon for it, right in the heart of the French Quarter. Immediately after checking in, I'd requested a female tattoo artist, and I'd gotten one in the form of the owner's wife, Lizzie Harvey. A pretty, perky woman who'd taken one look at the words I'd scribbled on a scrap of paper and said, "Yeah, men can be complete pigs sometimes. C'mon in the back and I'll take care of you."

While splayed out on the table, Lizzie had told me a story about an ex of hers who'd dumped her on social media—Instagram, of all places—and I'd nodded in sympathy, murmured my "no, he didn't!" comments in all the right places.

But a public dumping scandal didn't equate to a stolen life, and on the anniversary of my mother's death, there had been nothing I wanted more than to hunt Jay Foley down and give him a taste of his own medicine.

Even if Asher gave me a thousand orgasms, my mother's death was none of his business.

I slapped his hands away, not the least bit surprised when he slipped his grip higher, closer to the apex of my thighs. "C'mon, Avery," he drawled in that rough timbre of his, "don't keep me in suspense."

I could go tit for tat.

Give him an abbreviated version of events that truly told him nothing . . . in exchange for information on the list of names I'd found in his desk drawer. My mouth opened, the words hovering on my tongue.

But what came out wasn't at all what I'd intended: "You jealous, Asher?"

He grunted, then twisted his face away.

Oh, this was too good. Cupping his stubbled jaw, I forced him to look up at me . . . and as he was on his knees, it was with a burst of excitement that I realized that *I* was the one with the dominant hand this time around.

Well, well, well. How the tables had turned.

"Tell me, *Lincoln*," I said with a little smile, "have you ever bowed to a woman before?"

I felt the way his jaw clenched beneath my palm, and then there was no mistaking the way he spoke from between gritted teeth. "Trust me when I say that I only get on my knees before a woman for one reason."

A visual of him licking my core flashed before my eyes. It'd felt fantastic when he'd done it earlier, better than I could have ever imagined.

"Why do you have the tattoo?" he demanded. "Or did you lie about still having your *hymen*?"

The thoroughly disgusted way he uttered the word "hymen" made me roll my eyes. "Do you really have to ask that?" My hand slipped from his jaw to curl one finger beneath his chin, urging him to look up at me. "Or are you about to go all caveman and question my authenticity all the while you don't plan to sleep with me again? Hit and quit it, that's how my roommate always puts it."

"You have absolutely no faith in the male sex."

How could I?

My stepfather had my mother murdered in cold blood, and then had set out to do the same to me.

The men I'd run into while living on the streets had been only too keen to paw at me, even though I'd barely entered puberty at that point.

Nothing about the men in my life, thus far, leant to a positive image now—except for Pete and Sal, and they were way too in love with each other to ever look at another human being, let alone me.

Scoffing, I dropped my hand from Asher's face. "You're right, I have none. And in case you've forgotten, you already made it clear that sex between us was a one-time guarantee. Nothing more."

I patted myself on the back for not sounding like a bitter shrew.

Only, I'd greatly underestimated Asher.

In the blink of an eye, the sole of my foot was on his broad shoulder and his face was between my legs.

Oh. My. God.

It was too soon, right? Was there some sort of time restriction on how long you should give a recently de-virginized girl after demolishing her innocence? I didn't have the rulebook, and truthfully, sex wasn't a topic I talked about with anyone aside from Katie.

And Katie had lost her virginity long before I'd ever met her at the club she worked at.

"Ash—Lincoln," I corrected, heart hammering in my chest, "it's too soon, right? I mean, shouldn't we wait . . . or something?"

"Hold onto my shoulders," he husked out, and then spread me down below to lick up my slit.

Oh. *Oh, wow.*

My head fell back as his hands circled my hips to clasp my butt. One ass cheek for each palm, and two seconds later I understood why: he refused to let me wriggle away from the intense sensations.

He ate me like I was a feast made exclusively for him, his tongue lapping at my clit with determined fervor. And then he made the sexiest sound I'd ever heard in the back of his throat, like he was drunk on the taste of me.

I knew that feeling well.

I'd downed the Hurricane hours ago, but my whole body felt sluggish yet electrified, exhausted yet needy—Lincoln was the sole cause. Him and the magic of his hands and . . . other parts of his hard body. Desperate to see him work my body to distraction, I gathered the hem of my sweater and held the fabric behind me, knotted in one hand.

Lord, he was handsome.

All dark, messy hair and shut eyes and hard slopes and angles. There was minimal light from the window, but enough of the room was revealed that I could see the high color on his cheeks as he flicked me over and over again with his tongue.

A masculine finger probed my entrance, sinking inside. Curling inward. I was going to die, right here, right now. With Asher sucking on my clit like he was on a mission of his own design, his finger angling just right with every thrust.

It wasn't fair that he could work me up into this quivering mess within seconds.

And when he pulled away to rise to his feet, his height made me feel tiny, submissive, all over again. I whimpered at the loss of him, and then mentally berated myself for doing what I had vowed to never do: beg a man to make me feel complete.

It grated on my nerves, rubbed me raw—it was a power struggled I'd never anticipated.

In the end, I let newfound lust do the talking.

"That was . . ." I swallowed, allowing my gaze to hold steady on Asher's face. His full mouth glistened from my wetness and his eyes glittered. "We agreed to one-time sex, but technically, you broke that agreement. We could, maybe, I don't know, go for another round before you head out?"

He licked his lips, and I gulped down air because that right there, him absorbing the taste of me, was an image that would remain locked in my head for the rest of my life.

Then he spoke, and it went right over me, I was so entranced by the thought of him working me up to another orgasm. If I became an addict, it was all Katie's fault. She'd encouraged this, told me to live a little, and with Asher, I was all too willing to take the plunge.

One second passed.

Two seconds passed.

And then, finally, his words registered in my head.

My jaw dropped in pure outrage. "*Excuse me?*"

His gaze never wavered from mine. "You'll bow to me, Avery. It might not be today and it might not be tomorrow, but it *will* happen."

As though he'd taken a sledgehammer to my desire, it cracked in two like shards of broken ice. Fury curled my hands into fists at my side, and the blood pounding furiously at my temple had nothing to do with lust. That he thought he could just swoop up in here and lay down the law like he was some sort of . . . some sort of—

The outline of his gun under his sweater at his hip caught my eye, and I could have sworn that my right eye twitched. He might be a cop, he might have a shiny badge and the ability to lock people up, but he was *not* the law.

I'd be dead before I ever let him talk to me like that—like he owned me or had any say on what I did or did not do.

Finger thrusting in the direction of the bed, I snapped, "The only place I'm getting on my knees is if I'm on that bed and your cock is all up in my business." My voice vibrated with rage, my body trembling, too. "I will *never* get on my knees before you for any other reason. You better get that through your thick skull because I'm not going to say it—"

His lips crashed down on mine, swallowing my fight,

ending my tirade. The kiss was brutal, rough, and it was over before it had even begun.

Twisting away, leaving me breathless and panting, Asher shoved his feet into his shoes and strode for the door.

"Will I see you again soon?"

The question was out before I could stop myself, hanging in the air, humiliating in all of its transparent, longing glory.

Asher glanced back at me over his shoulder, the top of his face hidden in shadow. But I saw his mouth move, that mouth which had brought me to the brink of pleasure, and the words left me wanting to snag my taser from my backpack and put it to good use.

"When you get on your knees," he said.

It wasn't until I heard the *click* of the front door shutting that I erupted into motion. I snatched my shoes off the floor, my underwear, my jeans, dumping all but my boots into the laundry basket by the bathroom.

I would never, *never* give a man so much power as the kind Asher demanded. He was delusional if he thought I'd just hop to it, like some sort of badge bunny willing to do anything in the hopes of pleasing him.

I'd had sex with him tonight because *I* had wanted to. I'd wanted to feel the slick glide of his cock inside me, and I'd wanted to know firsthand that moment when my body burst apart like a firework, shattering as pleasure washed over me.

Asher had delivered on both accounts.

And that was that.

But as I got ready for bed some time later, I couldn't help but rewind the night to before he'd learned of my virginity—to those tense moments when I'd been crowded up against the wall on St. Phillip Street, my jeans unzipped, his hand clamped over my mouth, his fingers playing me into a frenzy.

Anyone could have spotted us.

And I'd wanted them to.

I'd wanted to feel their eyes on me, to *see* me, in a way that I'd spent the last twelve years hiding in plain sight. Feeling exposed—vulnerable in a way that I never allowed myself to be—had been just as freeing as letting Asher take control. The realization washed over me like a gallon of ice water yanked straight from the Artic.

I slid the bristle-boar brush through my hair, combing through the knotted strands. It didn't matter if I'd savored those moments for the control I'd given up. It would be a completely different case all the way around to submit to him the way he'd wanted on his way out the door.

Right?

It's what I told myself as I put Katie's sheets in the wash and set my alarm to wake me in forty minutes when the cycle was done. It's what I told myself when I pulled my blankets up under my chin after getting into my favorite position on the sofa.

Forty minutes later, when the washing machine beeped its completion, I was still fooling myself into believing that Asher's last command rubbed me raw . . . that it didn't hold a particular thrill, the same thrill I'd felt with my jeans around my thighs and his finger sinking into me.

Luckily for me, I had a long-standing relationship with such lies. After all, I'd been living the biggest one of them all for the last twelve years. What was another in the grand mix of things?

XII

THE HANGED MAN

MAJOR ARCANA

SIXTEEN

Lincoln

"**I**s that all for you tonight, Sergeant?"

Wrapping my hand around the Styrofoam coffee cup, I handed over my card. "Yup, all good, Sarah."

If my regular barista found it odd that I'd been in every night for the last week without wearing my Class B's, she didn't mention it. With a quick, red-painted grin, she swiped my credit card and handed it over.

"You know," she murmured, blue eyes flashing up at me, "some of the girls think you come in here for a reason. I mean, like for a *reason*. If you know what I mean."

I knew what she meant.

My wallet went into the back pocket of my sweatpants. I'd been a regular here at Café Vieux Carre since my promotion to sergeant. It sat two blocks from the eighth district precinct, and the brew wasn't half-bad. They had chicory coffee and lacked the touristy vibe that Café du Monde doled out in spades, two pluses in my book.

But the real reason I came here had nothing to do with the employees or the coffee—no, the place had ears, and even if I'd left Ambideaux's little whose-dick-is-bigger contest twelve years ago, I continued to show up here five days a week.

Knowledge was power, and power meant survival.

My lieutenant had an ulterior motive in not wanting to lose me, and it had nothing to do with how well I pushed papers. At the end of the day, I always had information he wanted—and I delivered, always.

Blowing steam off the top of my *café au lait*, I readjusted the ball cap on my head. "You're a little young for me, Sarah."

Her mouth drooped in an obvious pout. "Not *that* young," she muttered, "I mean, I'm twenty-five."

Avery's age.

Hot coffee burned down my throat, closing off my esophagus as I struggled to blink away the sudden tears in my eyes. I'd taken Avery without thought to her age, to the nine years that separated us. Aside from her sexual inexperience, she hadn't seemed young, not once I'd talked to her.

Over the years, I'd seen my coworkers walk down the aisle multiple times over. Hell, I'd even been invited to some of their weddings. When they'd spouted out their vows, rambling on about finding soulmates and knowing, without a single doubt, that there was no one who knew you better . . . Well, I'd chalked it up to be a load of romantic bullshit.

Until Avery.

Not that we were soulmates, by any means, but from that very first conversation, I'd been hooked. Her age hadn't mattered; the way she dressed hadn't mattered. All that *had* mattered was the fire in her hazel eyes and the defiance that radiated from her like a second skin.

And when I'd been cock-deep in her lush body, possession had been at the forefront of my mind, not the date on her birth certificate.

Cock twitching at the vivid memory of her tight pussy, I took another tentative sip of the chicory coffee and tried again with the barista. "How about that dude over there?" I pointed the cup to my right, indicating a guy wearing a black shirt and khaki pants. As though sensing he'd become the subject of our conversation, he blinked twice and then abruptly turned back to the open laptop before him. "He watches you, you know," I said to Sarah.

"Because *that's* not creepy."

"He owns five of the daiquiri shops here in the Quarter." In other words, he had money, and a lot of it. Although I'd venture to guess that only half of his net worth was on account of making liquored-up slushies for tourists—the other half was dirty money. Drug money. It wasn't uncommon for businesses down in the Quarter to double-dip, and Marco Carvino was a better bet than most. "And I can guarantee that he's been waiting for you to drop any sort of signal before he makes a move."

Sarah sighed. "You're just trying to boost up my ego since Tom dumped me two days ago."

Tom Townsend, number three on Ambideaux's list.

Like every other crook in New Orleans, Tom had made Café Vieux Carre his regular stop. We came in at different times of the day—him in the mornings, me at night since I worked the graveyard shift. *Had* worked the graveyard shift. Grimacing, I tipped the Styrofoam cup up to my mouth again, and then said, "I told you, I'd take care of him."

That prompted a laugh from her. "If murder wasn't totally illegal, I'd take you up on it." Chin down, she shrugged. "Humor me, how would you do it?"

I lowered the cup to the counter, throwing a glance behind me to ensure there wasn't a line building up. Satisfied that there was no one there, I shrugged my shoulders. Casual. "Gators, maybe. Let them do the heavy-lifting."

"Oh, my God, that's so gross."

Yeah, it was.

I rubbed the scars on my cheek with the heel of my palm, and bit back a hiss. Ambideaux's little pistol-whip had done more than rattle my brains—it'd created a new scar to overlay the old, turning my profile into something beginning to resemble Frankenstein. On a good day.

Saluting with my coffee, I stepped back. "Think about what I said." I jerked my chin toward Carvino. "His name's Marco, he's interested, and I can almost guarantee he won't break your heart the way Townsend did."

Sarah blushed. "That'd be nice . . . I'll think about it."

I paused outside the café, draining my coffee, tossing the cup into the metal trash bin to my right.

The door swung open behind me. "Thanks, my man."

I didn't glance in Carvino's direction as he stepped up next to me, our shoes parallel on the cobblestoned sidewalk. "Deal's a deal."

The Daquiri King audibly swallowed. "I didn't really think Sarah would even look at me. Honest to God, I'm not some creepy fuck, lusting after her. I'm just . . ."

"In love."

He released a heavy sigh. "Yeah, maybe. Okay, yeah that sounds about right. Between her dating Townsend and then having the hots for you, I figured I didn't even have a shot."

"Congratulations, now you do." My gaze caught on a familiar figure walking down the street, a nondescript gym bag slung across his back. Right on time. *Perfect.* "How much dope is he picking up?"

Beside me, Carvino fiddled with his laptop bag. "Two

ounces. Small run this time. He's, uh, desperate for some quick cash."

I almost laughed at that. Two ounces of heroin would have been a massive haul if I were at work. Officer of the Month, type massive, complete with a gift card and a damn plaque to hang on the wall with my name engraved in gold. But when you were a man like Tom Townsend— or a distributor like Marco Carvino—two ounces was chump change. Hardly anything worth mentioning.

"Listen, Asher, man"—Carvino cleared his throat—"I know it's not my business or anything like that, but you coming back into the fold? I, uh, never thought I'd see the day."

Neither did I.

But Jason Ambideaux knew how to bend me to his will, and if the last week had shown me anything, the bastard wasn't above manipulation tactics to get exactly what he wanted. And what he wanted was me playing executioner to his king.

"Go back inside and talk to Sarah," I said, already starting in the direction that Tom Townsend had taken, toward the back of the Quarter.

"I owe you!" Carvino called out.

I laughed, the sound hollow and devoid of all emotion. *Nah,* I thought as I held a finger up in the air as a see-ya-later, I owed *him.*

It wasn't every day that one of the city's top drug lords helped to arrange the murder of his number-two buyer, all in the name of a female who wouldn't even give him the time of day until she'd learned that he was loaded.

Then again, even Carvino feared Ambideaux.

And as Marco Carvino had personally witnessed one of my more notable "deals," before I'd joined the NOPD, he feared me too.

If knowledge was power, and power was survival, then fear ruled as king.

In exactly twenty-six minutes, I'd reclaim my crown— all for a woman who didn't give a shit that I was even alive. But blood was blood, and even if my mother refused to acknowledge my existence, I wouldn't be responsible for her death.

No matter how many times she begged for me to let her die.

EARLY THE NEXT MORNING, with the sun barely grazing the horizon, I drove back from my first Basin run in twelve years. Pulled over somewhere around the Gonzalez exit, halfway between Baton Rouge and New Orleans.

Rounding the trunk of my car, where I'd stored Townsend's body in a zipped bag—courtesy of Ambideaux —I collapsed on my knees behind the shelter of my car, my knuckles digging loosely into the damp soil.

And like I had on my sixteenth birthday so many years ago, I retched until there was nothing left in my stomach but utter self-loathing.

XIV

TEMPERANCE

MAJOR ARCANA

SEVENTEEN

Avery

"Tom Townsend, Owner of Kicks for Chicks, Goes Missing Late Tuesday Evening, confirms Police Chief Manuel Harlonne."

I stared down at the front page spread of the *Times-Picayune*, my heart in my throat as I sat on my couch. He'd done it. Asher had actually done it.

Suddenly, the meat-loaf sandwich on the plate before me looked entirely unappetizing. I shoved it away and pulled the newspaper closer. Fingers tracing the words, I skimmed the length of the three columns written up about the third man listed on Asher's damn list.

"Townsend recently came under fire for possession of heroin."

"Three weeks ago, Townsend and Jason Ambideaux, local real estate mogul, went into a bidding war for a 3,000 square foot, Art-Deco property on N. Rampart Street."

"Townsend was last seen entering one of Marco Carvino's popular daquiri shops in the French Quarter, this one located on Bourbon Street, around 9 p.m. Witnesses claim that he did not stay long, but his whereabouts afterward remain unknown."

Dread sank into my bones, heavy and unforgiving.

Not to mention the guilt—if I had slept with Asher prior to learning about his checklist of the damned that would have been one thing. But, no, I'd jumped his bones *after* finding it in his desk drawer, like some sort of hussy who couldn't even maintain her composure around an attractive man.

What did that say about me?

Nothing good, that was for damn sure, especially if I could hook up with a murderer and then still wonder when I'd have the chance to do it all over again.

"That doesn't look like some light reading."

And then there was Katie. My step-cousin. A girl who had no idea that she lived with a sort-of relative . . . well, if you factored in that her uncle was my stepfather. Former stepfather? The newspaper crinkled in my grasp.

Man, today was shaping up to be shitty.

Katie plopped down next to me on the sofa. Picking up my rejected meat-loaf sandwich, she set the plate on her lap and then took a huge bite of my store-bought masterpiece. Her face scrunched. "This is horrendous."

My gaze locked back on the newspaper. "Blame the deli at Rouse's. I picked it up on the way home."

"Ooo," Katie whistled, nudging me in the arm. "Were you with your secret admirer again?"

"No! I—"

"No need to be embarrassed about it, Ave. I mean, I

saw him at the club. Can I get an H-O-T, please? Hot damn, he was sex on a stick."

I shouldn't have assumed Katie had missed me leaving the club with Asher. Critical error on my part. She hadn't even been home long enough to pee before she'd shaken me awake with the order to, "Spill, sister. I orgasmed just looking at him looking at *you* tonight."

Katie knew nothing about Asher, save that he was a cop, and I planned to keep it that way. In fact, after what I'd just read in today's newspaper, I figured the less she knew about him, the better. As for me . . .

"Did this guy ever come into the club?" I asked, pointing at Townsend's name printed in bold on the front page.

Katie's eyes narrowed in thought as she shoved another bite of the sandwich into her mouth. Around the meat loaf, she said, "Hell if I know. It's so busy in there I don't even have time to look at the credit cards as I take them. Unless they look like they've never seen the inside of a bar before, I don't care."

"When the cops come around for another raid like they did last summer, you're going to be kicking yourself in the foot for not checking ID's."

"All right, Miss *I-Have-So-Many-Fake-IDs*." Katie laughed, her blond hair bouncing in its tight ponytail. "Listen, if we get raided, I now have the perfect out."

"Flashing your boobs didn't work for you last year . . . you do remember that, right?"

She pointed the meat loaf in my direction, and a dollop of BBQ sauce splattered on the plate. "Good news," she said, moving her knees so the plate was more evenly balanced, "you're now hooking up with a cop. Thank you so much for giving me the instant out I never knew I was missing."

Yeah, definitely *not* an instant out if he was a serial killer.

My heart lurched at the thought. How many murders constituted serial-killer status, anyway? Two deaths? Three? Thank God I hadn't even had the chance to take a bite of the meat loaf because I was feeling insanely nauseous now, just with the direction of my thoughts.

"So, no?" I pushed again, completely ignoring Katie's sneaky methods at getting me to spill my guts about Asher. "The name Townsend doesn't sound familiar?" I angled the newspaper to better face her, then stabbed a finger at a photo of the man in question. With dark hair and equally dark eyes, he looked like an attorney. Clean and impossibly stuffy. The kind of guy who liked his creature comforts and would never consider leaving them, unless the "leaving" was done involuntary. "Not ringing a bell at all?"

Katie flashed me a considering glance and then trained her attention on the black-and-white image. After a moment, she said, "Maybe he looks a little familiar. I don't know. I can't say for certain." She gave a loose-shouldered shrug. "Unless they look like your hot cop, every guy who waltzes into that place might as well be a copy-and-paste version of the last. So, maybe I've seen him. Why does this matter so much to you?"

Because of Tabby.

Because I can't be attracted to a killer—that sort of irony I couldn't handle. I wouldn't live my life in a cycle, and I wouldn't be blindsided by a fired gun in the middle of the night with my young daughter watching on.

I couldn't tell Katie any of this, of course, and so I fed her a lie: "No reason. I guess I'm always used to hearing the gossip at the square. You know how everyone knows everything about everyone there. But yeah, there's been nothing about this and it's Thursday. Just odd, that's all."

Folding the newspaper back in half along its crisp line, I jumped up to my feet. "I'm going to head down to Jackson Square now, actually. Get in a few extra hours."

"Want some company?" Katie asked. "I don't have to go into work until second shift tonight."

On any other night, I would have said yes.

Tonight, I just wanted answers.

"I might be stopping to see you-know-who beforehand."

Katie's blue eyes lit with excitement for me, and the knife of guilt twisted a little deeper. "Want a condom or two to take with you?" She tapped her forehead, then pointed at me. "Just thinking proactively."

"What? No!" Heat rushed up my neck. "No condoms are necessary."

"No condoms, eh? If you get pregnant, can I be the godmother?"

Waaaayyy too close to home for comfort there.

Stuffing the newspaper into my backpack, I slung the bag over my shoulder and stepped into my boots. "And on that note, I think it's time for me to head out."

"Is that a no?" Katie hollered at my back.

Hand on the doorknob, I cast a glance back. Katie half hung over the side of the couch, looking up at me while she was upside down. Her grin tipped the scale of shit-eating, and I laughed.

"You're insane."

"Nothing new there," she said, still grinning, "but is it a no?"

"It's a maybe."

When I shut the door, it was only to hear her exclaim, "I'll take it!"

MAJOR ARCANA

EIGHTEEN

Avery

The last time I'd stepped into the eighth district police station, Asher had been two steps behind me.

Now, I entered alone but with a very clear mission in mind: I wasn't leaving until I had either a phone number or a physical address where I could find him. I wasn't dumb enough to assume that I could influence him in any way, but I just . . .

My eyes briefly squeezed shut at the truth.

Whatever the reason, it felt imperative that I prove that he wasn't the man behind Tom Townsend's disappearance. The *how's* of managing this without giving myself away were murky right now.

Sometimes the best course of action was just to get out there and *do*, and that was exactly my plan as I entered the station, my gaze quickly skimming the lobby area.

"Can I help you, miss?"

I turned toward the voice, then spotted a bulky male officer seated behind a desk opposite the gift shop. I stepped forward, paused, and glanced back. *A gift shop?* How had I not noticed that the last time?

"Random, isn't it?" said the officer. "You wouldn't imagine the people we get through here." Chuckling low, he added, "Tourists, mostly."

"And they want NOPD gear as a souvenir?"

He grinned, his teeth shining pearly white. "I think they'd rather take an officer home, but they'll make do with the T-shirt."

It was the perfect opening to ask about Asher, and I laughed like I hadn't done that very thing in taking an officer home. Minus the T-shirt, obviously.

Approaching the desk, I let my hands fall loose by my sides to keep from awkwardly fiddling with the straps of my backpack. "I actually have a question about one of your officers . . . a sergeant."

Immediately, the man's shoulders snapped straight and the laughter faded from his expression. "Are you wanting to file a complaint?"

"What, no! No, of course not." Although if my suspicions were correct . . . Well, I figured it was better not to think of all that just yet. Innocent until proven guilty—wasn't that the way it worked in the justice system? And I truly, *truly* wanted to believe that Asher was innocent. I settled my hands on the lip of the desk, knuckles turning white with nerves. "Actually, this is going to be *so* embarrassing so I hope you'll forgive me beforehand, Officer"—I glanced at the gold tag pinned to his breast, above the shiny NOPD emblem—"Templeton."

He shifted awkwardly, his broad chest puffing out with clear indignation. "We don't normally give out any information about our officers, miss."

If working in Jackson Square had taught me anything, it was the skill of reading between the lines and deciphering what people wanted to hear. I tapped into that now, moving my hand so that my weight rested entirely on my right palm.

"I *fully* understand why so much information is off-the-record, sir. Privacy is integral, especially with what y'all do for a living." I offered a slow smile, hoping to put him at ease. "The thing is, I really need to speak with Sergeant Asher, and silly me, I never got his phone number."

The man's face contorted with an expression I couldn't even begin to read. "Sergeant Asher isn't here. I can give you his extension number, but I can't guarantee when he'll call you back. He's been . . ." He trailed off, muttering something incoherent beneath his breath.

Curiosity piqued, I leaned in some more. "What was that? I couldn't quite hear you." Tugging on my earlobe, I teased, "Let's just say that I made the mistake of listening to a street band for a few minutes before I came in. Great trombone usage. Unfortunately, all I hear is ringing. Would you mind repeating that?"

At his frown, I cringed. Okay, way too thick on that go round. *Rein it back, girl. Dial it down before you give yourself away*. I could fix this, I absolutely could.

"Just kidding!" I laughed loudly, only for it to peter out awkwardly when Officer Templeton didn't even crack a grin at my expense. Go big or go home—hadn't that been Katie's motto for the longest? I wasn't going home without Asher's phone number, and with no other way to contact him—aside from stalking the station until he came in to work, whenever that was—it was time to roll out the dice and take a gamble.

I palmed my belly and took a deep breath. "Officer Templeton, I'd like to start over." Rubbing my stomach, I faked a hitched breath and powered on. "It's been *so* hard for me to come here, especially because I'm not the type of girl who likes to admit to making a mistake. The thing is, I'm pregnant."

Templeton's mouth fell open unceremoniously.

Time to make the magic happen.

My left hand joined my right on my stomach, and I mentally toasted Katie for giving me the idea for this plan in the first place. If acting politely didn't get you far, then faking a pregnancy would absolutely do the trick.

"You *can't* tell anyone," I rushed to say, curling my shoulders inward as though parting with a very, very big secret. "Ash—I mean, Lincoln doesn't even know yet, which is why I need your help. It was all so casual between us, but then . . ." I dipped my chin, patting my flat stomach. "You can see how uncomfortable this all is, for me and for everyone else, including *you.*"

"I-I—" Officer Templeton coughed into one hand, his face the color of a Ponchatoula strawberry at the height of the growing season. "I never thought Asher would have children."

Since I was going to hell, anyway, I lied yet again. "He likes to say that he can't have them, but really he's just an inner softie. Didn't want to tell anyone that he was just waiting until the right woman came around. I'd say that he's changed his mind, don't you think?"

The officer's eyes ducked down to stare at my non-pregnant body. "Let me get you his number, Miss . . ."

I hesitated briefly, then told my first truth to another soul in years. "Laurel," I whispered, my hands turning clammy where they rested on my stomach, "it's Laurel."

"Right, Miss Laurel." With quick, efficient movements, Officer Templeton opened his desk drawer and pulled out a rather large binder. He popped it open, tongue to the tip of his finger, and began to flip through the pages, one by one. "Don't know why they alphabetized this damn thing by first name. Hold on."

"Don't worry, I've got all the time in the world."

Would Asher be shocked to answer my phone call? Knowing him, he'd find a way to turn it all around and ask me the one question I'd tried my best not to think about for the last few days: whether or not I'd get on my knees for him.

You wouldn't, especially not now after . . . everything.

In the darkest parts of my soul, however, I feared that I would.

"All right, Miss Laurel, here we go."

Hearing my real name made me twitchy, and I pasted a smile on my face and took the scrap of paper he handed me with a number scrawled across it. "I can't thank you enough for this, Officer."

Templeton's cheeks flushed red at the praise. "My name's Josiah," he muttered, eyes on the gift shop behind me, "if you're looking for a middle name or something down the road, and it's a boy, consider it as payment for linking the two of you up."

The way this day was going, I'd have a fake bedroom designed for the baby by the time the clock struck midnight, too.

Still, I owed him at least my left kidney, and so I played right along with the tangled webs I'd spun. "Josiah with an 'h' at the end?"

The corner of his mouth crooked upward. "Yes, miss."

"You got it, Josiah with an 'h.'" I backed up, one foot and then another, offering a little wave. "Thank you so much for everything!"

Twisting on my heel, I ducked my head and picked up my pace as I headed for the front door. Pregnancy lie aside, I'd gotten exactly what I'd wanted tonight.

Hooking my backpack to my front like a kangaroo pouch as I walked, I unzipped the front pocket and shoved the paper inside, too preoccupied with tucking it in safely to watch my step.

A body bulldozed into my shoulder, or maybe it was the other way around, and I released a soft *"oomph!"* when I twisted to the side from the unexpected contact.

And then I saw the person who'd bumped into me, and the soles of my boots might as well have turned into glue. My weight swung forward, hands clenching at my sides, and then, like one of those toys that pops back into place, no matter how hard you shove the plastic body, I rebounded.

Run.

My heart shrieked at me to go, to sprint through the front door and hail the first cab that could take me anywhere in the city . . . so long as it wasn't *here*. But my feet, my damn feet were still rooted to the ground where I stood.

Run! Run! Run!

"Watch where you're going, ma'am," one of my stepfather's bodyguards barked at me as they all stepped into the lobby as a uniform group, like a school of fish.

I fell back, hands locked on my backpack straps, my eyes never veering away from the man who'd ordered Momma's death. In my wildest dreams, I had imagined this moment a thousand-and-one different ways.

The most frequent reverie ended with a bullet to the back of his head, just as he'd done to Momma.

The most rational one, on the other hand, had me dominating the conversation as we sat in a courtroom. Before me, on a table, I would have every document linking my mother's death to Jay Foley organized, laminated, and tucked into files that I thumbed through without quivering hands.

But in every version of the events that existed in my head, I never imagined the one that actually played out.

Fear seeped into my veins, saturating every ligament, every tendon, every muscle, turning my limbs into useless appendages that did nothing but tremor. My legs, my arms, all paralyzed. After twelve years, I was in the same room as my mother's murderer . . . and terror gripped me like a poison I'd experienced only once in my life.

The night everything went to hell.

"Sorry, Mr. Mayor," said the bodyguard who'd spoken to me, "another lost tourist."

I prayed for Foley to keep his eyes on anyone else, to keep them off me. I prayed so hard that when his gaze *did* swing my way, it was as though I'd drawn on the invisibility cloak from *Harry Potter* that I'd begged so much for as a child.

I didn't dare breathe as his dark eyes slid over me, lingering for one impossibly interminable second, then dismissed me in the next.

Never in my life had I ever been so grateful to be deemed just "another lost tourist."

Feeling as though every nerve on my body had turned to ice, I swerved on my booted heel and beat it for the front doors. Toward safety.

"Ma'am?"

Oh, God.

"Ma'am!" Clipped shoes hit an even staccato behind me. "Ma'am, you dropped something."

You can do this, I told myself. *Just turn around and act normal, and for the love of all things good, do* not *break down into tears in this goddamn lobby*.

The mental pep talk didn't do me a lick of good.

I looked back over my shoulder, careful to keep my body trained to the exit in case I needed to bolt, only to see Officer Templeton standing there. Now that he was no longer sitting down, it was hard to miss how big he was, nearly the same size as Asher. But unlike the man who'd taken my innocence, Templeton looked at me with sympathy.

Probably on account of the whole baby thing.

Gaze skirting over to where my stepfather stood, I kept my voice low. "Is everything okay, Officer?"

Templeton thrust an arm forward, his hand closed in a fist. "This fell out of your backpack while you were leaving." Fist turning over, he flattened his hand. In the center of his palm was a crinkled ball of paper.

Heart thundering, I shook my head and looked back to my stepfather again. If he saw us . . . if he bothered to take another look at me . . . . Every word in my vocabulary tangled into nothingness. "I don't—"

Templeton invaded my space, palm out. "Take the damn thing before someone sees," he hissed.

The urgency in his voice had me obeying like a soldier in respect of a drill sergeant. The balled-up paper fit perfectly in the palm of my hand, and I nodded my thanks awkwardly. "I appreciate it. I'm going to go now."

His dark eyes flitted over my face. "Be careful today," was all he said, cryptic as all get-out.

Without wasting another moment, I ducked out of the police precinct, letting the curtain of my hair shield my profile from prying eyes—my *stepfather's* eyes, in particular.

Tourists jostled past me as I tumbled out onto Royal Street, and with a quick look to my left, I darted right, away from the more commercialized side of the Quarter with its bright lights and even louder music.

I needed the darkness. I needed the shadows.

At one in the afternoon, neither was a possibility.

Ten minutes later, I found myself in the very first pew of St. Louis Cathedral with the kneeler pulled down. To anyone walking down the center aisle as they roamed the historic church, I was sure I looked like a devout Christian in prayer.

And I did pray.

I prayed long and hard that Mayor Jay Foley forgot all about our accidental meet-up.

I prayed that Officer Templeton wouldn't repeat my appearance at the station to anyone else.

I prayed, most of all, for the fear to flee my body. In the span of minutes, I'd lost every ounce of confidence I'd gained in the last few years and turned back into that scared little girl with her face buried in her knees while her mother was killed just feet away.

Coward.

The word shot around in my head like a slingshot, repeating over and over again with every inhale that I drew into my body. I had lived where my mother had died, and instead of honoring her by standing tall and coming out to the public about what had *really* happened on that terrible night, I had run.

Twelve years later, I was still running.

All those years of *researching* took on an entirely new meaning as I knelt at that pew, my stepfather's face still so vivid in my mind.

I was a coward. I was still that little girl, still too terrified of her own shadow to truly step out into the light and make a change. I was the very depiction of deception, living with my step-cousin and pretending for all these years that our meet-up had been entirely accidental and not, actually, designed by my own hand, after I'd caught mention of her name in the newspaper when she'd made a fool out of herself at an event held by my stepfather, her uncle.

The sound of wood creaking snapped my head to the right.

An elderly lady pulled down her kneeler, and, like me, rested her forehead against the back of her clasped hands. As though sensing my stare, she lifted her head and looked over at me.

"Sorry," I muttered.

"Laurel—"

My weight wavered on that pew, eyes zoned in on that little old lady's face. "What did you say?"

She blinked. "Love thy neighbor, child. You're just fine there. No need to apologize."

Love thy neighbor.

Love thy—

Not Laurel. Never Laurel.

"Peace be with you," I ground out in a hoarse voice, just to return her kindness. Pay it forward and all that other shit.

Sinking onto the backs of my heels, I dropped my gaze to the maroon kneeler. *Templeton's note.* It was on the black-and-white tile, almost out of sight, and I silently berated myself for dropping it in the first place.

Reaching down, I scooped it up and snagged a bible from the pew behind me. I propped it open with one hand at the base, letting the pages fall as they wanted. *John 3:17.* If I were a believer, I'd have a laugh at the irony of the message behind the verse—that through God, you might be saved. Here I was, hoping for salvation or, at least, some place to hide. As it was, I used the bible to conceal the way I unraveled the crinkled-up paper Templeton had shoved at me, rolling it flat like a batch of gooey cookie dough until the words became legible on the page.

If chicken scratch could ever be completely legible, that was.

Letter by letter, word by word, the ink came into focus.

If you want to surprise Asher with the news, he'll be at Whiskey Bay down in the Bywater tonight. 10pm. Wear something nice. ~ T.

Whiskey Bay? There was no way that Templeton, a _police officer,_ of all things, was encouraging me to camp out tonight at a strip joint in wait for my fake baby's father . . . would he? I reread the note another time, then yet another time after that. I flipped it over, just to see if I'd miss something scrawled across the back.

There was nothing.

Approaching Asher at Whiskey Bay wasn't a good idea. Hell, it was downright terrible.

But after the day I'd had, terrible sounded just right.

FIVE OF WANDS

NINETEEN

Lincoln

W alking into Whiskey Bay was a bit like stepping into a time portal.

Nothing inside had changed in over a decade, not the red-and-black décor, with accents of gold; not the bouncers at the front door, who greeted me with a fist-bump and a "hell, man, it's good to see you again."

Perhaps the *only* differences lay in the dancers themselves, who clung to metal poles, spun in elevated cages ten feet above the hardwood floor, and were a good deal younger than I remembered. Or maybe it was just that I was older, and probably not a good deal wiser.

Kevan, a bartender from the olden days, slid a jack and coke across the bar to me. His once-curly dark hair had been shaved completely, his bald crown shining whenever the strobe lights hit at the right angle.

He nodded to the drink. "Just like old times, right? You look the same."

I ignored the way he stared a little too hard at the right side of my face. "You're as bald as a cock." Bringing the cocktail up to my mouth, I sipped from the rim, disregarding the tiny straw he'd popped inside. "New look?"

Kevan's eyes turned flinty before he tipped his head back and laughed heartily. "Still a goddamn asshole," he muttered, running a hand over his smooth skull. "Guess the NOPD didn't wash out your mouth with some much-needed soap, am I right?"

As usual when I let myself think about the NOPD and my suspension, bitterness swept over me. I downed a fourth of the jack and coke. "They tried, trust me."

"And failed?"

"I'm still an asshole, aren't I?"

I hadn't meant it to be funny, but Kevan roared with laughter, so much so that we caught more attention than I would have liked. Which reminded me of the other major difference here at Whiskey Bay . . .

I leaned in, elbow on the bar. "I've never seen so many Hawaiian shirts and Birkenstocks in my life." I nodded toward the other end of the bar where a dude stood, decked out in a pineapple-print shirt, tight pants, the requisite Birkenstock sandals, and an Apple watch on his wrist. "What the fuck happened to this place?"

Kevan eyed the customer, snapped his gaze to the other bartender, and then rubbed the back of his head again. "Hipsters happened, man. The Bywater's flooded with them."

"And they all can't wait to go to the strip club on a Thursday night?" I knew why I was here, and it had nothing to do with the dancers putting on a performance for the crowd. No, like some sort of lovestruck idiot, I'd only thought of Avery since our night together. *Even though I'd been a dick at the end.* Pushing her from my thoughts before I risked getting distracted, I said, "Don't tell me the Basement is overrun, too."

The Basement wasn't at all underground here at Whiskey Bay. Dig a little too deep under the surface in New Orleans, and you'd hit nothing but water. No, the "basement" was an insider's joke to those who knew Whiskey Bay best—on the second floor of the industrial building, it was home to everything that the first floor wasn't.

Gambling. Sex. Drugs.

Morals were checked at the door and the only thing praised within were human vices.

Putting his weight into it, Kevan dragged a white rag across the bar. "Same old shit up there."

I took another pull of my jack and coke. "Same old people up there, too?"

There was a minute pause, and then, "Always has been."

Perfect.

Setting my cocktail down by my elbow, I slid a folded twenty beneath the plastic cup. Pushed away from the bar with a nod of acknowledgement. "Good seeing you again, man."

Kevan's voice stopped me, and I glanced back, brow raised.

Behind the bar, he shuffled from one foot to the other, one hand lifting and then falling again on its way up to rub his shaved head. Clearing his throat, he sent me a quick glance and then looked away. "You haven't been here in a while, and I can only imagine what's brought you back. But I just . . . I'm actually GM around here now."

Did he want applause? I forced a grim smile. "Congrats, Kev. It's long overdue."

"Yeah, thanks." Mouth twisting, his cheeks hollowed with a rush of air as he exhaled. "What I'm trying to say is, we still operate by the same rules. No whiskey spilled in here. Not even the shitty, cheap stuff."

The thinly veiled warning felt like a slap on the wrist.

I hadn't been gone so long that I didn't catch his drift, though. At Whiskey Bay, "no whiskey spilled" was synonymous with "no bloodshed." Lucky for him, the club was just my meeting spot for the night.

Zak Benson, Number Four, had a reputation that surpassed him for frequently visiting the rooms upstairs and the gaming tables.

Playing craps, of all things.

Holding two fingers to my temple, I offered Kevan a salute that teetered on the line of sarcastic. "You got it, Kev. No whiskey spilled."

Whistling as though I didn't have a damn care in the world, I headed for the back of the club, sidestepping groups of people as they stared up in awe at the dancers twirling around effortlessly like Cirque de Soleil performers. If only the Birkenstock crowd knew that the Basement catered to live-sex acts, they'd probably shit themselves.

Just as it always had, the back of the club tapered off into a narrow hallway where the public restrooms sat. Passing the men's room and then the ladies' room, I paused outside the third door on the right, the one marked with a black sign that read GENERAL STORAGE. I lifted my hand and knocked twice.

No one answered.

Frowning, I rapped my knuckles on the door, a little harder this time.

Still nothing.

"For fuck's sake," I ground out, frustration biting out with every word, "Nat, just let me the hell in."

The door cracked ajar, and a female voice drifted out.

"What, does the big, bad Lincoln want entry to a place that he *raided*?"

Guess she wasn't over that yet. Leveling my shoulder against the door, I gave a little push to test whether or not Whiskey Bay's owner was still holding down the fort on the other side. When there was no resistance, I slipped inside and gently shut the door with the heel of my foot.

Nat, Whiskey Bay's Queen and Ambideaux's ex-wife, glared back at me, blocking entry to the stairs that led up to the Basement. To my utter lack of surprise, she was tapping her foot impatiently, her spitfire attitude all but palpable as she waited for me to apologize.

She hadn't changed a bit, though her hair was now more silver than brunette.

I cleared my throat. "If we're being technical here, I wasn't the one to make the call for the raid a few years back. The Bywater's not even in my district."

Wrong answer.

Her nostrils flared, and her tapping foot picked up in tempo. "All you cops are exactly the same. *Pigs*," she sneered with a hair toss.

The verbal insult rebounded off my shell without even making a dent. Nat was understandably pissed—Whiskey Bay was her key to survival, especially after Ambideaux cut her off without a single penny in their divorce settlement, which was even more screwed up since he was the one responsible for their relationship going up in flames in the first place. I'd been sixteen when they'd officially divorced, but there'd been no hiding from Nat's rage whenever her ex-husband's name was brought up in conversation.

Those who took Jason's side were dead to her.

Including me, the parentless kid she'd put up with after Ambideaux had taken me under his wing. The dirt on the soles of her shoes had been more tolerable to her than I ever was, and as I faced off against her now, I wondered if she even knew that my presence after all these years could be traced back to the man she despised most in this world —her ex-husband.

"I'll pay double for entry."

It was the opposite of what I wanted, but it was all I had to work with if I wanted Zak Benson in my back pocket. On the second Thursday of every month, the Basement matched the winnings for every other round of craps and roulette as a way of enticing their clientele to keep on coming back. After all, the gambling wasn't what funded the business—the cost of exclusive membership to the Basement did. And if the rumors had any truth to them, Benson had never been able to resist dice . . . or dipping his cock into some pussy right after his winnings from one of the Basement's girls.

As to why Ambideaux wanted to off him so badly—not my business.

At Nat's close-lipped silence, I shoved down my frustration. "Triple, but I get a round at craps thrown in for free."

"Done."

Her lips pulled wide, palm thrust out, and I bit back every curse word under the sun as I whipped out my wallet and counted six hundred-dollar bills. *Ambideaux's gonna have to start paying interest on this shit.* "Triple," I said, just short of slapping the money into her waiting hand, "now let me up."

"Well, of *course*, Sergeant Asher," she cooed in a tone that oozed like poison. She stepped to the side, her nose turning up as I passed her by. "You have fun in there now. You always did."

Years ago, I had.

When I'd still been on speaking terms with Ambideaux.

Tonight, I had absolutely no plans to take my cock out of my pants. Get in, get Benson, get the hell out, get shit done.

Talk about time portals.

When my foot hit the second-floor landing, Nat's voice rang out, high-pitched and all too smug: "Oh, Sergeant! It must have slipped my mind, but our schedules have switched since you were here last." I turned back just to hear her add, "The house matching the table winners ended an hour ago. I do hope you'll enjoy your stay anyway."

Nat twiddled her fingers in my direction and sashayed out of my line of sight.

Motherfucker.

NINE OF WANDS

TWENTY

Avery

In all the years that I'd lived in the French Quarter, Whiskey Bay must have been mentioned over a thousand times—and that was no exaggeration. It was a favorite among locals: the cocktails were good and the dancers even better. Over the years, as I'd closed out my readings with customers, they'd often pause, hands drifting back to their wallets and ask, "Do you by any chance know where I might be able to find Whiskey Bay?"

There were at least five on the map, all dotted throughout New Orleans, but only one that truly mattered.

The one that I was standing before now.

The one that I'd actually never visited . . . although all that was about to change.

The bouncer at the door stared at me, eyes all flinty as he barked, "ID."

Already prepared, I stuck out my fake and made a little prayer that he wouldn't question it. I had more than a few in case one was ever confiscated—though that rarely happened. I bought them off a guy on Basin Street, a tech wizard if there ever was one, and he had a hundred-percent customer return rate. To date, he'd created me a birth certificate and a Louisiana state ID. His true value came in with his hacking skills, which meant that "Avery Washington" existed in all the pertinent, state-wide databases.

I may not "exist" to the fullest extent of the word, but I came pretty damn close. Well, unless you stared a little too long at my records and realized that not everything lined up perfectly.

The bouncer passed my card back over. "Twenty bucks."

Fishing through my purse, I pulled out the cash and gave it to him for the cover charge. At his finger twirl, I flipped my hand over and he stamped the back of it. Black ink, a treasure chest submerged in swampland. How . . . fitting.

I flashed him a bright smile. "Thanks for that."

Grumbling beneath his breath, he motioned for me to duck under the leather cord keeping people out on the sidewalk.

And then I was in.

"Oh, wow."

Blinking in surprise, I swiveled at the waist to look this way and that. I couldn't help it; I said it again. "Oh, *wow*."

So. Many. Hawaiian shirts.

It felt like I'd entered a frat party, and the feeling only intensified when someone threw up their hands at the bar and shouted, "Give me all the booze!"

"And tits!" his friend hollered back. "Booze and tits! Booze and tits!"

I swallowed—it was either swallow compulsively or bust a gut laughing, and I figured the former was probably the better option. You never knew who was watching.

The hipsters, I thought to myself, *the hipsters are watching.*

This was not at all what I'd envisioned after hearing all about Whiskey Bay's notoriety. The red-and-black furnishings? One-hundred percent as expected. All the . . . I squinted, soaking up the scene before me to its fullest extent. Well, hell. There were more Birkenstocks sandals going on in this room than I'd ever seen in my life.

First impressions: this did not look like the sort of place Lincoln Asher would visit. Ever.

"You look a little lost, *cherie*."

Startling at the sound of the female voice, I turned and —my jaw dropped. "*Nat?*" I sent a look over one shoulder and then the other. Just in case I was about to be pranked. Facing the tall brunette again, I shook my head. "What in the world are you doing here?"

My number one client smiled serenely, though one brow remained arched. "I could say the same to you. You've never visited Whiskey Bay before."

And she knew that . . . *how?*

For the last number of years, Natalie Lauren had appeared at my table in Jackson Square at least once or twice per week. Always dressed demurely. Always a little shy as she sat opposite me, her gaze locked on my Thoth deck.

But *this* Nat looked entirely different—she wore a red, evening-length gown made of silk. Her gray-streaked hair was teased to sultry, voluminous heights, and her makeup . . . well, "vixen" would probably be the best word to use to describe it.

Forcing the words off my tongue, I asked the very lame, "Do you come here often?"

Dimples pierced her cheeks as her grin widened. "And here I thought you could see the unseen."

"Just what's presented to me in the cards."

"Ah."

This would probably be the best time to stop talking . . . just in case you haven't put your foot in it enough already, and you ever want to eat again.

Biting my inner cheek, I tried to think of an appropriate response to her telling one-word syllable. Unfortunately, nothing came to mind and I was forced to awkwardly sway on my rarely used high heels.

"Are you meeting someone, *cherie*? You look . . ."

Oh, thank God, a question.

Fingers going to the hem of my black dress—okay, *Katie's* dress—I tugged on the fabric and resituated it around my thighs. I hadn't truly felt exposed until this moment but standing in front of Nat made me wish I had even a few napkins to hide my naked legs. Like, a good three dozen would do.

Since there was absolutely nowhere to hide, I forced steel into my tone. When I sat at my table on the square, confidence bolstered my ego and I spoke with authority. Right now, it was a miracle I hadn't turned tail and fled into the night.

Stepping out of your element could do that to you.

I met Nat's kohl-lined eyes. "I am, actually. At ten." The confidence dissipated a smidge when I once again noticed the clientele. "But, actually, looking around . . . I'm wondering if he meant a different Whiskey Bay. I don't think this is quite his scene."

Or Templeton was just screwing with you.

No doubt about it, if that was the case, I'd be storming the eighth district station first thing in the morning with the mother of all complaints.

"Not his scene, hmm?" One red-painted nail tapping her lip, Nat cast a glance around the space. "Do you have a name? I know everyone who comes and goes within these walls."

It was official: I was confused.

Coughing awkwardly, I yanked on my dress again, already regretting asking Katie if I could wear it. As if I'd wanted to impress Asher or something. Which hadn't been the case—not exactly. I'd simply wanted to fit in.

I just hadn't anticipated that Hawaiian shirts would be a much better option than the cocktail dress I'd donned.

Figures.

"Nat," I said slowly, "this is going to be an incredibly random question but do you—"

Her dark eyes lit with humor. "I own Whiskey Bay, *cherie*. *This* Whiskey Bay, at any rate. I wouldn't touch the others in this city with a ten-foot pole."

"Oh."

"Now, if you don't mind, I'd love to return the help you've given me for so many years now. Your readings . . ." Biting down on her nail, Nat only grinned. "Well, shall we say that your readings have been a highlight for me? Always so spot-on when it comes to the business."

Odd as it was to hear someone praise me for what I did, I felt the most absurd urge to throw my arms around Nat and say thank you. Not for the compliment, but for the help she offered. It was something that friends would do to bolster each other up, and I couldn't deny how it made me feel ten times lighter.

"Thank you," I whispered. "Honestly, hearing that means a lot to me."

Nat waved me off dismissively. "Now, this gentleman you're looking for . . ." She glanced my way, eyes narrowed in speculation. "It *is* a man, isn't it?"

"Yes." Cheeks burning, I almost put a finger over my mouth to keep from spilling my guts about Asher.

"And you haven't seen him here yet?"

"No," I said with a shake of my head, "honestly, it's possible he stood me up. He didn't know I was coming—an acquaintance of ours set this up tonight. Told me to be here at ten on the dot because that's when Asher would be here too."

Nat's head jerked in my direction. "*Asher*, you said?"

"Yes." Feeling a little thrown off by the undertone in which she'd uttered his name, I cocked my head. "Do you know him?"

Over the soulful blues blaring from the speakers, I heard her rough laugh. Heard, also, the over-saturated note in her voice when she said, "Oh, I absolutely know Lincoln Asher, *cherie*. I've known him for years."

Years?

Sucking in a breath, the hem of my dress leapt up my legs again—and I yanked the damn thing back into place. The difference between Katie and me came down to top-heavy and bottom-heavy, and I fit solidly in the latter grouping.

"How do you know him?" I asked, which wasn't at all what I wanted answers to. The real question that had haunted me on my entire way over had circulated around one common thing. . .

Can I trust him?

Sensing my unease, Nat patted my arm. "He and my asshole of an ex-husband are great friends."

That'd probably be more useful knowledge if I had an idea of who her ex-husband was in the first place. I smiled like I knew what the hell she was talking about, and noncommittedly muttered, "Such an asshole."

"See!" she exclaimed, like we weren't the only two people engaged in this conversation, "I'm not the only one to think so! Instead, this entire city treats him like even his piss is liquid gold."

I came up spluttering for air, my entire chest contracting as I choked back a laugh.

Nat gave me a pitying glance. "You'll see one day."

I hoped not, but I supposed that answered my question well enough. Bitterness radiated from her like a tangible force field, and it didn't take a genius to recognize that Nat was *far* from over her divorce.

From my periphery, I watched as an unknown man tapped her on the shoulder and then leaned in to whisper something in her ear. Her dark eyes flicked over to me, sliding down the length of my body, before flitting over to something else. Her response came in a language I didn't recognize, and I didn't bother straining my ears to understand any of it.

Stepping back, the man gave me a single, polite nod before heading off in the opposite direction from where he'd approached.

"I thought you were French?" I asked casually, my gaze still locked on the man's back. For whatever reason, he seemed . . . familiar. The broad nose, the mole on the right side of his temple. He turned, and I noticed it then.

"He has a limp."

"Injured in Ramada in the early 2000's," Nat murmured as though my observation weren't completely rude, which it had been. But I couldn't shake the notion that I'd seen him before . . . that limp, that mole that was shaped like the state of Texas.

Aware that Nat was still talking, and I'd completely shut her out, I gave a quick shake of my head. *Be in the present.* "I'm so sorry. I didn't catch anything you just said."

Unlike the first smile she'd given me upon spotting me

in her club, this one was small and strained. "No worries, *cherie*. You don't need to hear about my parents' immigration from Hungary." She clapped her hands together, the sound like a shock to my system. "Now, let's return to the reason why you've come to Whiskey Bay in the first place, shall we? Follow me, please."

Taking the skirts of her dress in hand, Nat whisked around, the silk billowing with elegance. Despite the fact that the dancers were scantily clad—if "clad" at all—heads swiveled to watch Nat as she moved.

With my back straight and my feet aching from the stilettos, I followed right on her heel. If I gave her anymore of a lead, I'd lose her in the crowd. Following her in silence gave me time to think, too, which probably wasn't a good thing.

What had she meant that I'd see one day? If we'd been anywhere else, I'd have asked about her ex-husband. As it was, I made a mental note to do a little research when I went back home tonight. Nat would be easy to find as the owner of Whiskey Bay, even if she'd never given me her surname. And if her ex was as notorious of an asshole as she claimed him to be, then there was no telling what I'd find about him on the internet, as well.

"This way, *cherie*," Nat murmured, inserting a key into a lock at the end of the hallway. "Asher arrived not so long before you. He'll be just *thrilled* to see you . . . although, we did chat a little too long for you to technically be on time."

Considering he had no idea I was even here, I figured the lapse in time was a no-problem-type deal. "I always love chatting with you, Nat," I said when she encouraged me to take the stairs. It was true, too. She was one of my favorite customers, and it had nothing to do with the size of the tips she left me.

In a world that often looked at me like I'd spawned

horns mid-conversation, Nat had always treated me—and the other readers in the square—as though I had something incredibly special to share.

Behind me, her voice floated up the narrow, industrial stairwell. "Me too, *cherie*, me too."

Planting the heel of my stiletto on the last stair rung, I stepped up onto the landing of the second floor . . . and promptly felt the blood in my body rush everywhere all at once.

"Shocking, is it not?" murmured Nat by my ear as she swept past me. With my heart in my throat, I watched with wide eyes as she tossed her hair over one shoulder and skimmed a quick glance over the room before her, as though observing her kingdom. "Your Asher, *cherie*," she said, "is not a man of simple tastes."

No . . . it would seem not.

It suddenly felt too hard to breathe, like no matter how many times I opened my mouth to suck in air, I only ended up gasping. Or maybe I was simply panting—everything on this floor was a sure-fire reason to be short of breath.

Because, no matter which way I diverted my attention to, couples were engaged in hard, loud sex.

On top of the gaming tables.

On circular stages elevated some four feet off the ground.

On the bar itself.

And all around them were onlookers, their faces completely blacked out by the darkness as only the couples engaged in sex had any kind of spotlight on them.

Awareness prickled like a tangible touch as it danced its way down my arms and up my spine. When the hem of my dress inched dangerously close to riding up my butt, I didn't even bother to fix it.

Compared to the women being fucked openly in this

room, one panty-sighting wasn't going to be much of a jaw-dropper.

A bare shoulder brushing mine had me flinching, but at Nat's smooth, accented voice, my shoulders released their tension.

"Live sex shows have always been popular for as long as the French Quarter has existed, but with the city council and the NOPD shutting down long-time establishments for dancers just stripping . . . it seemed like the right decision to pick up and go elsewhere."

As much as I wanted to shut my eyes, I couldn't look away from the nearest couple. Hoisted up on a mini stage, the woman was on all fours, a black blindfold neatly tied around her eyes, a large man behind her. He stood, imposing in his stature—especially when compared to the woman—and trailed what looked like a crop up the gentle slope of her back. Up that strip of leather went, to the space between her shoulder blades, then down, down, down, until the tip rested on the curve of her ass.

When the man brought that strip of leather down on her behind with a *thwack!* I jumped as though Nat had clapped her hands all over again. A female whimper cut through the air, and I'd be dead before I ever admitted it, but even my own ass clenched as though *I'd* been the one to take the licking. Heat saturating my limbs, I shifted my weight on my heels.

Nat's hand found my back, and she gently brushed back my hair. "We like to be all-inclusive here, as it's one of the few places in the city you can still find such performances. Whether our clients are looking for some BDSM, missionary, men on men, or threesomes, we cater to all."

Lips dry, I wet them—and then wished I had a few ice cubes to toss down the front of my dress . . . and probably in my damn underwear, too.

"And downstairs?" I asked breathlessly as I spotted a new group off to my left. Positioned on a bed up on a circular stage, a woman and a man hovered over a second man, who was sprawled across the rumpled sheets. Through the crowd, I couldn't see much of the second man's face. But I saw his cock, erect and proud, and there was no mistaking it when the first man leaned down to swipe his tongue along that hard length, from base to crown.

My core tightened at the sight, and there was nothing —*nothing*—I could do to stop watching the scene unfold before me.

"Downstairs, *cherie*, there is a wait list for those who would die to ascend those steps. But they'll have to wait to join our little club." Bitterly, she tacked on, "We're prone to police raids though we do our best to stay off the radar. No one enters this space who hasn't already been checked extensively."

Tearing my gaze from the threesome, I refocused on Nat. "You didn't do a check on me."

She didn't even blink. "Ah, but you don't truly exist, do you, Miss Washington?"

Like earlier tonight when I'd run into my stepfather, Nat's offhand comment was like a douse of cold water over the head. My lust cooled instantaneously, my brain working overtime to think of something to say that would throw her off. Had the bouncer downstairs told her that my ID was a fake? *That had to be it.* Relief hit me like a sledgehammer to the chest, the built-up air filtering out as I exhaled again and again and again.

"Look how pale you are!" Pressing a hand to my forehead, Nat eclipsed my hands between hers and rubbed them together. "It was only a joke, *cherie*," she said, brows wrinkled in concern. "After all these years of you helping me, you are welcome here whenever you want." She paused, and I glanced up to meet her gaze. "I find it necessary to warn you, though, about your little *crush* on Lincoln Asher."

"What about it?" I asked, more sharply than I'd intended.

"It's nothing, nothing." Beneath her breath she muttered something, probably in Hungarian, and then piped up again. "I just . . . you ought to be warned that he is more likely to ruin you than to love you. Do you understand what I'm saying?"

Feeling the need to defend myself, I bit out, "I'm not looking for love. That's not why I'm here."

Why are you here, then?

Tom Townsend.

Tabby.

"Nat, I need to ask you—"

She cut me off, finger to her lips in the universal move for me to keep quiet. Behind that finger, her mouth moved, her voice cutting through the moans and whimpers and cries of the activity behind us: "If it has nothing to do with love, then I would like to introduce you to someone. Or, shall I say, some*ones*. Come along."

Leaving me no choice but to follow, we wound our way through groups of people until we reached the very back of the second floor. In comparison to the rest of the space, it was quiet here, almost deathly so. Shadows hugged the walls, and though I was aware of other people sitting and whispering to each other, their identities remained anonymous with the light trained only on the stage.

"Sit, *cherie*," she said, gently pushing on my shoulders until my knees gave up their protest and my butt landed on the velvet settee with a bounce. "They are about to begin."

Who was about to begin?

"Nat—"

Her silk skirts skimmed my swollen feet as she turned away. "I shall send him to you. Enjoy the performance, Miss Washington. You won't soon forget it."

SIX OF CUPS

TWENTY-ONE

Lincoln

T he very first time I came to Whiskey Bay, I'd had no idea that sex could be anything besides missionary or reverse cowboy. I'd watched porn like every other hot-blooded teenage boy, jerking off in the bathroom stall to the memorized visual of bouncing tits and shaved pussies and my one sexual experience in that fancy mansion.

On my fifteenth birthday, Ambideaux steered me up the flight of steps from the first floor to the Basement. He and Nat were on the verge of divorce by that point, but he had too much of a hand in the business—and keeping unwanted eyes *off* the business—that his estranged wife could never give him the full boot.

That night had been eye-awakening.

The next year, too.

Nat refused to let me touch any of her girls—I was way too young, she'd argued, and they were way too old.

Torture at its finest, especially to a fifteen-year-old who'd already been tasked with doing big-boy drug runs for Ambideaux. By the time I'd finally hooked up with one of Nat's girls, I'd orgasmed in under thirty seconds—the slow burn of anticipation, I guessed, since I wasn't a virgin by that point.

I'd never been particular good with looking and not touching, which was why I'd grown to favor the rooms along the right side of the Basement. All that was required of me was to pick a room and wait for the doorknob to twist, the door to click open, and a hot female to walk on in.

The chosen room dictated which toys were available, and no room had the same toys two nights in a row.

Russian Roulette, sex-style.

Those rooms had been my favorite, way back when, and according to my source, Zak Benson shared the preference, as well.

Unfortunately, missing the gaming tables tonight was turning out to be a major pain in the ass. With no way to know which room he'd chosen or even if he was still here at all, and with lights turned down, I was well and truly fucked.

"Harder!" a feminine voice shrilled. "Ohmigod, *harder!*"

Cock twitching in my pants, I crushed my empty water bottle and tossed it in the closest trash bin. All right, so I wasn't *that* fucked, but still.

Tonight was a wash, that was for sure. And instead of lingering around and hoping for a lot of something when it was more likely I'd get a whole lot of nothing, it was probably for the best if I just went home.

Or you could go and see Avery.

My eyes squeezed shut. Seven days since we'd been together—seven days of telling myself that I'd been too rough on her, that I'd pushed way too hard way too fast. Christ, she'd been a virgin and I'd sank into her heat like a fucking animal, with no regard as to how she'd feel after I left and she was alone again.

A good man would have spent the night with her tucked into his body, his hands smoothing over her arms, brushing back her hair.

I wasn't, and had never been, a good man.

My equivalent of getting romantic was making demands when she hardly knew me, and what she *did* know, probably wasn't much to her liking.

If I wanted to see her again—and, God help us both, but I did—I'd need some sort of grand gesture. Fuck if I knew what that entailed. Flowers were probably a given, though Avery didn't really seem to be a roses kinda girl. Chocolate, maybe. Although that brought in the question of white, milk, or dark.

Or maybe you should just wait to see her until this shit with Ambideaux blows over. I needed to at least try and be a decent sonofabitch who didn't go storming over to Avery's to take her all over again.

Dragging my palms down my face, I grimaced as my calloused right hand hit my equally calloused right cheek.

Yesterday I'd walked into a convenient store to pick up milk and a little girl had gone running for her mother, tears in her eyes as she cried, "Scared!" over and over again while pointing at me.

Nothing said "good times" more than sending a child into a tear-ridden fit, and all before noon.

"I've got to go home," I muttered.

Benson wasn't here, and the thought of watching people hook up all over this place while I went home alone was single-handedly the reason why the world invented the Food Network.

You couldn't feel total rage when you were watching

people make cupcakes and fight over whose frosting was better. It just wasn't possible.

Placing a fiver on the bar as a tip, I stretched my neck, giving it a quick *pop-pop*, and then made my way back to the stairwell. Ambideaux would be pissed about tonight, but sometimes shit didn't pan out the way you wanted.

During the old days, I'd been desperate to please the man who'd been like a father to me. Nothing would have stopped me from following through on his orders, not even a case of a guy like Benson not showing up when he'd been all but scheduled to do so.

Guess that was the difference a decade could make.

Plus, making Ambideaux sweat a little was just fine by me. The bastard needed to have his world shaken up some, and I wasn't above being the guy to do the shaking. Put that shit in a blender and flip the switch—

"Lincoln."

Nat.

I was *not* in the mood for another round with her tonight.

With my back to her, I drawled, "Something I can help you with? Or are you just looking for another Benjamin to warm your wallet?"

"So vulgar," she sniffed, as though she wouldn't nab my wallet if she had the chance . . . and we both knew she would. "And here I thought I'd be delivering some good news to you."

Shoulders tensing, I slowly turned to face her. "The only good news I'd like to hear is that your husband is dead."

"*Ex*-husband," she spat out, all pleasantry wiped from her face. "And, trust me, I'm waiting on the same thing. But that is not the news I have for you."

Apparently, it wasn't my lucky day after all.

"I was on my way out, so if you're wanting me to stick around for this, I'm going to need something more than just clues."

Eyes blazing, her hands reached down to fist her dress. "Then I suppose I shall just tell you this: a little birdie has arrived here for you."

Spinning on her heel, she turned to go.

My hand locked around her elbow, stalling her retreat. "What 'little birdie' are we talking about here?" I hissed, careful to keep my voice low.

Her eyes dropped to where my hand gripped her, and her mouth curled in a sneer. "You have always been so disrespectful."

Was she really that surprised?

I'd been dropped off at foster care by the age of three and had entered her and Jason's lives four years later. Most of my memorable years had been spent as her ex-husband's right-hand man . . . the one not brought to events or mentioned in public. No, Ambideaux had made use of my many talents in other ways that were better suited to running with drug lords, dining with murderers, and sleeping with prostitutes.

And the day I'd grown the balls to walk away, he'd shot me twice and had me hand-delivered to the swamplands.

I was as fucked up as they came, and she was lucky I didn't have a damn collar around my neck with a tag reading FERAL on it.

I tightened my grip on her elbow. "What little birdie, Nat?"

She smiled at me, then, her pearly white teeth on display. "Laurel is here."

My teeth scraped together as I clamped my jaw shut. Ambideaux had always said his ex was insane, and as I stared down at her now, I figured that might be the one thing he'd ever told the truth about. "I'm going home."

"Are you so sure you want to do that?"

"I don't know a Laurel," I bit out, releasing her. "Good night, Nat."

"Dark hair. The prettiest hazel eyes you'll ever see. One birthmark, just alongside her hairline. A certain lightness in her expression whenever she mentions your name."

Back stiffening at her pointed tone, my brain went into hyperdrive.

Did she mean *Avery* was here?

Christ, if Avery had been nervous about sex, this place had to have her absolutely terrified. It wasn't meant for people like her—good, innocent people who were better off believing sex was done in a bed, missionary-style, and that was that.

Guess you fucked up that already for her.

"Where is she?" I demanded, kicking my conscience to the curb.

Nat's smile twisted into the beginnings of a smirk. "Stage one. Your old favorite."

My lids fluttered shut.

I gave myself three seconds to breathe through the volatile hatred before I launched into motion.

I didn't even make it to two.

I needed to find Avery—hopefully before she saw what happened on that stage.

SIX OF PENTACLES

TWENTY-TWO

Avery

I t all started out normal enough.

Aside from the whole *we're-doing-this-in-front-of-everyone* bit, of course.

But when no one in the settees and armchairs around me seemed to bat an eye at the man and woman stepping onto the stage, naked as the day they were born, I kicked off my offensive stilettos and sat back to enjoy the show.

Nat's cryptic, departing message, however, made my brain spin like wheels caught in mud for the first few minutes of the performance, as did her promise to "send him over."

Had she meant Asher?

Stupid heart of mine had not stopped beating in overtime since she'd waltzed away, and I caught myself searching the darkness every few seconds for the sight of his approach.

Fess up, you just want to see him *tonight.*

The truth seeped like serum into my skin, and my toes tapped the wood floor anxiously as I waited.

I would be normal.

I would be calm.

My heart gave a shocked *ba-dump* as I watched the man on the stage fit a ball-gag into his lady friend's mouth, the strap going around her head. His thumb brushed over her pebbled nipple, stroking it until the woman's hips swirled, seeking his.

I squirmed in my seat.

Glanced around to scope out everyone else's reaction, but . . . nothing. If people were bug-eyed like me, if they were drooling with lust, it was impossible to tell. *Anonymity at its finest.*

A new thought lodged itself in my head: if the room was so very dark, would Asher be able to find me?

I had to imagine that Nat would tell him where I was seated . . . right? It only seemed logical, especially after she'd sat me on this *exact* sofa.

Swallowing my nerves, I checked out the couple again.

Oh.

The woman was flat on her back now, knees brought up to her chest, as the man lay between her legs and sucked hard on her clit. This time when I swallowed, I couldn't get it down all the way and I choked.

"Are you okay?" a masculine voice whispered in my ear, and I almost jumped straight out of my seat. A soothing hand swept up to the back of my head, under the curtain of my hair, to touch the skin at the base of my neck. "Easy, sweetheart. Just me."

Just me.

My lungs heaved as Asher lowered himself to the cushion next to mine. He was taller than me, though, broader, and he couldn't extend his legs without kicking the stage. He set them wide, instead, getting all up in my space and popping my bubble.

Two hours ago, I'd been ready to cut into him and demand answers.

Seated in the dark before a naked couple like the pair on the stage, I was just . . . turned on.

Even admitting that in the privacy of my own head felt embarrassing.

Asher and I leaned into each other at the same time, our opposite cheeks grazing as we spoke:

"How did you find me?"

"Why the hell are you here?"

At the fire in his voice, and cognizant that we were *far* from alone, I angled my head to hiss in his ear, "Wow, not even a nice-to-see-you? Classy, Sergeant. Seriously."

With his nose, he nudged my face to the side and did the same to me, hissing in my ear. "I'm not wasting time with the pleasantries, Avery. This isn't a place for someone like you."

Someone like me?

To the backdrop of the woman moaning on stage, I cupped Asher's scarred cheek. "I'm sorry, are you referring to my *virginity*, which you took?"

"I'm talking about your lifestyle—it's only been a week and I know you haven't forgotten what it's like for me to own your body. You were nervous then, and I get it. I pushed, and you submitted, but if you were worried about sex with me, then this shit is going to give you nightmares. I need to get you home."

He was . . . he was—

A head stuck between us, and then a man muttered, "Would the two of you shut the hell up? If I wanted to hear arguing, I would have stayed home with the missus."

Like two reprimanded schoolchildren, Asher and I jumped apart, and I fixed my attention on the couple.

A second passed and then another, and then, "*Fuck*."

I sent an askance glance in Asher's direction. "What, do you disapprove or something?"

His blue eyes, however, remained locked on the couple. "We're staying," he muttered.

I tapped his hand, which was squeezing his thigh. "Newsflash, I had no plans on leaving."

"Seriously," the man in the row behind us snapped, leaning forward again, "I'm not going home to my wife so we can argue about how to organize the damn socks again. Please, take pity on me and shut the hell up!"

We shut up.

While I'd been more than prepared to watch the proceedings on the stage *before* Asher had appeared, now I felt only more hyperaware to every flick of a tongue or circle of a finger.

The woman's face was a mask of pleasure, her eyes squeezed shut and her cheeks all flushed. Unlike some of the other acts which took place on beds or settees or pool tables, there was nothing but the stage here. Nothing but their two bodies as they moved in unison, the female taking, her hips moving downward to meet every thrust of the man's tongue. Her hand latched onto his dark hair while the other gripped the rounded curve of the stage, her fingers flexing, her palm sliding, never finding purchase, when he changed angles and her body spasmed.

It was . . . *erotic*.

So simple to put it that way and yet so very accurate, and as I sat on that settee, I became aware of the way my hand loosened and re-gripped the armrest of the sofa, as if in time to her moans that we did not hear.

Asher's hand landed on my naked thigh, my dress having ridden up. He leaned over, his voice a deep rumble that made me shiver. "Are you sure you want to stay?"

The man on the stage, with his face still buried

between the woman's legs, dropped a hand to his cock and gave it a long stroke. The determined set to his face wavered, his lids falling closed as he slicked his palm up and down, twisting at the crown, and my lips parted.

It was wrong, *so* wrong, but my mind's eye replaced the man's face with Asher's . . . and the woman's face with my own. I pictured Asher—*Lincoln*—above me, his mouth sucking on the sensitive hood of my pussy, his hand down between his own legs as his powerful body brought us both to the edge.

And all the while, I couldn't speak, not with that object in my mouth, my tongue resting up against the back of it, my eyes watering with the effort to withhold my moans, to enjoy as Lincoln took the lead and hand-delivered me to a Paradise I never knew existed.

Tongue swollen, I darted it across my lips, and whispered back, "I need to know what happens."

Asher's fingers flexed on my leg. "They come, Avery. *That's* what happens."

I shook my head, unwilling to get up and go before the act was over. Something in his tone, in that tortured heat I heard, whispered for me to keep my butt in this chair and stay still. There had to be a reason that *this* stage, out of all the others, eclipsed their viewers in total darkness and not just partial-shadows. A reason that it was ensconced in the very back of the room, isolated from the other acts, so that to even hear the moans and cries of *those* couples required me to strain my ears and listen hard.

The man on the stage rose to his feet, and, as he disappeared quickly off the stage, there was a general sigh of discontent from the audience—only to be replaced by chuckling when the woman set her fingers between her own legs and began to play.

Without her partner.

I swallowed, hard.

For years, masturbation had been my only source of pleasure, but it'd come with a price—a certain level of guilt that I wasn't supposed to be doing that, that whatever excitement I wanted in bed should be found with someone else . . . and not just my fingers shoved down my underwear, in the cloak of darkness.

Everything in me went tight at seeing this woman so carefree, *owning* her pleasure, rocking it out like she had not a single care in the world. I wasn't delusional—she was here, working, while to the rest of us, we were being swept up in an illusion of their creation.

I didn't expect for Asher's fingers to play with the hem of my dress, nor for the way he reached over and tugged my hand from its death grip on the armrest . . . and then set it between my legs, my fingers meeting the fabric of my underwear.

My breathing escalated, and I shot him a look that could have ranged anywhere from *what the hell are you doing?* to *is this okay?*

I heard, rather than saw, his swallow, and it pleased some part of me to know that he wasn't completely made of stone . . . that he wasn't so unaffected either.

"You'll see," he said, voice hoarser than I'd ever heard it. "You'll see."

He was the second person tonight to say that to me, and I opened my mouth to demand answers when every word in my head died on the tip of my tongue.

The man was back on the stage, and this time, he'd also fit a ball-gag in his mouth. Black to her pink, but otherwise exactly the same. With gentle hands, he caught her wrist and rolled her over, so that she was on all fours.

Involuntarily, my finger pushed down on the sensitive

nub beneath my cotton underwear, and my hips twitched at the hint of contact.

"*Fuck*."

Asher's groaned curse enflamed me, in a way that the couple on the stage never could. I wanted to hear it again, just as I had the other night when he rose up above me and pushed my knees to my chest and took me with nothing held back.

I stared at his profile in the dark, placing his features where I knew them to be: the strong jawline, the heavy brow bone, the nose that had clearly been broken on more than a few occasions. I imagined his throat working as he swallowed his lust, his throaty groans, and then the breadth of his shoulders as they rubbed up against mine. I heard the sharpness in which he inhaled from his barrel-wide chest, and then completed the visual with his hard-on, which had to be shoving mercilessly at his jeans, begging for relief.

I pictured it all, and I wasn't sure what that said about me, that I could question his intentions and still want to climb on his lap and fit his cock inside me, riding him as the man on the stage thrust into his partner.

Wriggling in my seat, it hit me then that I wouldn't want the restraint on my mouth.

Asher would need to hear what he did to me, so that every whimper, moan, and cry that spilled across my lips would be embedded in his memory for the rest of his life.

Maybe it was the thought of being loud that did it, but suddenly I realized that our little slice of the room, which had been so deathly quiet, no longer was.

I could see nothing, but I could hear it all.

The tiny whimper off somewhere to my right; the wet glide of a fist squeezing over a dick, and a man's accompanying curse that set my ears on fire; the whispers, the moans, the *"please, please, please"* that echoed like a sinful prayer as its owner strained for orgasm.

My fingers twitched over underwear as the implication behind the use of the ball-gags hit me: the couple remained quiet on this stage so that every noise you heard belonged to the man behind you, the woman to your right, the couple seated in the far-left corner.

Oh. My. God.

THE HIGH
PRIESTESS

MAJOR ARCANA

TWENTY-THREE

Lincoln

I'd entered a new circle of Dante's hells—and somehow, some goddamn way, I knew that it'd been arranged just to make me sweat.

Sliding a glance to the stage, I watched as Zak Benson gripped the female's hips and fucked her in a way that only a man who knew he was on borrowed time would fuck. His pupils were dilated, perhaps from the tight grip of her pussy around his cock or maybe from drugs. And no matter how hard he tried to fake it otherwise, his eyes continued to fixate on me, and not because he was thinking about batting for the other team.

No, someone had tipped him off that I'd be here, and had subsequently put him on that stage like a pig for slaughter.

Only, scratching off another name on Ambideaux's list had taken a backseat because—

Her delicate moan reached my ears, and, like an addict needing his fix, I searched for Avery's face in the dark.

The fact that she was here, that she was even enjoying this, felt surreal.

Way back when, Stage One had always been my go-to. If I cared to dig a little deeper into my soul, maybe I'd find the reasons why I liked to watch a couple screw, their voices muted in preference to those in the audience.

When it came to sex, I rarely chose to unravel my preferences.

But *Avery*'s preferences were a completely different ballgame, ones that I wanted to dissect until I knew the reason for each twitch of her legs against mine or the reason some of her moans were deeper-pitched than others.

In another lifetime, I would have dropped to my knees before her—in front of everyone—and knuckled her panties to the side as I ate at her pussy, forcing her to watch the couple fuck behind me while *I* was the one to make her finally orgasm.

Too much, I reminded myself as my cock twitched in my jeans. I'd already stripped the physical innocence from her body, and I'd be damned if I dragged her those final steps across the River Styx and into the hell that was my home.

She needed more.

She *deserved* more.

"Lincoln," came her quiet cry, her breath hitching on the second syllable of my name, her fingers landing on my arm and tugging.

What was left of my soul wrenched in half, the two camps battling it out for dictatorship of my body.

Take her.

Do your job and get Benson off that stage.

With another tug from her, my hand landed on her cloth-covered pussy. Her underwear was soaked, her hips undulating against my hand, and there was a good chance Ambideaux would feed me to the gators again when he discovered that I'd chosen Avery over killing a mark.

A seedling of doubt pierced the fog of lust, reminding

me that it wasn't just Benson I was ignoring, but also the woman who had birthed me.

She hates you.

Right or wrong, I clung to that hatred.

I clung to it, letting it fuel me into feeling validated and morally in the right when I fisted the fabric beneath my hand and yanked it straight from Avery's hips.

I was right where I needed to be—next to Avery, in Avery.

Nothing in my life had ever felt more perfect than meeting her gaze as I'd thrust into her for the first time.

Now, her shocked gasp was music to my ears as I hooked her closest knee over my lap, spreading her wide. Relying upon hearing alone, I smoothed my hand over the soft skin of her left leg, starting at her ankle and running up along her calf. Teeth clenching, I dragged my palm over where I remembered her tattoo was located, and it didn't surprise me in the least when Avery sank her fingers into my bicep and whispered, "I haven't forgotten what you said."

"Good."

I palmed her thigh, dragging the heel of my hand into her muscles, loosening the tension until she sagged in the seat and I heard the back of her head collide with the settee.

Under my calloused hand, she was temptation at its finest—and there was something utterly sacred about being the first to touch her like this, needy and exposed to everyone . . . though she sat perfectly hidden in the darkness.

My fingers trailed up to the apex of her thighs, skimming past where she wanted me most, to hop to her other leg and repeat it all over again.

Her breathing hitched, my name on her lips.

"Please."

One word, and I caved, just like that.

In the shadows, with the sounds of pleasure echoing all around us, I dropped to my knees.

What the fuck are you doing?

I had my back to Benson and God knows who else, but I was a man with a cause: to make Avery come so hard, they'd hear her all the way downstairs.

Her fingers sank into my hair as I kept her left leg bent and on the settee. I kissed her inner thigh, letting my lips linger, nipping her skin when she pulled on my hair in a silent command.

I was a man on my knees—but I was still in charge.

I took my time meandering my way over to her core, deliberately staking my claim with every imprint of my mouth on her skin. Avery Washington belonged to me. Her pleasure was mine to take, and by the time I reached her pussy, she knew that full and well.

Her hips pushed up against my mouth, my name on repeat, and I showed her no mercy.

Dragging her ass off the cushion, cradled by the palm of my left hand, I sucked her clit into my mouth and circled her entrance with my finger. Her sweet scent made my nostrils flare. So good. She tasted so damn good and there was not a chance in hell I'd ever let another man have what Avery gave me freely.

Mine. All mine.

Her leg quivered by my head, and I slipped my finger from her pussy and set my palm on the flat of her belly. Her stomach went concave under my touch, her lungs pulling in such deep breaths that every part of her shook.

And when she reached for my hand, the one that held her still, I was a goner.

She tangled her fingers with mine, bringing our clasped

hands up to her mouth to press a kiss to each one of my knuckles. My dead heart gave an erratic thump at the sweet gesture, even as my balls drew up and my vision blurred with desire.

I—*fuck*, but I couldn't finish this here.

Alone, we needed to be alone.

I pulled away, kissing her thigh once more, and pulled her from the settee.

"My shoes," she whispered, and I turned back to feel for them on the floor. My palm grazed a sharp heel, and I snagged it; the other was wedged tightly against the bottom of the stage.

"Take my hand," I growled, finding hers in the dark, slipping our palms together, "and don't look back."

I was a selfish bastard—I wanted her locked in *our* moment and not sidetracked by the way Benson screwed a girl. And there was not even an inch of me that felt remorse at wanting Avery to be thinking of me, and only me.

It seemed only fitting. Since I'd met her, she'd consumed me explicitly.

I waited until we'd left what was commonly treated as "Stage One" to yank her up against me, my mouth coming down on hers. The kiss, like my heart, was untamed: clashing teeth, bruised lips, warring tongues.

Avery rose on her toes, her hands locked on my sides, keeping herself steady as she let herself be devoured. I wanted to tug on her hair, fist the strands and pull, exposing her neck for me to kiss.

But my hands were otherwise preoccupied, and so I snuck in another kiss, nipping on her bottom lip, and then muttered, "Follow me."

As we neared the row of rooms that had once been my favorite, I searched for one with a tassel on the doorknob—

no tassel signified the room was already being used, and the occupants had brought the flagrantly gaudy ornament into the room with them.

A new twist on the telltale sock or elastic band on the doorknob.

My gaze locked on every door.

Taken. Taken. Taken. Success.

"This one," I said, squeezing her hand before releasing it to unlock the door and usher her inside. Snagging the tassel off the handle, I closed the door and hung the tassel's loop on a hook just to the right at shoulder level.

Some things never changed.

"Are there lights in here?" Avery asked.

Below the hook was the light switch, and I flicked it on.

A red glow, so common within the old-time brothels down in the Quarter, filled the room. It turned Avery's skin to a blush pink and the dark of her hair into a deep mauve. When she blinked at me, her eyes seemed almost black.

Questions pounded at my head, demanding to be voiced.

Why are you here?

How do you know of this place?

Why are you so goddamn perfect to me?

I asked none of them, not wanting to destroy the moment of carefree abandon. I'd ditched my mark, left Benson out there to his fucking, and, for the first time in years, put my desires first.

Not Ambideaux's, not the NOPD's, not my mother's.

Mine.

Sinner.

Saint.

Cop.

Crook.

Mouth dry, I swallowed. Then confessed: "I've never wanted anyone the way I want you."

With the hem of her dress hiked up high, Avery moved toward me, hips pushed forward seductively, shoulders back. Confidence brimming with every step, she reached for my belt buckle. The hook popped from its hole, and she slid the leather aside in exchange for the brass button of my jeans.

I squashed my excitement, trying my damn best to stay still and let her take her time.

Patience hadn't been my strong suit in years.

As the teeth of my zipper unhitched audibly, I swore my brain might implode.

When her small hand reached into my jeans to wrap around my hard-on, my damn knees wobbled with anticipation.

When she lowered herself to the floor, on her knees, her hands fisting my length, I died.

And when her lips parted, and she said, "You might want to take a picture of this historical event," a startled laugh climbed my throat.

Avery Washington on her knees, her mouth pursed to suck on my cock, was a visual I would never, ever forget.

At the first swipe of her tongue against the crown of my dick, I groaned, a sound so hoarse that it echoed off the walls. She circled the tip with soft, languid strokes that teased much more than they satisfied.

My hands fit along the back of her head.

Her soft chuckle around my dick was heaven on earth, her throat closing, and, *Christ*, I needed to slow her down. Back her up.

She cupped my balls and every thought went up in flames.

"*Fuck*," I grunted, my fingers impulsively spasming on

her skull, so that I brought her forward and her mouth opened wide, and that wet glide along her tongue as I hit the back of her throat . . . it was too much, all of it way too much, too tight, too wet, too fucking good. My hand moved from her head to her neck, my thumb pressing on her jaw. "You have to stop. Avery, you have to—"

She batted my hand away, her fingers latching onto my hips as she bobbed her head, taking my cock in deep on every swallow, her moans reaching my ears.

With my hand to the base of my dick, I pulled out from her mouth just before I was about to come.

Legs unsteady, I sucked in a heavy breath and forced my legs to move. Five steps to the nightstand alongside the pristine, sheeted-up bed. Fingers grasping the latch and pulling the drawer out. Foil being torn apart as I fit the condom over my length and turned back to the woman still on her knees.

The sight froze my feet in place.

With her dress hiked up around her waist, her full ass on display, she could have been any one of the dancers downstairs, out to make a quick buck.

But that wasn't Avery, and I could read her emotions plain as day as I took in all of her. The straight, proud set to her shoulders. The shy, almost uncertain way she touched her fingers to her mouth, as though wondering, *did I really just do all that?* The heavy blush that stained her cheeks, although that could have been on account of the lighting.

I didn't think so.

Fingers brushing her hair back, I murmured, "Put your hands on the bed, sweetheart, and keep your ass in the air."

I'd seen the way she'd panted as she watched Benson move the girl on the stage into position, Avery's hips circling as though *she* could feel him pounding into her from behind, her whimpers so clear-cut and seductive that even the asshole behind us had unzipped his pants and jerked off to Avery discovering what turned her on.

But it wouldn't be Benson's cock that fit between her legs and made her bury her face in the sheets.

No, it would be mine.

Avery planted one foot on the soft carpet, and then pushed herself up to stand. With the gait of a queen, she strode to the four-poster bed and climbed up, her toes hooking over the edge of the mattress as she got into place.

Her ass swaying in the air had my hand wrapped around my cock in an instant, squeezing tight, delaying the release I was so desperate to have.

I stepped up to the bed.

Slid my hands over the curve of her ass and down to the outside of her thighs.

Bent down and slicked my tongue from her clit to her entrance.

Did it again.

And again.

Until her moans were a litany of noises that she couldn't control, even when she bit down on her knuckle and came with a deep moan that had my chest reverberating with a deep-seated groan.

With one last swipe of my tongue, I straightened and positioned myself at her entrance. Put my hand to the small of her back, forcing her to arch a little more. Pushed inside, until I was balls-deep and there was no telling which one of us was louder.

Her hands gripped the sheets as I pulled out and thrust back in, and mine did the same but to her ass. I'd leave marks tonight, red fingerprints that she'd never see unless she spent time looking at her backside in the mirror. The thought alone made me want to reach forward and do the same to her neck, wrapping my hand around there so that she couldn't forget—even if she tried—who made her feel this way.

"*Lincoln,*" she cried out as I plunged in deep, my hips churning, my stomach flexing with the effort to hold off and wait for her to find her pleasure first. "*Lincoln,*" came her husky voice again when I buried myself in her pussy, and then gave in to temptation and gently circled her neck with my hand. She hissed, twisting her head to the side, just in time for me to see her sink her top teeth into her bottom lip. "Oh, my God, you feel so good—you feel . . ."

Back arching, she craned her neck as though trying to give me more room to play, and then sank her hips back on my cock, her pussy tightening. She was so wet, so tight, and I wasn't going to outlast her.

I gripped her hips, then wrapped one arm around her stomach like a band and hauled her up, backward, until it was only her knees that dug into the mattress as I stood behind her. Her nails carved half-moons into my forearms as she clung to me, her head falling back onto my chest as she let me take control.

She felt amazing, almost *too* amazing. Each glide of my cock into her heat was like a vice around my lungs. It hurt to breathe, hurt to swallow, and every time I looked down to see her dress around her waist, her small, perfect breasts bouncing under her fabric, I halfway convinced myself that this wasn't even reality.

In real life, Avery didn't grip my arms like I was her favorite person.

In real life, she didn't let me into her body—me, a former foster-stint kid with a track record that would make men on America's Most Wanted piss themselves.

"It feels so good," real-life Avery whimpered, her nails biting into my arms, "you feel so, so good."

Praying that I didn't blow my load too soon, I found her clit with my free hand and stroked her into a frenzy.

Her hair caught on my lips.

Her clammy back stuck to my chest.

She orgasmed with a cry ripped straight from her soul, and I followed a second later, hips spasming as I grunted out her name and emptied inside her.

In every way that mattered, it felt like the first orgasm I'd ever experienced.

Avery did that to me.

And you really think you'll be the one to ruin her?

I stared at her back, heard her deep chuckle as she arched an arm back to circle around the back of my head and bring me in for a kiss.

No, I thought. I was pretty sure that, between the two of us, I was the one about to be ruined.

MAJOR ARCANA

TWENTY-FOUR

Avery

I could be wrong, but I was pretty confident that my legs were still twitching from that last orgasm. Pulling air into my lungs was a difficult thing to maneuver with my face plastered against a pillow, and I twisted my head to the side and blew away a strand of hair from my mouth.

"I can't feel my toes."

Asher grinned one of his customary half-smiles. Leaning back from where he sat on the edge of the bed, he traced the neckline of my dress with a finger and dropped a kiss to my mouth. "Mind-blowing orgasms will do that to you."

My stupid heart warmed at his teasing tone, and I tried to play it cool. "I was actually talking about how my heels cut off circulation earlier. I still can't feel my toes."

His smile firming, he twisted at the waist and ran a finger from the heel of my foot to the top of my big toe. My knee thrashed upward at the ticklish sensation and I nearly clipped him in the jaw—or I would have if he didn't have quick enough reflexes to clamp a hand on my knee and stop the upward momentum.

"Duly noted," he murmured in a low voice, "Miss Washington has ticklish feet."

"Do *you* have ticklish feet?"

The glance he gave me was all stone-faced, composed cop. "I'm not ticklish. Anywhere."

"Of course you're not." Rolling my eyes, I sat up in the bed and wedged the hem of my dress down to cover up the goods. When Asher had ripped off my underwear, I'd been knee-deep in the moment and loving the show of dominance. Being sans panties now, however, didn't seem like such a bonus.

Searching the room for some hope, I said, "If they've got condoms, toys, and who knows what else in here, they've got to have underwear, too, right? I'm talking unused underwear—some drawers with lingerie just like if you were shopping at Victoria's Secret."

Asher pushed off the bed, jeans lifted to his lean hips. "Did they ever find out what secret Victoria had?"

You were so into it, you didn't even realize he still had pants on and *that he didn't even taken off his shirt.* Funny now that I thought about it—I'd never seen his naked chest. Assuming that this wasn't a two-off type of thing between us, we'd have to change that. I had a feeling he was gorgeous, all sinewy lines and tight muscles.

Shaking my head to get it back on straight, I said, "Well, we for sure know that at least she had some underwear—of which I do not."

Blue eyes narrowing in my direction, Asher's mouth turned up in what I could only call a smug smile. "You can pretend all you'd like that you didn't enjoy every second of me ripping it off you, but I know the truth."

I stared at him, unblinking.

That smug smile widened. "You were so wet when I touched you and no one can fake it that good."

The pillow was the closest object to me, and I hurled it at his rugged face.

And because the damn man had the reflexes of a panther, he caught the throw pillow between his hands and tossed it right back, where it bounced off my forehead.

"Romantic," I muttered, even though I couldn't fight back a round of laughter. I wasn't the flower girl, or the chocolate girl, but Lincoln Asher had me pinned: I wanted to smile, I wanted to laugh, in a way that I hadn't in years. He was good at making that happen. Even better at making me forget all about my vow to never kneel, to never give someone the power to hurt me.

In this room, I'd given him that slice of control.

And when he'd taken the offering, he'd stripped my defenses and made me hurt in an entirely new way that felt way too good to stop.

My fingers brushed my neck, and when he caught my eye, I smiled.

Perhaps the most honest smile I'd ever given a man.

Ducking my head in slight embarrassment, I scored the floor, looking for where Asher had dropped my shoes. "I'm so glad that I came tonight," I said, spotting them by the door. The rug was soft and springy beneath my feet as I crossed the room. "I was honestly a little nervous about how you'd react to seeing me."

And hearing me question your involvement with Banterelli and the others.

Shoving the thought aside, I pressed my back to the door to balance myself as I shoved my toes into a stiletto.

My toes were still numb.

Either the amazing sex was responsible or I was right and the shoes had killed off my nerve endings.

"You never mentioned how you knew I'd be here."

I searched out Asher's face in the red glow of the room, confusion slowing my fingers as I fit the stiletto over the back of my heel. "I thought that . . ."

"Thought that what?"

Swallowing past the lump in my throat, I admitted, "I went to the station earlier today." When he showed no outward reaction, I pressed on, foot back on the ground, standing ungainly with just one shoe on. "I needed to see you and since we never exchanged phone numbers or even email addresses"—I shrugged, then swallowed again—"well, I had to find you somehow."

Asher's hands went to his hips, chin dipped as he stared at the carpet. "No one at the station knew I'd be here tonight."

Oh.

As the implication of that sank in, I thought back to earlier in the day when Officer Templeton had shoved the crumpled note in my hand. I'd been so rattled after seeing my stepfather, I hadn't even given a second thought as to why he'd know where Asher would be and what time to meet him there.

After I'd left the station, I was a little ashamed to admit that I'd ridden on a high for the rest of the day. Picking out my heels, my dress, doing my hair.

Like tonight was a date.

The truth was decidedly less romantic: Asher hadn't even known I was coming.

The hurt came swiftly. Kicking me in the butt. Throwing a one-two-hook into my belly, like I'd been sucker-punched. Honestly, I shouldn't have expected anything else. Sex or not, Asher and I weren't an item, and there was absolutely nothing wrong with appreciating an orgasm and then going on my own merry way. I would *not* feel sorry for myself, and I refused to dip into the land of Pity's R Us.

Not happening.

Although none of this could explain why Nat had seated me with him or why she'd gone all strange after hearing his name—

"Who told you I would be here?"

The vehemence in Asher's tone stole another slice of my afterglow. And, yep, that made me angrier than learning that I'd been the only one prepping for a "date" tonight, no matter how ridiculous it sounded now. Fingers clenching at my sides, I answered, "Josiah Templeton. With an 'h.'"

"With an—" His fingers dove into his hair, tugging on the strands. It was the most worked up I'd ever seen him, aside from bedtime activities obviously, and when he began to pace the room, I didn't even bother to look away.

"It doesn't make any sense." With quick efficiency, he did up his jeans and fastened his belt. "Templeton wouldn't know this place if it bit him on the ass, and it's not like we ever had a discussion about . . ."

Trailing off, he reached into the back pocket of his jeans and pulled out a fancy cell phone. Then, without any warning, he crouched down low, lifted the hem of his jeans, and removed a gun from an ankle holster.

Holy. Shit.

"Hold on," I snapped, hands coming up in a T-shape. "You can't just—I mean, you weren't wearing that when we were . . ."

Asher's narrowed eyes homed in on my face. "I never take it off."

"So it's okay for me to go walking around without underwear but not for you to be without your precious—"

The rest of my sentence ended in a shriek that may or

may not have come from me when he pulled the trigger and put a bullet through his phone.

Like he was some sort of executioner or something.

"Are you *insane*? Someone could have heard you!" My hands flew up, knocking a lamp over to my right. Trying to catch it before it crash-landed, while also only wearing one stiletto, wasn't ideal, however, and the titanium stand went right through my fingers.

"It's called a silencer, sweetheart." He pinned me with a wry arch of his brows. "I could have sworn you said you knew how to use a firearm."

Currently, my gun was stashed in my apartment in the cabinet above the fridge, along with the rest of my documents. And if I were to ever use it as something besides a paperweight, I wouldn't demean the thing by shooting expensive-as-hell phones.

"I do know how to use one," I muttered defensively, and maybe, yes, a little curmudgeonly too. I wasn't going to even touch on the *sweetheart* comment. Ducking down, I snapped up my other stiletto and bit back a curse when I slid my foot into it. "I just don't understand why you'd opt to go shooting something that costs so much money."

"Because only one person knew I was coming tonight, and he has no connection to Josiah Templeton."

I wrestled my other shoe on, fighting the impulse to hurl it at his head and call it a day. "And, what?" *Jeez, the pain*. Why were stilettos such soul-sucking things anyway? "You think someone would actually bother to wiretap your phone? Only politicians and criminals bother to do anything like that, and you don't fit under either category."

"Let's go."

Re-holstering his gun on his ankle, Asher set his hand on my lower back. I hated how good it felt—how good *he* felt.

I dug in my heels, refusing to take another step. "Asher —*Lincoln*," I corrected when his blue eyes flared, "you didn't answer my question."

"It wasn't really a question."

"Just answer it anyway."

His shoulders lifted, a tick starting in his jaw. "What do you want me to say, Avery? I'm a crook." He leaned in, eyes blazing with a frustration I hadn't expected, his scars appearing even more dominant in the red cast of the room. "Newsflash, sweetheart, *every* damn cop in this city is a crook in some way."

It wasn't a confession, but I jerked back as if I'd been stung anyway.

Digging into my purse, I riffled through for the newspaper about Townsend and then shoved it at Asher's chest.

"Was this you?" The way the words escaped, I might as well have punctuated every one with a period. There was no room for him to evade the question, and when his Haint blue eyes darted down to stare at the front page with its massive photo of Tom Townsend, I saw all of the ghosts of his past brimming to life in his expression.

Jaw tightening, he growled, "Don't make me answer that."

The heel of my palm landed on his chest when he made a move to slide past me. Even in my heels, I was nowhere near as imposing as him, and yet his feet carried him no farther—like I had the ability to dictate his every move, just by touching him.

I took a deep breath, stabilized my thoughts, and said it again: "Was. This. You?"

His throat worked with a rough swallow. "You're reaching for shit that isn't true. Trying to stir up trouble." He tore the newspaper out from under my hand and shoved it back into my purse. "I don't know how it works with you tarot readers in the square, but I'm going to nip this rumor in the bud."

If he thought I was going to listen to his bullshit, then he had another thing coming to him. "Then you might want to look at this list, because the way I see it, a crook is when someone steals extra candy out of the jar. But this would make you a murd—"

The jiggling of the doorknob snagged my attention, as did a male voice that sounded eerily familiar: "No tassel, huh, Asher? Looks like you got well and truly laid, just like the good old days."

"We need to go."

I looked from the door to Asher and then back again. "I'm sorry, but where exactly . . . ?"

"You got your taser on you?"

"Yes?"

"Great. Keep it close. We're going out the back way."

EIGHT OF CUPS

TWENTY-FIVE

Lincoln

I hadn't done a window jump out of the Basement in twenty years, but there was no time like the present.

When your choices came down to scaling a building or walking into a bullet, there was only one option: out the window we went.

Unlatching the window, I slid the plaster sill up and thanked God that Nat hadn't moved from the French Quarter into a nineteenth-century residence. No, Whiskey Bay could be found in an old cereal-making factory, and the windows were both tall and wide. I shoved it up, leveraging my shoulder beneath its weight so I could re-hinge the latch.

Then I turned to Avery, my palm held out.

"This is the 'back way'?" she asked, and I didn't miss the way her voice hitched on the word. She was nervous, and I understood that, but there was only one reason why Josiah Templeton would have teamed up with someone who wasn't the NOPD, and that meant my ass was on the line.

And because I'd been idiot enough to get caught almost-kissing her against the precinct, now my old boss believed that Avery meant something to me. Collateral, at its finest.

I just wished I hadn't been so blind tonight to see that it'd all been a setup.

The craps table winnings being doled out an hour earlier.

Zak Benson on Stage One, instead of seated at the gaming tables.

Nat rushing me to sit with Avery, when she hated my guts with every fiber of her being . . . and had never, not once, lifted a finger to help me in my entire life.

Laurel.

The name sprung to mind, and I shoved it away. We had to go—*now.*

I swung my arm around Avery's waist, hauling her onto the windowsill. "Move your legs there," I instructed, pointing to the fire stairwell just three feet beneath the ledge.

When she spoke, her voice was ten layers of annoyed. "You let me believe we were literally jumping out of this window."

"It was a joke."

"You don't make jokes," she quipped, dropping her feet onto the platform.

Eyeing the door to the room—and hearing Templeton calling my name—I followed her through and slammed the window shut. "Seemed like a good time to start," I muttered, angling her so that she could file through the narrow path that led us down along the building, some forty feet up in the air.

Her gait incredibly uneven, she tossed back, "I'm

pretty sure I liked you more when you were all brooding and surly."

"Don't worry, that Lincoln will be back soon enough and then you'll remember how much you prefer me cracking jokes."

"Just in time for you to kill someone off that list of yours."

Hearing the fury in her tone, I snapped, "What the hell are you even talking about?"

At the end of the building, we turned down, stepping onto the circular stairwell that would lead us to a small, grassy bank just next to the Mississippi River. *If it's even still there.* Christ, if it wasn't—if the river had assumed that spot of land—we were screwed in every meaning of the word.

Avery's stilettos echoed like pin drops with each wobbly step she took. "Your *list*. Josef Banterelli—dead. Micah Welsh—dead. Tom Townsend, missing."

I stared at the back of her head, my heart pumping blood that seemed to skip my head completely and head straight south to my legs. They were frozen, unable to move, and I snaked out a hand to grind Avery to a stop, too.

Her right arm flung backward as she turned to me, her nostrils flaring. A second later, her precious taser was trained on me—aimed right at my crotch. "*Don't* touch me."

On anyone else, that might have worked.

On me, she didn't stand a chance.

I gripped her wrist, popped the taser free, and dropped the damn thing over the side of the stairwell.

It took ten seconds for me to hear the *plop!* of it hitting muddy river water.

Only a second after that for Avery to lose her ever-lovin' mind.

"Are you *insane*?" she hissed for the second time tonight. "You tell me to keep that on me and then you . . . you—" With sharp jabbing motions, she gestured to where it'd fallen below. "That! You did that!"

I hooked a hand on her shoulder, turning her back around, and began to march her down the metal steps. "It was safer than you shooting me with it."

"Says who? *You*?"

"You're fucked without me, sweetheart. What are you going to do, tell Templeton and his lackeys to hold off a second while you wait for a cab to drive you home? Because, yeah, that's going to go over real well."

Her silence was a personal win, until she cut back with: "Because your car is going to work any better? Like they don't have it completely swarmed already?"

"Ah," I murmured, my tone laced with sarcasm, "but I didn't park in the lot with everyone else."

Shoulders twitching under my hands, she glanced back at me. "Was Zak Benson here tonight?" Her gaze was steady as she waited for my answer, and I had a feeling that no matter which way I answered this for her, she was going to be disappointed.

Surprise trickled down at my spine as I remembered what Ambideaux had told me—about how he'd stashed another list in my desk drawer as a way to incriminate me if needed.

Apparently, Avery Washington had filched it when she'd been in my office the other night.

If I weren't so furious, I'd applaud her.

As it was, I just wanted to keep us both safe long enough that we could hash this out somewhere else.

"Number four," she said, a little more forceful this time, "was Zak Benson here tonight?"

I didn't know what possessed me to tell the truth when

I so rarely did in my life. Maybe it was the way she stared at me or maybe it was that I was so damn tired of the lies and everything else. Either way, as soon as I opened my mouth, I should have known it'd be a big mistake:

"He was the guy on Stage One. The one we watched for close to an hour."

PAGE of SWORDS

MINOR ARCANA

TWENTY-SIX

Avery

Betrayal was such a funny emotion.

You could dole it out in spades, never batting an eye as you cut someone to the quick.

But the minute it turned your way, exposing your weaknesses and highlighting your insecurities—well, suddenly, it seemed like something you'd never recover from.

I tore my gaze from Asher, away from the inscrutable expression on his face, and continued down the stairwell.

Why are you even upset right now? You knew all this going in.

I'd suspected but I hadn't known for certain.

Turns out, hearing the confirmation wasn't what I'd wanted to hear at all.

And if he'd been here for Zak Benson tonight—no matter that he'd spent time with me instead—that meant that Tabby was up next. I couldn't let that happen.

My fingers twitched, missing the option to yank my taser out of my purse and put it to good use. Without it, I felt vulnerable, weak, and when Asher put his hand on my shoulder to draw me to a stop, I wondered if I could trust him at all . . . or if this was part of some bigger plan to toss me to the wolves.

"Let me go first," he muttered, stepping around me. "It's a ten-foot drop to the grass and you'll break an ankle if you attempt it."

"You sound like you've done this a time or two before."

Blue eyes touched on my face as he turned his body and gripped the base of the fire stairwell. "From the age of fifteen to sixteen, I was allowed upstairs but was never given permission to enter the rooms. How do you think I learned this stairwell even existed?"

His body went into freefall before I had the chance to respond. Heart sinking, I lurched forward, hands on the railing, to see him land in a body roll in the grass below.

I hate how sexy that was.

Climbing to his feet, he motioned for me to jump.

I looked down at my heels.

They were going to have to go.

In record time, I'd stripped them both off and threw them overboard.

There was a *plunk!* of a heel hitting the water, and then a denser *thud* sound, like it'd landed on the ground below.

I guess it was a good thing I'd decided that I hated them after all these hours.

Positioning myself just like Asher had, ass out to the wind, I took a deep, steadying breath. "You can do this," I whispered to myself.

"I got you, Avery," came Asher's voice below. "It's not far from you to me."

I'd spent most of my life watching out for myself, and it was no different now. If I survived tonight, it'd be because I stayed on top of my game and trusted no one.

Not even Lincoln Asher.

The thought twisted my stomach, and I chose that moment to push free.

My body fell, dropping, dropping, dropping, the cool air rushing up under my dress and hitting my panty-less crotch—

Sturdy, masculine arms caught me, dragging me inward and keeping me close.

"Brave girl," he whispered against my hairline, and I tried, I tried so hard not to melt at the words.

I was brave.

I'd always been brave.

Lincoln Asher didn't know the half of it.

"Can you run with no shoes?"

"I've done worse," I told him, and I could see it in the firm line of his mouth. He wanted to ask questions. He wanted answers.

What happened tonight wouldn't happen again, though.

I'd survived this long by staying cautious, and Asher had slipped under all of that when I'd least expected it. He was dangerous . . . and it wasn't simply because he'd murdered.

His hand wrapped around mine, tugging me behind him.

The soil was damp from being so close to the river, and my toes squished every time they hit the ground with another step.

We could have run for an hour. We could have run for only ten minutes.

The darkness was a thief stealing time, and it was only when Asher slowed, disengaging our handhold, that I felt myself breathe a little easier. The field ahead was blessedly empty, aside from one SUV so far off to the right that it was nearly concealed in a thicket of cypress trees.

"Take this."

I glanced at him, shock no doubt written across my face as he held out his gun. "I-I—"

"You're getting some life lessons today," he drawled, shoving the pistol into my hand and slipping my finger over the trigger guard. "Don't touch the trigger unless you actually plan to shoot. Goes without saying—don't shoot at me." Then, he bent down and pulled another gun from his left ankle.

The man was a dispensary for guns.

It would be obscene if it wasn't so sexy.

No, not *sexy*.

"Is the SUV yours?" I asked, fondling the gun like I knew what the hell I was doing.

"Yup." He glanced over at me. "You can yell at me and pretend to shoot me once we're way out of here. Until then . . . stick behind me and don't say a word."

I followed his order, biting my lip to keep from mouthing off.

In the far distance, I could almost hear the notes of jazz playing. Closer up, there was the gentle rush of the Mississippi River lapping up against the levees. Beneath me, my bare feet shuffled through the short grass.

Watching Asher as we approached the SUV was like something out of a movie. He dropped to his knees and checked beneath the car. Flicked on the light attached to his pistol and peered into every window. Only when he gave me a nod of approval did we hop inside.

He started the ignition, put the SUV in drive, and peeled out of the vacant field as though the bats of hell, themselves, were chasing us down.

"You're not trembling," he muttered a few minutes later when we pulled up to a red light. "I figured you'd be shaken to the core."

I was, but I wouldn't let him see it.

"I think I'll honestly just feel better after putting on some underwear."

That made him laugh, and it was such a nice, deep, reassuring sound that I joined in. The laughter spread like wildfire between us, until we were going at it so hard that the car behind beeped to get us moving when the traffic light switched to green.

The giggle monster, my momma had always called it. *When you're scared and relieved all at the same time, you'll laugh until you die.*

Maybe I would.

Maybe it'd be better that way, to at least know that the laughter was better than the tears.

When we pulled up at the next red light, the laughter was gone.

I turned to him, determined to make him open up about his plans for Tabby, only to see the barrel of a gun staring back.

And Asher wasn't the one holding it.

A whimper escaped my lips, and I peered up to see a matching pistol positioned beneath Asher's jawline.

"Well, if I haven't just stumbled right into a little family reunion," said a voice from the backseat of the car, "the spawn of our lovely city mayor. Or should I say, his bastard son and long-lost stepdaughter. How utterly *quaint*."

To be Continued…

MARIA LUIS

I am both a sinner and a saint, but I bleed vengeance.

For years, I've lived in the grey… until her.

Avery Washington didn't belong in the shadows, but I dragged her into the darkness anyway.

One kiss, and I would stop at nothing to possess her.

One caress, and my need to destroy wavered.

Our attraction was poison and pleasure.

They say the devil recognizes his own, but I never saw Avery coming.

She's determined to light the matchsticks, and I can't resist going down in flames...

Cover Designer: Najla Qamber, Najla Qamber Designs

Editing: Kathy Bosman, Indie Editing Chick

Proofreading: Tandy Proofreads

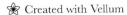 Created with Vellum

For my girls in Book Boyfriends Anonymous - thank you for encouraging me to write Lincoln & Avery's story when I shared a snippet of the prologue months and months ago. Without your interest, without your encouragement for me to take a leap of faith, the Blood Duet would still be gathering dust on my laptop. Thank you for always having my back, and I love you guys, tons.

Good job, honey.

TEN OF SWORDS

ONE

Avery

The chill of the metal gun to my temple was like ice skittering down my spine.

Every inch of me was frozen—fear working its way through my limbs, immobilizing me until all I could do was struggle to breathe.

In.

Out.

In.

Out—

The muzzle of the pistol slid from its place against my temple to that sensitive spot behind my earlobe. Chills erupted over my skin, and there was nothing I wanted more in that moment than to cup my hands over my mouth and quiet the humiliating whimpers escaping me on every exhale.

Be brave.

Be bold.

The stranger's words finally registered, pushing through the blood pounding furiously in my head, and suddenly the ice turned to heat, and I worried I might vomit all over the front seat of the SUV.

My gaze latched onto Lincoln, the man who'd just brought me to orgasm not even an hour ago. *Multiple orgasms*, my brain offered up, *not just one*.

"Ahhh, I see," the man in the back of the SUV drawled pleasantly, like we'd all sat down for tea instead of a feast of guns and terror, "you didn't know."

How could I have known? My stepfather had never spoken of having kids when he'd been married to Momma. There'd only been me. His stepdaughter. His only child. *Apparently he'd lied about that too*.

The urge to throw up returned, tugging on my gag reflex, but not because of who Lincoln Asher was—we had no ties to one another. Nothing to bind us. His father had my mother murdered in cold blood, and the way I saw it, that one fact destroyed any familial bonds society could have ever deemed existed between us.

No, I wanted to vomit because that was yet another lie Jay had fed us.

Another lie, another way to keep us in the dark and create an illusion of gentlemanly behavior that held no truth to it.

And Momma and I had believed every word, sucking them up like they were a paragon of all that was right in the world. *He'd never lie to us*, he'd always whispered—but he had.

Every. Single. Day.

"Take the gun off her," Asher clipped out, his voice pitched so low I could barely hear him over my thundering heart. "If you're going to kill someone, it's going to be me. Not her. Do you understand?"

The gun on the underside of his jaw shoved up,

pushing hard enough to cant his head into an awkward angle.

"The one with the gun at your head is the one who gets to call the shots here, Sergeant. And that ain't you."

In the light of the vehicle, Asher's scars flexed as his cheeks hollowed with a dark laugh. "*Ain't*, huh? You suddenly forget every bit of schooling you learned back in the day, Joshua? Or is it that when you're slumming, you feel the need to speak like us regular folk and forget all about your fancy Pershing presidency?"

My eyes went wide. The Pershing presidency?

The man holding me at gunpoint was *Joshua Hampton*?

It was so absurd that I almost laughed out loud. Maybe I would have, if it weren't for the pistol getting so closely acquainted with the back of my skull. As it was, my voice tremored when I spoke, like the very devil himself was the one seated behind me. "What do you want from us?"

"So, she speaks." The backseat cushion squeaked as he shifted his weight. "There are *many* things that I want, Laurel, but first . . ." He cocked the hammer on the revolver at Asher's jaw, the sound swallowed by the hum of cars honking their horns as they passed us. "We need to take a little trip. In case you're concerned, Sergeant, you've got enough gas. I checked when I had Templeton break in for me and hide me under all your uniforms back here. I'd suggest bringing them to a laundromat soon."

"*Motherfucker.*"

In the driver's seat, Asher jolted, twisting at the waist and hands lifting into motion, and then—

Click.

This time, it was the hammer to the revolver at the back of my head, and I wasn't the only one who stiffened in fear. Asher's limbs locked in mid-air, his jaw working as he went still, his familiar blue eyes fixed on me.

Dread. Terror. Grief.

I read it all in his gaze just before he blinked and his customary mask slipped back into place.

Would he tell Hampton to pull the trigger? When it came down to it now—him or me—had he changed his mind? He looked at me like he cared. But there was no denying the fact that we barely knew each other, and at the risk of saving his own neck . . . would he sacrifice mine?

I wouldn't cry out. I wouldn't *cry*. But there was no stopping my lids from falling shut as the realization set in that I was at Hampton's mercy for reasons that were completely unbeknownst to me. I would die, probably, not knowing. Without having peace. Without vindicating my mother. Without *living*.

"Put your hands on the wheel, Asher." Hampton lifted the revolver from the base of my head to my temple. "Unless you want this SUV looking like a crime scene, you're going to do exactly as I say. You understand?"

With reluctant slowness, Asher's hands went to the steering wheel, gripping at ten and two.

The pressure holding the gun to my head didn't slacken.

"Good," came the Pershing president's soft murmur. "And if you think, for even a second, that I won't put this bullet through her head, all you have to do is take a glance in the rearview mirror or at the cars on either side of us and check out the drivers. She'll die before you even have a chance to make a move." There was a small pause, and then, "Now drive straight until I tell you otherwise."

EIGHT OF WANDS
reversed

TWO

Avery

W e drove for close to an hour.
Joshua Hampton's revolver never wavered.

Between fits of panic that I was one trigger away from having my brains blown out remained the nagging fear that I was missing something crucial here. Besides Asher's relationship to my stepfather, besides the fact that I'd never even heard Asher's name before two weeks ago, was one lingering thought: "Big" Hampton knew my name.

My *real* name.

Which meant that he somehow knew my stepfather was full of shit, pretending after all these years that Laurel Peyton had committed suicide.

It was both a relief to know that I was "alive," so to speak, and also terrifying.

If Hampton knew, who else did?

Who else could use my identity against me?

With the revolver kissing the base of my skull, I watched the street lights speed past my window as Asher drove down Airline Highway, somewhere just east of Baton

279

Rouge. The fact that Hampton had no worries about us knowing our final destination meant that he either planned to kill us before the night was over *or* the location was a setup for tonight only, never to be used again.

I desperately hoped for the latter.

"Up here," Hampton murmured, "take a right up at the next traffic light."

He spoke like we were being directed to a restaurant or somewhere equally unassuming, but when Asher made the turn and the street went from gravel to dirt, there was no mistaking the fact that we were in the middle of nowhere.

My fingers dug into my thighs.

For all his pompous air, Hampton wasn't an idiot. Within minutes of us driving out of New Orleans, he'd forced us to hand over both guns. There was no telling him to screw off when we were sitting ducks—every which way I looked there were black, unmarked SUVs, and I wasn't enough of an idiot to think that they were simply accessories to a man who liked to make a grand entrance.

No, each one was packed to the brim with men who carried firearms. If I squinted hard enough, I could make out their outlines through the tinted windows.

Our own SUV bumped along the uneven road, the seatbelt locking me in place.

I'd rather go through the windshield than be stuck in here.

The thought came just as quickly as it went.

It wasn't true, not really. I hadn't managed to escape my stepfather's notice for over a decade just to roll over and give up now. Momma would never forgive me for giving in. I wouldn't forgive myself.

"Are you going to kill us?" I demanded, my voice scratchy from pent-up nerves. "Is that your plan?"

Pershing's president chuckled. "Want to answer this one, Sergeant?"

With my heart in my throat, I stared at Asher. Even after an hour of sitting on the new information, I couldn't believe . . . I couldn't even fathom that we . . . that Jay—

I dropped my gaze to my thighs, breathing through the jitters, only to hear his deep timbre to my left: "We're not dead yet, which, if memory serves correctly, means we're likely to keep our heads on our necks for the time being."

"You remember so well," Hampton murmured with an air of snobbery. "I figured our last run-in made enough of an impression on you, and I suppose I was right."

"Our last run-in had nothing to do with me. If your side-piece wanted some better cock—some *younger* cock— than what she was currently getting, that's not on me, you piece of—"

Pft! Pft!

Glass shattered before me as my ears rang from the shot of a pistol, my hair swinging forward as the SUV slammed to an unexpected stop.

Lincoln.

I tried to turn to him, but the seatbelt jerked me back —and the revolver at my head never eased. Asher's arm shot right, across my chest, keeping me in place as though he worried I'd go flying from my seat and through the splintered window.

My lungs inflated with much-needed air, and it was only in the far recesses of my mind that I realized I was clawing at his bulky arm, trying to draw him closer.

He was okay. *He was okay.* He wasn't dead.

"Put the gun down," Asher bellowed, his voice harsh in the dimly lit car, "if you fucking shoot one more time, I will—"

Behind me, Hampton's breathing came loud and heavy. "Finish that sentence, Sergeant, and I'll put the next round through you. Better yet, I'll aim for Laurel here.

How does that sound? You mess with me and she ends up as collateral."

It sounded like Joshua Hampton had spent too many years watching blockbuster thrillers at the theaters, but I wasn't about to risk my neck by giving voice to the sarcastic retort.

One second passed, and then another, and then Asher stiffly pulled away from me and set his hand on the steering wheel again. A single glance at his profile was all I needed to know that he was a man balancing on a very thin tightrope.

Like me, he was no good at obeying.

In pure silence, Asher hit the gas again and we rolled on, farther into the darkness, farther into unknown territory. I watched the digital clock on the dashboard like my life depended on knowing the precise moment everything went straight down the gutter, and by the time Hampton instructed Asher to park the car, another thirty minutes had trickled past.

"Don't move," Pershing's president grunted as he popped the back door open and slid out from the SUV.

A half-second later, the passenger's side door swung open and an unfamiliar man stood there. "Put your hands out," he ordered. I wasn't given the opportunity to do a damn thing—he clasped my hands in his, drawing them out, and then efficiently circled them with a set of metal handcuffs. The lock clicked into place, and then he was hauling me out of the SUV.

Was Asher being subjected to the same treatment? Was he getting manhandled just like me?

My bare feet tripped over the dusty soil as I stumbled forward, my weight off balance from the man's hand directing me forward. Although "directed" was too gentlemanly sounding. No, the man at my back shoved relentlessly.

Temper snapping, I twisted back to glare at him. "Ease the hell up before I eat dirt, asshole."

Dark brows lifted, and to my satisfaction, the pressure at my back slackened.

It didn't make me feel any better.

Off somewhere to my left, I heard Asher protesting, volatile curses falling from his mouth, and then . . . nothing at all. *Oh, God.* I craned my neck to stare at where he'd stood before, searching for him, needing to catch sight of his powerful frame, only for the jerk behind me to push me roughly all over again.

"Keep walking," he growled.

Within the binds of the cuffs, my hands curled into fists. Rage claimed my every step, the soles of my feet beyond the point of protest as I stomped over gravel, dirt, pebbles. My dress rode high on my thighs, every step inching the hem up to expose more skin. I was far beyond embarrassment, though, and I didn't touch it. Didn't try to yank it back into place, even though I was still panty-less.

I wanted someone to make a comment.

I wanted someone to leer.

And when I finally got my hands on a damn firearm, I'd wipe that stupid look right off their faces with a single bullet to their most precious jewels.

Boom.

Head up, chin lifted, I stormed forward. Crying did nothing for me. Worrying only wasted my time. If Asher was wrong, and we were going to be killed tonight, I'd go out in a blaze of glory. The particulars hadn't formed into a solid plan yet, but I refused to roll over and call it quits.

Be brave.
Be bold.

I always had been, and I wasn't about to change now.

The scent of swamp infiltrated my senses, pungent and smelling of rotten eggs. Cypress trees dotted the horizon, swarming my periphery, concealing the moonless night sky above, and up ahead was a small wooden shack that looked like it belonged to Huckleberry Finn and not the twenty-first century. Seated on tall pilings, the house hovered some ten feet above the water with wooden steps leading from the ground level to the front door.

"Up we go," Jerk muttered, giving me another push when we reached the base of the steps. "Don't even think about getting frisky."

The wood grated the soles of my bruised feet, and I bit back a curse when a jagged splinter cut just below my big toe. Hissing, I sucked in a quick breath and shoved past the pain. If I couldn't hear Asher, then that had to mean he was dealing with more than just a wounded foot—at that thought, the rage in my system burned hotter.

It wasn't until my eyes registered the figure sitting at the table in the brightly lit, one-room shack that I blinked and then blinked again, just for good measure. Maybe Big Hampton had accidentally knocked me over the head without me realizing it because there was *no* way I could be seeing who I thought I was.

Nat sat at the table.

My Nat.

My friend Nat.

Betrayal struck me straight in the heart, savage like an unexpected blade to the chest when you were expecting a hug. If she was here . . . if Joshua Hampton knew who I really was, then that could only mean . . . I swallowed the hurt—the lies that Nat had fed me all these years as she sat at my table in Jackson Square.

Somehow, she'd found me out. Deduced the truth.

Kept my secret until it suited her to spill the tea and throw me to the wolves.

"How long have you known?" I didn't bother getting more specific. From the way her gaze flicked over my body to my shoeless feet, she knew exactly what I'd gone through tonight . . . and I had the sneaking suspicion that she'd been part of its orchestration.

"Long enough," she answered in that maybe-French-maybe-not lilt of hers. Her lips pursed. "Your feet look horrible."

That was what she had to say? Seriously?

Back stiff, I snapped, "I didn't have the luxury of keeping my shoes on when someone was trying to kill me."

"Not you, *cherie*. You were never meant to be in any harm."

I blatantly looked down at my cuffed wrists, lifting them up as though to say, "Stop with the bullshit."

Nat tilted her head, one shoulder lifting in a delicate shrug. She was still dressed in her gown from earlier in the evening. Still looked just as elegant, as though she weren't sitting in a shack in the middle-of-no-where-Louisiana. "Inconvenient, of course. I do hope you'll understand why we'll need you to leave them on."

A startling *thud* echoed in the room. The tiny hairs on the back of my neck prickled, and I spun around—or as far as I could go with the jerk still holding me in place.

My heart dropped clear to my feet, my stomach roiling at the sight of Asher.

His fists were cuffed like mine, although his were locked behind his back. But his face . . . Bile rose in my throat, threatening to put on a performance for everyone to see, as I absorbed the horrid sight of him. The half-closed right eye, already purpling from what had to have been a fist. The blood trickling from his nose, a single droplet glistening on his bottom lip. His scars, already tinged a faint pink, were a brilliant red as though he'd been roughly shoved up against something—and held there with force.

I wasn't even aware of darting forward, of my voice splitting the quiet of the room, until arms banded around my chest and yanked me backward, toppling me into a chair. Hands pressed down on my shoulders, limiting my movement, as a thick cord of rope wrapped around my ankles, tying them together.

"Shut her up," Hampton said, entering the room in my periphery and moving to stand at Nat's side. "I don't want to hear a single word from her."

When a palm closed over my mouth, I bit down on the calloused flesh without regret.

"Fuck!" my jailer shouted, just as Asher surged forward, my name on his lips: "*Avery*."

He didn't get far.

I watched in horror as a fist from one of the men collided with his stomach, and he folded at the hips, dropping to his knees as he coughed harshly, hands still linked together behind his back.

My gaze went to Nat, tied feet twisting on the floor as I squirmed in my chair. "What the hell is *wrong* with you?"

She didn't look away, simply returned my stare. Calmly. Easily. Like this was the norm for her. "I wish you hadn't come to Whiskey Bay tonight," she said. "You weren't supposed to be involved in any of this." She tipped back her head when Hampton shockingly slid a hand over her hair.

Holy crap.

Were the two of them *together*?

I stared at Hampton's hand, at the way he smoothed her hair, tucking the strands behind one ear in a typically sweet gesture. She reached up to grasp his wrist and tug his hand down to rest over her collarbone, where she played with his fingers.

Pershing's president met my gaze, startling me with the lack of warmth in his expression. "You'll have to excuse my behavior, Laurel. It wasn't my intention to frighten you."

There he went *Laurel*-ing me again, without even dropping a hint as to how he knew my identity. Everything in me tightened, especially when Nat gave a short nod, like she was pleased with Hampton's half-assed apology.

I wasn't pleased by it, and one glance at Asher told me that he wouldn't be pleased by it even two centuries from now.

"You're worried about him," Hampton murmured, returning to stroking Nat's hair like she was some sort of precious pet. He jerked his chin in Asher's direction. "It's sweet of you, of course, Laurel, but I wouldn't stress. Your sergeant has been through so much worse."

Worse than being pummeled while handcuffed?

A beat later, Hampton tacked on, "Isn't that right, Sergeant?"

Asher swayed on his knees, his bruised eye swelling rapidly as he blinked his good one in the president's direction. His full mouth twisted in a sneer. "Fuck you."

Hampton's ridiculous hair-stroking paused, his hand suspended mid-air. "He's as crude as you warned me."

Nat's eyes turned to slits. "Some things never change."

Through a rough laugh, Asher drawled, "Screwing your husband's competition is definitely a new change. Ambideaux have any idea that you're taking it up the ass from enemy number one?"

"*Ex*-husband," Nat snapped, practically vibrating in her seat with fury. The part of me which considered her a friend wanted to shout at Asher to watch his language; the part of me which felt betrayed by her deception silently urged him to keep going. "Don't be mistaken—Jason and I haven't been on speaking terms for *years* now."

Hampton cleared his throat. "In actuality, that's the reason you're here, Sergeant."

"To listen to y'all's bullshit?" Asher straightened his shoulders as much as he could with the cuffs, and my heart squeezed at seeing him—a strong, independent man— struggle to keep his balance. "Fuck no," he growled, "I'm gonna take a hard pass."

"Will you, really?" Stepping away from Nat's side, Hampton closed the space between him and Asher. The president didn't kneel to Asher's level, nor did he crouch down, but he did stand less than a foot way. The close proximity forced Asher's head up in order to maintain eye contact.

He's in so much pain.

To the outside observer, they'd never notice . . . but I could. I could see it all: his shoulders flexing from his restrained position, the uneven way his chest lifted and fell, the slight pinch to his brow. The way it took all of his strength to climb to one foot, with no use of his hands, and then to the other, his chest muscles flexing under his shirt as he rose to his full height and moved toward Hampton.

He towered over Pershing's president, imposing and brutally beautiful.

Hampton visibly stiffened.

In a low voice, Asher spoke. "This shit ends now. I'm done playing games."

The entire room descended into silence, and it struck me then that when Hampton had quipped that Asher had dealt with worse in his past . . . perhaps he'd meant that Asher had personally dealt *out* worse. *It would explain all of the guns trained on him, like they expected some savage to pop up in his place at any moment.* And it would explain why no one said a word when he slowly limped to a man standing by the door.

Not a soul moved. Not a soul breathed.

"Take out your gun."

SEVEN OF WANDS

THREE

Avery

E ven I startled at the deathly quiet way Asher uttered the words, my bare heels digging into the floor, my back shooting straight.

The man's eyes volleyed from Asher to Hampton and back again, a look of frenzy in his expression. "I-I—"

"I said"—Asher stepped closer, invading the man's personal space until his back collided with the wall behind him—"take out your gun." I couldn't see Asher's face from my position, but there was no mistaking the way his head ducked down as if he'd run his gaze over the man and found him lacking.

"Mr. Hampton," the man edged out weakly, "I—"

My gaze fixed on Hampton, who clenched his hands into fists at his sides. "Do what he says, Charles. The sergeant clearly wants to make a point."

With awkwardness and a visible tremor, Charles fumbled with the gun at his hip. The distinct scent of urine saturated the air, and it sure as hell didn't belong to me.

The man had pissed himself.

His legs shifted from a squared-off stance to squeeze

together, and the misery on his face said it all. Embarrassment cloaked him like a second skin as he clutched the gun in his hand, his gaze bouncing everywhere but never landing on the man directly before him.

Asher would not be ignored.

He knocked the man's wrists with his bound right arm, and the guy was so on edge that he nearly let the gun drop to the floor. Scrambling, he reassumed his position, gulping audibly.

Turning around to face the room, Asher rasped, "Put the gun to my head."

Wait. *What?*

Was he absolutely *insane?*

My ass came off the seat in an instant, and I managed one step before remembering that my ankles were tied together. My elbows broke my fall.

As did my chin.

Teeth crashing together painfully, vision swirling, I lifted my face to see Asher staring at me, his expression tight. His one good eye narrowed with concern, his lips pulling thin, and then he seemed to come to a decision in his head.

He wrenched his gaze from me just as masculine hands went to the back of my dress and hauled me off the floor. It was a miracle the damn material didn't rip in half, and God knew how many people had just seen my naked crotch.

If I came out of this alive, I really needed to stop for new underwear.

Walmart would do.

Walgreens would do.

Anywhere would do.

"I'm not getting any younger," Asher barked like a drill sergeant, and the gun he was so desperate to have aimed at his head lifted up, up, up until the mouth was in place, and every single person in the room took a collective inhale, all at once.

Except for Pershing's president.

Haint-blue eyes homed in on Hampton. "I'm giving you one chance for this. You pissed I decked your precious kid? You ticked off that I'm a crude motherfucker?" He stepped back into that gun like a man without fear, and that icy feeling returned to my skin, raising the hair on my arms. "I've giving you one chance. You skip it? The next time you even try to come after me, I will snap your neck before your next breath."

He paused, the silence lengthening, and then added, "But maybe you're trying to prove that you can play with the big boys—and we both know that you don't have the balls to kill someone, Hampton. You'll rough them up, hold them at gunpoint, but at the end of the day, you're still that rich asshole sitting in your perfect mansion behind twenty-foot walls with twenty-four-seven security ensuring no one disturbs a blade of grass on your damn lawn. But, hey, maybe for the first time in my life, I'm wrong. Maybe you'll follow through." Asher's bloodied lips lifted in a smile that would send children scurrying for their mothers. Hell, it made *me* want to scurry away. "Tell him to shoot."

My mouth fell open.

He. Was. Insane.

There was only one reason why he'd do something so asinine as to tell someone to *shoot him*. And where the hell did that leave me?

Dead. That's what.

If we lived, there was a good chance I'd bust his other eye—just for giving me a heart attack. The bastard deserved it. One-hundred percent.

Hampton's expression tightened, hands balling into fists at his sides as he glanced over his shoulder at Nat.

Nat, who'd tricked me into this mess.

Nat, who'd lied to me for *years* when she'd known all along that I was Laurel Peyton.

If given the chance, I'd bust her eye, too.

The metal handcuffs chafed my wrists, and I settled down, temporarily resigned to my restraints.

"Make up your mind," Asher clipped out.

Hampton slammed his eyes shut. Then, "Take the cuffs off him."

"Surprise, surprise." Not even relief or smugness registered on Asher's face. Like he was completely composed of marble, he nodded stonily in my direction. "Avery first. Now."

The jerk who'd cuffed me earlier moved before me, unlocking the handcuffs, untying my feet. My limbs, already accustomed to the constraints, felt heavy, my toes numb. I wriggled them, but I might as well have been watching someone else's appendages move because I couldn't feel a thing.

Hampton spoke up. "I brought you here because I have a proposition for you, Sergeant."

"Then you should have called me like a normal fucking human, instead of playing the Hollywood villain and staging an abduction." Asher sneered, rubbing his wrists after they were freed. "Give me my guns and my damn car keys."

Pershing's president dipped his chin, and someone off to his right scurried forward with the goods.

"We have a common enemy between us, Sergeant," Hampton said, trying to get Asher's attention when he stepped forward, into Lincoln's line of sight. "Your father . . . he has something that I want."

Asher's father.

My ears perked up, and I shifted forward, biting back a howl of pain when my poor feet scraped along the floor. Asher's eyes flicked to me again, went to my feet, and then he immediately crossed the distance between us.

His arm went around my waist, and he hoisted me close to his side.

His familiar scent felt like safety, but I couldn't . . . God, it was weird. So weird. We shared no blood, and I waited for disgust to sit low in my belly. I waited, and yet it never arrived. My fingers clutched the back of his shirt, holding onto the fabric for stability.

When Asher spoke, I felt his chest reverberate against my cheek. "I don't give a fuck what you want. You don't own me. You don't get a say in what jobs I take on. You are *nothing*."

A hard light entered Hampton's dark eyes. "Perhaps I'm nothing, but is she?" He indicated to me with a casual tilt of his chin. "It seems imperative to note that our lovely mayor fully believes *Laurel* is dead. Clearly, he went so far as to bury the poor girl before the masses when she's standing before me now, breathing, alive." Mouth curving in a sinister grin, he added, "But a single word from me will change all that. I, for one, would love to see his reaction to her *miraculous* return from the dead. So, let me repeat my question to you, Sergeant. I might be nothing to you . . . but is she?"

Asher's arm tightened around my waist, which may as well have been a hand around my lungs, squeezing, squeezing, squeezing until they burst with a climactic *pop!* My vision blurred at Hampton's words.

I was the pawn.

Since that day twelve years ago, I had run my life as the

queen of the chessboard. I directed the ship. I operated everything from behind-the-scenes.

In the span of a breath, Hampton's words had demoted me so swiftly I feared suffering whiplash.

I opened my mouth, fully prepared to take control of my fate.

There was no opportunity to do so.

"Take your threat and shove it up your ass, Hampton," came Asher's gruff reply.

His arms swept me forward, directing me toward the front door of the shack. I jerked to look back at Nat, at Hampton, at my fate dangling on the precipice. Pity lined Nat's pretty features. There was nothing but resolute hatred in Hampton's.

"No," I whispered, "no, I—"

Asher's heat left me, and I whipped around just in time to see him grip the man who'd pissed himself by the throat and shove his face into the wall. There was a crunching sound—the wall or the man's bones splintering upon impact, I didn't know—and then Asher was leaning in, his hold so tight that Charles's face began to purple from lack of oxygen.

My hands went to my mouth, holding in my gasp.

"You *ever* throw another fist at me like you did earlier tonight," Asher said, voice deathly low, "and I will end you." His knuckles whitened as his grip tightened. "Understand me?"

"*Lincoln.*"

That was me. My horrified whisper. My rapidly beating heart. My unrelenting fear.

His lips thinned at my tone, and then he brutally tossed the man to the floor, where he curled in a fetal position, his hands at his throat as he gasped for air.

"Let's go," Asher muttered, hands reaching for me.

I stepped back.

I didn't want his hands on me.

I didn't want him *touching* me.

He was—he was . . . I looked at Charles with the imprint of Asher's hand around his neck, and this time when the bile rose, it had nothing to do with my stepfather or his lies and everything to do with the monster masquerading as a man before me.

In the end, my feet stole the fight from me.

They wobbled under my full weight, burned with an intensity from the scratches and cuts that scored the soles.

Asher's arms swooped below my butt, hauling me into his arms, bridal-style, as he strode from the shack.

Cop.

Devil.

It didn't matter what you called him—in the end, Lincoln Asher carried me all the way back to the SUV, his rugged face bruised and bleeding, his limp shortening his usual long-gaited stride.

He thought he was doing me a favor.

He thought he was helping me.

In reality, by turning down Joshua Hampton's offer, he'd just sealed my fate.

And I was as good as dead.

FOUR OF CUPS

FOUR

Lincoln

S he wouldn't talk to me.

Hell, she wouldn't even *look* at me.

If I'd been alone in this SUV, I would have bellowed out my rage. Buried my fist in the dashboard. Hit the gas, burning rubber so fast that I could forget everything that had happened tonight as the outside world sped past me.

None of those were options with Avery sitting in the passenger's seat.

No, not Avery.

Laurel Peyton.

Christ. I shoved a hand through my hair, tugging on the strands relentlessly.

It made sense that I'd have no idea who she was—I was nine years older. Had spent my entire youth bouncing from foster care to foster care after being dropped off with the Ursuline nuns as a toddler. Until Jason Ambideaux had stepped into my life, I'd had little understanding of my parents or why I'd been unwanted. Even then, there'd been no mention of Jay Foley. Not until much, much later.

I'd gone to the Ursulines with nothing—not even a surname, or so they said.

One of the nuns had named me "Asher," after a man she'd once fancied herself in love with, long before joining the cloister.

I wasn't a Foley, like my father.

I wasn't a Meriden, like my mother.

And I'd never been treated as such, always the forgotten bastard son left to his own devices.

Squeezing the steering wheel, I fought to see the road out of my good eye. Did my best not to let my frustration seep through like an infectious poison when I muttered, "We're stopping for the night."

That got her attention.

Her shoulders twitched though she didn't turn to look at me. Only sat there, face forward, shoulders squared off. "It's only an hour or so drive back to N'Orleans."

My muscles tightened at the distrust I heard in her voice. "You know how to drive?"

At that, she turned to glare at me, her chin lifted stubbornly. "No."

"Thought so." She'd told me nothing, but I'd survived thus far in life because I paid attention to the details. And the details were obvious: when I cut a hard turn, when I took a second too long to start easing off the brakes, Avery remained at ease. She never reached for the oh-shit handle or pressed down on a nonexistent foot pedal on the passenger's side. Another driver would be terrified; Avery was completely unaware.

And it all made sense.

Laurel Peyton had died from suicide in her early teens, that much I remembered from reading the newspapers. Long before she would have studied for her learner's permit. Long before she'd have had the chance to steal her parents' car and go for joyrides.

Long before she would have learned to trust anyone enough to give up her virginity.

A visual of her backside as I thrust into her body hit me, and—*fuck*. I couldn't go down that road, not right now.

Grip tightening on the steering wheel, I focused on evening out my breath and not squeezing my eyes too hard. The swollen one hurt like a bitch, and regret swarmed me for not ending that asshole's life when I'd had the chance.

One word from Avery, however, and I'd dropped his ass to the floor.

I'd heard the terror in her voice.

Had seen the fear in her hazel eyes.

Good. That was . . . good. No matter the fact we were barely related, Avery—*Laurel*—didn't deserve to deal with my bullshit. I'd never win an award for upstanding citizen of the year, even on my best day.

Rough. Brutal. Deadly.

Those were the words which best described me.

Poisonous, too.

Ill-timed laughter filled my chest because wasn't that the damn truth? Nothing good in my life ever lasted for very long. Like an infectious disease, the sinner in me had a way of converting everything I touched.

Avery didn't deserve that.

Especially not after the life she'd lived.

Trying to soften my voice, I took the next exit and veered left at the merge. "There's not a chance in hell that I'll be able to make it back to the city." Spotting the first bright neon motel sign on the quiet interstate, I pulled into the parking lot and found the first available spot. "I can't see worth a damn. We're lucky I haven't already driven us into a ditch."

There was a small pause and then, "Your eye does look like shit."

"Yeah, well, it feels even worse." Turning off the ignition, I sat back in the driver's seat, head resting on the cushion behind me. My good eye fluttered shut and I drew in a deep breath. "I can barely see," I muttered, "and I'm in no mood to teach you how to drive. Staying the night is the only option."

Six hours ago, we'd been fucking in the Basement, not a care in the world.

Now, she couldn't even relax beside me, like she was worried that I might launch myself at her and tear her limb from limb.

I was a monster. I was cruel. But only to those who deserved it.

Letting my head fall to the right, scarred cheek pressed to the headrest, I stared at the woman who'd made me believe, even for a moment, that more existed in this world than what I'd always believed possible. *And she's your stepsister.* Sort of. Barely.

I palmed the car keys in one hand, squeezing so tight that the serrated edge tested even my roughly calloused palm. The pain, unlike the one in my heart, felt good. A reminder that, at the end of the day, you could always count on reality to dump you on your ass and level out the playing field.

Happiness wasn't in the cards for me.

If I didn't understand that now, at the age of thirty-four, then there was seriously no hope for me.

Opening my mouth, I hesitated on the words I so desperately wanted to say:

You can trust me.

I wouldn't hurt you.
Please don't be scared.

In the end, I didn't say a damn thing. Cranking open my door, a grimace on my face, I stepped out and slammed it shut behind me. Crossed around the hood of the SUV to Avery's side, just as her bare feet connected with the dirty, glass-ridden concrete.

She could hate me again in ten minutes when we had a set of rooms and there was nothing but carpet everywhere.

Without any warning, I scooped her up in my arms, tugging her in close to my chest, hating that the instant her body collided with mine, my cock twitched in my pants.

"Put me down!"

Her voice was throaty, audibly exhausted.

I ignored her protests. Ignored the pain in my right knee, thanks to one of those bastards coming at me with a crow bar when I'd least expected it outside that damn shack.

Avery's hands scrabbled for purchase as I limped my way to the front door of the shitty motel. Dead potted plants sat on either side of the door, and a junkie reclined on the circular front drive, a matchstick in one hand and a spoon in the other.

Nothing said romance like staying the night in a shit-hole like this.

Not that romance should be anywhere on your mind after tonight.

"Asher," Avery snapped, sharply tugging on my shirt, "put me down. I can walk on my own. I don't *need* you."

Propping the front door open with my elbow, I angled us in. "Your feet are worse off than my eye."

She snorted derisively. "You're only saying that because you haven't seen your eye yet. It looks—"

"*Oh!*"

"—like shit."

The receptionist behind the front desk blinked up at Avery in my arms. Except that her eyes weren't on Avery. They were trained on me—on my swollen eye.

Guess it is that bad.

Readjusting Avery in my arms, I returned the receptionist's stare. Short and with skin weathered like worn leather, the woman had to be over eighty. On a good day.

I forced a grim smile. "We need some rooms."

"Oh." The woman's smile dipped, losing some of its luster. "I . . . Listen, sir, but I'm sorry to tell you that we"—her cloudy blue eyes refocused on Avery—"are booked solid for the evening."

Booked solid, my ass.

"Is that why you got a junkie on your front doorstep? Because you're *booked?*"

"Lincoln."

"No, Avery." I didn't believe for a single second that there wasn't even one room available for the night. We were in Bumfuck, Louisiana, not New Orleans, and if the druggie outside was any signifier, then this motel was hurting. "Two rooms," I ground out, feeling Avery's eyes on me. "If you'll sell to a junkie, then you'll sell to us. I need two rooms, second or third floor, with windows facing the parking lot."

The receptionist stiffened. "I don't like demanding guests."

"Yeah, well, I don't like—"

A hand clapped over my mouth, silencing the rest of my sentence.

Avery threw me a harsh look, eyes narrowed into slits, before turning back to the woman. "You'll be doing us such a huge favor," she murmured softly, "and we'd be so appreciative. Unfortunately, we were camping when Lincoln here came in contact with a black bear . . . let's just

say that the bear won. He's a little embarrassed about it."
She cupped a hand around her mouth and dropped her
voice to a barely audible murmur. "Actually, he's a little
emotional. We've been driving for hours and we simply
can't go on any longer tonight."

Black bears?

If the state had any black bears at all, they weren't
south of Baton Rouge, that was for sure.

The woman's straight brows eased, unpuckering until
the crease at the center of her forehead finally smoothed.
"That's *horrible,* dear," the receptionist whispered.

"It was. It *really* was." Avery nodded, her cheek
brushing up against the planes of my chest. "You know
what's worse? The fact that . . . well, the fact that the bear
somehow managed to steal *all* of our clothes. Including my
shoes . . . and my underwear."

Christ.

The receptionist gaped at Avery's fabricated tale, and I
didn't know whether to applaud or jeer, demanding that
she tell the truth about her missing panties. The panties *I'd*
torn right off her before dominating her body.

With a shaky smile and a quick glance around me to
the front door, the woman behind the desk turned to grab
an old-school key fob off a hook. "Two-twenty-one," she
edged out, "second floor, facing the parking lot." Her blue
eyes went to Avery again. "I live here on site. I don't know
if . . . I don't know if you'd be interested, but I do have an
extra pair of underwear. They might be a bit big—"

"She's fine," I bit out, letting Avery slide down my
body so that I could pull out my wallet. It was almost a
miracle it'd survived tonight's activities. "We'll just take the
rooms."

Avery's hands latched onto the lip of the chest-high
front desk, holding herself steady as she settled her weight

on her heels. "That is such a kind offer . . ." Leaning forward, her hazel eyes drifted over the elderly receptionist, pausing at the woman's pinned name tag. "*Sue*. I'd love a pair."

"They're clean," *Sue* said, all brilliant smiles and crooked yellowed teeth.

Avery returned the smile with one of her own. "Even better."

God save me from—

I slapped my credit card down on the counter, startling both the receptionist and the woman hell-bent on driving me insane. "We'll take the two rooms." Beside me, Avery bristled, and I gave in with a grunt. "And the underwear."

Sue shifted her weight, taking my card. "Just the one room, Mr. . . ." She peered down at my name embossed on the credit card. "Asher. Two-twenty-one, as I said. It's all I got."

One room.

Something told me that I'd have a pillow smothering my face before the night was over—Avery did *not* look pleased. Even so . . .

I nodded curtly. "We'll take it."

"We won't."

I ignored Avery's protest, grimly picking up the key and tucking my credit card back into my wallet. "Knock when you have the panties, ma'am. It's much appreciated."

Bending at the knees, I let out a tight breath at the twinge in my right leg, and then—

"I can walk, Lincoln," Avery snapped. "No, seriously, I'm fine—"

She bounced high on my chest as I stepped away from the front counter and headed for the hallway off to the right. I needed a shower and a bed, the sooner the better.

Catching the flowery scent of Avery's shampoo, I swallowed.

Maybe it was a good thing we were sharing a room. We had a wide array of shit to discuss, starting with the fact that she was Laurel-fucking-Peyton. *You knew she'd been bull-shitting you when she gave up her name.*

Yeah, I'd suspected that she'd fed me lies.

But there was no way I could have suspected *this*.

My good eye narrowed at the computer paper taped to the elevator with chicken scratch scrawled across it. Broken —of course.

"This has got to be the shittiest motel in the history of motels," I growled, turning my head in search of the stairwell.

In my arms, Avery snorted. "You chose a place called Bedding Down. Beneath the logo was the tagline, 'No more than twelve people per room.' What else did you expect?"

"That's not a tagline. That's a calling card for orgies." I hooked my thumb through the door handle to the stairs and drew it open with a low groan. "If I'd actually been able to see that, I would have kept driving until we hit a Motel 6."

"You should have kept driving until we hit N'Orleans."

"Then we wouldn't have made contact with the only pack of black bears in this part of Louisiana. Who knew they liked women's lingerie so much?"

"You should feel lucky they don't fancy dicks even more." With *that* comment, Avery squirmed in my grasp when my foot hit the first stair rung, muttering, "I can walk. Stop treating me like I'm an invalid."

She wanted to walk? Fine.

I checked back my grimace when her mouth twisted in pain as her feet made contact with the cool tile of the stairs. I wanted to swing her back into my arms, but she was right.

She was capable.

She was independent.

And I was smothering her like a man obsessed.

Resigned to letting her crawl up the steps if that's what she really wanted to do, I turned back to the stairwell and stifled a groan at the pain in my knee. She wasn't the only one feeling the course of the night, and with each step I took, my mood soured several more degrees.

By the time we reached the second floor, Avery's face was three shades paler than normal and I was minutes away from coming unhinged. I'd spent twelve years separating my life from the corruption of our city's finest leaders—unless it directly involved work for the NOPD.

Twelve years of keeping my head down and trying to do the right thing.

Twelve years of staying in my lane and off the radar of men like Jason Ambideaux.

Twelve years of trying to build a life that wasn't blood and terror day-in and day-out.

I didn't miss the way Avery skirted out of reach when I let her slide past me into our shared room for the night. And I sure as hell didn't miss the way she slid a distrustful glance in my direction when I drew the blinds shut over the windows, as though she questioned my need for privacy.

Frustration welled up, suffocating in the way it clawed at my chest, until I finally let loose the words that had been on my mind since she'd watched me shove that man into the wall at the shack.

"If I wanted you dead, *Laurel*," I growled, "you'd already be lifeless."

THE DEVIL

XV

MAJOR ARCANA
reversed

FIVE

Avery
_____

Funny how more than one person had called me
Laurel tonight, and not a single time did I feel like
they were talking to me.

I'd always thought that hearing my real name would
come with a sense of freedom, like I'd broken free from my
jail cell after so many years of being locked away in the
darkness.

That wasn't the case.

In reality, it felt foreign. Strange.

I wasn't Laurel, not anymore. Laurel Peyton was a thirteen-year-old girl with starry-eyed fantasies of becoming a
well-known vet and saving any animal that entered her
practice. Avery, on the other hand, was simply content to
foster strays and give them enough love so they never felt
unwanted while they waited to be placed with a permanent
family.

Laurel knew nothing but family picnics, an obsession
with Brad Pitt in *Mr. and Mrs. Smith*, and that her momma,
despite her affinity for drinking a little too heavily, never

put up a fuss about random karaoke jam sessions with her only daughter.

None of that even related to me as Avery.

"Nothing to say to that?"

Asher's deep timbre yanked me from my reverie, drawing me back into the shadows of my reality. "Don't call me Laurel."

With the blinds drawn shut, I could barely make out his features and his scars were completely obscured. His dark chuckle, however, was perfectly crisp in the otherwise quiet room. "You've got to be kidding me—the secret's out and you're still trying to keep up the act. Listen, *Laurel*, there's no reason to pretend anymore."

I bristled at his sneering tone. "Do you really want to play that game?" Biting back a howl of pain, I took a step closer to him. "At least my biggest sin is pretending to be someone who I'm not. How many people have you murdered, *Sergeant?* How much blood truly stains your hands?"

His chest heaved, mouth twisting harshly. "You have no idea what you're talking about."

"No?" The memory of him squeezing that man's throat was not one I'd ever forget. It made me sick to think of it. Sicker to think, even for a moment, that I'd enjoyed Asher's hand around *my* neck as he'd fucked me. What did that say about me? What did that say about the kind of person *I* was? My stomach churned at the disturbing thought, threatening to upend the dinner I'd eaten hours earlier.

I turned away, unable to meet him in the eye.

"Just say it, Avery. I can practically taste your desperation to be the saint here."

I wouldn't face him, no matter the fact that he was right. My brain was on fire, thoughts rioting through me, demanding to be voiced. Struggling to maintain my cool, I let my head hang low and kept my gaze rooted on my still bare feet.

I must have taken too long to speak or maybe it was that his patience was threadbare. Whatever it was, I didn't expect to feel his hand on my elbow. He whipped me around, and my toes burned from twirling so fast on the scratchy carpet. Our chests brushed, and if that wasn't enough to make me feel unbalanced, being the sole focus of the hard glint in his one un-swollen eye was like experiencing vertigo.

The room swirled, my lungs heaved, and I bit down hard on my bottom lip to keep from gasping out loud.

"Say it," he growled, his hand still locked like a vice around my arm. "*Say it.*"

He pushed and he pushed and he pushed, and it wasn't my fault that I snapped.

Teeth clenching, I stared up at him, refusing to back down. "If I hadn't said anything, you would have *murdered* that man without thinking twice. I could see it in your eyes, the resolution there. And, for what? Because he punched you?" Shaking my head, I gave a dismissive laugh. "That doesn't make you a hero—it makes you a cold-blooded killer."

Silence.

It reigned in the scarce space between us, suffocating in the power it held.

And then, in a tone that sounded like it'd been pulled from the depth of his soul, Asher growled, "You're right, sweetheart. You want to know the number of people I've taken out?" He leaned in close, his hot breath wafting across my face. "I don't know. How's that for a confession? *I don't know.*"

Eyes widening, I tried to pull back, away from the

anger in his expression, away from the shock of heat that hit me square in the belly. "Lincoln—"

He didn't let me go. Didn't let me flee.

Instead, he invaded my space. Step for step until my back bumped into the wall and his arms came down like iron bars, locking me into the space between his chest and the plaster behind me.

"Should I confess some more?" he whispered like the devil himself. "I want to fuck you, Avery." His mouth dropped to my left ear, nudging at the soft skin there with the crooked bridge of his nose. When I gasped, he answered with a rough laugh. "Does that shock you? That even now that I know my asshole father married your mom, it doesn't make me want you any less?" He nipped at my skin, keeping me caged within his muscular embrace. "I want to bend you over and fuck you. Me, a *cold-blooded killer*. I want to mark your skin and wrap my hand around your neck just the way you like it and thrust into your tight pussy until you confess."

With every word that left his mouth, my breathing grew more erratic. I needed to breathe; I needed to remember that Lincoln Asher was not the man for me, for more reasons than just the recently made obvious. And yet, my response wasn't a set down and it wasn't a rebuttal.

To my utter humiliation, my response could be summed up with only three words:

"Confess to what?"

One masculine hand landed on my hip. "That you want me as I am. A murderer." His palm skimmed up my body, past my ribcage. "A cop." Over the curve of my small breast. "A sinner." Gently circled the base of my throat as his lips made contact with my hairline and a shiver worked its way down the pearls of my spine. "A man who is, beneath it all, just a man like any other."

But Lincoln Asher wasn't like any other man.

He stepped into a room and people cowered in fear.

He took a breath, and grown men pissed themselves.

Tonight, one of the most powerful men in the city had sicced his lackeys on Asher, just so that they could have the slim chance at an upper hand.

And *still* they'd failed in grandiose fashion.

My tongue darted out to wet my dry lips, and Asher's blue eyes tracked the movement hungrily. He said he was a man like any other, but I'd spent too many years watching and observing to take the words at face value. If I gave an inch, he'd steal a mile.

And if I submitted, he'd continue to believe that I was his for the taking.

Whenever he wanted me. *However* he wanted me.

How long until he turned those fists on me? How long until I ended up just like Momma, dead on my dining room floor, at the hands of a man who spun pretty words and yarns of lies?

At the hands of my stepfather's own blood—his *son*?

Chin kicking up, I fixed my gaze on his battered face and made a confession of my own: "I'm not Laurel Peyton anymore. I'm not naïve or trusting or looking for a savior. I'm not in the market for one. And the next time you make a decision for me, taking my voice away because you think you know what's best, just remember that I am *not* like other any other woman who will heel just because you tell her to."

Haint-blue eyes burning furiously, he rasped, "Is that so?"

I would not cower, not like the rest of the population who saw him and ran. "Yes, it is."

His lips pulled downward, jaw clenching tightly, and

then he wrenched around with a violently uttered curse. "Any other confessions tonight?"

Fighting the urge to sag against the wall, I stood tall, shoulders back. My heart thundered in my chest. "I saw it the very first night you sat at my table in the square," I said, struggling to keep my voice steady as I watched his back flex with his labored breathing. "You're a man who's haunted by your past, Lincoln. I won't go down in that fire with you. I've got my own flames to put out."

With a bitter laugh, he glanced at me over his shoulder. "And what flames are those?" His tone baited me, daring me to rise to the challenge swirling in his gaze like a chaotic sandstorm. "Hiding in the shadows for another decade? Pretending to be someone you're not? Sitting at your little table with your deck of fortune-telling cards and *collecting* information? You can judge me all you want, but don't be mistaken. The only flame you're fighting is your own cowardice."

He might as well have stabbed me in the heart, slicing at the beating organ until every self-doubt of mine was splayed open for all to see.

I couldn't catch my breath. Couldn't see beyond the rage clouding the periphery of my vision.

"That's what I thought, *Laurel*," Asher murmured, his bruised lips turning up smugly. "Keep sitting on that high horse of yours. I'm sure the smell of bullshit is *real* sweet where you're at."

My feet were frozen, my limbs unmoving, as he turned for the door.

"Where are you going?" I heard myself ask, my voice faint in comparison to the blood pounding in my head.

He didn't look back. "To sleep in the SUV where the air is a little less judgmental. I'll get you in the morning."

Fisting the doorknob, he drew it open and then froze,

broad shoulders stiffening. "Ms. Sue," he murmured, "thanks for bringing this by."

She said something I couldn't quite catch, and then Asher was turning around, a slip of white fabric in his big hand. He held it out, a silent challenge for me to step up and take it from him.

With wooden feet, I closed the distance between us.

Just before I would have clutched the material, he jerked it back and waited until I looked up, past his wide chest, his thick throat, to his hard blue eyes.

"White," he said, voice low, his gaze crudely skimming my body, "how fitting for someone determined to be such a saint. You of all people should know that the world isn't black or white, sweetheart." I watched, eyes wide, as he purposely let the receptionist's underwear fall to the floor at our feet. The tips of my ears burned with embarrassment as he tacked on, darkly, "I can't wait for the day when you're forced to make the decisions I've made in my life. What's that saying again?" He snapped his fingers dramatically. "Oh yeah, I remember. *How the mighty have fallen.*"

Heat swept over me, and it was hard to distinguish between the anger and the humiliation at knowing what he wanted—for me to get on my knees in front of him if I wanted to pick up the underwear he'd dropped.

"Fuck you," I whispered, my voice vibrating with fury, my hands balled into tight fists.

"I wouldn't want to stain your pristine innocence all over again, sweetheart, no matter how much you liked it." He lifted one brow and then idly dropped his gaze to the scrap of white fabric on the floor. "But, maybe," he drawled, "if you begged for it, I'd be down to tear off your panties again. We can blame black bears for their disappearance, if it makes you feel any better for sleeping with a murderer."

With a wink, he disappeared out the door and closed it shut behind him.

I don't know how long I stood there.

I don't know how long the rage lasted, burning in my veins, threatening to drown me.

I *do* know that I went to bed panty-less, refusing to even touch Ms. Sue's kind offering.

And as I stared up at the dark ceiling, I had only one thought: Lincoln Asher wasn't just dangerous. He was the devil.

I punched my flat-as-hell pillow, turning onto my side, slamming my eyes shut.

Sleep eluded me, and by the time the sun began to peek through the blinds less than two hours later, I couldn't shake off our heated conversation and the horrid realization that, like the devil himself, Asher had sussed out my inner truth.

I was a coward hiding in the shadows.

Had *always* been a coward hiding in the shadows.

It was time I did something to change that.

THE EMPRESS

III

MAJOR ARCANA
reversed

SIX

Avery

F or the second time in less than twenty-four hours, I
was back at Whiskey Bay.

Unlike yesterday's visit, it was broad daylight
now and unseasonably warm. The mid-afternoon sun beat
down relentlessly, warming the crown of my head, turning
my back so sticky that my T-shirt clung to my damp skin.

After driving back to New Orleans this morning with
Asher—in pure, unforgiving silence—I'd only stayed at the
Sultan's Palace long enough to shower and pull myself
together before grabbing a cab to the Bywater.

You're an idiot for coming back.

Or maybe I was finally just making a move. Albeit,
hopefully not an idiotic one.

The bouncer from last night was missing as I tugged
open the door to the strip club. The dim lighting inside was
an instant relief, especially compared to the hotter-than-
hot weather outside.

Whiskey Bay might as well have been a different bar at
this time of the day. The tables were scarce of gamblers,
the dancers missing from their stages. Hardly anyone

mingled at the bar, and I spotted only three Birkenstock-wearing fellows over by an old-school jukebox.

Movement behind the bar caught my eye.

Time to bite the bullet—not literally, of course.

With fake confidence, I ambled over, picking my way around tables and chairs. Slid onto a stool, elbows on the bar top. Like I'd seen in the movies, I lifted one hand casually, hailing down a bald bartender from where he was taking pint glasses out of a steaming dishwasher on the other side of the register.

Be brave.

Be bold.

"Hey there!" I exclaimed when he was an earshot. Pinching the fabric of my black T-shirt at my neck, I pulled it away from my clammy skin and made a show of fanning my face with my free hand. "Jeez, it is *so* hot outside."

Dark eyes, glazed over with a lack of enthusiasm, didn't so much as blink. "It's N'Orleans in spring. That's what happens."

Huh. Guess bartenders weren't generally happy at this time of day. I could have sworn I'd seen him here last night, mixing up cocktails and laughing with patrons. Then again . . . I squinted at his face, taking note of his blood-shot eyes. Maybe he was hungover.

It seemed silly to wish that *my* problem could be as simple as a hangover, but no, I got the shit end of the stick.

A stepfather who wanted me dead.

A sort-of stepbrother who I both wanted to bash over the head with a heavy object *and* climb onto his lap for non-bashing activities that involved both of us being naked from the waist down.

I never said it was great to be me.

In fact, I wouldn't recommend it.

"I'd love a cocktail," I said when the bartender seemed uninclined to ask me what I wanted.

"It's two p.m." Somehow, he managed to sound both disinterested and disapproving all at once. "And I'll need your ID."

"Yeah, sure!"

I pulled my wallet from my purse and handed over my fake. Like last night at the door, this guy gave the laminated plastic a cursory glance and handed it back over. "You look young for twenty-five," he said after I ordered a screwdriver.

I lied about many things—my age wasn't one of them.

"The perks of high-end skincare products." With a casual shrug, I added, "And good genes. My mother had *perfect* skin."

"Great."

This guy wasn't much of a talker.

Time to scrap the casual conversation and go straight for Plan B.

I edged my elbow a little farther on the bar, then scooted my ass to the very edge of the barstool. "Listen . . ."

He slid the screwdriver over to me. "Wanna open a tab?"

"Uh, sure."

"Great."

Any more of that Great-ing and he'd be giving Tony the Tiger a run for his money. "Right, thank you." *Because you're any less awkward?* This was so much harder to do now that I was here. And if I really wanted to dig deep and be honest with myself, I was suffering from a bad case of cold feet. Taking an irreparable step was a lot more terrifying when I had only myself to blame if shit went south.

Deep breaths.

Wrapping my hand tightly around the cocktail glass, I swallowed my nerves and mentally whipped my ass into gear. It was now or never.

"I'm looking for Nat."

The bartender's dark eyes flitted over me, assessing. "Yeah?"

I gave a curt nod. Forced steel into my stone. "I read cards for her weekly. Unfortunately, she couldn't make it down to Jackson Square for our usual appointment and asked for me to meet her here instead. Do you mind letting her know that I'm here for whenever she's ready?"

Half terrified to breathe too sharply and give myself away, I waited and waited and waited for the bartender to make his call. White rag in hand, he wiped down the bar near the register, then swapped towels for another set, the latter which he used to buff the wine glasses dry.

"Nat's been in a meeting all day," he finally said, hooking the rag over one shoulder as he put those glasses up and grabbed another four by the stems from the dishwasher. "But I can see if she'd like for me to put you in one of the rooms while you wait."

One of the rooms.

Immediately, I thought of Asher and myself at Stage One, him on his knees with his face buried between my legs. It was wrong, *so* wrong, and there was a good chance I'd be more likely to shoot him than hug him the next time we saw each other, but I still wanted . . . Well, I guess it should be noted that I'd been on edge all day.

Sitting next to a man for over an hour while wearing no panties—not my finest moment.

Also not my finest moment? Spending the entire hour of that drive wondering if hate sex was as magical as everyone always boasted that it was.

Sipping my screwdriver for fortitude, I waited in my

corner of the empty bar until the bartender returned some twenty minutes later, tossing the rag from hand to hand. "She's ready for you."

Four little words, and yet I grinned like he'd spouted out the entire dictionary from start to finish.

"Great!" Now I sounded like Tony the Tiger, too. Pushing the cocktail away, I belatedly tacked on, "I'll close up my tab after I speak with her. Any chance you can point me in the right direction?"

He closed a fist around my discarded glass. "The Basement. She said you know where to go."

An uncomfortable laugh bubbled up in my chest. Yeah, I knew where that was. Both the stairwell that led up to it and the fire escape that led *out* of it. Twenty-four hours was definitely not long enough to scrub the memories from my retina. Twenty-four *years* seemed only slightly more likely.

"I'll help myself there, then." Clapping my hand on the bar, I hopped off the stool and offered a short wave. "Thanks for the drink."

It was time to put on my *I-can-do-this* attitude. Remember that—

"Want a suggestion, Miss Washington?"

No. I was actually rather convinced that I'd already hit my suggestion quota for this quarter. But because I wasn't an unthinking asshole like Lincoln Asher, I kept my opinion to myself. Plastering a smile on my face, I peered over my shoulder with what I hoped was a friendly expression. "Sure," I said, grinning way too brightly. There was a good possibility that my smile read *screw you* instead of *you're so nice to help me out*.

That was the problem with reaching the end of your rope—you were incrementally closer to giving less and less fucks about playing nice with the world.

The bartender stacked one dry pint glass on top of

another. Then, finally, he spoke: "We all know you were here last night, Miss Washington. Nothing stays secret in this place for long." He added another pint glass to his tower, eyes on his masterpiece and not on me. "Nat's not your most subtle creature, and she's never been particularly fun to be around when she's pissed."

"Is anyone?"

Dropping the rag to the counter, he fixed his attention on me. "She came in this morning and fired one of my guys for serving an Irish coffee without whipped cream. Kid's been with us for six years. Guess what I'm trying to say is, Nat's in a special mood today, and if you've got any sense of self-preservation, you'll turn around and head right back out that front door."

Slowly, a smile worked its way across my face. "How fortunate, then, that I'm in a mood, as well."

I didn't give the bartender the chance to convince me otherwise.

Turning on my heel, I erased the distance to the hallway. Men's bathroom. Women's bathroom. Ah, here it was —the elusive General Storage Room. Sending a quick glance down the hall, I pried open the door, surprised to find it unlocked, and entered the so-called closet of Whiskey Bay. Then immediately took the stairs two at a time.

Like the main room downstairs, the Basement lacked a lot of its mystery during the day. Light glistened from the large windows, the curtains flung open wide to reveal a view of the winding Mississippi River and the grassy West Bank just across the width of the water. The stages were idle, empty, the chairs and settees and couches that circled each platform all arranged neatly in preparation for tonight's activities.

"I see you've decided to show your face, *cherie*. How utterly daring of you."

At the delicate sound of her voice, I breathed hard through my nose, expelling my nerves, and then turned to face her. Her evening gown had been swapped out for a skirt with larger-than-life patterns and a deep, V-neck top that plunged down to expose the inner swells of her breasts.

Straining for a nonchalance that I did not feel, I smiled. "It's surprisingly less difficult than I thought it'd be." My smile stretched a little wider. "Tell me, was it incredibly hard for you to lie to me for all these years? Or are you surprised that it wasn't that hard after all?"

If I hadn't been watching her face so closely, I would have missed it—the gentle arch of her brows and the twitch of her upper lip. Casually, cruelly, she murmured, "To be surprised entails that I was emotionally invested in the outcome of your life. I can't say that I've given much thought to it until recently."

Ouch.

Her words were like little pinpricks needling my arms. As though they were an actual physical threat, I ran my hands over my arms, swiping the little bastards away. If I could flick Nat into nonexistence, as well, I would have without second thought.

At the very least, I couldn't let her see how she'd wounded me, however minimal the puncture.

Slipping my hands into the back pockets of my jeans, I swept my gaze over the Basement, touching on everything and nothing all at once. Rocked back onto my heels when I said, "I won't lie, Natalie—from your cards, this isn't so far off from what I thought you did for a living." I paused, drawing in her curiosity before slipping in the verbal knife: "Only, I always assumed that you were the one putting out.

Although perhaps that's a more *recent* venture with the city's favorite university president?"

It didn't take long for my implication to click with her, and Nat's elegant hand lifted, hovering like she wanted nothing more than to strangle me, before snapping back to her side. "Acting a cunt doesn't become you, Laurel."

I turned to Whiskey Bay's queen, refusing to shrink before her. "How fortunate," I drawled, "that me and Laurel had a falling out some years back. Turns out I was too much of a *cunt* for her liking."

Her brows arched.

I stood my ground.

Seconds passed, and I watched her—a woman I'd considered a friend until yesterday—work through the scenarios in her head. Pristine white teeth sank into her red-painted lower lip. "You're here for a reason."

It wasn't a question. Wasn't even a statement, really— more like a thought voiced out loud.

"Yes," I said. Striving to appear casual, I kept my hands in my pockets, thumbs hooked over the denim fabric. With no one around to overhear, I opted to skip beating around the bush and go in straight for the kill. "Whatever deal Hampton planned to offer Asher, I'd like to take it on."

Take it on?

Because *that* sounded convincing or even halfway lethal.

And it seemed that Nat agreed with me.

Unblinking, she stared at me. "You couldn't handle it."

If I argued or protested, I'd sound like a petulant child throwing a temper tantrum—and I couldn't afford to lose this opportunity.

Big Hampton's threat still rang loudly in my ears, and I'd yet to shake off the worry that I was hours away from meeting my fate: death. Whatever Joshua Hampton wanted, whatever he needed of Asher, I was willing to make happen.

For that to even be a possibility, I needed to play it cool. Stay unfrazzled.

If only my heart would get with the program.

I shoved aside the concern that Nat could hear its incessant thumping in my chest and zeroed my gaze on her face with a silent prayer that she couldn't read my inner feelings. "What's he want?" Pulling my hands from my pockets, I dropped my arms to my sides. *Look confident. Act confident.* "For Mayor Foley to die?"

Nat's mouth quirked. "You'd like that, wouldn't you? To be the one who finally ends your stepfather's life?"

Yes. I wanted nothing more. Had *never* wanted anything more than to see the blood pool around his body, his eyes unblinking, just like he'd had done to Momma.

Still, I said nothing.

Waited, hoping, for Nat to give up because of my silence and divulge more information.

She didn't . . . at least, not in the way that I'd hoped.

"I've always found this city so fascinating," she began, moving toward the closest stage and leaving me to follow. With an elegant fluff to her skirt, she settled into a velvet-padded chair. Her hands curled over the lip of the armrests, and she glanced at me as though she were actually peering down at me from a throne. Without waiting for me to take a seat, she continued. "You never know who you can trust. It was such an odd adjustment when I moved here."

"From Hungary?" I asked, thinking of her accent and her mention of her immigrant parents.

"No." She gave a thin-lipped smile. "Baltimore, actually."

Right.

I took the seat opposite hers, careful to remain facing the stairwell up to the Basement. Just in case. After last night, I'd never look at Nat with a sympathetic eye again— and I'd come armed with my gun in my purse since my taser was probably in the Gulf of Mexico by now.

"It took me no time at all to understand that I would *never* understand the way New Orleans works. My first year here, a few of our finest men in blue murdered a man just over there"—she pointed toward the window, and I had the feeling that she meant across the river—"but, of course, they couldn't just let that slide. Couldn't risk having a target on their back if anyone found out that a drug stop had gone so wrong." She propped an elbow up on the armrest, positioning her chin in the palm of her hand to watch me with glittering eyes. "So, they torched him. Shoved his burnt body back in his car. Drove him up onto the levee and fled."

Bile climbed my throat, and I swallowed hard.

Nat smiled, slowly. "But, of course, that wasn't enough. They set the car ablaze before they left, too, just to be sure."

"Why are you telling me this?"

"Because I can understand why you wouldn't have gone to the police when your mother died." Forehead creasing, Nat's expression turned sympathetic. "You must have been *terrified*, *cherie*, not knowing who you could trust. Not knowing where to go. A man like your stepfather is supposed to be one of the most trustworthy—a family man, an overseer of our precious jewel of a city, a protector for those who can't protect themselves."

My soul cried out at the truth in her words, and just like that, she'd shoved me back into my thirteen-year-old body. Listening to my stepfather argue over my disappearance, my nose buried in my bent knees, my arms clasped around my shins. The fear that clung to me as I scrambled to my feet and slipped out a cracked-open window on the first floor.

Physically, I'd escaped that night unscathed.

Mentally, emotionally, it felt as though the chains of those long-ago fears would never break.

"Jay Foley is a bastard," I whispered, the curse sounding so underwhelming in contrast with the pure hatred I felt for the man. A word like I needed just didn't exist—not in English, at least, and I didn't know any other languages. I'd dropped out of school the year we were finally offered a language elective.

Nat nodded, her hand dipping with the force of the movement with her chin still in her palm. "Yes, *cherie*, he is. But I must say . . . of all the cocks I've sucked in my life, his is perhaps the best."

"I—"

The words died on my tongue.

Everything went rigid: my limbs, my heart, my blood, if that was even possible. It *felt* possible. In this room, in this old factory seated along the Mississippi River, in this *city* which had stolen so much from me, every iota of heat dissipated from my body.

"What did you say?" My tone was hard, unforgiving, and Nat smiled like she'd been waiting for this moment. Possibly even for years.

"You were right," she said after a moment, crossing one leg over the other, her skirts moving like silk, "I did put out. I *do* put out, as you so politely put it. And Jay is by far one of the best customers I've ever had. Your mother was a very lucky woman."

Hatred seethed like poison in my veins, twisting and

turning and nearly strangling me with the force of it. "My mother was *murdered*."

"Oh, I'm aware. He let that slip, once, when he was deep in the liquor bottle." Nat straightened in her seat, hands clasping together in her lap—the very image of demure respectability. "He has a photo of her by his bed, his precious *Catherine*. Anytime he fucked me, it was with me on my knees, your mother's picture inches from my nose. I could have kissed it, especially when he got carried away in the fantasy and thrust too hard."

Stop. Stop, no more. Please.

The urge to dry-heave overwhelmed me, and it was only a testament to my strength that I didn't turn and vomit all over the floor. I despised the images she planted in my head. Didn't want to think of Foley—

"*Catherine*, he'd whisper into the crook of my neck as he fucked me," Nat went on, a nasty smile curving her red lips. "And next to her picture was one of *you*."

I couldn't stop it.

My body twisting, my hands landing on the chair's armrest, nails biting down into the fabric, my chest dropping as my stomach unloaded itself.

"With the number of times I *put out* for him, I had the opportunity to learn your face very well, *cherie*. The crook in your nose with the scar right over the bridge. The birthmark near your hairline. The smattering of freckles over your cheeks, and the green ring around your hazel eyes. You may have swapped out your blond hair for black, Laurel, but one glance at you in the square was like a time portal to every fucking I ever received in your stepfather's bed."

Eyelids screwing shut, I exhaled through my nose. "Please," I edged out, my palm scraping across my lips. "I don't want . . . I can't—"

I heard the creak of Nat's chair, and then her hand gently landed on the back of my head, stroking my hair in much the same way Hampton had done to her last night. Her touch reminded me of Momma's, soft and soothing—and that alone had me wrenching away, jumping up from the chair before the sensations of wanting love, my *mother's* love, could sink me back under.

"No wonder you came to see me so often," I worked out, my stomach still queasy as I stood out of reach, arms locked around my middle. "How much did you report back to Jay once you found me, huh? Everything?"

Nat's nose scrunched as she glanced down at my vomit, then hooked a foot around my rejected chair, her hands on the back, and dragged the chair over the spot where I'd literally lost my lunch.

Satisfied, she returned to her seat, turning her head slightly so I remained in her line of sight. "Nothing. I told him nothing."

Highly doubtful. Suspicion laced my tone as I spoke, "And why should I believe you? You clearly told Hampton about me."

"I like to have people in my debt, *cherie*. It doesn't work in my benefit for your stepfather to know anything."

"And it works out for you if Hampton knows?"

Her shoulders lifted in a delicate shrug. "It earned me his trust. Joshua is a powerful man, and he and Jay claw at each other's throats at every chance. So, yes, him knowing about you put me in place for what *I* wanted."

There was something in her tone that I didn't like.

I stepped back, gaze dropping to my purse—which had fallen from my lap when I'd made the leap of faith from the chair. Dammit. *Amateur move.*

Nat's voice cut through my thoughts: "I wouldn't do anything drastic just yet, *mon amour.* I'm about to offer you the deal of a lifetime, and it'd be a shame if you were to grow too hasty before you could enjoy it."

The deal of a lifetime, huh?

Casting a quick glance over my shoulder, I was once again treated to pure emptiness. The sense of isolation was both a blessing and a curse, and I chose to focus on the blessing part of it all as I asked, "Is this the same deal Hampton planned to offer Asher last night?"

Head cocking to the side, Nat brought her hand up, index finger and thumb millimeters apart. "With a change or two, but yes."

"And if I take on the job, will you continue to keep my secret from Jay?"

The room seem to still, the energy itself grinding to a halt, and then: "*Cherie*, there won't be a secret to keep once you kill him."

THE MAGICIAN

I

MAJOR ARCANA
reversed

SEVEN

Avery

"**W**hy?"

Like a queen, Nat leaned back in her seat. "Don't play the idiot, Laurel. You know exactly why."

Yes, but—

I shook my head, trying to right my thoughts when everything seemed so terribly confusing. "I know why Hampton does, but why would *you* want him dead? Because he, what? Called you by my mother's name and hurt your feelings? That's enough to kill someone?"

Visibly stiffening, Nat kicked up her chin. "Those reasons lay with Hampton, and he was *incredibly* disappointed with Sergeant Asher's decision to walk out last night."

"He shouldn't have kidnapped us."

"He prefers to do things on large scales." Nat sniffed. "He's just that sort of man."

"A limo pickup service would have been better appreciated by all parties. Maybe pass the information along."

Dark eyes narrowed in my direction, and I had the distinct feeling that my most frequent tarot client was running through all the reasons she'd like to kill me off—in her head.

Out loud, however, she only slipped back into the role she played so well: the owner of Whiskey Bay, elegant and all too proper. "You want Foley dead, *cherie*. Hampton wants him dead. So, dead he shall be."

My mouth gaped. "I'm sorry, but are you hearing yourself right now? *Dead he shall be?* First, who talks like that— you're from Baltimore, Nat, not the Gilded Age. Second, you're expecting *me* to kill him? Me. Kill the mayor of N'Orleans. I didn't spend the last twelve years hiding out just so I could end up in prison and someone's lady friend."

"So, you what? Hid for twelve years to . . . keep hiding?"

Well, no. Obviously not.

It'd always been my aim to kill my stepfather, but the *how's*, the *where's*, and the *when's* had always eluded me. They *still* eluded me.

After all, I wasn't Lincoln Asher—murderer extraordinaire.

I didn't even know how to use a gun, let alone stage an elaborate plot to kill the city's most elite politician.

Opening my mouth to tell Nat that she had the wrong girl, I was soundly cut off.

"I'll set up everything, *cherie*. It's what I'm good at, after all, and I do have a few people who I can ask to help with the logistics."

Throat dry, I croaked, "If you're handling all of the logistics, then why don't you or one of your minions take him out?"

"I was under the impression that you wished to avenge your mother. Here I am offering you everything you've ever wanted and you're balking. Am I to assume that you *want* your stepfather to learn about you?"

"*No*, of course not." Why couldn't I breathe? Why was it suddenly so hard to draw air into my lungs? I fisted my right hand and set it against my heart. Through my black T-shirt, I could feel the heavy thud of my heart against the fleshy outer part of my fist. "I-I want this."

"Then why the fuss?"

Because I was a coward, as Asher had so politely told me, and that was something that needed to stop. Now. "I want to bring justice to my mother," I said, voice shaky. "I can do it."

Nat's answering smile was wide and serene. "You've waited a long time for this."

I had, she was right.

I'd lived in fear and worry, slept on the streets and on the hardest beds the city had to offer in the homeless shelters. I'd been pawed at by greedy, masculine hands and had been told countless times over that all my troubles would disappear if I just opened my legs and gave up my self-worth for a quick buck.

"Is this like a calendar-coordinating thing?" I asked. "Planned far in advance with maps and backup plans so I don't end up incarcerated after?"

Tipping her head back, Nat released a healthy laugh. "All of the above."

Maybe it wasn't so difficult to be Lincoln Asher, after all. Maybe he looked at each kill with a series of pros or cons. The way *I* looked at it, the pros far outweighed the cons in my book for murdering my stepfather.

Hell, the only con, really—besides the possibility of

getting caught—was the matter of my own moral conscience.

I wanted to save the world. I wanted to save every stray animal. I wanted everyone to feel safe and loved and happy.

At the end of the day, however, I could handle my guilt over ending a life.

I had to do it for Momma.

I had to do it for myself.

If I wanted to make myself feel even more justified, then I was also doing it for Nat, who'd been forced to screw Jay Foley while he called her by another woman's name. *My mother's name.*

"Great," I said with a short nod. "I'm glad we got all this settled and squared away. I'm just going to grab my purse"—I crouched low and snapped it off the floor—"and be on my way. I'll wait for your call or something. Give you some time to figure it out. It's all been a great talk."

My feet beat it to the stairwell, and I had *almost* managed to get the hell out of dodge before her voice stopped me in my tracks:

"*Mon amour*, a deal is two-sided."

"Yes . . ." I glanced over at her, where she'd yet to move. "I want the same thing Hampton does. What you would have offered Asher last night."

"But it isn't what *I* want, and as I'm the one who could personally ruin you, it seems imperative that I get what I want, as well. Perhaps even more so . . . unless you don't mind having your *heartbreaking* tale told to everyone tomorrow."

She rose, crossing the space between us, until she was less than two feet away.

That spidey sense was back. Her tone had turned sly, which matched the devilry that I saw in her dark eyes.

I clutched the stairwell railing. "And what is it that you want?"

She leaned forward, eyes glittering.

"I want Lincoln Asher dead, *cherie*, and you will be the one who kills him."

THE HIEROPHANT

MAJOR ARCANA
reversed

EIGHT

Lincoln

It was probably an omen that no one stopped me as I busted in Ambideaux's front door to his fancy St. Charles Avenue townhouse. Not a single house alarm went off as I stormed through the powder-blue parlor or the blood-red dining room.

In a different life, this townhouse had been the hub of all activity.

Politicians smoking cigars with the city's richest real estate mogul.

Elegant women reclining on the settees in the parlor.

New Orleans was a city that clung to its traditions—and no matter how many years passed, its snobbery remained intact without a single crack.

Money and pedigree guaranteed entry to the upper class. Without it, you'd be lucky if your ass was even allowed to stand on the front step.

I should know.

In Ambideaux's eyes, I'd always been the perfect fit when it came down to his Basin runs. Entering his house, on the other hand, had always been off-limits. Like the dogs, I'd been kept outside to watch the perimeter of the property.

Always on the outside looking in.

Always experiencing life through the windows I'd crack open just to catch the scent of a cigar or hear the titillating sound of feminine laughter.

Don't go down that road, man.

Molars grinding, I checked back my impulse. Snapped my hand back to my side from where it'd been flirting with a priceless antique vase Ambideaux had once sent me to "collect" from a man named James Mayer.

The vase sat on the gold-leaf table at the base of the circular stairwell.

James Mayer sat at the bottom of the Atchafalaya—or he had when I'd dropped his body in when I'd been nineteen.

My lips twisted in a sneer, which I caught in the table top's reflective mirror. Swollen eye from last night's activities out in the swamp. Cut lip. To say nothing of the right half of my face, where the flesh remained raised and red.

I was tired, *so* tired of dealing with all the bullshit.

And you're in a shit mood because of Avery . . .

Fingers twitching, I stared down at my reflection. Reached out to wrap my hand around the base of the vase. It wasn't massive, and my thumb and middle finger easily touched as I took its weight in my hand.

One million dollars sat on my palm.

In the next breath, one million dollars had been hurled at the wall.

It shattered upon impact, bursting apart like fireworks composed of centuries-old Chinese porcelain. Fell to the marble flooring like shards of ice.

A single piece skipped along the flooring, aiming straight for me—I crushed it with my right boot, finding a sick sense of satisfaction when I felt the delicate pottery crumble beneath my weight.

"That was from the Yuan Dynasty. Almost a thousand years old."

Following the direction of the familiar voice, I looked up to see Ambideaux meandering down the stairwell.

I flicked my gaze down to the mess I'd created. "It had a good run."

My former boss stopped at the base of the stairwell, one hand on the balustrade. "You never understood the significance of antiquities."

No, I didn't.

Antiques were for people who could appreciate them— those who had the luxury of raking in millions of dollars each year, or more, and who never had to wonder when they'd eat next.

Antiquities were for men like Jason Ambideaux, who practically shit wads of cash on command.

They weren't for me.

"I didn't come here to talk about your vase."

"My *broken* vase."

Ignoring him, I pulled out the notebook full of names he'd thrown at my feet a week ago. Then waited until he'd locked eyes on it before continuing, "Why do you want them dead? Josef, Zak, these are people you know . . ." I dropped the notebook on the table, and its coiled-spirals pinged as it landed on the mirrored top. "You've always been a cold-hearted bastard, but why them? And don't bullshit me on this."

Growing up, I'd never trusted Ambideaux to give me the full truth. When I'd been real young, he'd kept some things secret to "watch out for me," he'd always said. By the time I'd hit my teens, I'd learned that he liked to manipulate the truth, stretching it and forming it until *his* version of reality was so skewed from real life that I was convinced he believed every lie he told.

Probably explained the state of his marriage—which was to say, his *non*-existent marriage.

Not even Nat, the Queen of Bitches, could handle his shit.

I flipped open the notebook, flipping through the lined pages, and then stopped when I reached the handwriting that looked exactly like mine. "You played me pretty good, Jason," I said, referring to our little *meeting* in my kitchen from the week before. "You always have. It's what happens when you grow up with no family but one asshole prick—you latch on. Grow soft. Hope, maybe, that they won't stab you in the back when you look in the other direction."

Without giving him the opportunity to speak, I went on in a low voice. "You've stabbed me a whole hell of a lot, some instances worse than others." His gaze lifted to my scars, and I didn't look away. *Refused* to look away. "So, we can do this one of two ways. You can either give me a good enough reason to go after Zak Benson and Tabitha Thibadeaux *or* I can solve a lifelong problem I've had and permanently shut you up."

Ambideaux's blue eyes opened wide. "You wouldn't."

"You don't know that." Pushing away from the table, I strolled near him, hands loose at my sides, until only a foot separated us. He was decently sized, but I was bigger—taller, stronger, broader. "Fact is, Jason, you don't know *me* any longer. So, let's operate on the assumption that I wouldn't give a damn if you stopped breathing." I paused, cranked my grimace into something resembling a smile. "Now why do you want them dead? What the hell made you so desperate that you went so far as to blackmail me out of my job and go out of your way to hit Big Hampton where it hurts?"

Silence reigned, stretching and growing, until finally he bent at the knees to survey the broken porcelain. "He's leaving Pershing to run for mayor when Foley's term is up."

Every response that had been ready to leap from my tongue died in an instant.

And then I tipped back my head and laughed. Hard.

So hard that Ambideaux grumbled something beneath his breath and snapped, "Why the fuck are you laughing? I've been in the political world for years now. The people want—"

"The people don't know what they want." When he reached for a shard of pottery, I kicked it out of his way. He was a sneaky asshole, and I wouldn't put it past him to plan out an entire plot to kill me off with nothing but some Yuan Dynasty cast-off. "You think they want another eight years of dealing with bullshit politicians who have a tendency to run their opponents—*any* opponent—into the ground?"

With narrowed eyes, Ambideaux straightened to his full height. "That's politics for you, son. Everyone is determined to win."

"Sure they are, but I can guarantee that the public isn't expecting death as a result." Fingering the coiled notebook, I tacked on, "And we all know that death is something you dole out exceptionally well. I'm guessing that Josef and Micah were your handiwork—too lazy to make the drive all the way out to the Basin?"

His mouth flat-lined, and I had my answer.

Got you.

"Did your recruits bail?" I asked, resting my ass on the table. It was sturdy enough that I gave it my full weight, folding my hands over the edge as I studied him. "Let me guess. You went over to Central City . . . Galvez and Fourth—nah, Galvez and Third would be more your speed." I drummed my fingers on the underside of the table, straining my ears to listen for approaching footsteps. I'd be dead before being caught off guard again. "What'd you offer them? Crack?"

Face flushing, Ambideaux's jaw clenched. "I offered them enough that they took it."

"They played you, Jason." I grinned, slowly, methodically. "You want to run this city and you can't even figure out the difference between a group of junkies and their dealers. Let me clue you in on how that works: dealers don't work for *you* but I'm sure they appreciated the free cocaine."

"They're idiots if they think they can get away with—"

"They already did, and that's why you got desperate and ditched Josef and Micah in the river yourself." Pushing away from the table, I ambled toward him. "You've lasted this long without getting caught because you're smart. Dumping bodies in the Mississippi? That's sloppy work." The shattered porcelain cracked under my boots when I stopped, a foot separating us. "What made you fuck up after all this time? We both know there's a reason—and don't give me a bullshit excuse about you and Big Hampton competing for office."

Ambideaux's blue eyes shot to the side, avoiding staring at me straight-on.

I waited, already knowing the answer that he'd give.

And because I was a ruthless bastard, I twisted the knife a little deeper, backing him into a proverbial corner that he couldn't escape. "You blackmailed me into taking out people who worked for *you*. I remember Josef and Micah from back in the day, and if there's an idiot here it's not me. Every single one of them has your damn tattoo branded on their skin. You marked them. Promised them protection. Now you're taking them out one by one. *Why?*"

He cracked.

Shoulders hunching, eyes hard, Adam's apple dancing down the column of his throat as he swallowed. "Because they chose *her*. All of them."

Bitter laughter nearly suffocated me. "You're too old for that shit, man."

"Nat is—"

"A crazy bitch who won't stop until you're dead and she's watching you bleed out."

Ambideaux shot a hand out at me, clearly aiming for my throat. Speed and age were on my side, though, and it took me only a half-second to register his intent and reciprocate. Weaving to the left, I caught his elbow in my fist and spun him around like a middle-aged ballerina. His back slammed up against my chest and I locked his wrists at the base of his spine, my hands holding him in place.

He'd taught me the move when I'd been ten and desperate for some sort of guidance.

Now, his dyed dark hair was all I saw, and his heavy breathing was all I heard.

"Sloppy," I muttered, shaking my head. "Without Godzilla here to protect you, you're fucked." Squeezing his wrists in warning, I let him go—but not without a move of my knees at the back of his legs that had him toppling over.

He crash-landed with a *thud*, the broken pottery going every which way as his arms flailed to catch his weight.

Before he'd fed me to the gators, I probably would have felt a measure of guilt in seeing the only man who'd ever been like a father figure to me splayed on the ground.

But it wasn't guilt I felt now—more like regret that I'd lived.

That I was stuck in a damn cycle that I couldn't break free of, no matter how desperately I wanted to. I was chained to this city, both emotionally and physically, and I was beyond ready for the shackles to shatter just like the Yuan Dynasty vase I'd broken.

"You killed her brother," I said, voice low, my temper tightly leashed, "because he counted cards at a friendly game of poker with his *brother*-in-law."

Ambideaux hoisted himself up on his hands and knees, and I watched as his palm sank into a splinter from the vase. He reeled back with a curse, lifting his palm to examine the wound. With it cradled to his chest, he glared at me. "*You're* the one who did him off."

It would be so easy to angle my boot and push him back to the ground, to let off the steam boiling from the last twenty-four hours.

The goddamn "abduction."

Learning that Avery's mother had married my father.

Watching Avery as she stormed out of my SUV this morning and slammed the front door behind her as she disappeared into her building.

My foot shifted back, and I set my weight on the sole. Repeated the action again and again until there was a safe enough distance separating me from the city's richest bastard. I needed some patience—at the very least, I needed to not act when provoked.

"I'm not gonna take responsibility for your divorce. Like any good soldier, I did what I was told. You ordered. I made it happen."

Blue eyes hardened in my direction. "You're not making it happen right now."

"You don't own me anymore."

"You still marked?"

At the invasive question, my hand shifted to the base of my skull. Egotistical prick that Ambideaux was, he enjoyed knowing those who worked for him were always aware of who held the upper hand. The placement of the quarter-sized tattoo always changed—mine had required me to shave my head so that the tattoo artist could ink the back of my head. Women, generally, were marked in more prominent areas—their collarbones, their arms or their faces, like Tabitha Thibadeaux.

The men worked under Ambideaux's employment.

The women for Nat at the Basement—either as dancers in Whiskey Bay or on the stages or rooms upstairs.

Sexist. Masochist.

Jason Ambideaux reigned as king of it all, threatening to tear down any pawn that didn't fall into line.

And he thought he'd be a successful mayor? I'd rather have my asshole father for another eight years.

"Don't want to answer that?" Ambideaux taunted. "You're marked, Lincoln. You took a vow. You—"

"Yeah, well, you took a vow that you'd let my mother out of her goddamn cell."

His nostrils flared. "It's not a cell—"

"She hates it," I growled, hands curling into fists at my sides before I did something ridiculous—like strangle the man before me. "You don't get to choose what's best for her just because the two of you were childhood friends. She's suffered."

Jaw working, Ambideaux got up close in my face. "If there *is* anyone who knows what she went through, it's *me*." His knuckles connected with my chest—but even with the weight behind his shove, I didn't budge. Not even an inch.

It was like the last twenty years hadn't even passed. I was the troublemaker kid pushing all the right buttons, knowing what to do and what to say to send the people around me into a downward spiral.

And maybe he was right about my mom.

Hell, it wasn't like she'd wanted me. When I was two,

she'd given me to the Ursuline nuns. I had no memories of her from that age, no splices of a vision of her cradling me against her chest. Nothing. It hadn't been until Ambideaux entered my life when I'd been seven that I was even made aware that my mom was still alive.

Ambideaux had fashioned himself as my mom's best friend. A neighbor from when they'd been kids. Promised me that if I did everything he said—if I behaved—he'd take me to her.

So I'd behaved.

Everything he'd wanted of me, I did without question.

I was desperate, and it didn't occur to me until years later that in those intermittent five years between when I'd met Jason Ambideaux and when I'd first seen my mother, he'd stripped every bit of my conscience.

I stole. I cheated. I threw my entire body, soul, and mind into being good enough to run with the older guys who worked for Ambideaux. At eighteen, the tattoo on the back of my head had felt like a rite of passage.

A reason to live. A reason to fight.

Particularly when only Ambideaux had ever cared if I lived or died.

Nat hadn't cared.

Neither had my mother.

And yet I still gave a fuck, even when she didn't give a damn about me.

When I opened my mouth, my voice emerged like I'd smoked a pack of cigarettes all in one go. "I'm taking myself out of this equation. You pissed that your crew ditched you in favor of Nat? Find someone else to do your dirty work. And when it comes to Big Hampton, maybe try doing shit legally for once. You never know—you might find that it's not so repulsive."

I turned to leave.

Had made it two steps when Ambideaux's hand at my elbow pulled me to a stop.

"What about your mother?" His voice echoed in the room, hammering on my dead heart as I stared at the broken shards of priceless pottery on the floor.

The doctors had always said that a concussion like the kind my mom had experienced after her car accident could change a person. I wasn't a doctor, had never studied medicine, and had technically only "met" my mother, Victoria, after she'd survived the traumatic four-car pileup on the Greater New Orleans Bridge. She'd lost the use of her legs, the metals of the car twisting and turning and crushing the lower half of her body. I'd only been allowed to see her at the age of twelve; I'd never known her any other way.

When I'd first met her, she'd been hooked to a ventilator and had spent her days binging on *Jerry Springer* and every court show TV had to offer. Although the ventilator was long gone now, her bills continued to be expensive—more so than I could ever afford to pay— and Ambideaux used my limited funds to his own benefit. He ensured my mother's welfare, kept her healthy, and I paid the price for loving a woman who'd never love me back.

I'd heard her laugh, once.

When I'd been down the hall, a bouquet of flowers clutched in my seventeen-year-old fists, ready to surprise her for her birthday.

Her laughter had died the moment I rapped on the hospital room door and entered the space. Disgust had lined her features, and the hatred that narrowed her eyes was one I'd always been familiar with.

As were the words she greeted me with: *I don't want you here. You aren't my son.*

"The concussion," everyone always assured me. "She doesn't realize what she's talking about."

I wasn't stupid.

I'd been two when the car accident stole the use of her legs, and it seemed unlikely to me that fifteen years could pass with the same old excuse of her concussion working like a charm. No, for a reason I'd never understood, Victoria Meriden hated me. Despised me.

I wasn't her son just as I wasn't Jay Foley's son.

By blood, maybe, but nothing more.

I shook off Ambideaux's hand like he was nothing but an obnoxious fly, then sent a quick glance up, my gaze following the curve of the oak stairwell. Somewhere in this townhouse, my mother was set up in her room like the princess she never was, which had to be an improvement for her from her routine hospital visits.

"Lincoln," Ambideaux demanded with an unwavering stare, "I warned you what happens if you screw off on this. I want Benson and Tabby taken care of. If you don't, your mother will regret it. *You'll* regret it."

I met his gaze unflinchingly. "She's not mine to regret. She never was."

The only thing I heard on my way out was the pottery cracking one last time under my weight, and then the nonexistent sound of Jason Ambideaux's plans withering like wood set ablaze.

The smile that slipped onto my face as I stepped back into the world was perhaps the first genuine one I'd ever experienced in thirty-four years.

And while I wasn't free from the bullshit of New Orleans politics, I would be. Soon.

I refused to have it any other way.

TWO OF WANDS

NINE

Avery

I was experiencing déjà vu.

Me at my table in Jackson Square, shuffling my Thoth deck mindlessly as I waited for someone to look my way and ask to have their cards read.

Him storming toward me, emerging from the shadowy Pirate's Alley alongside St. Louis Cathedral.

Except this time, I knew the taste of his lips and the hard brush of his athletic body alongside mine. I knew what it felt like to be wrapped up in his embrace as he thrust into me, the pressure so acute with each shift of his hips, the pleasure in his blue eyes only that much more erotic when he groaned my name.

And I knew now, though I wish I didn't, what it meant to look a man in the eye and realize that it came down to him or me.

I hadn't agreed to Nat's proposal, but I hadn't turned her down either.

The guilt was eating me alive.

Guilt which only surged forth like a thunderous wave as Lincoln Asher took the seat opposite mine. Forty-eight hours since I'd seen him last, and I soaked up his presence like I'd been starved of sustenance.

You can't. Don't even go down that road.

I couldn't stop.

My shuffling slowed, the backs of my hands resting in my lap, each half of the deck clasped in my palms. He said nothing, and I didn't either. We'd parted ways in anger, our words dripping like poison in that motel room, and the awkwardness of this moment stole my words and kept my mouth sewn shut.

Should I apologize for speaking my mind? For trying to push him away and avoid the future hurt?

Or maybe you should whip out the I'm sorry's for sort-of agreeing to kill him?

Fingers tightening around the deck, I dropped my gaze to his plain clothes. Dark jeans paired with a plain black T-shirt. Unwanted approval hummed in my veins because there was no denying that he looked good tonight. "You're not wearing your uniform."

For a conversation starter, it could have been better. I'd maybe rate it a C-minus on the scale of A-F—nothing higher because, really, *that* was the first thing to come out of my mouth considering everything that had gone down between us? Utterly pathetic.

But it seemed to break the slab of ice, even just a little, because Asher let out a low chuckle that sent shivers of awareness twirling down my spine. I sat up a little straighter when he said, "Guess I never broke the news to you. I've been suspended."

"*Suspended?*"

The bottom of his chair scraped against the concrete as he positioned it directly before mine, the toes of our shoes touching when he sat down. "Suspended," he confirmed with a small dip of his chin, his right forearm landing on the table. "Want to take a guess as to why?"

Knowing him, it could have been a number of things.

He was stone and fire, all at once. Unreadable and yet in possession of a temper that ran on a short leash—if there was a leash at all.

"Did you talk smack?" I asked, all too aware of our shoes getting closely acquainted with one another's.

His mouth hitched, the side with his scars, and as I watched them crinkle and stretch, I felt a wave of protectiveness sweep over me. Could I do it? Could I be the one to take away the vitality in his Haint-blue eyes?

Lincoln Asher wasn't a good man, and I wasn't entirely sure he was even likable when he went on one of his ridiculous alpha bents, but that didn't mean I had the right to take his life.

Now you're just being a hypocrite—do you have the right to take Jay Foley's either with that logic?

No, I didn't.

And yet I'd thought of nothing else since leaving Whiskey Bay yesterday.

What would it be like to walk free in this city without watching my back? Would each breath I brought into my lungs taste a little sweeter?

My cards slipped from my grasp, and it took my brain a moment to register the fact that Asher had stripped them away from me and was setting them out on the velvet-lined table.

"You're not doing it right," I muttered, reaching forward to take them back.

His shoe eased against mine, a silent warning for me to give him space. He followed it up with a husky, "Let me try."

After our argument—after being called a coward,

however right he was about that—I should have raised my foot and plowed it straight into the apex of his thighs. He was a cocky bastard, and there was not a single reason why I had to put up with his bullshit. Not. A. One.

But I was a junkie and Lincoln Asher was my chosen vice, and so I caved without verbal admission, falling back into my seat and folding my arms over my chest as I watched him sort the cards with his brows furrowed and his teeth sinking into his lower lip.

He would never be sexy, not in the classic, model sort of way. He was altogether too rough for that, too rugged and way too dominant. And yet as the sun set behind St. Louis Cathedral, its cream-plastered walls turning red and pink and yellow from the dipping sun, I couldn't look away from this man who I so wanted to hate.

"Turns out some of my rank didn't enjoy me coming to your rescue three weeks ago," he said, gently flipping over the tarot cards as his gaze tracked every minute detail of their illustrations.

My mouth dropped open. "They suspended you for *that?* You were helping me! And Casey, too."

Giving a curt nod, he turned over one last card, so that three were spread out before him. The rest he bundled up and slipped back into their velvet pouch, which had been resting next to the lit candle. "It was a use-of-force. I got a nice slap on the hand. They didn't want to piss off the kid's father, and I get it. Although I think it's safe to say that after recent events, me and Joshua Hampton won't be attending any crawfish boils together or anything like that."

Joshua Hampton? The kid who'd attacked us was Hampton's son?

I felt like a fish, my mouth snapping open and shut—or at least like a snapping turtle—but it was hard to digest all that information. If it had been Big Hampton's kid that night . . . "Was it staged?" I asked, already dreading the answer.

Blue eyes lifted to meet mine. "It wasn't staged by Hampton, if that's what you're wondering. Little Hampton showing up at the right time and the right place was just icing on the cake."

"Then by *who*?"

"That's who I came to talk to you about." Lips curling in a small grin, he gave a soft laugh that was so at odds with the harshness of his features. It lit me up like a match and kindling. "But, first, I'm gonna read your cards. Put you in the hot seat. What do you think about that?"

"I think the fist you took to the head the other day may have popped a screw loose." It wasn't at all what I wanted to say, but it sounded a lot more confident than the thoughts running on repeat in my head: *what are you doing here? Why are you being so* nice?

"You can learn anything off YouTube." Tapping the center of the first card with the tip of his finger, he dragged it close, shifting his big body so that he could get a good look at the illustration. "I spent a few hours today studying."

My mouth betrayed me by quirking up at the boyish way he confessed it all. "So, a few hours of YouTube later and you feel comfortable enough to read tarot?"

"Nah," he said with a shake of his head, "but I feel comfortable enough to read *yours*."

Something about that struck a chord, and I sucked in a sharp breath. If I let myself get lost in the tailspin of wondering *why* he was here reading my spread, I'd never venture up for air again.

Mentally, I shoved the *why*'s aside, sending them fluttering into the evening air.

"You're already off to a rough start." Wrapping a hand around my mug of hot chocolate, I lifted it from the table to my lips, blowing away the steam. Asher's blue eyes tracked it all, but whatever emotions he felt weren't out for open season. He watched me steadily, carefully, but the heat I'd come to recognize from him was nowhere to be found.

Obviously, you idiot. Y'all aren't just strangers anymore.

The hot chocolate burned on the way down, its temperature a few degrees too hot. Coughing and swallowing happened all at once, and I cranked forward, hand to my throat, as I tried to catch my breath.

Asher's fingers went to my chin. "Look up. It'll help."

In between gusts of coughing, I croaked, "I thought that was just an old wives' tale."

His fingers didn't move away. Instead, he gently angled my chin so that my face tipped up, my gaze latching onto the darkening sky. Beyond the spire of the cathedral was a full moon in all of its glory.

My hand hooked onto his wrist, just as his deep voice rumbled, "Not sure about the old wives' tale, but it's what the nuns always told me."

The . . . *nuns*?

Tearing my gaze from the beauty above us, I fixed my attention on his face. "The nuns? Did you go to Catholic school?"

He pulled back, his touch leaving my skin bereft of his warmth, and he returned to the cards. "Nah, public," he finally answered. "But, before that, I was with the Ursulines for a time. I don't remember much."

Had Jay truly cast him aside at birth, just like that? It was beyond extreme, and until the day he'd ordered Momma's death, he'd never veered to the extremes. Even-keeled might as well have been his middle name.

Although it wouldn't be shocking to learn that all of that was just another lie.

"Did Jay . . ." How to even put this into a question that wasn't fully offensive? Swallowing, I tried again. "Were you ever close with him, at some point? I mean, with you growing up here in N'Orleans, you had to have seen him at some point, right?"

The following second felt as though it lasted months, and then Asher was sighing, dropping his elbows to his knees, lacing his fingers as he stared at our feet. "We're going to have this conversation right now, aren't we."

It wasn't a question.

Or, if it was, it'd totally been rhetorical.

"We don't have to," I murmured, and then risked another sip of my hot chocolate. *Mmm, much better.* "I mean, if you'd rather we discuss our meltdown from Thursday night, we can do that too."

His façade cracked, a grimace peeking through. "We both said some shit we didn't mean."

That wasn't true. "I meant every word I said."

Letting out a dry laugh, Asher lifted his head to meet my gaze. "I did, too. Should I be worried that you're gonna take that candle and shove it down my pants in retribution?"

"I'm not crass, Asher."

His arched brow was the only response he gave me.

Rolling my eyes, I crossed my right leg over the left. "All right, so I can be crass. Sometimes. Rarely." Uncomfortable under his astute gaze, I squirmed in my chair. Then reprimanded myself for acting like an immature brat who couldn't get comfortable. *Time to get this conversation back on track.* Hopefully.

"Go back to Jay." I tapped his shoe with mine. "What was he like?"

His big hands shifted over the cards once more, the pads of his fingers lazily tracing the illustrations while his gaze remained locked on my face. "We're going to do this the unconventional way," he said. "You good with that?"

"I don't even know what you're talking about."

Alongside my foot, his jumped into a small rhythm—like he couldn't keep his emotions in check. Or, maybe, it was actually his nerves.

"The unconventional thing is that I'm going to sit here and read you your cards. That work for you?"

I stared at him, refusing to show any hint of trepidation. He clearly had a plan with this tonight, and who was I to tell him to screw off without even allowing him the chance to give it a go? Maybe it'd be revelatory.

Or maybe he should learn that you aren't supposed to sift through the cards and pick the ones you want before a reading.

Maybe that was the case, but curiosity trumped every other emotion for me.

"Avery?"

A small nod tilted my head down. "Yeah, all right. It works for me."

A brief, grateful smile ghosted across his lips before he plucked the cards right off the table and clutched them in his big hands. Turning to me completely, his feet sandwiching mine and the table to his right, he flipped his pickings around, with only the first one showing.

The Three of Swords—Sorrow.

My nails dug into my palms as I noted the familiar card with its black and purple coloring, and a sword puncturing a rose. It wasn't a card I pulled often for myself, but it was nevertheless one that always made me feel a measure of sadness seep into my bones.

I pushed the question out: "What's that represent?"

Asher's lips parted on a short exhale. "This is your past."

The laugh that broke free from my chest was more air than joy. "Pretty accurate, I guess."

I don't know what I expected from this so-called reading. Perhaps for him to simply call the card out and move onto the next. Maybe for him to create a fanciful tale that was nothing more than unicorn bullshit, all gussied up with glitter and rainbows but containing little substance.

I'd expected those things, going so far as to gear myself up for them, but I couldn't have expected *this*.

"I never knew about you, you know." He set Sorrow to balance on my knee, forcing me to touch the card or see it teeter off and fall to the ground. "Until I was around twenty-five, I had no idea who my biological father was. I was given to the Ursulines at two. Dropped in foster care at three and stayed that way until I was a legal adult. Jay Foley never came around. Never showed his face." Blue eyes flicked up in my direction. "And when I finally met my mother, she never mentioned his name either."

Awkwardly, I shifted in my chair. "I . . . I don't know where you're going with this."

Clearly uncomfortable with the turn of the conversation, Asher raked his fingers through his messy hair. His hand hesitated at the back of his skull, forearm flexing as he studied me. Then, he spoke, that familiar husky timbre of his making me shift for an entirely different reason. "I was twenty-two when I heard about your suicide in the news."

In my head, I jumped up from my chair and stormed away, hands over my ears to stamp out the sounds of the words I didn't want to hear.

In reality, I didn't move a muscle.

"Foley was on the City Council at the time," Asher

went on, hands linking together as his elbows went down on his knees. "And all I remember thinking as they showed your picture on the news was that you must have known so much love from your mom that it was impossible to live without her." A ragged laugh came from his mouth, and, as though embarrassed by the sound, he scrubbed a palm over his lips. "In that moment, I was jealous of your sorrow. Jealous that you'd loved and been loved, and all I knew was pain and disappointment."

Why was he telling me this?

The fact that he could sit down and tell me something like that was just—

"When Big Hampton dropped that little bomb," Asher said, cutting into my thoughts, "I realized you'd known a sorrow of a different kind." He nodded his chin in the direction of the card, which was still balanced on my knee. "You've been alone, isolated, and yet you still survived."

I had no other choice.

It was either survive or give up, and Momma had never raised me to roll over and take it. *Be brave,* she used to tell me, *and always be bold.* For years I'd repeated the words in my head, over and over again until it was either believe in what my Momma had preached or just accept that I'd been spoon-fed yet another lie.

Asher's foot nudged mine. "It wasn't true, what I said about you being a coward. I've known my handful of people who've pissed off Foley and they couldn't manage to do what you did. What you're continuing to do right now—live."

Every word that fell from his mouth pushed the blade of guilt yet another inch into my sternum. I wanted the anger from him. I wanted to feel that familiar fury swirling in my gut. I wanted, above all else, not to think of Lincoln

Asher as anyone but a calculated killer who could snap my neck in two without remorse.

The words he spoke now didn't belong to a man who took lives apathetically.

And that . . . that only made me want to look closer and peer into his soul. Discover anything and everything I could learn about him.

Fingers pinching Sorrow, I positioned it on my thigh so it wouldn't fall off. "What did you pick for my present?"

With a quick glance in my direction, he revealed the next card that he held in his grasp.

Seven of Disks.

"Failure," I muttered, staring at the dark illustration with its Roman symbols embedded in what looked like a myriad of black feathers, but which were meant to represent dead vegetation. Forcing a smile, my teeth ground together. "How ironic."

Asher set Failure atop Sorrow on my leg, his fingers momentarily brushing the fabric of my black skirt. He sat back, arms on the flimsy armrests of his lawn chair. "You wanted to hide, Avery. You wanted to run from your past, and I brought you right back into it. That failure is mine."

But it wasn't, not really.

No matter the fact that Nat claimed to know him, she had followed *me* for years. I'd been in this mess for the long haul, no matter the fact that I hadn't even realized it all along. And it didn't help that he'd settled the card on my thigh with it reversed—in Thoth, Seven of Disks came with a darkness that always held light at the end of the tunnel. But if the card was drawn backward, and set down that way, that light was eclipsed. Negligent. The struggle never-ending.

I was so tired of fighting.

I set both Sorrow and Failure on the table, face down.

"Here's the third card I pulled," Asher murmured, yanking me from my reverie. "Dominion. I'm no card reader, Avery, and that's something we both know. YouTube can't make you a pro, and I pulled cards that I thought resonated, but this . . ." He wiggled it back and forth in his hand. "This is gonna happen."

Plucking the card from his grasp, I stuck it back on the velvet-lined table, my palm echoing with a *thud* against the rickety frame. I should leave well enough alone. Accept that maybe he was trying to make amends after being an arrogant prick who thought he could say and do whatever he wanted.

But I couldn't leave well enough alone.

"What game are you playing at, Lincoln?"

His blue eyes never wavered from my face. "No games."

"I don't believe you."

"And why is that?" he asked, voice low. Behind him, the St. Louis Cathedral bells chimed the new hour, but he didn't so much as glance back. No, *I* was the center of his attention, and even though he sat in his chair and I sat in mine, I nevertheless felt crowded by his presence.

"Can we not—"

"We have to." His hands caught my wrists in a move so quick I barely had time to register it. And then he was tugging me forward until my hands were gripping his knees to stabilize my weight, and my butt was hovering inches off the fabric of my seat. "You don't know this world, this city, sweetheart, not the way you think you do." Thumbs caressing the delicate bones of my inner wrists, he met my gaze. "It was my failure that landed you in this mess, and I'll be damned if I let you get burned because of me."

"I can handle myself." Right? I'd done so, well enough this far, at any rate, and if push came to shove, I could carry on for another twelve years—if I wanted to. If Nat didn't flip the script on me and send her wolves sniffing at my ankles. If my stepfather didn't think back to our almost-meeting at the police station and wonder, *was that her?*

So many *if*'s, but they were all I had.

The man holding my wrists was the biggest *if* of them all.

His lids fell shut, and I took the moment of solitude to study his features up close in a way that I hadn't had the chance to before, when we were too busy having sex in the dark. A thin, white scar marked his tan skin just above his left eyebrow. Dark stubble lined the lower half of his face, longer than it'd been when I'd first met him, but not yet a full beard. His scars—

I hated the way I ached for his pain. I wanted to keep my walls in check and my empathy at the bare minimum. I wanted, so very badly, to blame his dangerous life on the choices he'd made and the decisions that he'd set forth out of his own volition, and not as a consequence of anyone else's influence.

It was easier than facing and accepting the truth, and the truth was that I so desperately wanted to understand the inner workings of his mind. He'd saved me, at the Basement, when he could have so easily thrown me to the wolves. Even when it'd come to uncuffing us in that shack in the middle of nowhere, he'd demanded that I go first.

He wasn't a good man.

But he had a conscience, I had to believe that.

Once again it seemed like we were tethered together by a string because as I pulled from his grasp and laid one hand over the raised flesh of his scars, his lips parted to murmur, "Ask me what happened to my face."

KNIGHT of PENTACLES

MINOR ARCANA

TEN

Lincoln

_____

If Avery truly thought she could take on the likes of Foley, Ambideaux, and Big Hampton, then she'd be dead before she even had the chance to draw a breath to scream.

It was the reason I'd sought her out tonight.

The reason I was willing to share the one moment of my life that I'd vowed to carry to the grave, forever unspoken.

It's not the only reason.

No, I was a selfish bastard to my core. I craved her, even though I'd been a complete asshole when we'd last seen each other. I craved her, even though logic said she should be the last woman I should ever desire.

I didn't give a fuck about any of that.

There was something to be said about making amends —I could do that now, even though the ones of my past weren't so easy, or possible, to erase.

I opened my mouth, heard the words as they left—"Ask me about my face"—and then felt softness land on my cheek. My scarred cheek.

My heart lurched, the damn thing flopping around in my chest like a beached fish desperate for water, for safety, for the familiarity of its everyday reality. Just like that, her gentle touch yanked me from my numb existence, like the flick of a switch, and emotion ricocheted through me.

We'd fucked, me and Avery.

But when was the last time anyone had ever touched me willingly outside of getting naked? When was the last time anyone had ever sought to soothe me or care enough to even try?

Never.

Not in any of the homes I'd lived in growing up.

Not Jason, and sure as hell not Nat.

Not my mother, who couldn't even bring herself to look at me.

If the Ursulines ever had, I'd been too young to carry the memories along with me into adulthood.

And, Christ, but the reality of my life hit me like a sledgehammer, pummeling my chest, forcing out a breath that echoed in my ears like a foghorn.

Words. I needed to speak, to say something so Avery didn't think I'd gone mute, but I found myself incapable of doing anything but soaking up the feeling of her hand against the ugliest part of me. I was ruined, as she'd told me when we'd first met, and she touched me now anyway.

Like I was someone worth her time and energy.

Like I wasn't a monster clothed in human skin.

"Lincoln."

Fuck, she could have lit a fire and told me to run through it, and I would have stripped naked to go the extra mile and then stood in the middle of the flames. Welcomed the heat. Welcomed the pain. If only I could pretend, if only for a second, that I was a man worth loving.

I blinked my eyes open.

She blinked down at me. "Where did you go?" she whispered, and I didn't even have to ask what she meant.

My throat constricted with a swallow. "To a place I generally like to pretend doesn't exist." In other words, my heart. My soul. Two things I'd thought were dormant until I'd found her in Jackson Square, exactly where we sat now. I reached up, hand circling her wrist, and startled even myself by settling her palm even more flatly against my cheek.

I waited for the disgust to twist her features, but it never did.

Instead, her hazel eyes went to our hands against my face and didn't flit away. "Tell me what happened."

Starting from the beginning wasn't an option, so I settled with the truths that could be told without landing her in even more hot water. "I worked for Nat's husband growing up. Jason Ambideaux."

Her features scrunched. "Like an intern sort of work?"

I wished. Maybe life would have played out differently if I was only one of the kids he hired from the local high schools to plan his social events and schedule his Facebook posts and coordinate his meetings in a fancy little calendar that cost more than my prized Glock 19. "No, not like an intern."

At the risk of seeing that disgust appear, I added, "I ran drugs for him, Ave. Murdered people."

Her nails scraped against my cheek, a gut reaction from her, I knew.

I plowed on—there was no other way.

"I told you that I don't know how many people I've killed, but that's not true. I know every person—their birthdate, their parents, their kids, if they had any." My chest would remain forever marked by their losses. A tattoo for every kill. Pain for pain, as the Romans would have once put it. My chest was covered, as were my upper arms. I was a walking tombstone, and I'd have it no other way. It was regret and shame that I carried on my shoulders alone, though, and it was the single reason I rarely removed my shirt in front of others.

I didn't want the questions, the curious glances.

They'd never understand, and it wasn't in me to try to explain what they would never, ever, comprehend. The ink was my penance alone.

"Jason had this . . . I hate to call him an enemy because it sounds so damn cheesy."

Avery hooked a foot around her chair and drew it forward, so that it was almost on top of mine, and then lowered herself onto it. She never tried to remove her hand from my face, simply angled her body so she could maintain contact. "He was an enemy," she said evenly, "just call it like it is."

My lungs squeezed with a heavy sigh. "Yeah, they were. They hated each other, for reasons that I still don't know, not then and not now either. Jason had learned something about Foley, though, and he called me in. He had something he wanted me to take care of, and I'd never told him no before. I was always the reliable one."

Her teeth sank into her bottom lip, and I could practically see the wheels spinning in her head. "Do you like . . .?"

Knowing the answer she wanted, I gave her my truth: "I'm good at it, but I've never taken pleasure in seeing someone die." No, I'd been worse. Indifferent. Resigned. Determined to please a man who wasn't my father but was the only person who even came close to filling the role. "Except then he'd told me the mark's identity, and I almost balked."

"Why?"

I met her gaze, and unraveled the words that I'd kept bottled up for so damn long. "The target was a kid," I said, pulling her hand away from my scars. As much as I wanted her touch, I didn't deserve her empathy with this story. I never would. "An innocent kid who'd done nothing but exist, but Jason wanted retaliation for something his so-called enemy had done."

Avery's gasp felt so very loud. *Just keep going. Get to the point of the story.* It was hard, so hard to know that my actions had set so much into motion.

"I agreed—"

Dark brows furrowing, Avery watched me carefully. "You said that you *almost* balked. Please—please tell me you didn't go through with it."

The weight of her quiet disappointment felt like chains circling my neck. I was going to hell, that was for sure. A first-class ticket engraved in gold, just for me.

"I agreed, at first. Ambid—Jason was like a father to me, and I hated the thought of disappointing him. But in the end, I couldn't go through with it. I went to Whiskey Bay, determined to get the fuck out of that life and confront him. He was waiting for me already, knew exactly how I'd failed to follow through."

My mind's eye brought forth a visual of Ambideaux waiting for me at the bottom of the stairs of the Basement, arms crossed over his broad chest. To say that he'd been pissed was an understatement. *Furious,* more like. I'd never seen him in such a rage before, and my gut had told me to whip around and get the hell out of dodge.

I'd stood my ground.

And he'd shot me in return.

My voice emerged like I'd been silent for years instead of seconds. "I told him he was a fucking predatory asshole for bringing a kid into the mess. I wanted out." Forcing the lingering panic away, I tucked my elbows on my knees and let my hands dangle between my legs. *Stay calm, man. Don't lose it.* "I remember turning away, and then feeling hot fire ripping through my right thigh. And, then, a split second later, more flames just above my knee."

Avery's eyes went wide, and her full lips parted like I'd ordered them open on my command. "He *shot* you?"

"Yes."

"What an *asshole*," she ground out, as though horrified on my behalf. And, hell, but it felt good—even if her sympathy was all wrongly misplaced.

"I woke up in a car, blood all over me. We weren't in N'Orleans, and it was like some twisted sort of fate that I knew exactly where they were bringing me—Whiskey Bay." At her lifted brows, I corrected myself: "The Atchafalaya Basin. It's where we—*they*—brought the bodies we were dumping. The river would bring the dead straight out to the Gulf of Mexico, and if that failed, then they'd end up as food. I wasn't dead, and they knew that." But they'd stripped me of all my belongings—my ID, my guns, my sanity. "And before they threw me over, Jason made one last order."

"What else—" Breaking off with a low growl, Avery stared hard at my face. "Please tell me they didn't."

"Held me down." I could picture it all now, my limbs restrained as I tried to fight the fuckers off; the tip of the knife drawing first blood; my already tepid heart rate growing slower with extreme blood loss. "They carved my face with a *J*. One guy made the comment that he could see bone, and then they threw me in."

It should have warmed me to see the way Avery reacted, the utter shock that lined her delicate features as her hands went to her mouth to hold in a small cry. The chill was back in my limbs, though, the memories of that day still so vivid in my head that I could almost taste the bile that had stolen up my throat.

"How did you—" Shaking her head, Avery whispered, her eyes shimmering with unshed tears. "It doesn't look like . . ."

I laughed, but there wasn't a single ounce of joy in it. "Trust me, I wanted to die. There wasn't anything I wanted more. And I won't lie, I don't know what twist of fate had me washing up on a grassy bank like some sort of bastard prince, but there I was when some shrimpers were coming out to set some traps." Reaching up, I skimmed my palm over the jagged scars. I couldn't remember a time when they weren't there, but now, much like the tattoos, they were symbolic of my guilt. Visual suffering for all to see. Jaw unclenching, I said, "As for the scar, I fixed it."

Avery blinked. "You *fixed* it?"

I waited for the implication to sink in.

I didn't have to wait long—not even three seconds had passed before she was swallowing convulsively and tearing her gaze from my face, the first time she'd cut eye contact since sitting down. "Lincoln—"

"No one owns me, sweetheart. Not Jason, not Foley, not Hampton. I would rather have a face that scares kids for the rest of my life than live a single day with that asshole's initial etched into me."

"I-I don't even know what to say. He's awful—and awful isn't even a good enough word for it at all. You shouldn't have had to suffer like that, just for wanting to do the right thing. The *noble* thing. It's not okay. None of it is okay, and I can't even imagine what that must have felt like, having your—"

"There's nothing to say. That was my reality and so I walked out. I'm a damn lucky bastard, but that's not the point to why I brought up all this up." I picked up the card that I'd selected for her future while stalking the internet for any and all understanding of tarot. Dominion had fit for what I wanted for Avery, according to the website I'd found. Illustrated with yellow and orange swords and flames, the card was supposed to represent boldness and courage. Something about the spirit rebelling against boundaries in order to find a resolution.

What it meant besides that—or, hell, if that meaning was completely wrong in the first place—I had no idea.

Guns were my area of expertise, not fortune-telling.

Twirling the card between my index finger and thumb, I husked out, "My point is, Avery, I don't want that for you." I tapped the corner of the card to my face, just below the raised flesh. "*This* is not going to be your future. I'll be dead before I let them touch you. So everything we said the other night, all those bitter feelings? We're squashing the fuck out of them right now. You need me, I'm here. You *don't* need me, I'm still gonna be right here, waiting."

Looking shaken up, Avery licked her lips. "You could be waiting forever. I highly doubt anyone is looking for me."

"You don't think Foley will be if he finds out?"

Her hazel eyes squeezed shut. "I don't know. I hope not."

He might not be right now, but he would be soon. If Hampton was stirring the pot, and so was Ambideaux, it was only a matter of time before Foley caught wind and started paying notice to everything around him.

My father had grown comfortable during his term as mayor—it wasn't a secret. But shit was changing, and one wrong move could land Avery back on his radar.

Unless I stepped in and watched her back. I was a

glorified hitman with a suspended badge, not a bodyguard. *You can't walk away—not again.*

Not from her, Avery.

Laurel Peyton.

The reason for the scar on my face and the age-old pain in my right leg.

She was the kid I'd been sent to take out. Only, I'd never made it past the front lawn of Foley's mansion. A visual of her running from the house and falling to her knees stained my retina. I recalled her vomiting, her young face inches from the grass, her long, blond hair brushing the ground, as I heard a gun fire from the grand mansion.

I'd assumed Ambideaux had sent someone else after sensing my hesitation.

Who Foley was to Jason, I'd never known. Who he was to me, well, I hadn't discovered that until much later.

But I'd failed her that night. Heartless to the very end as I'd left and climbed back into my car. At any point, I could have warned Foley about Ambideaux's plans. What man wouldn't want to know that his family was being targeted? And yet, I'd left, all the while knowing that someone else could be sent in my place to do the job I couldn't carry out.

A year later, when I'd heard of her suicide on the news, I'd vomited just as she had—on my knees, stomach roiling from pent-up guilt and self-disgust. I may not have been the direct reason for why she was dead, but I'd felt responsible nonetheless. And, beneath it all, her death was a reflection of how far I'd sunk: stealing lives was never honorable, but to even consider killing someone so young? There was nothing worse. Nothing more disgusting or deplorable.

I settled a hand over my heart now, my fingers brushing

my sweater, right over where I'd tattooed her number on my chest.

47.

I may not have made her take those pills, but the way I'd looked at it back then, I'd had a direct hand in her death anyhow.

Except she wasn't dead.

She was alive, breathing, and thriving just in front of me, and I was stuck in limbo, wanting to capture her lips with mine and beg for forgiveness while simultaneously wanting to keep our relationship strictly professional.

Hampton's little bombshell had thrown me for a loop, for more reasons than one.

I was the sinner.

The executioner.

The man who belonged in every circle of hell.

With my hand over my heart, I met Avery's gaze and dropped my voice to a low murmur. "Let me be there for you."

Let me find some sort of atonement.

Her lips parted on an inhale. "Okay," she whispered, "okay."

THREE OF CUPS

ELEVEN

Avery
_____

*S*oooo, how long exactly are we going to pretend that Mr. Hot Cop himself isn't downstairs and acting like our very own Captain America, all chivalrous and gentlemanly?"

Dammit. Clearly, today wasn't going to be the day that Katie suddenly learned not to pry into everyone else's business.

I shoved a pillow under my arm just as the front door clicked shut behind her. "He doesn't have a shield," I said, turning to face my roommate and best friend, "so Captain America probably isn't the best comparison."

Dropping her work bag by our tiny entryway table, Katie gave me a crooked grin. "Ave, let's get this settled." She jerked her thumb over her shoulder at the door. "A man like that doesn't *need* a shield. He looks like he breaks bones for a living and takes names."

Andddd, we've officially gotten too close for comfort now.

Even after telling Lincoln that I didn't need him hanging out in front of my apartment building tonight, he'd refused to listen to reason.

"What are you going to do if someone shows up looking for you?" he'd demanded, arms over his wide chest, jaw working tightly as he stared down at me. *"You're already out one taser, sweetheart. I'm the next best thing."*

The way I looked at it—he was selling himself short. He was way more capable than the taser would be, electroshock prongs and all.

Plus, the stubborn man was the reason I was "out" one taser in the first place.

Clamping the pillow beneath my arm so I had a good grip on it, I slung a blanket over my forearm, and then dipped low to grab the assortment of snacks I'd picked up earlier on the way back from Flambeaux. For the first time in years, I was thankful for having interacted with one of Pete's employees and not Pete himself—not with Lincoln Asher waiting just outside on the street. I could only imagine what sort of questions that would bring up.

"Oh, Ave."

Hearing the plaintive note in her voice, I lifted my gaze to meet Katie's. "What?"

She gestured at all the items in my arms. "Girl, you're nesting."

Wide-eyed, I glanced down at the weight in my arms and shook my head. "False. I'm just bringing him—"

"You're nesting." Without giving me the chance to protest, she stole the yellow package of M&M's from the plastic sack hanging from my index finger. Ripping it open like a savage, she popped a red M&M into her mouth, molars grinding as she crunched away. "Let me ask you this," she said, "*why* is Mr. Hot Cop down in his SUV right now, hanging around?"

Another M&M went into her mouth as I stood there and contemplated my next move.

Finally, I muttered, "How did you even know he was there?"

"His face. Totally dream-worthy. It's the kind that's totally hard to forget."

I highly doubted that "dream-worthy" was a name that Lincoln Asher heard frequently about his looks. Gritty. Powerful. Raw. Those seemed undeniably more appropriate.

Then again, when he actually allowed himself to wear his heart on his sleeve, as he had earlier tonight, then, yes, "dream-worthy" was actually a perfect description.

"Avery."

Jeez, she wasn't shaking the claws off tonight.

"Have you ever found yourself drawn to someone who wasn't any good for you?" Rolling my shoulders, I awkwardly gestured for her to return the M&M's to the bag. "And I'm not just saying they're a night owl and you love waking up at the crack of dawn."

Katie's gaze skirted away, landing everywhere but on me. "Oh, you know," she murmured in a blithe tone, "just like every relationship I've ever had."

Right. Somehow, I didn't think it was exactly the same thing.

Katie might love getting outrageous in the bedroom, but her relationships were frequently much more conservative. She fell for the rich types who strolled into the club on a weekly basis. The sort of men who were in town on business, and who felt the inexplicable need to party it up like they were in their twenties.

How many times had Katie come home heartbroken when yet another jerk dumped her three months after his visit to New Orleans?

It was a vicious cycle, one sporadically broken up by hot sex with whoever she fancied at the moment, but was still, in no way, the same as the situation I'd found myself in.

"Asher is trouble," I said, struggling to maintain a neutral expression.

Blue eyes flicked down to my armful. "Then why are you bothering to go downstairs at all?"

Because I can't stop myself.

I hadn't asked him to stay, but now that he was here, I couldn't stand the idea of him sitting in his SUV alone all night without a single creature comfort. No matter the fact that he probably did this sort of stake-out for a living. Just because he was *accustomed* to it, didn't mean that I wouldn't worry.

My forced smile slipped a notch. "No questions tonight. Please."

Katie's blond ponytail swung sharply as she shook her head. "After years of listening to you go on and on about how you didn't need a man, you've made a real quick turn-around." She tapped her chin, lips pursing. "Is this when I tell you that I told you so?"

I grimaced. "Maybe a little too soon?"

"Nah, never." Grinning, Katie surprised me by pulling the pillow from my grasp along with the snacks. "C'mon, I want a formal introduction."

A formal . . .

"Wait!"

Katie waved an arm up above her head, the plastic bag of goodies dangling from her index finger as she turned on her heel and headed for the front door. "Come along, Ave. I don't want to look like an idiot when I knock on his window."

A visual of Katie startling Lincoln—and, naturally, him reacting aggressively—shot me into motion. My legs churned toward the door, blanket in disarray within my arms. "Really," I muttered, slipping out of our apartment to tail Katie down the wooden stairwell, "we don't need to make this a whole big *thing*."

"Who else is going to make it a thing for you? A grandma? An aunt? You have me, Ave. Just me."

"*And?*" Never had I been more thankful to be rocking my solo life than in this moment. "I'm perfectly okay with that."

With her back to me, and her feet making headway down the last flight of stairs, Katie announced, "Listen, girl. Not once in all the time we've lived together have you ever even *flirted* with a guy. So, this sergeant? It's big news. Before you throw your heart into it all, I just want to do a little reconnaissance to make sure he's up to speed on how everything goes down."

"Reconnaissance? I thought you stopped watching *CSI*." Confusion splintered the fog of my thoughts. "And how *what* goes does down?"

"He screws with you, and he'll hear about it from me."

The front door cracked open, and Katie spilled out onto our front stoop. She barely waited for me to appear at her side before she was stepping out onto the cracked sidewalk and glancing from right to left before ambling across the one-way street, calm as can be.

"Katie," I bit out, trailing after her, "seriously, please don't embarrass me."

Her laughter was all I heard. And then, "Don't worry, I'll keep the good stuff to myself. For now. Oh, look! Here he is." She flashed a smile in my direction, and then, with typical Katie-flair, simply knocked on the SUV's window with full-on confidence.

Hurrying toward her, tripping on a corner of the blanket, I yanked the material out from between my legs and picked up my pace. "Katie, c'mon—"

I watched her spine snap straight, the plastic bag falling to the cement.

Oh, crap.

Then, sounding like she was being strangled, my best friend coughed out an awkward laugh and said, "Captain America is packing, Ave. You're right—I would've preferred the shield."

TWO OF SWORDS

TWELVE

Lincoln

I stared at the blonde outside my window, watching her from the interior of my SUV as she mouthed something that looked a hell of a lot like "Captain America."

Before I even had the chance to make sense of that, she was being bulldozed to the side by a woman who looked eerily similar to Avery.

My eyes narrowed.

Fuck. It *was* Avery.

Flinging the door open, my feet hit the concrete just as Avery's dark head whipped in my direction from where she stood, body angled in front of the blonde. "Gun down, Sergeant."

My empty hands flexed at my sides, and I felt the absurd urge to lift them and wriggle my fingers. Just to show that I wasn't a complete savage. "Gun's not out, *Avery*."

Behind her, the blonde piped up. "Why are we talking about guns?"

Glancing behind her, Avery let out a very strangled sounding, "You said he was *packing*."

"Oh, right." She stepped out from around Avery, then tacked on, "I was making a joke. He was . . . well, he was eating a po'boy."

Satisfaction sliced through me as I watched the reality of the situation hit Avery. Her lips parted and her cheeks turned a pretty blush shade and I was just enough of a bastard to murmur, "Fried catfish, in case that was in question, too."

The blonde let out a boisterous laugh.

Avery looked like she was just hoping for the ground to swallow her whole.

And that's when I noticed it.

All of it.

The pillow clutched to the blonde's chest; the blanket half-tangled around Avery's legs. A plastic bag lay torn on the cement, its contents spilling out.

Peanut M&M's.

A bag of chips.

Two triangular sandwiches still tucked safely in their plastic containers.

One bottle of water.

A sensation I didn't recognize pulled low at my gut, warm and completely foreign. My gaze inched up, over Avery's baggy sweatpants to the Saints T-shirt she'd pulled over her head. She looked like she was ready for bed. Rumpled. Sexy. So damn off-limits.

Voice husky, I asked, "What's all this?"

The blonde answered in Avery's stead, striding toward me with her hand outreached. "I like to think that I'm watching my best friend finally fall. Anyway, I'm Katie! Avery's roommate, friend, sister from another mother. And you're Captain America."

"Oh my God, Katie, please stop talking."

Laughter rumbled in my throat at Avery's miserable-sounding tone. I couldn't resist getting under her skin. "You give me that nickname?" I asked her, altogether enjoying the way she bit down on her bottom lip in clear consternation.

Her mouth dropped open. "No—"

"She totally did," Katie interjected, her expression one of pure joy. "She's just feeling a little embarrassed that I've called her out on it. She thinks the *highest* of you." Ducking down, she grabbed the plastic bag and shoved the food right back into it. "Which is why she planned this picnic for the two of you."

Christ, I knew I shouldn't find it funny.

But in the grand scheme of competing politicians and rising death tolls, this was the highlight of my week.

If we didn't count me having sex with Avery, obviously.

Mirroring the roommate, I crouched down and grabbed the water bottle from where it'd rolled right next to my tire. Gently pulled the pillow from Katie's grasp and then did the same to the blanket wrapped around Avery's legs. To Avery, I said, "You know of somewhere we can go to enjoy the spread?"

That seemed to startle her out of whatever trance she'd been in.

Hazel eyes blinked at me, and then lowered to the goods. "I thought you said we needed to stay local?"

Yeah, it was probably best—only, I wanted to feel again, just like I had at Jackson Square earlier. Would we be making a major mistake by leaving home base? Only one way to find out.

Opening the back door, I set the pillow and blanket down on the leather seat. Then, motioning to Katie for everything else, I tied off the top of the plastic bag, so shit wouldn't get loose again, and placed it on top of the blanket.

Somedays you just had to take the risk and hope you didn't get scarred in the process.

I turned toward the women and gave a quick nod in the blonde's direction. "It was nice meeting you, Katie."

"You, too, Cap'."

I almost laughed. She was a nut—the perfect balance to Avery's more somber outlook on life.

An outlook, I reminded myself, that she had every right to.

Guilt slithered up my legs like overgrown, wild vines.

Hand curving over the top of the door, I fixed my attention on the woman I wanted with every fiber of my being. "Get in the car, Ave. I've got the perfect place for our picnic."

A picnic at almost midnight.

If my heart hadn't been thundering with anticipation, sending blood pumping to two different hemispheres of my body, I would have questioned my own sanity. *Why the hell are you going out of your way to make this happen?*

Without a glance in the direction of her roommate, Avery closed the distance between us. Her hand landed on the door frame next to mine, our pinkies tangling like we were high schoolers feeling each other out for the first time.

It wasn't enough, not for me.

My hand covered hers, our fingers interlacing, my breath catching the loose tendrils at her hairline when I leaned down.

Chin tipping up, she met my gaze and said the words that stole the proverbial rug out from under my feet: "I need this."

I needed it, too.

Her heat.

Her slow smile.

Her dry wit that challenged mine.

I squeezed her hand and stepped back. "Get in the car. We're going for a ride."

I TOOK her across the Mississippi River to Algiers Point, a cornerstone of New Orleans that rivaled the French Quarter when it came down to quaint, nineteenth-century character. The historical neighborhood sat directly opposite the Quarter and the downtown Central Business District, and its views were ones for the record books.

And for dates.

If this *was* a date, which logic told me it wasn't.

There was too much convoluted drama surrounding us, threatening to drag us under, but I couldn't—for the life of me—walk away from how I felt around her. Alive. Human. A numbed man finally unthawing to the world.

Putting the SUV in park, I glanced over at her. "Have you ever been to this side of the river before?"

"Once." Staring straight ahead at the tops of the highrises peeping out over the twelve-foot tall grassy levees, she added, "He brought us here for a dinner. One of those fancy parties where I was shoved into a dress with sequins at the age of eight, and my tight shoes pinched my toes for the entire night. All I remember beyond that is the amount of food that covered the dining table. It could have fed my entire grade at school, including the teachers."

A party like the sort Ambideaux had held all the time —the kind I'd watched from outside the windows, a silent voyeur to a life I'd never even dreamed of having.

Swallowing past the lump in my throat, I turned off the car and waited for the quiet hum of the engine to settle down. "Ready to go up? I promise the view's even better at the top."

"Yeah, let's do it."

We gathered the goods, me with the pillow and the blanket, and her with the food. The levee was a steep climb, a modern-day outer wall to protect the neighborhood from any flooding. Algiers Point was quiet at this time of night—a bar down the road had old blues playing, and there was some laughter and music emerging from the two restaurants just behind us.

Otherwise, it was just the sound of our shoes crunching over grass as we rounded to the top of the levee, where a concrete path was located for cyclers and walkers.

I nudged Avery in the arm, gathering her attention. "Wanna live life on the edge?"

A soft laugh escaped her, and in it I heard all of the longtime exhaustion of actually existing on that cusp of no-return. "Why not?" she said, lips turned up in a smile. "Might as well go all out."

"Brave girl."

Her shoulders jerked, and the plastic bag tangled in her hands whipped to the right as she twisted to face me. "That's the second time you've said that to me. You say it like you admire me."

I didn't want to lie but given recent news about our respective connections to Jay Foley, I didn't want to make her feel uncomfortable either. Over the years, I'd learned that if I wanted something, no one would ever be there to offer it to me.

I took, or the opportunity passed me by without a second chance.

With Avery—*Laurel*—it had to be a two-way street. I couldn't take without her giving approval first that she wanted me in return, and I couldn't assume that we were both on the same page.

"You're a force to be reckoned with," I finally said, meeting her gaze without hesitation. "I'd be an idiot if I didn't admire that."

She chewed on that, literally biting down on her lower lip as she gave me a onceover that had my cock hardening in my pants. "I can't imagine Captain America ever being an idiot." With a wink and a smile, she turned away, her long ponytail swooshing with the movement. "Now where are we going? I'm ready to take a risk. You've convinced me."

My feet were rooted to the concrete.

And, for the first time in my life, I wished for something other than death.

If I closed my eyes, I could almost pretend that *this* was my life—having a midnight picnic up on a levee with a beautiful woman who made my cock hard and my heart warm, and who made me want to toss her over my shoulder, just to hear the sound of her laughter as I teased her with the possibility of throwing her right into the water.

The reverie got away from me, and then it wasn't just Avery and me here at the riverfront, but also a dog pouncing around after a tennis ball. He'd be muddy, feet dancing with the water, before tromping back and shaking himself dry at our side while I wrapped him up in a towel and looked to Avery. Her dark hair draped over one shoulder; her face glowing with happiness; her one hand settled over the curve of her pregnant belly.

"Lincoln! Are you coming?"

Just like that, the vivid visual dissipated like mist on a hot, sunny day.

The chill coming off the Mississippi River cooled my

racing heart, even if it did nothing for the hard-on I was now sporting below the belt.

"Yeah," I muttered, my voice rusty with want, "follow me."

Just like we'd climbed up the levee, I led her down the other side of it, toward the water. We'd had weeks without rain, which meant that the river was lower than usual and grassy banks had popped up along the waterfront. One glance at the exposed knees of the cypress trees was enough to tell me that we didn't have to worry about the river's current coming this way—they were as dry as the Sahara.

I picked a spot with a view of the skyline and the GNO Bridge we'd taken to drive over to Algiers Point. Down here on the banks, with the lights from the Point eclipsed by the height of the levees, there wasn't a chance that anyone would spot us if they happened to be meandering down the bike path.

"It's gorgeous," Avery murmured, as I laid out the blanket for us to sit on. "I was so young when I came here last, I don't even think I paid any attention to a view like this."

Sitting down, I patted the empty spot next to me. "At home, I've got a picture frame up with this view. I got it down on Royal—someone was selling artwork on the street and I had to have it."

"And Sergeant Asher always gets what he wants."

She said it in a teasing tone, but it rubbed me raw, anyway. "Sometimes you learn the hard way that no one is out there handing you freebies just for breathing."

That made her laugh. Picking up one of the sandwich containers, she popped it open and handed it over. I took it with a husky *thank-you* and waited until she'd done the same to her own sandwich before taking a bite into mine. Chicken salad on rye bread—not bad.

"We're such a jaded pair," she said after washing down a bite with a swish of water. "Katie likes to joke around that I'm too wound up, but I just . . . I don't know how to let my guard down. After my momma . . ."

Rumors circulated enough in the underbelly of New Orleans that I'd always suspected Foley had done away with his wife the same way I'd been sent to do away with Avery. At the time, though, I'd selfishly only thought about my life and wanting out of it.

Sandwich clasped in my right hand, my knee bounced under the weight of my elbow. *Tell her everything. Own up to it.*

My mouth opened, and an apology wasn't what emerged: "Go on. I'm not going to repeat what you say to anyone."

"And I should trust you . . . why?"

You shouldn't trust me. I didn't say that either.

I tapped her knee with the back of my hand, the one holding the sandwich. "Thought you said you wanted to take a risk."

"I do."

"Then lower your guard," I said, hating myself with every word for not doing what I preached, "and let me in. No tarot cards, this time—just me and you."

She treated me to her profile as she glanced out across the river. In the dark of night, the water appeared almost black, though the lights from the CBD and Quarter reflected off its swirling currents. She huffed out a soft laugh. "Funny how sitting on this side of the Mississippi makes me feel like I've got an entirely different perspective on life."

Someone could have held me at gunpoint, and I still wouldn't have wrenched my gaze away from her face.

Moonlight kissed the crooked slant of her nose, caressed the crests of her cheekbones, highlighted the length of her neck.

"Tell me why," I rasped.

"Give me your guns."

Incredulous laughter climbed my throat and bubbled out. Only, she didn't laugh with me. Chest tightening, I stared at her. "You're not fuckin' with me right now, are you."

It wasn't a question.

She only patted the empty space between us, much like I had, the palm of her hand landing on the chip bag and making it crinkle. "I'm evening out the playing field. You want me to trust you? Then I want you to lower your guard, too." Her mouth quirked up. "Unless you're too much of a chicken to do as you preach?"

Do as you preach . . .

Christ, she didn't pull any punches.

Flicking my gaze up to the levee, I submitted. Not that I was happy about it. "Hold my sandwich," I grunted, already questioning my sanity as I passed the damn thing over and bent one leg. Lifting the hem of my pants, I unholstered my sidearm and placed it on the corner of the blanket. Still in reach if we needed it, but far enough to make a point.

I was lowering my guard—literally.

Only for her.

After repeating the process with the gun at my hip, I motioned for her to give me back the sandwich. It wasn't that great, but eating it beat worrying about the fact that I was unarmed—

"Other gun, too."

I lifted my arms, my brow raised. "All out of guns to give up, sweetheart."

Her gaze roved over my torso, then paused and cocked her head. "Anything else you want to put in the pile?"

Fuck, but she was pushy.

Popping the rest of the chicken salad sandwich into my mouth, I chewed, frustrated, and then lifted the hem of my shirt. From its leather band, just behind the holster for my gun, I withdrew my trench knife and dropped it next to the firearms. "Happy?"

She chewed on a bite from her sandwich. Swallowed. "Feeling naked, Cap?"

I was feeling *something* all right, but it was probably for the best that I kept all grumbling to myself. "The captain thing isn't going away anytime soon, is it?"

"I like it."

"I'm not a hero, Avery. We both know that."

"Maybe not, but how about, for tonight, we both pretend to be something we're not?"

My mouth went dry. And my hand went to my chest, right over where her number was inked into my skin, and then I voluntarily stepped in front of the proverbial bullet: "What're you pretending to be?"

"Yours."

ACE of SWARDS

MINOR ARCANA

THIRTEEN

Avery

I was playing with fire.

And there was not a damn thing I could do to stop myself.

Sitting here in the calm of the night, away from the bustle of the city, made me feel like anything was possible. For the first time in years, my head felt clear. There was no Jay, no fear, no need to be brave for the sake of survival.

What had that lady said at my table in the square some weeks back?

I want to be wanted.

It felt like some odd twist of fate that Lincoln had walked into my life that night. Here I was, three weeks later, almost to the day, and I was just like that woman, smoking a cigarette, hoping beyond hope that all would be well in the end.

I wanted to be wanted—by no one else but him, the man who was wrong for me on every level.

"Avery."

He said my name like it was the last word he'd ever utter, and I took the opportunity to appreciate the way the moonlight glossed over him. He was on his knees, hands on his belt, and I took the plunge.

"Ask me whatever question you want, and I'll answer." I eyed his shirt, the way it flirted with his pants. God, I wanted to strip it off him and finally see *all* of him. "I'll do the same in return."

His face turned away, toward the river, exposing the unmarred side of his face. Sinful. He looked downright sinful with his big muscles playing under the fabric of his shirt, and the messy way his dark hair fell over his brow. He needed a cut, just like he needed a shave, and yet I didn't want him to do either one.

One hand lifted to scrub over the lower half of his face. "I need two questions."

"That's being greedy."

He flashed me a wicked grin, his teeth appearing extra white in the evening light. "Put it this way—one question is for me and the other is for *us*."

Us.

Two little letters and yet they warmed my heart like no other.

"You push a hard bargain," I said, trying to sound playful and not nervous, "but I accept."

Sitting back on his heels, his hands went to his thighs. "Tell me what happened to your mom."

Murdered. Brutally so.

In theory, it should have been as easy as that to admit. It wasn't like it was the first time I was telling someone— Katie knew. And yet, my tongue felt swollen as I sat there, fingers reaching for the water bottle to quench my sudden thirst.

He was patient in waiting, expression solemn, body completely still.

Just say it.

I took a sharp breath. Clenched the water bottle in a tight fist. Forced the words out: "He killed her. The one man who the whole world of N'Orleans has put on a pedestal. He . . ." My throat closed with anger, and I swallowed a fistful of water. "He hired someone—I don't know who he was—and that man shot her. I-I heard it all."

Lincoln let loose a volatile curse, and then he was shifting forward and wrapping his big arms around me. "Don't cry, sweetheart," he said into my hair, "fuck, don't cry."

I wasn't crying.

I hadn't cried in *years*.

But as he rocked me in his large embrace, I touched a finger to my cheek and was startled to find it damp.

Crap. I *was* crying.

"He's a bastard." Lincoln cupped the back of my head, cradling it as he encouraged me to look up and meet his gaze. My heart went into triple-time at the strained set to his face—he looked ready to commit murder, and I had a sneaking suspicion who the mark was in this case.

And it wasn't me.

As though he'd opened the dams, I couldn't lock them back up. The words flooded forward, a tangled mess of things better left unsaid. "I hate him. Every day I wake up and I"—my hands flexed against the strong muscles of his biceps—"I think about how much he took from me that night. My mother, my identity. I'm *no* one, and there is nothing—nothing—more that I want than to return that favor."

Lincoln's body froze against mine. "You can't."

Can't?

Pushing backward, I landed on my ass—and the chip bag. With a *pop!* it wheezed out air. I swatted it to the side, frustration sharpening my motions. It made my voice even sharper. "What? You don't think I can do it? I'm not a kid, Lincoln. If I wanted to kill him, which I do, I would have no trouble—"

Strong hands wrapped around my wrists. "Stop," he growled when I tried to twist away, "just stop and look at me."

Perhaps it was the imploring note in his baritone voice, but I gave in. Just like that, the struggle fled my frame.

"Look at me, Ave. Fucking look at me."

I looked.

And suddenly wished I hadn't.

His blue eyes were eerily intense in the sporadic light that slashed across his face, and there was something almost ruined in the way his gaze searched my face. "You asked, once, if I knew how many people I've killed. I told you tonight that I did." His hands tightened around mine. "Sixty-one. Sixty-one people I've looked in the face like I'm doing to you now and betrayed them in the next breath." Breath drawn in tight, he blew it out like a gust of wind. "There's no pleasure in it."

"I'm not doing it for *pleasure*, I want to do it—"

"For vengeance," he finished for me with a quick shake of his head. "You asked me if I killed Tom Townsend. You were so determined to know if I had or not. So, ask me again."

My stomach turned over. "Lincoln . . ."

"I won't bite. Ask me the question."

God, it wasn't supposed to be like this. He wasn't supposed to make me question myself. For years, beating Jay Foley at his own game had been all I'd ever wanted. And here was his son, trying to convince me otherwise. The irony was almost painful.

Bitterly, I bit out, "Maybe you just want to change my mind so I don't hurt your precious dad."

A half-second later, I found myself on my back, Lincoln's body pressing me into the blanket. I gasped for air, sucking it down into my lungs.

Our legs tangled. His elbows planted themselves on either side of my face.

His lips—oh man, they were temptation at its finest, just inches away from my own.

"Let's get this straight," he rumbled, his chest reverberating against mine. "I don't give a fuck about Foley, but I'll be damned if I have you ending up just like me."

"There's nothing wrong with you—"

He tossed his head back with a harsh laugh. "Don't lie, sweetheart. You called it like it is in that damn motel room. I'm a killer. Coldhearted to the very end. *You don't want to be me.* Don't you get it? I'm fucked up. I don't sleep. I walk around like a fucking armory. Given the opportunity, half this city would take me out." His breath wafted over my face as my breasts rubbed up against his hard chest. It wasn't intentional, but that didn't stop the two of us from groaning at the contact.

His arm muscles flexed by my face. "You think you know what it's like to walk around with a target on your back, but I can promise you"—he lowered his face, our noses almost touching—"you don't want to find out."

"What did you do to Townsend?" I didn't want to know the answer, not truthfully, but it felt like it was something I needed to hear. Maybe hearing the graphicness of it all would slap me back to reality, back to a place where I was perfectly content getting on one of those MegaBuses down at North Claiborne and Elysian Fields and leaving the state.

Blue eyes never wavered from my face. "I put a bullet in his skull and left him in the Atchafalaya."

I wanted to vomit at the visual, as well as the senseless loss of life.

And then I wanted to punch Lincoln for being so blunt, as though he knew that if he said it all matter-of-factly I'd wobble in my decision.

My neck strained as I glanced up at the sky. "Will you kill Tabitha?"

"Tabitha Thibadeaux? No. I walked out on the job. Jason—Nat's ex-husband—didn't take it lightly. They all . . . shit, how do I say this?" He coughed awkwardly, and then rolled to his side, resting on his elbow as he kept his gaze locked on my face. "Your girl got herself mixed up with the wrong crowd."

"How do you know that?"

He blindly reached for my hand and then lifted it, curling my fingers so that they brushed through the dark strands of his hair. Until my middle finger was pressed to a spot at the base of his skull.

"I don't understand."

"Jason's got a superiority complex. He brands those who work for him—I have one here, where you're touching me now. Didn't you ever get curious about your friend's tattoo on her forehead?"

"She said she got it on a whim."

"Not the way it works." Dropping my hand, he added, "She worked for him—who knows for how long—and at some point she decided to work for Nat instead. Jason took exception. Hence, the bodies of Banterelli and Welsh, who also ditched him. And, no, I had nothing to do with them two."

It just didn't seem possible that Tabby would be working for any of that. And yet, Lincoln had no reason to lie to me about her either. Hell, he'd been sent to *kill* her, which said it all, really.

She was still breathing, which meant she was just fine. For now.

I pushed up onto my elbows, my gaze landing on the cityscape just across the river. "We both know why I'm still here in N'Orleans. Why are you?"

"Too many connections," came his low response. "You can't leave a city when you've got unfinished business."

Intriguing. My thumb drummed a steady tempo against the rumpled blanket beneath me. "And when that business is done, you're going to leave?"

"Never let myself think that far."

"Because you don't think you'll ever take that step?"

He paused, the silence drawing out. And then, "Because I never really believed I'd be alive long enough to make a decision like that."

MAJOR ARCANA

FOURTEEN

Avery

M y stomach dropped at his gritty confession.

"Cap," I whispered, trying to stifle the horror in my tone, "don't talk like that. You're invincible."

He chuckled. "No one's invincible, sweetheart. Not even me."

Sweetheart.

Lids squeezing shut, I edged out, "It's my turn. Let me ask my question."

There was the soft ruffling as though he were repositioning himself, and then, "Shoot."

Dammit. Did he *always* have to bring me back to that? The man liked his guns—a fact I knew pretty well by now. Rolling up onto my shins, I set my hands on my baggy sweatpants at the knees. It was now or never.

You can do it.

I reached up to tighten my ponytail, just to buy myself time. A second trickled past, and then another. Swallowing hard, my chest heaved with courage. Fake courage, but courage nonetheless.

"I want you." *Keep going.* I squeezed the band of my ponytail loop again. "I know I shouldn't. I mean, for one, we're all wrong for each other. And second . . . about what Big Hampton told us—"

"I don't give a fuck what he said."

I blinked, startled. Glanced behind me in case he was actually talking to someone else. "I'm sorry," I said, "what?"

Lincoln's hands touched mine, lowering them from my ponytail and setting them on the hard planes of his chest. "I don't give a fuck what he said. You and me? Strangers until three weeks ago. I didn't know you. You didn't know me. If anyone has something to say—and why the hell would they when you don't even go by your legal name?— then that's on them."

Laughter warmed my chest. "You make it sound so easy."

"It is that easy." With a gentleness I didn't anticipate, he cupped my cheeks, his thumbs brushing over cheekbones. "I admire you. You admire me—"

"Don't push it, buddy," I muttered, though I was sure my smile belied my short tone.

He continued on as though I hadn't interrupted him at all. "You admire me, Ave. It might just be for my cock, but hell, I'll take it."

I set my hands on his knees, nails digging in as I waited for him to make a move. Although I'd never go so far as to say that I was submissive, by any means, he was the aggressor in our relationship. The one who'd pushed me up a wall and made me pant into the curve of my arm. The one, when seated in a room of people all having sex, who tore my panties straight off my hips and proceeded to make me come with his tongue and his fingers.

He pushed and I gave back, tenfold.

It was our thing.

But as I sat there with his thumbs caressing my cheeks and my hands on his knees . . . he did nothing but watch me. Haint-blue eyes tracking my face, dipping down to my neck, but he never moved closer. Never crashed his lips down on mine and made me beg for more.

A minute passed.

Then a second.

And all the while, my core tightened and my toes flexed in my shoes and my breathing grew more erratic as I wondered when he'd push me back and stake his claim.

"Take what you want."

My gaze snapped up to his. "What?"

His head dipped, mouth finding the curve of my ear to nibble on the flesh, and *oh God*, but that felt good. Mouth rasping against my skin, he murmured, "I'm teaching you a lesson." Another sharp bite at my ear, and then his tongue smoothed away the sting. "I told you—sometimes you gotta take what you want or you'll end up with nothing."

"What are you saying?"

"Don't be coy, that's our first rule." His hands fell from my face and he sat back, so that my fingers slipped off his knees.

"And our second?" God help me, but I already sounded turned on. I squeezed my knees together, but the pressure did nothing to alleviate the way my core pulsed.

Lincoln shook his head. "Tell me, Ave, what did you like about the times we hooked up?"

I laughed nervously. Reached up to tug at the neck of my T-shirt and pull it away from my skin. "It, ah, felt good."

"Goes without saying," he said, "but that's not what I mean. What did you like about it all? What made you go from, *I want to smash this guy over the head* to *I just want to fuck him?*"

Oh. That.

Shifting my weight farther back on my heels, I mustered up the confidence to get the words out. To really *think* about what it was that sent me from zero to one hundred in under a second. "I . . . I liked—" Jeez, this was not easy. I wet my bottom lip, then swung my gaze over to the brightly lit downtown area. "I liked—"

Without waiting for me to finish my sentence, Lincoln stood. He let out a low groan when his right knee straightened, and I grimaced in sympathy. No doubt he was still feeling the pain from Big Hampton's asshole lackeys.

My gaze trailed him as he moved the food off the blanket, and then as he circled around me to stand at my back. He kneeled there, my lower body sandwiched between his legs. The unexpected close contact made me jump, but I settled down as soon as his hands fitted themselves at my hips.

"I'm gonna tell you exactly what I liked."

Oh, God.

A shiver carved down my spine at his deep baritone by my ear, rustling the baby-hairs that hadn't made it into my ponytail. "All right," I managed to get out, wondering what protocol was when it came to my hands. Should I put them on his arms? Let them hang by my sides? Tangle them in his hair?

In the end, it didn't matter.

Not when he spoke as though the words were a piece of his soul, selected and chosen just for me. "I like the way you fit against me." His hands swept up my sides, following the indent of my waist to the slight weight of my breasts. "I noticed these first, how perfect you were on top."

Small as my breasts were, I still gasped when he pinched my nipple over the fabric of my T-shirt, pelvis bucking unintentionally.

"I like that too." His mouth dropped to my jaw, and he pressed a kiss there. "For a woman, your voice is so unique. Throaty, I thought once. But that's not the way you sound when you're in my arms. Your gasps"—he slipped his hand under my shirt—"make me hard in an instant. Your cries" —*please*, I thought, as he circled my nipple and tugged, hard—"are addictive enough that you've ruined me forever."

"Lincoln—"

His other hand went to the center of my back and gave a gentle push. It caught me off guard, and I went down willingly, landing on all fours as I twisted my head to try to look back at him.

"I like this, too," he growled, that big palm of his sliding down, down, down the ridges of my spine until it rested over the crevice of my butt. "I like how quick you are to put someone in their place, but with me, all you want is pleasure."

I want to be wanted.

"You look gorgeous, but I think . . ."

I waited for him to finish that thought, my ass suspended in the air, my braless breasts loose beneath my shirt. My neck strained as I held the position, my arms quivering with every effort it took not to turn around and demand to know why he'd stopped.

But then I felt a rush of cool air on my backend, and—

Oh. My. God.

He'd tugged down my sweats until they were pooled at my bent knees.

Thighs squeezing, I slammed my eyes shut. I should argue. Tell him to cut the shit and then yank the material right back into place.

"Spread your legs for me, sweetheart."

Cutting a glance through the darkness to the levee, I did as he ordered. There was no one around. Just him and me, *us*, with a Louis Armstrong song playing off in the distance and the quiet hum of cars as they drove along the other side of the levee.

At the barest touch of his finger to my inner thigh, my head dropped and my fingers curled into the blanket beneath me.

"You know what else I like?"

The pad of his finger hit home base, circling my clit with the slightest hint of pressure, wrenching a sob from my mouth. He pressed down on the sensitive nub, brought another finger into play, circling and circling and circling until my voice cracked out his name.

His low chuckle echoed in my ears. "I love how wet you are. How eagerly your pussy drips for me. How just being out here, with the possibility of anyone seeing us, turns you on so much that you're already shaking." He thrust two fingers inside me, curling them just right, right off the get-go, so that my spine arched and my core squeezed around him.

"Why is that?" he demanded, and then my ponytail was lifting off my shoulder and being wrapped around a masculine fist. "Don't be coy."

His first rule.

His *only* rule.

The truth hovered on my tongue, but his thrusting fingers stole my attention. Greedily, I sank my hips back, seeking more of that deliciousness. God, it felt so good. I wanted more of that pressure, more of that friction that only he could give me—

He pulled on my ponytail, and my teeth cracked together.

Like he'd flicked a switch, the words spilled from me on a harsh gasp: "I'm tired of hiding." His hold on my hair loosened and I immediately missed the contact, however wrong that was. "I want to feel alive. I—Lincoln, *please*. Yes, *yes*, just like that."

He worked another finger into me, that sensuous slide feeling that much tighter. It was almost too tight, but I knew—oh, I knew, that his cock was bigger. Thicker. Sweat beading on my forehead, I bared my soul and whispered, "I want to be loved. I don't care who knows. I want to scream it from the rooftops, and not care who sees me, *us*."

"*Fuck*."

As his fingers slipped from my core, I bunched the blankets in my fists and prayed that I hadn't just made the biggest mistake of my life. But I wouldn't hide—he'd asked for my truth, hadn't he? He'd asked me what I liked.

I'd be damned if I apologized for any of it.

"The next time we do this," came Lincoln's hard voice, "it's gonna be somewhere private. Iron bars sort of private. But there's not a chance in hell that I can . . . Christ, you're beautiful. Turn over onto your back, Avery. I want to see your face when I sink into your body."

I flipped over—like there was really any other choice.

There wasn't.

For some reason, Lincoln had walked into my life. I wasn't a huge believer in fate, despite the fact that I read tarot cards for a living.

And yet, it seemed like fate had a hand in tonight. Not a single soul walked past up on the levee. It was just me and Lincoln, and when he reached down to pull off his shirt, I felt myself grow warm. Or warm*er*, as the case might be.

"Cap," I said, almost reverently, kicking my sweatpants and underwear off completely, "you've got some ink on you."

It was too dark to make out the details, but there was enough light to note the dark tattoos covering his chest and the upper parts of his arms. His shoulders were big, biceps even more powerful. Unable to stop myself, I propped myself up on one elbow and traced the hard ridges of his abdomen with my other hand.

He was . . . godlike.

"Thor."

I felt him tense. "What?"

"I think that"—oh man, now was *not* the time to begin suffering from verbal diarrhea—"Katie may have been mistaken in calling you Captain America. Thor might be more . . . appropriate."

There was a minute pause, in which I ran over every other idiotic thing that could possibly come out of my mouth, and then his hand was pressing me down into the blanket before sweeping it over my body to cup me between my legs.

A hiss escaped me, to which he only let out a dark laugh.

"Good thing I come equipped with a hammer."

He slipped a finger into my pussy, and I didn't know whether to moan or laugh, it felt so sinfully good. The sound that *did* emerge was strangled. "Put the hammer to good use, please."

"Take off your shirt and I will."

He didn't have to ask me twice.

I whipped that bad boy off in the next breath, then

used the fabric to hook around the back of his neck and pull him down onto me.

He caught his weight on his palms and didn't waste another second before claiming my lips. The kiss was obsession personified—needy, raw, demanding. His tongue swept along the cushion of my lower lip, and I opened to him. Giving him anything and everything he wanted.

And he took, like he'd taught me to do.

But I'd learned the same tonight.

Letting go of one side of the T-shirt, I skirted my hand down over his chest, his abs, and then circled his cock with a tight grip.

"Not tonight," he grunted, trying to bat my hand away. "I'm two seconds away from fucking you."

I nipped at his jaw. "Then I have two seconds to make you lose your mind this way."

I made good on that vow, swallowing his dick with my fist. Squeezing tight on the ride up to the head, twisting at the crown the way he'd enjoyed when it'd been my mouth doing the work at the Basement, and then diving back down to the thick base. Over and over again, until his mouth was open, and his eyes were shut, and he was cursing me and praising me all in the same breath.

Only then did he shove my hand away and reach for his wallet. There was the telltale sound of a condom wrapper being torn open, and then my legs were being pushed wide and I didn't even have the chance to prepare because—

"Oh!"

He buried himself to the hilt, pausing only long enough to mutter, "Feel free to shout how you're feeling to the rooftops," before he pulled out and thrust back in.

Forget shouting from the rooftops.

If I didn't hold on, I'd be shoved all the way out into the Mississippi River.

Wrapping my legs around his waist and clutching his inked shoulders, I looked up at the man whose soul, he claimed, was as dark as the devil's. But that wasn't true—he'd let his guard down tonight, peeling back his layers until he'd been completely exposed.

Neck muscles straining, he angled his hips differently. With every thrust, his pelvis ground against my clit, and it was too much. My head thrashed to the side, and as Lincoln dominated my body, I caught sight of the city that had buried me in the underworld of New Orleans.

If it weren't for my past, I wouldn't be here now.

Clinging to a man who could pass for a Norse god.

Moaning his name like I'd never get enough of him.

Rubbing my hands along his inked skin.

This close, I could make out that the tattoos were of numbers. They weren't in a line. They weren't in order. And in the back of my head, I realized what they had to be.

His kills.

Each and every one.

My breath caught, and he leaned down to capture my lips with his, tangling our tongues together.

He was powerful. He was deadly.

"More," I whispered, one hand landing directly over his heart, "don't hold anything back."

Lincoln cursed, his hips momentarily pausing, before continuing the pace that sent my toes curling and my heart thudding. "You were made for me, Avery," he whispered back, his breath harsh as he took me, "everything that you are . . . was made for *me*."

He reached down, one finger landing on my clit, and that was all I needed to go over the edge. I came, calling out his name, and he followed a moment later, back strained, mouth pressed in a firm line, blue eyes focused solidly on my face. Like he never wanted to forget a thing about this night.

He was powerful. He was deadly. And for tonight, he was mine.

FIVE OF SWORDS

FIFTEEN

Avery

We fell asleep on that blanket, our discarded food scattered around us, the horizon turning into a smattering of orange and yellow and pink.

Lincoln had mentioned that he rarely slept, but his chest lifted and fell evenly under my cheek.

With the sun rising like a spotlight on my sins, I gently pulled out from his embrace and righted my tangled T-shirt. Like any other stubborn man, Lincoln had foregone wearing his shirt when we passed out, and I took the opportunity now to study the tattoos inked into his tan skin.

Numbers.

So many numbers.

Some were single digit, others two digits, some marked as though they were birthdates. In the early morning glow, it was easy to see that he'd sought to give his kills some sort of haven. Angel wings stretched across his chest, and the numbers were seemingly "stitched" into the feathers themselves.

He'd called himself a sinner.

And me a saint.

But he had it all wrong.

My gaze latched onto the firearms I'd urged him to remove last night. They lay exactly where he'd set them, and, on silent feet, I moved to that corner of the blanket and dropped to my knees. Picked up the knife that looked like something out of an action movie. Tested its weight in my grip, and then glanced back at the man who'd rocked my world for hours without tiring.

One expertly placed thrust of the knife and I could have everything I'd ever wanted. Jay Foley dead, at my hand. My freedom, finally.

Be brave.

Be bold.

Blood thundered in my ears, as loud as the tugboat foghorns we'd heard late into the night as they powered down the mighty Mississippi.

I readjusted my grip on the knife, twisting my head so I could look at Lincoln again. He shifted in his sleep, arms reaching out as though missing my heat pressed against him.

Yeah, he had it all wrong.

I was the saint, the sinner, and at the end of the day, I was the one who bled vengeance.

XI

JUSTICE

MAJOR ARCANA

SIXTEEN

Lincoln

There was something to be said about waiting for your boss to show up when your ass was already on the bench—especially when you had news that could potentially change the game.

"Next!"

I stepped up to the counter at Café Vieux Carre, and promptly swallowed a groan when I saw it was Sarah at the register. Her eyes were bloodshot—tears, not weed, if I had to guess—and she looked like she'd just rolled straight out of bed.

Putting it bluntly, she looked like hell.

"Mornin', Sarah." I paused, waiting for her usual flirtatious greeting and, because I was still riding on the high of sex with Avery all night, tried to be nice. "You doing okay?"

Her ponytail slashed through the air as she angrily twisted around, already grabbing a Styrofoam cup from its stack. "I'm just *fine*."

Oh, Jesus.

Even I knew what "fine" meant—as did the guy behind

me in line. He muttered something that sounded suspiciously like, "Fuck that," and then hightailed it out the front door. Smart man. If I didn't have to be here this morning, I'd do the same thing.

With a hard *clang!* Sarah dumped new coffee grinds into the machine, and then shoved the cup into the appropriate spot. "Milk?" she snapped, hand on her hip as she faced me.

"Uh . . ." My gaze darted to the left and then to the right. No one seemed to be noticing the café's barista having a meltdown. Either they were oblivious or had already received her special treatment for the day and were determined to keep their heads down and out of sight. *Wish I could do the same.* "Yeah, milk's great. I'll take the usual."

As if I ever chose something else besides a *café au lait.*

Bending at the waist, Sarah flashed me her jean-clad ass and yanked open the mini-fridge.

Yup, something bad was about to happen, and I checked behind me and counted the number of steps it'd take for me to escape. Six. But only if I wasn't running.

"Here's your milk, *Sergeant.*"

I whipped around just in time to see her pour soy milk into my coffee. My eyes went wide when she didn't stop pouring, and the coffee that should have been toffee in color was suddenly looking like shit that had just been pumped out of a cow's udder.

She slammed the carton down on the counter, and the coffee splattered over the lip of the cup. Palm out for my debit card, she said, "I hope it's as weak as Marco's dick."

Halfway wanting to protest paying for what had to be the shittiest coffee in the city, I pulled out my wallet and handed over the card anyway. "Guessin' y'all went on a date and it didn't go well?"

"*Didn't go well?*" Sarah's brows furrowed together. "His dick was as big as this straw." She pointed to the straw in question, and I winced.

I opened my mouth. "Not everyone can be—"

"He's overcompensating. *Five* daiquiri shops. Literally, who the hell needs *five*? You try one slushy, you've tried them all."

It probably wasn't the best time to tell her that the daiquiri shops were just a front for passing drugs through the city. She waved her hand around as she continued her rant, my debit card clutched between her fingers, and I made a quick dodge of my hand to snap it out of her grasp.

I missed the first time. Snagged it on the second.

Shoved the bastard into my wallet and picked up my mutilated coffee.

"You have a good day now, Sarah."

"I bet you have a small dick, too, if you're friends with him!" she shouted at my back. "It's the small dicks club!"

"What the hell have you been joining since I suspended you, Ash?"

Fuck. As if the morning wasn't going just fantastically shitty already.

Swinging my head toward the direction of my lieutenant's voice, I watched his approach with a sip of my coffee. Nearly came up choking when I tasted how awful it was.

When Stefan Delery was less than a foot away, I muttered, "How badly do you feel about booting me off the force?"

His mustache twitched. "First," he grunted, "you're *suspended,* not fired. I'm not interested in getting the union involved in this shit. Second, not bad at all. It's been fucking sunshine and rainbows showing up to work without having to see your mean mug."

Yeah, I was going to ignore all of that. "Great. For the greater cause, get me something else." I dumped the cup into the closest garbage can. "You don't want me having this conversation without coffee, and I sure as hell can't go up there again."

He glanced past me toward the register. "Don't tell me you fucked her, man."

I'd been coming here for years and had never given her a second glance. And now that I was all wrapped up—literally—in Avery . . . yeah, that ship was never sailing. Not a chance in hell.

"Nah. Set her up on a date with Marco Carvino. Turns out the man's loaded in every place but his pants."

"That's unfortunate."

"So's my coffee that was just subjected to soy milk." I clapped him on the shoulder. "*Café au lait,* large. I'll even smile for you when you hand it over."

Not wanting to give him the chance to turn me down, I was out the front door in six steps and taking a seat at one of the outdoor picnic tables in ten. My back to the café, I slipped my sunglasses on my face and watched the street. If I'd had the opportunity to have this conversation at the station, I would have, but with my suspension still looming over my head, there wasn't any other choice.

L-T was weird about meeting at people's apartments, and rarely—aka never—allowed others to visit his house.

So, we were doing this shit here, and all I could do was hope that no one overheard.

The door to the coffee shop swung open, and Delery ambled over, two coffee cups in hand. He slid one over to me with a dry, "Soy for you," and didn't even blink twice when I flashed him the bird and took a small sip.

It went down smoothly, albeit scorching its way down my throat, and I nodded in satisfaction.

"What're we doing here?" Delery took the bench opposite mine and clasped his cup between his hands. "You know we're not even supposed to be talking right now."

We both knew I had the upper hand in this situation. Maybe in the walls of the precinct, Stefan Delery reigned superior, but we weren't on NOPD property. And the shit I had for him was completely off the books anyway.

Months of work in the making.

Years, if you counted the time that I'd been making moves without the New Orleans Police Department behind me—and even when they had, I'd always skirted the line of illegal. Rank like Delery turned a blind eye when I got them the results they wanted. But this sort of break . . . it could change things. Hell, it could change *everything*.

And then Avery would be free.

She hadn't asked for a savior, and it wasn't like I had a damn halo above my head—but involving her in this would mean setting aside years of my life and taking a damn breath of my own.

Just like her, I was ready to live.

Reaching into the inner pocket of my jacket, I cast another glance toward the street and then slipped a small notebook from its sleeve. I dropped it on the table, thumbing it open to reveal a folded sheet of paper.

"Look at that," I said, then took another pull of my drink.

I waited, stomach clenched, for my lieutenant to palm it flat.

His surprise registered in the twitch of his mustache. "You have a point in showing me the obituary for the mayor's stepdaughter?" He rubbed his jawline. Tugged on his right ear. "Jesus, that was some sad shit."

Guilt thrived in my veins like I'd taken a shot of a depressant, and I purposely distracted myself by flipping to the next page of the notebook. Withdrawing the ID from where I'd quickly stashed it this morning, I slid it over to Delery. "Notice anything?"

Fingers to the laminated plastic, my lieutenant dragged the ID closer and peered down at it. "Avery Washington." He glanced up at me. "Am I supposed to recognize her name?"

My gut told me I was overstepping boundaries here. Not even overstepping—*leaping.*

You have the chance to save her while keeping her safe.

Up until three weeks ago, I wouldn't have questioned my decision. When you cared for little, not a damn thing mattered. I did my job, just like I had, once, for Ambideaux. At least this one was closer to the state line of being legal. But with Avery to consider . . . shit, no more second-guessing.

It was the right move.

It *had* to be the right move.

Clearing my throat, I nodded my head toward the ID. "It's one of Rafael's," I muttered, referring to the tech whiz over on Basin who was known for making fake ID's, to say nothing of the crazy sort of magic he wielded over the internet. "You stare at enough of those like I have in the past, and you start to recognize the small details."

Like the extra space he added after the person's birthdate.

And the hologram that was a damn near replica to the real Louisiana ID but was off . . . just enough for someone like me to notice.

"Ignore the dark hair, Stefan. Look at her face."

Sitting in my SUV after commandeering one of Avery's "spare" ID's from her wallet, and dropping her off at her apartment, it was hard to believe I'd been such an idiot. How had I not spotted the similarities before? The green ring around her hazel eyes and the defiant set to her chin, and a myriad of other small quirks that were intrinsically *hers*.

Maybe because you didn't want to.

Delery's mouth dropped open. "Ash, you're not saying that . . ."

Don't do this to her. Don't expose her.

I swatted the thoughts away like a fly getting smacked into nonexistence.

Elbows on the table, I spoke, voice low. "It's her. I know it's her, which means this shit with Foley can finally be put to rest."

Delery's gaze went back and forth between the obituary picture and then the ID. "You think she'll testify?"

"To the fact that her stepfather has got a sick fetish for underage girls? Why the fuck *wouldn't* she testify?"

It was the reason Ambideaux had sent me to murder her, after all. What better way to strike back than to take out the one person your enemy prized most of all? There *was* no better way. Me going after Avery at thirteen was like cutting Foley off at the knees. If any of my investigations over the last few years had proven anything, it was that he liked them young and innocent. Avery had been that way, perfect pickings for a man like the mayor.

And it was the reason I'd spent the last number of years working underground in this city I called home. Tailing leads, talking to all manner of girls who'd found themselves connected to my bastard father in some way.

And sometimes, the rage got a little too much to handle. Sometimes it wasn't Foley's victims I came across but other juveniles who'd been dealt an unlucky hand of fate. And, sometimes, I voluntarily chose to do what I do best and take out the predators—I wasn't a modern-day Robin Hood by any stretch of the imagination. Had never wished to be someone else's hero.

But when you split your time between working the beat with your coworkers and then living in the trenches with the vilest humans the world had to offer, being a little trigger-happy wasn't necessarily a bad thing.

Not if it let someone else breathe a little easier when they went to sleep at night.

And even if it carved another sin into my rapidly growing tally.

Delery sat back, the ID in one hand and the obituary in the other. "I'm not going to lie to you, Ash. If this . . . Miss *Washington* doesn't come forward with solid proof, I'm not sure how much longer the NOPD can have your back on this."

My mouth curled in a sneer. "Christ, do you *hear* yourself, Stefan?" I planted a hand down on the notebook. "Don't be like every other pussy in this department, bending over to take it up the ass. He's a mayor. He's not fucking *God*."

My lieutenant swallowed. "You know Harlonne's in his back pocket. You *know* how hard it's been for me to keep this on the down low when no one's willing to go against the prick—at least, not until he's out of office."

Fury boiled deep in my gut as I pushed my chair onto its hind legs and tried to rein in my temper. Exploding on my boss wouldn't do me any good—not for keeping my job and absolutely not for landing Foley in prison. Let him be someone else's bitch and see how much he liked it.

Air pumped into my lungs as I inhaled deep. *Be calm, man.*

"So, what you're saying is, I can either convince Avery

to testify or I'm shit out of luck on this. Even with all the other evidence I've gathered."

"You don't have evidence when those girls won't repeat to a judge what they told you. What they wouldn't even tell you over a damn *audio* recorder because they're terrified of the consequences. You've got stories, Sergeant. Grotesque, ugly stories told to you on street corners in the dead of night, but nothing more."

It all boiled down to Avery, and wasn't that the true irony in this situation?

When she'd spoken of Foley, she hadn't mentioned abuse. It was possible he hadn't messed with her yet, just biding his time until she was ripe enough to pluck off the proverbial tree branch.

And she'd been a virgin . . . until you.

Delery sipped his coffee, then wiped a hand across his mouth. "You've been a cop for a real long time, Lincoln. You're a good one. A damn good one. But you know what'll work and what won't. You're too close to this case to even be remotely objective anymore. *There's not enough evidence.*"

Head pounding with undiluted frustration, I slammed the notebook shut. "Sometimes, I think the reason this 'case' hasn't gone anywhere is because none of you want it to."

My lieutenant slid the obituary and ID across the table. "For whatever reason, you've got a vendetta against the man. I don't like him—never have. But I know my place and I like my job. Not everyone's you, Sergeant. Not everyone cares."

He made it sound like I wore my heart on my sleeve.

That couldn't be further from the truth. Hell, the only person I'd even come close to sharing any part of myself with was Avery, the one woman I had to convince to come clean and *not* kill her stepfather, so that all the work I'd done for years could finally be done.

She wasn't the only one running.

She wasn't the only one whose life had been brutally torn in half by the man running this city.

But she was the only one who had complete power to end it all—for good.

FOUR OF PENTACLES

SEVENTEEN

Avery

U niversity students were everywhere—and I did
mean *everywhere*.

The good news: Pershing University was
equipped with maps throughout the campus, which meant
that it *should* be easy to navigate my way to the head
administration building.

The bad news: there was some sort of sporting event
happening today. I'd never seen so many bare chests with
letters painted in green across their lanky forms.

A P stumbled his way into my line of sight, the paint
on his chest half washed away as he shook a water bottle
then dumped it over the top of his head. "Fuck yeah!" he
hollered, throwing the bottle into the crowd.

It bounced off a girl's head some seven feet away.

I'd always thought I'd missed out on the whole college
experience, but one glance at the chaos around me told me
maybe *I* was the one who'd ended up getting lucky.

You're way too old for this.

In terms of years, maybe not so much.

Based on life experience, I might as well have arthritis,

a cane, and a tomb picked out at one of the city's notorious aboveground cemeteries.

"Excuse me," I muttered, giving up all pretense of playing nice. I palmed a guy's shoulder and shoved him roughly to the side. Slipped into the next open pocket within the crowd—and then repeated the process until I was nose-to-one-of-the-campus-maps, trying to determine exactly where I stood in relation to the admin offices.

Pershing University was seated in the center of New Orleans' Uptown neighborhood, right on the streetcar line that started in the French Quarter and cut through the city. Unlike the campuses I saw on TV, Pershing wasn't massive in acreage but more jam-packed into a centralized area, its perimeter flirting with surrounding residential homes.

My gaze tracked my location—the quad by the main dining hall—and then followed through to my end destination. Not far, maybe a five minute walk.

With one glance at the mayhem happening on the quad, I turned my back on the campus party and stepped on the pebbled pathway. Limestone buildings reached toward the sky on my left, and what had to be the smoothest street in the city graced my right.

Pershing was beautiful—if only its president wasn't a total kidnapping prick.

By the time I climbed up the front steps and then rode the elevator to the third floor, I was sweating under my armpits, and the unease once again began to cling to my confidence. Visiting Big Hampton was a bold move, albeit an unexpected one. I hoped.

A bell jangled up above as I pushed open the glass door and stepped into the seating room. Luxurious artwork covered the walls, and potted plants sat atop every small table.

The receptionist's head jerked up at my entrance, and

a wide smile spread across her face. "Oh! Hello, dear." She pushed the glasses that were perched on her nose up to the top of her head. "Do you have an appointment with one of our counselors?"

Luckily, I'd thought ahead.

Closing the distance from the door to the front desk, I smiled down at the woman, taking note of her nametag. "Hi there, Ms. Betty. I actually called earlier this morning? About the article that I'm doing for the *Times-Picayune*?"

Snapping her fingers, she exclaimed, "Ah, right! Yes, yes. Ms. Samantha Lovelace. Yes, I'm so sorry. I've got you all marked down for your appointment with Mr. Hampton." She tapped a finger to her nose, staring at the expanse of her messy desk, and then snapped up a sheet from the far-right corner. "Here we go. He's expecting you —2 p.m., right on the dot."

I forced a smile. "Sorry I didn't get here a little earlier, as promised. I wasn't expecting the campus to be so busy today."

"Oh, you're just *fine*, dear. It's Pershing's one-hundred-year-old anniversary this week, so there is celebration aplenty." Beneath her breath, she muttered something that sounded very much like, "and so much booze."

My fake smile flirted with a real one. "So long as Mr. Hampton still has room for me today, I think we can include something about the anniversary along with my article."

Green eyes blinked up at me. "He would *love* that. Good press is the best kind of press."

I was pretty sure that the saying went "any kind of press was good press," but I wasn't about to correct her.

"Why don't you follow me?" She pushed back her chair and came around the corner of the desk, gesturing for me to step ahead of her. Clamping my purse close to my side, I held my chin up and kept my shoulders pressed back.

Act like you belong here.

"Coming here today, I can't believe I chose to go to Loyola University instead." The lie nearly made me grin, and because Samantha Lovelace had always been a more naïve version of myself, I blithely added, "It's just so *beautiful* here. Oh my God, the campus is like something out of a fairy tale."

"Isn't it?" Betty patted me on the shoulder like I was a good dog. "Don't worry, dear, we won't hold it against you that you went to *that* school over Pershing."

That school.

Wouldn't she die a little inside if she knew I'd never even graduated high school?

One day I would, though. I'd get my GED and then my college degree. And maybe, when all this had blown over, I'd apply to vet school, just to see.

I was one step closer to freedom, but first Joshua Hampton had to get me there.

Betty knocked, twice, and then at a booming masculine voice calling out "enter!" she edged the door open and popped her head in. "You all ready for your two o' clock? Ms. Lovelace is here."

"What the hell kind of name is *Lovelace*?"

A fake one. Definitely a fake one.

Not to mention I'd come up with it when I was thirteen —no one should judge a girl that age.

"Is that a yes, Josh?" Betty asked.

"Send her in."

Facing me again, good old Betty gave me an encouraging grin that could have read anywhere between *go get 'em tiger* and *bless your heart*.

One quick nod of appreciation later and I was in the

office, the door shut behind me, as I looked to the man of the hour behind his desk.

His eyes narrowed. "*You.*"

Time to make the magic happen.

Perky smile on my face, I took the available seat across from him, purse in my lap. "How amazing to see you again, Mr. Hampton. It's been what . . . three, maybe four days since you held me at gunpoint?"

He blanched, gaze skirting behind me to stare at the door. "What are you doing here, Ms. *Lovelace*?"

"What? No small talk?"

"My secretary said you were here for an article about the mayoral race."

My lips quirked. "I am. Unfortunately, the information will go no further than me, but I can't imagine how you'd have a problem with that." I leaned in to whisper, "I mean, no offense, but considering recent behavior, you'd have a lawsuit on your hands if word got out about your ventures in kidnapping."

"My . . ." His brows went high, and his hand, which had been balled into a fist, smoothed out over the desk. "I'm not going to repeat myself again—what do you want?"

I gave a small shrug. "I want what *you* want—Foley dead. Although I'm going to harbor a guess that our reasons for why we're praying for a miracle that our lovely mayor drops dead are for two different reasons." Reaching into my purse, I pulled out a manila folder and propped it open on the desk. "You tell me what you know, and I'll do the same. I think you'll find that we're both reaching for the same outcome."

An outcome that didn't include Lincoln Asher dead.

My heart twisted at just the thought of it alone, and I suppressed the emotion for the sake of staying on my toes.

I couldn't allow myself to dwell too deeply on him—not right now. Not when this was a life or death situation, literally.

At Hampton's stubborn silence, I sifted through the leaflets of paper I'd brought along. The copious notes I'd taken over the years were finally paying off. Although if Hampton failed to cooperate with the plan I had in mind, it wouldn't matter what I said today.

"How did you meet Nat?" I asked casually, hand coming down to rest on the final sheet of paper in the bunch.

Hampton stared at me. "What does that have to do with anything?"

I met his gaze unflinchingly. "Haven't you ever wondered how she's so wrapped up in the politics of this city? She married Ambideaux, worked on her back for my stepfather, and now"—I offered a little smile—"she's fucking *you*. The richest man in the city, the mayor, and an esteemed university president like yourself. Why?"

"Maybe she's got good taste."

Doubtful. All three of them were creeps of the first order.

Shaking my head ruefully, I murmured, "Or maybe she's got an ulterior motive."

He barked out a laugh at that. "Of course she's got an ulterior motive. She's a hustler, Ms. *Lovelace,* and that's what hustlers do. They'll social climb until they're either dead, in jail, or living under a fake name in Mexico. I have absolutely *no* delusions that she wants me for anything but my money and my status."

Jeez, he was a cocky bastard.

Not that I'd expected anything else.

Drumming my fingers on the desk, I drew out the

silence until his cheeks began to redden with impatience. Then, "And why do you want her?"

His stance stiffened, mouth going flat as he stared at me. "She has a great rack and an even better pussy. Does that answer your question?"

"Not even close, but the sarcasm is appreciated."

His molars ground together and he shoved away from the desk, chair nearly toppling over until he caught the back. "This *appointment* is getting old. I have no interest in playing games. Either say what you came to say or get out of my office."

The sweat that kicked off its marathon under my armpits spread to my chest, between my breasts. It'd be so easy to succumb to the fear and the nerves, but neither fear nor nerves would get me out of this mess.

"I don't believe you're a bad man," I murmured, dragging my folder close and flipping to the front of the stack. "Sometimes good people do bad things." *Like me right now.* "Sometimes"—I flicked my gaze up to check out Hampton's expression—"you find yourself in a tough position. Right or wrong, good or bad. You can only do what you think is right."

His eyes narrowed into slits. "How lovely to know that you don't believe me to be an asshole."

Pretentious asshole, more like it.

Shrugging off his bad attitude, I returned my attention to the folder before me and to the notes that I'd faked just this morning. *Sometimes good people do bad things.* My new motto—for better or for worse.

"Nat's come to visit me for years in Jackson Square, Mr. Hampton. I've read her cards enough to think I know her reasonably well."

"No one knows Nat well. Not you, not me, not her damn ex-husband. *No one.*"

My plan was risky, and there was a good chance Big Hampton would laugh in my face. But if there was anything I'd learned from watching the world behind the curtain of reading cards, it was that there was nothing more destructive—nothing more *implosive*—than pitting two self-centered people against each other and watching the sparks fly.

Flexing my fingers to subtly shake out the nerves, I pulled out the three tarot cards I'd layered at the back of the folder. "Tell me, have you ever had your tarot cards read?"

Mouth curling in disgust, Hampton snapped, "Do I look like someone who believes in that shit?"

Judgmental jerk. I wouldn't even deign him a response for that one—although it did make me feel better for what I was about to do. One by one, I laid out the three cards before me on the oak desk, pushing my chair back with the hope that curiosity would bite Joshua Hampton in the ass and propel him to see the cards I'd pulled.

"The thing is," I drawled, dropping the pitch of my voice to match the throaty tenor I always used in the square, "tarot is a lot like Murphy's Law, Mr. Hampton. If you believe something *will* go wrong, it no doubt will. But within tarot, I like to think of it like . . . if your mind is constantly obsessing over one thought or idea, it'll naturally manifest in the cards you pull."

From my jacket I pulled my velvet pouch where I stored my cards. Emptying them out, I set the deck on the desk, to the left of the three splayed cards. With my palm, I rolled the deck out, so that they formed a shallow arc.

Stepping back, I met Hampton's gaze. "Humor me, sir. Why don't you pick a card?"

Jaw clenching, he looked from me to the desk and then

back again. "Nat does this?" he asked, and there was no denying the hesitation coating his tone.

My lips turned up in a smile. "Weekly. She's quite the *fanatic* about coming to see me."

Indecision danced across his features.

The seconds dragged on. I refused to let my smile dip, refused to holler like a maniac when he caved and approached the desk like he had chains locked around his ankles.

"I can pick any card?" he asked, sounding doubtful.

"Whatever card speaks to you."

Please let this work.

I was desperate to fiddle with something, just to work out the excess nerves, but I forced my hands to my sides.

His hand hesitated over the middle of the arc, hovering. He glanced at me over his shoulder, scrutinizing me with narrowed eyes, and it took everything in my power to keep my expression passive . . . even though, on the inside, I was dying for him to make a pick.

Over the years, it wasn't only people's stories I'd recorded, but the cards they typically picked from the spread—and which number they were in a lineup. Confident people tended to pick from the front end of the deck, as though assuming that even in their readings, they were always ahead. Those who were more sensitive chose from the middle, like they were shoving through the murky in-between and looking for some kind of guidance.

Joshua Hampton was a confident man.

A man who didn't believe in the art of tarot or anything that he couldn't touch tangibly.

It was obvious that he wanted power and money. Even more obvious that the only thing he despised more than someone messing with his kid was a person who threatened his power *or* his money.

His fingertips flirted with the very first card in the spread, and then, turning his body to face me, he selected the second card.

Pulled it from its spot.

Turned it over and squinted at the words at the bottom of the card.

He cleared his throat. "Four of Disks."

Also known as Power, the card I'd placed in that exact spot for him to select, knowing that it would stroke his ego and make him more malleable. *Thank you, Lincoln, for showing me the way to* not *read tarot properly.* After all, if he hadn't decided to teach himself to read tarot, by picking my cards in advance, I would never have even given thought to doing the same to Hampton now.

Only, unlike Lincoln, I had no plans to tell the university president that I'd had a hand in anything at all.

"How interesting," I purred, stepping close to make a show of craning my neck to see the card he held in his hand. "And how appropriate."

"Yeah?"

I tapped my temple then pointed my finger at him. "I was under the impression you wanted to be mayor."

He frowned, staring down at me. "I do."

Without giving him the chance to protest, I plucked the card from his grasp. "Then there's no better card to pull. Being mayor is like being the most powerful man in N'Orleans. Seems like you've been thinking real hard about this, Mr. Hampton."

"I think of nothing else."

"No?" I gestured to the spread again. "Why don't you pick another card? See if Murphy's Law is working in your favor again—the tarot version of the law, I mean."

His Adam's apple bobbed down the length of his neck, but unlike with his first selection, he wasted no time in reaching for the cards again. Palm open, he waved his hand from the front to the back, hesitated, and then his fingers were pushing at the third to last card, removing it from its pack.

I stifled a sigh of relief.

I'd put three possible cards for him at the back, but my first choice was the one he'd gone for.

Must be my lucky day.

He flipped it over and immediately held it up for me to view. "Six of Disks."

Success—literally. I gave him a bright smile. "Looks like your path to mayor will be greeted with success. How fortunate."

"Yeah?" He pulled back his arm to stare down at the card. "Just like that?"

I shrugged. "Nothing is guaranteed, and free will can change anything."

With another glance down at Success, he set it down, and promptly let curiosity bite him in the ass—just like I'd hoped it would.

Knuckles pressed into the desk, Hampton leaned his body toward the three cards I'd first laid out. "Are these for you?" he asked.

Not even close.

Twisting around, I leaned up against the desk and folded my arms over my chest. "Those?" I shook my head. "Unfortunately, those were the last cards I picked for Nat."

Hampton jerked in my direction. "Why are you showing them to me?"

Because I'm hoping you're dumb enough to fall right into the trap.

And then, like I was putting on a stage performance on Broadway, my tone hardened as I murmured, "Honestly, after what you did to Lincoln and me, I had no desire to help you whatsoever. For all I care, you could rot in hell. The hotter the flames, the more satisfied I'll be."

His nostrils flared. "And yet here you are."

"And yet here I am." Reaching over, I tugged the three cards close to me. "You see, Mr. Hampton, I'm the type of person who'll stop a group of idiot boys from assaulting a young woman." If he caught my reference, his expression didn't even twitch in acknowledgment. I pressed on. "For all I've been through, I just want to help people. Nat's been coming to me for years now, and I've read cards for her at every stage of her life."

I lifted my gaze, climbed the tight fit of the man's suit, and fixed my attention on his face. "I would love to let this go. The idea of helping *you* of all people turns my stomach, but here I am, once again playing the saint because I just can't help myself."

Voice tight, he bit out, "And your point is?"

"Here are the cards that I last pulled for Nat. Read them to me."

Hand balling into a fist, he dropped it to the desk and leaned forward to look at the first card. "Eight of Swords."

I swallowed a smile. "That'd be Interference."

He visibly stiffened.

"Read the next, sir."

Free hand coming up to run the course along his jawline, he looked to the next card. "Death."

Wincing for dramatic effect, I placed my hand to my chest. "How unfortunate."

This time, I didn't even need to prod him into telling me the next and final card. He stared down at it, his cheeks turning red from what could only be rage or embarrassment.

"It's The Emperor," he breathed out, turning to me. "What does this even mean? Is this about Whiskey Bay?"

Sometimes good people do bad things.

I took the card from him, drew in a deep breath, and then lied. "It's about you, Mr. Hampton. She came to me wanting to talk about a love interest, and then . . ." I shrugged. "Well, I saw the way you acted toward her the other night, and as much as I'd *love* to see you go down in flames—"

"Yes," he ground out, cutting me off, "you mentioned that."

"—it seemed only fair that I tell you what she told me. She was *very* pleased when she left, which is a little alarming, obviously, considering the nature of the cards. I mean, for her to feel so strongly against you, clearly you must have something that she wants. Right?"

His nails scraped along the desk as his shoulders hunched. "She keeps mentioning how happy it makes her when I give her money to spend how she pleases."

No surprise there.

"Hmm." I bit down on my thumb, pretending to give the situation a lot of thought. "And she *has* mentioned marriage to me before in our sessions. So, that's troubling. Unless, you know, you aren't particularly concerned about her wanting to marry you for your money and then, well . . ." I tapped Death, just to make him squirm.

And squirm he did.

Back going ramrod straight, Hampton twisted from the desk, hands on his hips. "If that's all you've got for me, Ms. *Lovelace*, I've got to get back to work."

"Oh, I don't want to hold you."

I slipped the cards back into their velvet pouch, tucked my folder into my jacket again, and moved toward the door. Only when my hand was on the doorknob did I pause and glance back to say, "Free will is such a powerful thing, Mr. Hampton. Just remember that nothing is ever set in stone."

He didn't offer a response, but I wasn't looking for one.

I'd planted the seed of distrust. For an already suspicious man like Joshua Hampton, I had a gut feeling that the seed was all he needed to attack anyone who threatened his kingdom.

But kingdoms rose and kingdoms fell, and one by one, I wouldn't stop until they all came tumbling down.

XVI

THE TOWER

MAJOR ARCANA

EIGHTEEN

Avery

"You need a date, and I don't care what Captain America says, I was your one and only first," Katie hollered from the doorway. "Which means that I deserve the chance to sweep you off your feet."

The eggs on the stove sizzled and popped as I flipped them over in the pan. "By that sort of logic," I repeated to Katie as she entered the kitchen, still in her work uniform of a skimpy tank top and even skimpier short-shorts, "you should be cooking *us* lunch today instead of the other way around."

Grabbing two plates from the cupboard next to the fridge, I tacked on, "And what are you going on about, anyway?"

"A fancy party, that's what I'm talking about."

Out of my periphery, I watched her toss an unsealed envelope on the counter. It slid to a slow stop inches from the pan. Curiosity weighing heavy, I moved the skillet off the hot burner to the back of the stove and then picked up the envelope.

"Party's set for tomorrow evening."

I lifted my gaze to my roommate's face. "Since you already opened it, why not just tell me what it is?"

"I'd hate to take away the fun from you."

I bit back a laugh. "You've already opened the damn thing up. I mean, the party bus has already left the scene."

"Good point." Tugging the envelope from my grasp, Katie promptly pulled a cream-colored card from it, and then cleared her throat. "Tomorrow evening at seven on the dot"—she wiggled her brows playfully—"you've been invited to a party being held in support of the announcing of a new mayoral candidate for the upcoming election." Pausing, Katie sucked in her bottom lip. Then, "Not going to lie, it's a little weird that they'd send you an invitation like this on such short notice. Who do they think you are? And what the hell sort of clients have you been seeing in the square that you nabbed an invitation like this in the first place?"

The kind who wanted me to play puppet to their puppeteer.

Stomach dropping, I gripped the edge of the kitchen counter for stability's sake. There was only one reason I'd be sent an invitation like that—and there was no doubt in my mind who'd sent it.

"Give me the card," I muttered, extending one arm.

"You look like you just bit into a lemon." The card was slapped into my waiting palm. "Newsflash, Ave, people *die* to get invited to stuff like this."

Yeah, that was my fear.

That, and the fact that the event was less than twenty-four hours away.

Twenty-four hours until I came face-to-face with Jay, my stepfather.

456

Twenty-four hours until I finally laid to rest the retribution I'd been determined to dole out for years now.

Forcing my gaze to the card, I skimmed the flowery prose of "winning back New Orleans" and the mention of "representing the people for the greater good."

Bullshit, bullshit, and more words.

Politicians in the city were all one and the same in this city—dirty and corrupt to their core.

Only, the name at the bottom of the card wasn't Natalie Lauren, as expected. Nor was it Big Hampton.

No, Jason Ambideaux was the man behind the invite.

Nat's ex-husband.

Lincoln's former boss.

My bare toes curled into the linoleum flooring, and I swallowed, hard. Had . . . had Lincoln mentioned me to him in passing recently? Or maybe Nat had dropped some sort of info about me, even though I thought they no longer spoke to one another anymore?

Maybe I was on Big Hampton's radar; maybe I was on Nat's.

But Ambideaux, the man who'd ordered someone to carve Lincoln's face? There was absolutely no reason for him to know me. Not to mention . . . how had he even known where to deliver the card? I wasn't listed in any registry, and no one knew I lived here at the Sultan's Palace aside from Pete, Lincoln, and Katie.

But the apartment and rent were in Katie's name, not mine—which meant that *someone* had to have told him where to send it. And that someone . . .

My cheeks hollowed with a harsh exhale. Or maybe it was a broken laugh.

I was so, so stupid. Still that naïve little idiot on the streets wanting to believe the good in everyone I met. And

I'd trusted Katie—maybe not with who I was, but in every way that mattered, she was my family.

My *only* family.

Heart thundering, I dropped the card on the counter like it'd caught fire. Took a step back, and then yet another, until the cool expanse of the refrigerator was at my back. I wanted to run—to dart out the front door and down the stairwell, until the breath I drew into my lungs tasted like freedom. Freedom, and a new identity—the way I'd always done.

Be brave.

Be bold.

Hands shaking at my sides, I curled my fingers in, clamping down on my thumbs. Kicking up my chin, I reined in the shock to grind out the words that needed to be said. "It's weird that I received an invitation at all, considering the fact that I don't know a Jason Ambideaux."

Katie's blue eyes went from my face to the glossy invitation. "Really? That's definitely . . . unexpected, then."

"Unexpected" didn't even cover it.

As much as I wanted to manipulate her into a confession, I wanted answers more. And I didn't believe, not even for a second, that Ambideaux's invitation was just a casual, *let's get to know each other* type of deal.

Not from the way Lincoln had described him.

One wrong move on my part and I'd have a damn *J* carved into my face, just like him.

"Did he pay you off?" Bitterness dripped from every word, and my trembling hands were suddenly trembling for an entirely different reason. Betrayal. Anger. And the underlying layer of hypocrisy—because hadn't I kept her in the dark, too? Hadn't I staged our first meeting because of *who* she was?

Jay Foley's niece.

My cousin by marriage.

Family, for whatever worth that word even held.

In silence, Katie grabbed the pan off the stove and made a show of dumping the eggs in the trashcan like the action was some sort of metaphor for our relationship. Straight down the trash it went.

Patience wearing thin, I snapped, "Aren't you going to say anything?"

After roughly dropping the pan in the sink, Katie's hands went up to tighten the elastic band of her ponytail. "What is there to say? Here's your invitation." Her gaze cut to mine. "You're throwing a bitch fit for absolutely no reason. Most people would be excited to party it up with the city's elite."

Most people didn't have to worry about staying in the shadows for reasons they *still* didn't understand. And since it wasn't like I could stroll up to my stepfather and pop the question—*hey, why did you want to kill me so badly?*—I was stuck in a permanent position of ignorance that kept me forever vulnerable.

Suspicion crawled like spiders over my flesh, raising the tiny hairs on my arm. "Just answer the question, Katie. *Where* did you get the invitation? Because we both know that it wasn't sitting in the mailbox for me downstairs."

Mouth tightening, she twisted away, presenting me with her back. "He saw you, you know."

My mouth went dry. Did she mean Ambideaux or Jay? *Who would be the lesser threat?*

I wasn't given the opportunity to voice the question. With a hand on the wall, her shoulders hunched, Katie's voice practically seethed with tension. "Outside of the police precinct with Captain-fucking-America. You had him all over you, so the way I look at it, you brought this on yourself."

Because I'd finally wanted a man? Because I'd finally grown the nerve to let down my guard and let someone touch me? How in the world was that *my* fault? Hell, it seemed like something Katie would usually applaud me for.

Only . . . "You're not making any bit of sense. *Who* saw me and what the hell does *that* have to do with this?" I pointed at the card. "You're speaking in riddles."

It was the wrong thing to say.

Arms flying up in the air, Katie whirled around, her expression so hard, so unlike her, that if I could have backed up without climbing into the fridge itself, I would have.

"Speak in *riddles*?" she hissed, storming toward me. "Are you fucking kidding me right now? You want to throw stones, then how about this? Ambideaux saw you that night, and then he saw you at the club with your precious sergeant." Her gaze glittered with fury, and my shock must have registered on my face because she let out a caustic laugh. "Oh, yes, *Laurel*, he saw you with the good sergeant's hand down your pants. Then Ambideaux visited me at work. He wanted to know who you were, how long I'd known you. Maybe if you'd been forthcoming with me from the start I would have told him to fuck off. But, no, I wanted answers, and I found them."

Laurel.

The fear was back, clogging my throat, turning my limbs to concrete, submersing me beneath the water.

"Katie, I would have—"

Her hand came up, cutting me off. "I gave you the opportunity to come clean after I went through your precious file cabinet and the rest you hid above the fridge. Was it wrong of me? I don't even care. And though the blond hair might let you believe otherwise,

I'm not an idiot. I sat on that damn couch and called you out and waited for you to say *something*." She breathed out a laugh that sounded like tangible disappointment, and I couldn't deny that I wanted to shrivel up where I stood. "But you only fed me another lie, which I should have expected. I mean, who *don't* you lie to?"

Her pointed question landed like a sucker punch to my chest.

Lying was my key to survival, but hearing it out loud was . . . oh, God, I couldn't breathe.

At my silence, my roommate snorted derisively. "That's what I thought."

I needed to apologize. Hell, there was a *lot* that I needed to do to make amends with my only friend, but as I stood there, my brain working in overtime, I only whispered, "Jay Foley killed my mother. *He's* the one who murdered her, the reason I've lived on the streets. You've got to understand that there are some facts I couldn't tell you in fear that you'd tell *him*."

Fear ran my life.

Ruled my emotions.

And as Katie stared at me, her expression tight, I realized that my fear had also caused the death of my only friendship.

"Call me unreasonable or a bitch," she said in a thin voice, "but I'm gonna need space. And, ironically, I tried to warn you that running forever would land you in trouble."

She couldn't be . . .

Head pounding with panic, I muttered, "Twenty minutes ago you were demanding to go to this party with me, and now you're, what? Kicking me out?"

Katie snapped up the card from the counter and crumpled it up in one hand. "It's called finally coming to my senses and knowing when to call it quits. Maybe if you haven't totally fucked over your sergeant, he'll take you in."

Like a stray seemed to be her unsaid implication, and the thought alone was like having steel injected in my bone marrow.

I was completely aware of the fact that I'd lit the matchsticks for our imploding friendship. I'd approached her first. Warmed her up to me and broken down the walls until we hung out regularly and then we were picking out apartments together.

She'd trusted me, and I'd betrayed that over and over again for years.

You're not so much of a saint after all, are you?

My chest tightened at the truth. I could pretend all I wanted that every single one of my actions was justified, but at some point along the way I'd become unrecognizable even to myself.

A woman so determined to right a wrong that I didn't even blink at using others to put myself in a better place to manifest my own goals.

"I'm so sorry," I whispered. It was an apology to Katie, yes, but also to myself. For letting my rage overrule everything else, including my common decency. "I just—" I broke off, unable to put into words how I'd waged war within myself for years. "I'm sorry."

Katie nodded, then turned her head, as though she didn't want me to read her expression. "Don't go to that party alone, Avery. That's all I'm going to say. If you're smart, just don't go alone." Stepping back, she spun on her heel and headed for the bedroom. Over her shoulder, she said, "You can let yourself out. And if it makes you sleep any better, no, I won't tell my uncle about you. Your precious secret is safe with me—for whatever that's worth to you."

She closed the bedroom door, and I heard the lock click shut.

My palm closed over my mouth, and I bit down on my knuckle to keep from letting a sob break loose. I was strong, had always been strong, but never before had I wanted to admit defeat as much as I did now.

Jay Foley had stripped me of my identity.

But he wasn't responsible for the way I'd stripped myself of who I was at heart.

And, if I wanted to dig deep, I didn't even know the answer to that question.

Laurel.

Samantha.

Ruby.

Avery.

A figment of mashed identities, whose only purpose in life, for over a decade, had been to murder the man who'd had my momma killed.

Beyond that, I was no one.

And that, it seemed like, was the greatest loss of all.

FIVE OF CUPS

NINETEEN

Lincoln

I t wasn't Avery's face that greeted me after I'd spent five minutes banging my fist on her apartment door.

No, it was her roommate's.

The blonde.

I couldn't remember her name—but there was no mistaking her bloodshot eyes or the way her coloring was all off. She looked like shit, and I had a feeling that I looked no better.

Guilt could do that to a person.

"If you're looking for her, she's not here."

I went rigid. "You mean, she's at the square for work already?"

It was way too early in the evening for her to be reading cards. Hell, it wasn't even 6 p.m., which meant the gates of Jackson Square weren't even locked for the night yet.

The blonde lifted her chin. "No." She shook her head, then quickly averted her gaze to stare at my right shoulder. "I mean, I don't know."

There was something in her tone . . . something that

didn't sit well with me, and even though I knew it was inherently wrong to scare her, I set my palm on the door-frame anyway. Used the size of my body to intimidate her.

I'd never said that I was anything less than a callous asshole.

My voice was low, hard, when I said, "I read liars for a living, and I know when someone's trying to bullshit me. So, let's try this again—where is she? And we both know Avery's not the sort to go somewhere without saying something first."

If she had been, she would have left this damn city years ago.

Like me, she had unfinished business.

And she has me.

Christ, I couldn't go there right now. Not until I'd unloaded everything I had to tell her about the case—and not until I confessed about the night I'd been sent to kill her. I had to come clean, even if it meant she'd never want anything to do with me again.

Avery's roommate folded her arms around her middle. Then, softly, she whispered, "I asked her to leave."

Ice slid down my spine, and my nails scraped the door-frame as my hand balled into a fist. "Why?"

"She . . ." Lifting one hand, she ran it over the bridge of her nose and drew in a deep, shaky breath. "That's between me and her. I shouldn't have—" Shoulders squaring off, she met my gaze and I could read the worry in her blue eyes. The blatant regret.

Join the party—there's more than enough room.

Clearing her throat, she muttered, "She turned off her phone. I've tried calling. I've been waiting here in case she . . . That doesn't matter. I'm rambling, and I doubt you give a shit."

If it had to do with Avery, I cared. More than I wanted

to admit, and honestly more than I liked. She'd wormed her way into my life, staking her claim and making me believe in shit I'd always assumed was a bunch of bull.

"Where would she go?" I couldn't quite hide the urgency in my voice, and the blonde noticed.

Her shoulders twitched and the smallest smile tipped up her lips. "Shit, you like her."

I wasn't having this conversation. Pushing off the door-frame, I made a solid effort to wipe any trace of kindness from my expression. "No bullshit," I bit out, "where would she go? If she's not here, what's the most likely place?"

Shifting her weight, Avery's roommate dropped her hands to her sides. "She left yesterday. I don't . . . I don't know where she slept, but she's resourceful. Probably the most resourceful person I've ever met."

A visual of Avery sleeping on the street hit me like a fist to the face, and it was a testament to my self-control that I didn't let loose the rage sweeping over me. My periphery blurred. Heart rate went into overtime.

I stepped back, half fearful that I'd react physically.

Do something I'd always regret.

As a teenager, I'd obsessed over studies—was human nature learned or genetic? Were the things that I did, the way I acted, a reflection of learned actions over time or something I'd inherited from my parents and their parents before them?

The way I looked at it, I was fucked either way.

I'd been taught to kill, taught to react with violence and anger. No one had ever shown me a kind hand, a loving touch.

But as I stared at the miserable-looking woman before me, I rejected both cases, learned and genetic.

Only opened my mouth and rasped, "I need one place you can think of—just one."

I'd go from there.

I'd tear this entire city apart until she either turned her damn phone back on or I found her—whichever came first.

The blonde wet her lips, like she was nervous to be standing near me. Then, "Flambeaux. The corner store over by St. Phillip. She's . . . she's friends with the owners."

It would have to be enough.

One curt nod later and I was taking the steps two at a time—but the roommate's voice stopped me just before I opened the door.

"Captain America," she called out, and I glanced up the stairwell. "When you find her, tell her that . . . tell her that I'm sorry. I overreacted and I just—it's not home without her here."

I had my own groveling to do, without adding someone else's into the mix.

"Sorry, Blondie, you're gonna have to tell her that yourself."

SIX OF WANDS

TWENTY

Avery

I was too old to be sleeping on city streets.

    Also too old to have, in the midst of fleeing the scene yesterday with Katie, made the critical error in forgetting my cell phone somewhere in the apartment.

Neither were particular highlights of the last twenty-four hours for me, but hey, what doesn't kill you makes you stronger. Right? Right.

I shoved my hand into the bag of cheddar popcorn and popped two kernels into my mouth, watching as two patrons meandered down the tiny aisles of Flambeaux. After almost a decade of having Pete pester me into working for him, I'd taken him up on the gig—temporarily—in return for letting me crash on his and Sal's couch.

Couches I could handle—streets weren't my thing anymore, and I'd never loved Pete more than when I'd come crashing into the corner store yesterday, holding back tears, and he'd told me to pull up my britches, dry my eyes, and get in his car before he threw me in, head first.

I was twenty-five and more than capable of finding new living accommodations, but there was something to be said about sticking with the familiar when you were bleeding from the heart.

"Y'all got any jambalaya mix in here?" called out one of the guys who'd wandered in a few minutes ago. "Told my wife I'd come back home with it."

I'd visited Flambeaux enough times to know where everything was located. "Aisle two! Next to the microwavable rice."

The bells jangled above the door with a newcomer. Hand shoved into my popcorn bag, I turned to welcome the person—and promptly dropped the snack on the floor as a muscular body leaned over the counter, hands wrapping around my biceps, and hauled me close.

Lincoln's lips crashed down on mine, domineering and possessive.

The other problem about being phone-less meant that I'd had no way to reach him, especially as I didn't even know where he lived. But, holy hell, he was here and there was *no* denying the tension that reverberated off his body.

His hands were tight on my arms, his kiss choppy but so damn hot, and I could almost taste his desperation as he devoured me. It was heady, addicting, and like a junkie of the first order, I swept my tongue along his lower lip, wanting more. Needing more.

With a rough groan, he broke away and stared at me, his familiar Haint-blue eyes flashing fire. "We're getting out of here. Now."

Beyond his right shoulder, I caught sight of Mr. Jambalaya eyeballing us, mouth gaping open. At my stare, he blushed and waved a hand. "Sorry," he muttered, "in a dry spell with the wife. I'll just, uh . . . find that jambalaya she wants so damn bad."

Before I could say another word, he'd hightailed it down the aisle, and then Lincoln was lowering me back onto my feet, his muscles bunching under the fabric of his shirt as his arms unfurled.

I blinked up at him. "What are you doing here?"

His thumb came up to swipe over his bottom lip, like he was still absorbing the taste of me, and it was . . . I wanted him to do it again—preferably after he settled himself between my thighs.

"Your roommate told me I'd probably find you here."

My heart twisted at the thought of Katie, and I dropped my gaze to the register. "We had a . . ." A falling out? A breakup? It sure felt like a breakup. I squeezed my eyes shut. "She told me that Ambideaux saw us together, me and you. Outside the precinct. And then again outside the club when we'd—"

Lincoln let loose a rough curse, one hand coming up. "I'm going to need you to back up. He did what? And how the fuck does your roommate know Jason?"

"She didn't. She *doesn't*, not really, but he—"

"Five boxes of jambalaya, please."

I cut a sharp glance to the right, where Mr. Jambalaya himself was standing. He emptied his basket, tossing box after box of the pre-cooked New Orleans cultural dish onto the counter. My brows lifted, and he offered a casual shrug in return. "I'm praying that each box ends up with another round of sex with the wife."

"I . . ." Clearing my throat, I picked up the first box and ran it under the scanner. "You know, I really hope that works out for you."

"God, me too. You'd think she would want jewelry or some shit from here, but no, jambalaya was her only request. Honestly, it's weird, but if she sucks my—"

Lincoln growled, pulling himself up to his full height, and Mr. Jambalaya immediately sucked in a sharp breath. "Damn, man," he whispered in awe, "you can do that on command? I'm not even into dudes but I'd bang you. Wait, hold on. You think you can do that again while I record it this time? Gonna send it to my wife and see if I can convince her it was me—"

It only took one step from Lincoln in the guy's direction to have Mr. Jambalaya shoving a twenty in my direction before nabbing his plastic bag off the counter.

He backed up, feet tripping over each other, and he headed for the door. "You two have a great day. Like, have awesome sex for me." His gaze flicked to Lincoln. "I want to be you when I grow up. Seriously, man-crush status over here."

Before Lincoln could make another move, the man was out the door and the flimsy door was clanging shut behind him.

"Fucking tourists," Lincoln grunted, and I held back a snort.

Bending down to grab my discarded popcorn bag off the floor, I tossed it in the trash can. "You've got a secret admirer."

"The only admiring I want to do is with you riding my cock and my gaze on your tits."

Heat erupted over my cheeks. "They're small."

Lincoln leaned in, hands on the counter. "They're perfect. Especially when they're in my mouth and you're moaning my name."

I hissed out a breath, and then sent a quick glance to the rest of the store. Empty, aside from one grandfather-looking fellow checking out the fridges housing the dairy options. He appeared completely in his own world as I returned my attention to the powerful man before me.

As much as I wanted to keep flirting, I couldn't quite disguise the worry in my voice when I said, "Not trying to get all Negative Nancy here, but why . . . why would Jason

Ambideaux even care to follow me? Us? I mean, you—okay, I can see you, considering everything with Tabby and the others, but me?"

Expression sobering, the heat in his blue eyes cooled to a low simmer. "You're a way to get to me."

He said it so simply, so easily, and yet my mouth opened and fell shut in an embarrassing rhythm that was only broken up when I finally muttered, "He invited me to a party tonight. It's to announce a new mayoral candidate, and to be honest with you, I'm getting the feeling everyone in this city is trying to play the *whose-dick-is-bigger* contest and throw their hat into the ring." I paused, then belatedly tacked on, "They should probably be thankful that you're not entering."

Lincoln choked out a startled laugh. "My hammer would like to stay out of this narrative, thanks."

I grinned—it was big, and it was all teeth, and best of all, it was *real*. He did that to me, for me, and it was pure instinct alone that had me abruptly hooking a finger into the neck of his shirt and pulling him down for another kiss.

He let me, moving freely under my command, and that led to a rush I didn't expect. My hand left his shirt, skirting up to cup his cheek, and then *I* was the one who angled his face for a better fit. Lips brushing, tongues tangling.

I wanted to alternatively climb his body and force him to submit to me, just as much as I wanted to beg him to bend me over and take me from behind.

And, as much as I was loath to admit it, I almost wished that I wasn't on the outs with Nat, just so we could revisit the Basement again and experience more of the rooms.

Dropping back onto my heels, I broke off the kiss and pulled one of his moves—thumb brushing my lip, eyes lifting to meet his gaze.

He looked ready to jump the counter and fuck me right here, right now.

"We need to get out of here," he rasped.

"Because we need to talk about Ambideaux?"

Haint-blue eyes glittered. "Because I need to sink into your body, sweetheart. Because I'm fucking dying, and if I thought I could get away with taking you right now, I'd do it. No questions asked."

I eyed the elderly man again speculatively. "Not going to lie, I'm tempted."

"You're supposed to be the voice of reason."

I swung my gaze back to Lincoln. "When have I ever been the voice of reason?" Lowering my voice, I taunted, "When I let you put your hand down my pants on a not-so-private street? Or maybe it was when you went down on me in front of just about everyone and their mother in a sex club?"

His chest heaved with an inhale. "We're leaving."

I gestured to the store. "Can't go until Pete comes back."

There was a very good chance this was the first time I was seeing him close to coming undone. Stoic Lincoln, hard-ass Lincoln, dangerous Lincoln, reached down to subtly adjust himself. "How long?" he demanded roughly.

"How long until what?"

"Until Pete comes back."

I rocked onto my heels, thrusting my chest out, and peered at the digital clock on the wall. "Another hour."

"Another—" He broke off with a curse, hands going to the counter like he needed physical support.

I didn't know what possessed me to do it, but I patted his chest—like he wasn't the most feared man in the city—and drawled, "Must be karma."

Blue eyes narrowed on me. "Karma for *what*?"

I shrugged. "Tossing my taser into the Mississippi? Stealing my underwear? Or how about—"

"Who's your friend, Avery?"

Pete.

I turned to the man who'd been a friend to me since I was a teenager, and although it wasn't at *all* like introducing a man to my father, nervous butterflies erupted in my stomach anyway.

Swallowing nervously, I made the introductions as quickly as possible. Awkward, so awkward, especially since my core was still throbbing for Lincoln.

Lincoln, who ditched his badass persona long enough to exchange a word or two with Pete about the Saints and the NFL draft.

Lincoln, who grinned just slightly when he asked if he could steal me away early.

Lincoln, who ushered me out of Flambeaux five minutes later, gently nudged me into the passenger seat, and then climbed in behind the wheel.

We weren't even two minutes into our drive to Destination Unknown before he turned down the volume of the car radio and husked out, "Drop your panties, Avery. Karma is making me so hard that I can't even see straight, and I'm in the mood to return the favor."

THE EMPRESS

MAJOR ARCANA

TWENTY-ONE

Avery

S tartled, I twisted my head to stare at Lincoln.

Mouth feeling parched, I croaked, "What?"

Fingers white-knuckling the steering wheel, he slid a quick glance over to me. "Underwear, sweetheart. Lose 'em."

Lose them? I laughed shortly. "Excuse me a moment while I have a flashback to me dropping ten feet from a fire escape stairwell while being *completely* bare below the waist."

"You enjoyed every moment that came before that."

"Yeah, *before* it." I watched the buildings pass us by as we left the French Quarter. "I can't say that I enjoyed everything that came after, especially the whole being-held-at-gunpoint bit."

"That shit isn't happening again." He flashed me a dark, serious look. "I promise. None of them are going to touch you. Not again, not while I'm here."

I thought of what Katie had said about Jason Ambideaux . . . about him watching us. A shiver of trepidation slid down my spine. It was one thing for Lincoln and me to hook up at Stage One, when we'd willingly participated in everything that was happening.

It was something else entirely to know that Ambideaux had followed us, watched us, and had gone so far as to even approach Katie about me after no doubt seeing us talk while she'd tended the bar.

That sick feeling returned, pushing aside the lust, the need, to settle like lead in my stomach. And that—that made me angry. That I could so easily let someone else taint my experiences with Lincoln that I hoarded like shards of treasure.

Sex with Lincoln was like piecing together fragments of my broken soul.

Without giving myself the chance to rethink my decision, my fingers went to the button of my jeans. I flicked it open.

The zipper coming unhinged was what caught his attention—his nostrils flared at once, his cheeks hollowing out.

It was the right side of his face that was presented to me, and it seemed almost fitting that he gave me his worst, unflinching under my perusal, and I barely noticed his scars. They were there but they weren't my sole focus. No, I just wanted him. Any way that I could have him.

I shimmied my jeans down to my knees, butt lifted off the seat, underwear going with the denim.

Lincoln hit the brakes a little too hard, and the car behind us let loose three consecutive beeps.

"Distracted?" I teased in a low murmur, drawing my finger up the length of my inner thigh just to play the seductress and make him sweat. Watching him lose control was hands-down my favorite part of sex with him. Besides the orgasms, of course. "I wonder . . . can you drive when you're focused on me?"

"Hands on the back of your seat."

I blinked. Then blinked again. "What?"

"Karma." Slowing to a stop at a traffic light, he took the extra second to look my way. "I get to tell you a little story—and you get to wait until I let you touch yourself."

"That seems like a bullshit deal."

"You'll like it."

Doubtful. But even as the thought crossed my mind, I couldn't help but think I was lying once again—this time to myself. There hadn't been a single thing Lincoln had done so far that I hadn't enjoyed.

And it was for that reason alone that my hands slowly lifted to the seat, as he'd said, and wrapped around the back of the headrest. Nails digging in, I glanced down— my legs were as wide as they could be with my jeans still hiked around my knees. It was a heady sensation, knowing that each time he dragged in another breath, it was on account of the fact that I was half-naked and driving him crazy.

"How long are you going to make me wait?" My arms flexed in the position, fingers re-clasping the seat. "Until we get wherever we're going?"

"If it came down to me circling the block ten times just so I could get you off first, I'd do it."

"I knew you were a gentleman under all that . . . bad-assery."

He shifted in his seat, his gaze momentarily landing on my legs with enough heat that I was surprised my skin didn't singe. "I'm no gentleman, sweetheart. Never have been, never—"

"Will be," I finished for him with a wink he didn't catch. "Let's stop ahead of the clichés, what do you think? I'm pretty much naked, the AC is cranked a little too high and I can tell *down there*, and I'm waiting to be wowed by whatever you have up your sleeve."

That brought out a startled laugh from him. "I think I liked you more when you were a virgin."

"I can't say that I feel the same."

"Fuck," he worked out after another bark of laughter, "you were made for me. I didn't laugh until you. Didn't see a glimmer of light within all the darkness." One big hand lifted from the steering wheel to run over the scruff along the bottom half of his jaw like he was embarrassed. "And now you've got me spilling my soul like I'm some sort of poet."

I couldn't deny it—*cliché* or not, my heart fluttered at the awkward way he continued to glance over at me before quickly fixing his attention on the road again. Smiling, I offered up, "I don't mind poetry. Are you any good with haikus?"

Adam's apple bobbing as he swallowed, Lincoln directed the car off the main throughway and onto a side street with a row of townhouses that were all identical. Painted brightly hued colors like they were straight from the Caribbean, each one was complete with a small area of grass out front and a narrow driveway.

Neat.

Orderly.

Cute.

For whatever reason, I'd pictured Lincoln living on the cusp of the bayou where wilderness thrived and the only thing more untamed than the man who owned the land were the feral animals that prowled the swamp.

"Change of plans," he said as he pulled up into one of the driveways in front of a teal house, "we're taking this inside."

My hands unclenched from the headrest, biceps sore

from holding the position. "The disappointment is real, Sergeant. Here I am willing and waiting, bare to the world, and—"

The rest of my sentence ended in a gasp.

His big body invaded my space, seat creaking under his weight as he leaned over the center console, his warm hand between my legs. His thumb flirted with where I wanted him most, hovering just above ground zero. Palm squeezing my inner thigh, his lips grazed my ear. "Playtime's over, Ave. You like to be pushed to the edge. You like it when I'm rough. So, let's put it this way—pull up your jeans and go inside. I can promise you that the only disappointment you're about to feel is when you've come too many times and your body is too tired to go for another round."

Lips parted, I met his gaze as he pulled away.

Then I confessed: "I liked what we did at the Basement."

Thumb cresting over my clit, making me twitch with want, he lifted his hand and cupped my jaw, that same thumb brushing over my bottom lip. "I know you did."

"Is it wrong that I'm annoyed that we can't go back?" Even the pad of his thumb was calloused, and it was such a contradiction between the gentle way he touched me and the innate roughness that was so very much *him*. Giving in to pure lust, I licked the tip of his thumb just because I could. "Not unless we're keen to find ourselves jumping from a fire escape again, obviously."

His blue eyes darkened. "We don't need the Basement for you to feel like you're pushed to the edge. All you need is me."

He said it so casually, so easily, and as he twisted his body to climb out of the SUV, I scrambled to pull up my pants. Didn't even bother to slip the brass button through its hole.

I was out of the car in seconds, slamming the door shut behind me, lengthening my stride to the front door to cut the distance. Logically, I understood that I needed to be talking to him about Ambideaux's invitation—about the ultimatum Nat herself had given me—but Lincoln never failed to make me lose sight of everything but him.

And as he'd put it, if I wanted something, then I needed to take it.

I chose to take him, putting everything else on the backburner, even if only for a few hours.

He keyed open the door. Pushed it wide. Ushered me inside with a hand to the small of my back. Quickly, I skimmed the space: a living room that opened to what had to be the kitchen through a doorway.

Lincoln's hand slid from the base of my spine up to the space between my shoulder blades. "Go sit on the couch."

He didn't have to tell me twice.

I swept forward, stepping around a small side table, and took a seat in the center of the sectional. Immediately I reached down to kick off my shoes, tossing them off to the right as Lincoln lowered himself to the single chair opposite the wraparound.

"I feel like you're a little far away." I motioned to the space between us, then tacked on, "You're big, Sergeant, but not *that* big."

His mouth twitched at my innuendo, but he otherwise didn't outwardly react.

Instead, he settled in to his seat, legs spread wide in that masculine way that seemed to be part of a guy's genetic makeup. His forearms landed on the armrests, like he was seated on a throne.

"The Basement caters to everyone," he murmured.

"No matter what kink you've got, they'll take real good care of you. It's the reason they've got a waitlist a mile long."

I swallowed, hard. "You got a kink I should know about, Sergeant?"

He smiled, just a little. "I like to be in control."

"Right." I bobbed my head in a nod. "I was thinking more along the lines of . . . like whips or chains or something."

"Is that what you want? To be whipped?"

I rolled the image over in my head. Discarded it on second thought. "No. I'm sure it's . . . fun. But I just—"

"It's not for you."

"No."

"I spent a good amount of time at the Basement, back when I was too young to do anything more than sit and watch." He reached down, grasped the hem of his shirt, and pulled it up and over his head. It was the first time I'd had the opportunity to see his upper body in broad daylight, and it was . . .

Brutally savage.

Both the power that existed in his heavily corded muscles and the tattoos that were inked in his skin.

No, I thought as I stared at him, *he was beautiful.*

With his scars and his tattoos, he looked like a man who'd been through hell and come out the other side. And when he spoke, his voice a rough timbre, everything in me strung tight with desire.

"Kinks often reflect what a person has suffered in their past life. A man who has never had the opportunity to speak his truth, for example, might find that he likes to wear something during sex that limits his vocals."

Like Zak Benson.

I opened my mouth, prepared to mention that exactly,

but Lincoln rolled on, his gaze impossibly astute. "I'd say that goes for you, too."

"What?"

"My hand around your neck, sweetheart. Years of keeping your secrets and never telling a soul." He rose, then. Came around the backside of the sectional until he was there, behind me, his arms wrapping like bands around my middle as he bent over the back of the couch. "You have no fucking idea how wet you get the second my fingers touch you here."

The pads of his fingertips brushed the underside of my jaw.

My core tightened, and I hated that I was so damn transparent.

"Not everything is about whips or chains," he husked, those fingers of his coursing down, over my chest, down past my belly, until they were resting on the waistband of my jeans. My breath caught when he silently encouraged me to strip off the denim.

They were gone in a heartbeat. Kicked off to the side.

And his hand was pushing me gently forward, until I was seated on the very edge of the seat cushion.

I twisted my head to look back at him. "Lincoln?"

My eyes went wide as I realized he'd shucked his pants, too. He was fully erect, fully naked, and I was fully in lust. Limber like an athlete, he jumped the back of the couch and dropped into the space behind me.

Reached forward to clasp me at the hips and pull me back into him.

Oh, God.

Despite the thin fabric of my shirt, I could feel his cock like a brand against my back. Could feel the heat radiating from his skin as his arms wound around me, keeping me in close.

I was surrounded by him.

His heat.

His power.

He grazed my earlobe with his tongue, sending shivers firing down my limbs.

"Should we see how wet you are?" he teased.

"*Yes.*"

Chuckling, he pressed a kiss to my shoulder. "Go ahead."

I swallowed, hard. "What?"

"Take what you want, Avery." Clasping my hand in his, he set it on my inner thigh. "I'll give you what you want . . . but I want to watch you first."

Oh, God.

My heart thudded in my chest, so hard that I was surprised we didn't hear it. It was one thing to touch myself at the Basement, when I wasn't alone in doing so. Another thing entirely to do it on my own.

Butterflies fluttered to life in my belly. I flexed my hand under his, then brought it to the apex of my thighs.

"Brave girl." His hot breath rustled my hair and I felt him harden even more against my back.

I wanted to be that brave girl, the way I was in everything else in life, but never here. Never with a man. Letting my head fall back onto the hard planes of his chest, I stared down at my hand as if it was someone else's but not my own.

Those fingers curled, the middle seeking my clit. It was swollen to the touch—and I was on edge. The slight brush of my finger sent my toes digging into the carpet and my free hand went to Lincoln's thigh, where my nails carved half-moons into his flesh.

"Fuck, yes," he growled behind me.

The clear-cut lust in his voice powered me on. I dipped

my finger, sliding it along my slit, tracing my entrance. My core tightened, and I brought my thumb up to circle my clit as I teased my pussy.

There was something heady about playing for him this way, like I owned his pleasure, dictated its ebbs and flows. Lincoln Asher was a man who enjoyed being in control—but what happened when he lost it?

A grin flickered along my lips, and I tossed my head back in retaliation. I'd give him what he wanted, but it'd be on my terms. Not his.

"Oh, my God," I moaned, slipping a finger inside, curling it just right so that when I cried out, it was all too real. Putting on a show for Lincoln just might be the best sort of performance I'd ever attended—literally.

Releasing his leg, I skimmed my palm up my belly to my left breast. Tweaked the nipple over my shirt. Fingers thrusting down below, I hiked up my left leg and laid it over his, spreading myself wide.

"Christ," he grunted, his hands landing on my hips. "Don't stop."

I didn't.

Pulling my fingers from my pussy, I spread that wetness over my swollen clit. Rubbed in incessant little circles until my vision blurred and I was gasping for relief. Relief that Lincoln was determined to hold off, as though punishing himself just as much as he was punishing me.

He shifted me forward, his hard-on slipping between my ass cheeks.

It was a shock, the girth of him, the heat of his cock there.

All words fled my brain. My hand left my pussy to land on his knee. Using him as leverage, I lifted and fell, needing the pressure of his cock even though he wasn't inside me.

I wanted him to lose control, and I wouldn't stop until he did.

Turning around, I straddled his hips and sank my weight down on his body. Wrapped a hand behind me as I circled my fingers around his erection and rubbed the crown along my slit. Up I went, grazing his cock with nothing but the tantalizing hint of what was to come. Down I came, the crown teasing *me*, rubbing up against my clit and making my legs twitch.

It was seduction in its finest form, and Lincoln's blue eyes were wild.

His chest rose and fell with short breaths, and his fingers curled into the cheeks of my ass. "Holy fuck," he grunted harshly, "I need a condom. Avery, I need—"

I leaned in with a short kiss to his mouth. And then I said, "I think you can suffer a little longer, Sergeant."

If his gaze had been wild before, it was not even close to now.

He launched off the couch, me in his arms, bridal-style.

"I'm calling the shots on this one." His nostrils flared as he kicked open what had to be his bedroom door before dropping me on the bed. "I'm in charge."

My fingers dipped back between my legs again after I stripped off my shirt, and sure enough, his blue eyes tracked the path of my hand like a starved man. "No," I said, "I think it's safe to say that *I* am."

His big body stilled like he was cataloguing what I'd said.

And then he moved into action, and I didn't stand a chance.

My ass was in the air, my hands pinned to my sides, my face planted into the sheets. I heard the crinkle of foil and then a drawer slamming shut so hard that I was pretty sure he'd knocked over the bedside table.

The blunt head of his cock aligned with my entrance.

"You'll come when I let you come." His palm smoothed out over my lower back, keeping me in position. "Do you understand? If I want to hold off your orgasm until you're crying you're so desperate for relief, I will."

I turned my head, nose rustling with the cotton, and taunted, "Sounds like you might have to prove you're not a five-minute man."

His hand came down on my right cheek. It was pleasure and pain, all mixed into one, and my skin felt aflame as he pulled back and did it again. I bit back a cry, clamping down on my bottom teeth, as I fisted the sheets and held myself back from begging for more.

I wanted Lincoln as everything that he was: rough, wild, dominating.

I shoved my butt back against him, silently daring him to do his worst.

He thrust inside me a moment later, and I knew then that he hadn't given me his worst, but only his best. And he backed my theory up when he pulled out and buried himself to the hilt.

Oh.

My.

God.

I muffled my cry in the sheets, unable to stop myself from thrusting backward to meet him. I craved him like no other. Wanted him like no other. And then he was dragging his hand down my back, making me arch my spine like a cat lazing in the sun. His palm slid over one cheek and I prepared myself for the sting, for the want, for the way my core squeezed in excitement and anticipation and desire.

His hand never connected with my ass, not the way I'd expected it to. Instead, he spread my cheeks wide, and—

I swallowed. Fisted the sheets.

His thumb circled the puckered rim of my ass, and I didn't know whether to beg for more or run in the opposite direction.

But his cock kept hitting me at just the right spot and the pressure—oh, God, the pressure—of his thumb felt insanely good. He circled there, just like he'd do to my clit, and I moaned so loud I was sure they'd hear it in the townhouse one over.

"Your pussy is mine," Lincoln growled, "your ass is mine."

I cried out at the alternating pressures of his surging cock and the soft brush of his thumb. Struggled to gather my breath when I edged out, "You're at three minutes, Sergeant. A-almost there."

I was almost there.

I was spiraling in an abyss I'd never known existed, addicted to the feel of him dominating my body like he truly owned my pleasure. Dictated it, just like he ordered about all the cops in his unit.

Pleasure swept over me, my hair falling across my face, my sensitive breasts rubbing up against the sheets.

The pressure grew, his strokes more insistent, his thumb dipping down so that I felt him along my slit as his cock continued to power into me. And then the pressure at my ass was there again, heavier.

I couldn't breathe. Couldn't think.

Lincoln reached around, his free hand going to my clit, circling with two of his fingers. Stringing me so tight that I felt him everywhere, heard his deep groans and the way he said my name like I'd been made for him.

Like he'd been made for me.

Another circle of his fingers at my clit, another thrust of his hips, and I came, shaking so hard that there was nothing I could do but enjoy the ride. My lids slammed shut, and I felt Lincoln tumble along after me, his pace quickening, his hands on my hips as he fucked me.

He came, groaning my name, tucking me under him as we accidentally rolled off the bed and onto the floor. I tossed my head back with a laugh, the base of my skull connecting with the side of the mattress.

Lincoln chuckled, his blue eyes on me. "Wasn't quite the grand finale I was hoping for."

Shamelessly, I looked down at his cock. "All I need to know is . . . if my pussy belongs to you and my ass belongs to you, do I get to own *that*?"

As though aware that he was up for discussion, Lincoln's dick twitched. "All yours, sweetheart. He's all yours."

Stealing a big breath into my lungs, I watched him climb onto his knees and then move toward the small waste bin in the corner of the room.

"We made a mess." I lazily kicked the drawers that had tipped out of the bedside table. "A total mess." There was a deck of playing cards on the floor, a strip of condom packets, a bottle of Advil, and . . .

My heart stopped.

Shifting onto my knees, I leaned forward, my fingers grasping the bracelet that was jumbled in with the rest of everything else. I knew this bracelet. It'd belonged to me— once. Back before Momma died and I ran from the house. Back when I'd been happy.

"Lincoln." My voice was raspy, and I cleared it. Ignored the ringing in my ears and tried again. "Lincoln, where did you get this?"

SEVEN OF SWORDS

TWENTY-TWO

Lincoln

"Lincoln, where did you get this?"

I was fucked, didn't matter which way I looked at it.

Lies tangled in my throat, each demanding their own chance to smooth over the situation and put everything back to rights.

Rights would be Avery and I in bed together, her tucked up against my side while I skimmed my hand up and down her frame and memorized every dip and curve.

Christ, I needed pants for this conversation.

With my dick still half hard, I scoured my bedroom floor for a stray pair—then moved swiftly toward my dressers and yanked the second drawer open. I threw a T-shirt back for Avery, then drew on a pair of sweatpants up my legs.

It'd have to do.

"Lincoln," Avery said, her naturally throaty pitch elevating enough for me to know that she was trying to hold it together. That space in my chest—which I'd always assumed was empty and dead—gave a pitiful jump at the sound. "Where did you get that bracelet? Don't lie. Please don't lie."

I wouldn't lie.

But she wouldn't like the truth either.

Hands on my hips, I faced her. Felt the strained look in her expression like a punch to the gut. If I were anyone but me, that look on her face would have brought me to my knees. They wavered now anyway when I stared into her hazel eyes and gave myself away: "From your family's tomb."

The words were like a sledgehammer to her knees.

They gave out without warning, and her ass hit the mattress a moment later. She didn't pull the shirt on over her head—didn't do anything but sit there, her chest rising and falling rhythmically, her bare toes curling into the carpet flooring like she was seconds away from bolting out of this room.

She was naked, exposed.

And, this time, I was the one responsible for the devastation that lined her features.

"I-I don't understand," she whispered hoarsely, the T-shirt tangling between her fingers as she fisted her hands in her lap. "Did you go there recently? After you found out who I was? Who I am?"

In ten seconds, maybe less, she would hate me.

I experienced my own slice of devastation, then. My fist came up to rub at my chest, directly over my heart where her number was tattooed. I wished . . . fuck, but I wished we'd been other people than who we were. That I'd met her at a restaurant or on a blind date or *anywhere* else but our true reality.

At the end of the day, though, *this* was our reality.

"I went there a week after they put your body to rest."

Her pretty hazel eyes went wide, the color draining from her face. "No."

It was all she said, and that dug the knife of guilt more deeply into my chest than if she'd asked me to repeat myself.

I was so sorry, so damn sorry, and seeing her gutted expression stripped my emotions raw. I was dangling, hanging from a precipice where I went from a man she thought she could trust to the enemy.

Now she knows what the rest of this city does about me.

I'd never been a good man. Never been a hero. I lived in the darkness and relied on violence to get my point across.

And I'd never hated myself more.

Knowing it would only make the situation worse, I tried to explain. My tongue felt swollen, though, and when I spoke, it was a jumbled, chaotic mess of shit. "The kid—the *teenager*—that Ambideaux ordered me to kill . . . there's no good way for me to say this. I wish there was. I wish I was somebody else, and not the man who—"

"No."

She launched from the bed, slipping my shirt over her head as she moved around me.

I couldn't let her go. Call me an asshole, a bastard like my father, but I couldn't let her leave. Before I even realized that I'd done it, my hand was locked around her arm, dragging her back. Keeping her from fleeing, from leaving *me.*

Please don't leave me.

Desperate. Pathetic. But to a man like me—a man who'd lived without light so long—I wasn't willing to let this relationship go down in a ball of flames without trying to fix it.

"Avery, please—"

497

She stared down at my arm like it was the source of the next Bubonic plague. Her lips pulled back, nostrils flaring, and then she yanked away sharply. Stepped out of my reach. "You weren't the man who killed my momma. I know that you weren't . . . your voices aren't the same."

"No. I have no idea who that was, but I can guarantee it wasn't me." Not wanting to frighten her off, I took a single step in her direction. My hands came up like she was a terrified colt. "The guilt ate me alive for years," I muttered, "that I'd sunk so low in my own life that I considered, even for a second, taking—"

"For taking my life?" Avery shook her head with a bitter laugh. "Is this where I thank you for not putting a bullet through my head?" Her hands landed on my chest and pushed to no avail.

I'd take whatever punishment she doled out.

It was my penance. My atonement.

My hands wrapped around her wrists, my thumbs pausing over her pulse. "You were a mark, a way for Jason to strike back at Foley. The same mark that, not just a few days ago, you comforted me over." I jerked her in, getting my face close to hers. "I know it feels different switching out the unknown kid for being *you*, but I didn't know who you were. Or why Jason had a hard-on for your stepdad. *I didn't know.*"

Her lip curled. "Then what *did* you know?"

This was not the way I'd planned to tell her about Foley and the case, but if I didn't come clean from start to finish, there'd never be another opportunity. Squeezing my eyes shut, I exhaled through my nose and sought the calm that was quickly eluding me.

"Foley likes teenage girls." The words sounded so clinical, too hard, and I tried again. "Jason . . . he was pissed off at Foley. He's hated him for *years*, and I suspect he knew that if you were killed, that would send Jay in a tailspin he'd never recover from. I could be wrong—it's speculation on my part, pieced together from information I've gathered over the last few years. Rumors I've heard." *Stories I've been told.*

Avery stared at me, her eyes glassy and unfocused. "He was obsessed with my mom."

"Maybe it was a front—"

"No!" Her throat worked with a rough swallow. "You don't understand—he was *obsessed* with her. Cooking her breakfast daily. Always coming home with these little chocolates that she could eat by the box. There wasn't anything he wouldn't do for her. Until he had her murdered."

Fuck, I hated seeing the pain in her eyes. I wanted to wrap her up in my arms, but it wasn't the right time. *If it will ever be the right time again.*

"Avery, I'm telling you—I've been in the trenches, trying to bring this thing to light over the last few years. Trying to get him locked behind bars for the shit he's done to these girls. None of them will come forward to testify. None of them will say *shit*, but they all have admitted to sleeping with Foley. Every single one."

"How old?"

My heart slammed against the cage of my chest, like I'd been in a car going from eighty to ten in under thirty seconds. "What?"

"How old were they? These girls you've talked to?" She didn't mention the case or the testifying, and I had a feeling she was trying to prioritize all the information I was spewing out like a broken sieve.

She was the strongest person I knew, and it gutted me to think that life experiences had molded her this way.

That she could compartmentalize her own emotions in order to focus on the conversation at hand.

I'd called her brave before, but it was pretty obvious that "brave" was a gross understatement.

Releasing her, I shoved my fingers through my hair. "All ages. The youngest was sixteen. Two, rather. Two of them were sixteen."

Avery seemed to be working through something in her head—mouth moving, though no words emerged, and she pushed past me to head for the living room. I trailed her, trying to work the fuck out where her brain was going.

I was a cop and even I was lost.

"Looks?" she asked as she shoved one foot in her jeans, then did the same with the other. "What did they all look like?"

"Young. Young—I don't know, Avery. Where the hell are you going with this?"

Hands on the button of her jeans, she turned to me again. "Did they look like me?"

Since none of the girls had been willing to go on record or even come forward at all, my database with their information was slim. Practically nonexistent. I'd been running on fumes for years now, trying to make something of a case that no one wanted to bring to court but me.

But I was a man obsessed with redemption. Vengeance. It drove me every day, was the force that woke me up at morning, and was the reason I hardly slept.

"They didn't have dark hair like you," I said, "hell, I don't know. Maybe a few did, but it was clearly dyed. Heights were all over the place, no sort of similarity there. Eyes . . . I don't fucking remember."

"He used to fuck Nat," she said in an almost off-hand kind of way, "and call her 'Catherine' as he did so. She's not blond, but a man like that . . . a man like Jay doesn't kill his wife for no reason or sleep with girls because he can." She shook her head, then moved to shove her feet into her shoes. "No, a man like that screws anyone he can, and pretends that they're all his dear wife."

"Whom he *killed*."

"Sometimes good people do bad things." With a raised brow, she bit off, "I mean, I technically agreed to kill *you,* but I don't think I'm a bad person."

MAJOR ARCANA

TWENTY-THREE

Avery

The minute the words were out, and I registered Lincoln's look of betrayal, I wished I could stuff them back into my mouth.

Yes, he'd once been sent to kill me, but that was ages ago.

I'd accepted Nat's offer just last week.

It didn't quite matter that I never planned to follow through, that I'd only entertained the idea for so brief a period that it barely counted. Because somewhere along the way . . . Lincoln had stolen my heart.

I didn't know anything about love—had gone years without even a glimpse of it.

Momma, once, had lulled me to bed with talk of the language of love. I remembered little of what words she used or the stories she spun, but I'd never been able to forget the warmth that radiated from her voice as she murmured in my ear and tickled my sides to pull giggles from my six-year-old frame.

The minute I'd heard the gunshot that had stolen her

from me, that warmth and joy was replaced with fear, isolation, vengeance.

Until Lincoln had strolled into my life, my version of the language of love had encompassed dark streets and even darker secrets. Then he'd touched me, and I'd come alive, gasping, wanting, my skin ablaze with heat and my chest rumbling with laughter.

And maybe it was just that the stupid organ in my chest was so desperate for affection that I was making more out of my emotions than I should.

"Lincoln," I whispered, hating the tumultuous way he watched me, like he was torn between reacting out of his basic instincts and killing me before I struck first or crumbling right there before me. "I'm telling you right now that I had no plans to—"

"Who," he ground out, blue eyes locked on my face with an intensity that was almost unholy. "And don't lie, Avery. Who the fuck put you up to it?"

From the first time we'd met, I'd never completely feared Lincoln.

I'd been wary. I'd been suspicious of his attention.

Fear had never entered the equation—until now.

Rage radiated from him, making the whites of his eyes brighter, his muscles stiffer, which in turn only made him look that much bigger. More imposing.

With my fingers tangling in his shirt, which hung down to my thighs, I stepped back in trepidation. "Does it matter?" I asked, not because I wanted to protect Nat, by any means, but because I hadn't gone through with it.

Just like he didn't go through with killing you.

We were two pieces to a puzzle built long before we'd ever entered the equation.

"Was it Nat?" he demanded. "Hampton?"

"Let them implode."

Haint-blue eyes turned in my direction, and I despised the inner struggle that I saw there. My heart twisted at the sight of his pain, his hatred, which so mirrored my own.

"Let them both implode," I said again, voice gathering strength. "I pulled a card for you, that first day we met. The present you didn't want to know. It was Cruelty, Lincoln." Squaring my shoulders, I approached him with caution. "Cruelty is a mind game. It's driving yourself into the ground, never allowing yourself to move forward. You're stuck in the same cycle. *I'm* stuck in the same cycle."

Chest hitching, he cut eye contact. "The cards mean shit. This is real life, Avery. And, in real life, you don't sit around waiting to be picked off while your guard is down. That's not the way this works."

"So, what are you going to do? Just *waltz* into their homes and kill them all?" I'd be the first to admit that I'd spent years wanting just the same, but from the look on Lincoln's face . . . it wasn't nearly the same thing.

He was spiraling. Retreating back to the violence that had been ingrained in him since childhood. And it seemed like a strike of fate that I realized . . . I couldn't do the same. I wanted the love my momma had whispered to me about so fervently. I wanted to live, my conscience clear, knowing that I had taken the high road to my redemption. Through the courts, the way I should have done so long ago if I hadn't been so fearful of my own shadow.

Be brave.

Be bold.

My momma had guided me for years now, and I'd never listened over the furious pounding of hatred that seethed like poison in my veins.

I had to listen to that guidance now.

"I'll testify." Jaw clenching, I swallowed my fear and stepped in front of Lincoln, so that he had no choice but to look down at me. "Whatever you need to lock Jay up for what he did, I'll testify. He never touched me, but he killed my momma, and he can rot in hell for that."

Heart catching in my throat, I gently touched Lincoln's chest. Over his heart. Over the numbers and dates that reflected a life of horror and death. Somewhere in all that ink, I had a sneaking suspicion that he'd marked my death with a number, too.

"Tell me what you'll need me to do," came my whisper, "tell me, and I'll do it."

Hard blue eyes dropped to my fingertips on the even harder planes of his chest. And I knew it—I knew it before he even spoke—that this wasn't my Lincoln, the man who brought me to orgasm and protected me from anyone who dared to pose a threat to my safety.

"*Lincoln,* c'mon. Don't be impulsive. Think clearly. I lo—"

He spun away, leaving my hand to suspend in mid-air, forever grasping a ghost.

My momma.

My identity.

Him, a man who stood before me, though the ghosts of his pasts were drowning him still.

"I need you to stay here."

My jaw dropped. "Are you serious? You're not going to just *leave* me here while you go do all of—"

"You're a liability." Without waiting to see if I'd follow, he strode down the hallway. Ducked into his bedroom.

I followed like a lemming, ducking into the bedroom a heartbeat after him. "How the hell am *I* a liability?"

He stripped off his sweats. Naked as the day he was born, he yanked open his closet and began pulling out dark clothes. Pants. Long-sleeved shirt. Boots. One by one, he pulled them on—but not before arming himself. His trench knife, his two guns.

A walking armory, always and forever.

My gaze flicked to the rumpled sheets, and then fury displaced all else as I snapped, "I'm not a liability, Sergeant. I can take care of myself. I'm not—"

"You're a liability to *me*." The words shattered the otherwise silent bedroom like a crack of thunder. "I can't think straight when you're near me. If it came down to making a move against Jay or protecting you, I'd choose you. Every. Single. Time."

"Then why—"

His mouth came crashing down on mine, stealing my fury and giving me his own in return. The kiss was brutal, unromantic, a stake of claim and possession—but who was claiming who . . . I didn't know, not anymore.

Tearing away, his blue eyes flashed with heat. "I don't deserve you, Avery. You're . . . you're light where I'm dark." He shook his head, a wry laugh escaping his lips. "I picked the Dominion card for you, and I'm going to make that happen."

"And what about you?" I worked out, an edge to my voice.

"You picked Death for me, remember?" He gently nudged me to the side, stepping out of the room. "Stay here." One glance over his shoulder revealed a touch of sadistic humor in his gaze. "I once asked if you knew how to obey—here's your chance to prove that you can follow an order."

The slamming of the front door coincided with me picking my jaw off the floor from his high-handed arrogance.

And even though he was gone, and the house was

empty, my soul fractured anyway, belting out my anger in a way that I'd always kept locked inside before.

"I lied!" I shouted to no one. "I *lied*!"

Death was meant to be his new beginning, *not* a suicide mission that landed him in a tomb with me grieving yet another person I'd loved being taken from me too soon.

The man thought he was invincible.

He wasn't.

Would never be.

But I'd be damned if I let anything happen to him.

Be brave.

Be bold.

There wasn't any other choice.

THE MOON

XVIII

MAJOR ARCANA
reversed

TWENTY-FOUR

Lincoln

Anger had long been my biggest motivator.

It ruled my heart. It sabotaged my hopes for something more than the life I lived. It wrapped its claws around my ankles and dragged me back into the flames whenever something good entered my world.

Avery was that slice of good—and like all those who'd come before her, she'd been forced to make the decision between taking me out or letting me live.

Unlike the others, she'd given me life.

But that was the thing about anger. It was hard to shake. Harder to ignore. And as I flung open the door to Whiskey Bay, anger was the sole force driving me forward.

"Asher?" said a familiar voice to my left. "Man, I'm gonna be honest, you're persona non grata over here right now. Nat's not going to want to see your face, so I'd get the fuck out—"

Kevan's sentence died when my hand wrapped around his throat.

Our eyes met.

Fear swirled in his, and his hands came up to grasp at

my hand, desperation making each move sloppy. Blunt nails scratched my flesh. His mouth popped open, and I heard his ragged gasp. Noted the reddening in his cheeks as I kept him suspended an inch off the ground.

My grip never slackened.

"You're going to let me upstairs." Quiet, lethal, my voice barely reached a pitch high enough to draw attention to us. The Birkenstock crowd was too concerned about the women dancing to even glance in our direction. *Perfect.* Jerking Kevan close, our noses almost brushed. "You tell Nat that I'm here and I'll finish what I started." My gaze dropped to my hand encircling his throat in a clear threat. "Don't fuck me over, Kev. It never ends well."

Lips purpling, his tongue darted out to wet the bottom one. "P-please—"

"It's a yes or a no. You let me upstairs and tell her nothing. That's the way this shit is going to play out."

His head bobbed, fingers scrambling for purchase, and I dropped him a breath later.

Legs quivering, his hands went to his knees as he dragged in air. "W-what the fuck is *wrong* with you?"

In a rare moment when Nat hadn't explicitly showed her hatred for me, she'd once ruffled my hair and teased, "Lincoln, our resident killer."

That'd been before I'd murdered her brother on Ambideaux's command.

Before she and Jason had separated and then divorced.

Before she'd requested Avery handle the honors and end my life.

For twenty-seven years she'd been at my throat, waiting for any opportunity to throw me under the bus and watch me suffer. I was done playing by the rules. Done letting her have the upper hand because she didn't have a penis and should be left alone.

I wouldn't kill her—she wasn't worthy of being taken out quickly—but I'd make her life hell.

I turned my gaze on Kevan, who'd always been Nat's part-time fuckbuddy when she wasn't busy screwing dignitaries as a full-time gig. "Unlock the door to the Basement."

He laughed, the sound crude and hollow. "It's your head or mine if I do that, Ash, and I like mine just where it—"

He didn't see it coming.

My arm around his wiry chest, the other locked over his mouth to keep him from shouting and making a scene. I knew Whiskey Bay like the back of my hand, and I dragged his thrashing body back, back, back, until we were ensconced in a side closet brimming with cleaning supplies.

"I hope she fucking kills you for this shit. You're no better than Jason—"

His words died with my fist colliding with his cheek. Head swiveling to the left, a grunt broke free from his mouth—and I didn't miss the irony with this little setup. Ambideaux had done the same to me in my townhouse. Had shoved me into a chair and tried to break me.

I wasn't trying to break Kevan. Wasn't trying to kill him either.

But I'd be damned if he ruined my chance to catch Nat unaware.

Snagging a length of velvet cord off a shelf, I spun Kevan around and wrapped the rope around his wrists. Once I'd tied him off like he was Thanksgiving dinner, I sat him down on the floor—back to the wall.

His eyes were fluttering, breathing uneven. Groans were pitiful.

I'd dealt with worse, and I had no doubt that he'd live.

Dropping to my haunches, I quickly dug through his

pockets for the building keys. They were hooked to his belt, and five second later, they were hooked to mine.

I shut the door behind me on my way out, locking it from the outside.

With a quick glance from right to left, I moved toward the back of the room, heading for the long hallway that'd lead me to the Basement. No one said a word as I brushed past them, my head down. They were too busy drinking, too drunk on the sight of almost-naked women twirling on the poles throughout the room.

Shoulder to the General Storage Closet door, I flipped through each key individually until I found the perfect match. Inserted it into the lock, twisted the metal door handle, and quietly entered the darkened room.

At this time of night, the Basement would just be rearing up to go. The gambling tables would be popping though the stages would still be quiet and unused. Which meant that Nat would be circulating each table as she observed her den, watching for weaknesses in the players, instructing the house to make certain moves.

I took the steps up to the second floor, two at a time.

By the time the night was over, Nat would rethink ever trying to eviscerate me—*or* using Avery to do so.

My heart thudded at the thought of how I'd left her. I'd sensed her disappointment in me. Hated the desperation she'd voiced in wanting me to step back, to rethink, to not act impulsively.

She didn't understand.

Jay Foley may have tried to kill her *once*, but my neck had been positioned under the guillotine by too many people over the years. I was done with the threats. I was done with stepping back and keeping my head down and trying to stay away.

If they wanted to dance, then I'd fucking dance them right into their graves.

My eyes adjusted to the dark slant to the room, its seductive shadows rippling like water along the walls and the floor. Only two of the almost ten stages were open so far: a female masturbating on one, and then a couple fucking on the other.

I turned away, clinically skimming my gaze as I searched for a glimpse of Nat. Hand on the butt of my gun at my hip, I hunched my shoulders and sank deeper into the shadows along the wall. She'd be here, I knew she'd be here.

And if I had any luck, Hampton would be here too.

I'd given him the benefit of the doubt the night at the shack in bumfuck nowhere. A benefit that had bitten me in the ass when I'd turned my back and given him room to play.

That was my fault.

My mistake, but one I wouldn't make again.

I tracked each figure that entered my periphery, and then—

"Bingo," I muttered beneath my breath.

There was only one woman who'd be dolled up in a gold dress that shimmered and glowed like that. Like a beacon of falsehood, she threw her head back with a tinkling laugh, her hand pressed to a man's shoulder as he sat at one of the tables.

Limbs loose, I waited. It was part of the hunt, the waiting. Couldn't move too soon for fear of giving myself away.

Two minutes later, a man appeared at her side and bent to whisper in her ear.

Her laughter died. Giving a brief nod at the man, she made her exaggerated goodbyes at the table, and then followed the newcomer away from the gambling. They bypassed the rooms where I'd owned Avery's pleasure, and then breezed past a doorway just left of the bar.

Her offices.

Time to go.

I trailed them at a safe distance, and either the guy bartending was new and didn't recognize my face or he didn't give a damn because, just like Nat and the stranger, I breezed past the bar, too.

Flexing my fingers, I angled my body to hug the walls.

It'd be too easy to pull out my firearm now and unload a round the moment I saw either her or Hampton—but I was a civilized bastard, as much as was possible, anyway, and I only listened for the distinct sound of their voices.

Stepped down the hallway.

Paused. Listened.

Kept going.

"I'm glad you were able to meet me. It's been so very *long*, and I have such an interesting bit of information to tell you."

Here we go. Back to the wall, just beside the door, I strained to hear the response—tried to gather how many people might be beyond the closed door.

"It has been, Natalie. Quite long." There was a small pause, and then the masculine voice added, "Wasn't expecting to find Quinn here with you."

Feminine laughter drifted out into the hall. "Quinn's loyalty has been on my side for a *very* long time, sir. Since the end of my marriage, at least."

"How fascinating."

My eyes slammed shut as I recognized that voice—Jay Foley. My deadbeat, socialite of a father.

Fuck.

He never traveled without security which meant that

there were at least four people inside: Nat, Foley, the stranger Quinn, and at least one detail assigned to my asshole father. Give or take another one or two, just depending on how paranoid Foley felt this evening.

The situation wasn't ideal.

Actually, it was *far* from ideal.

But I'd been in worse positions. Hell, the first and only time I'd ever met my father had been during one of the annual first-responder galas. I'd had no interest in going, but Delery wouldn't have it—and it'd been with a shock of disbelief when the mayor walked up to me, out of nowhere, and said, "Heard through the grapevine that you're my son."

The introduction had been impersonal.

And the fleeting happiness that had entered my heart at being recognized—maybe even wanted—was extinguished in the very next second when the mayor cut a glance at me and muttered, "I've heard of you, of course, and what I've heard is disturbing. Man to man, I thought you should know who I am to you but"—he'd looked away —"I've got no interest in having a son, Mr. Asher, and particularly not one like you."

Particularly not one like you.

If I'd been quick enough on my feet, and not reeling from shock, I would have gotten in his face. Told him that the only reason I was *like me* was due to the fact that I'd been dumped as a child. Maybe if I'd been shown love, hugged on occasion, told that I was more than "our little killer," the mere mention of my name wouldn't have disturbed *him* or anyone else.

I never learned who told him about me.

It could have been Ambideaux, my mother's close childhood friend.

Could have been Nat, on a bender after the poker

game gone wrong with her brother, and wanting me to hurt. Years had separated her brother's death and when Foley had approached me, but she held grudges longer than even I did.

Back to the wall, I drew in air, filling my lungs, and debated my next steps.

There was no other way about it: I'd have to stroll in there like a casual son of a gun. Act like it was all part of my plan to be the odd number out.

Now or never.

MINOR ARCANA
reversed

TWENTY-FIVE

Lincoln

Pursing my lips, I whistled like a damn lunatic and popped the door wide open with the toe of my combat boot.

Then slammed to a dramatic stop as I went faux wide-eyed at the lot of them in the room. "Hot damn," I drawled with pure sarcasm, "I must have strolled into the wrong room."

For a solid two seconds, there was pure silence.

And then everyone launched into motion: Nat leapt up from her seat and Foley dragged her back, while Nat's lackey—Quinn—hurled himself toward me, the mayor's detail in tow.

I ducked the swing of Quinn's arm on instinct alone. Came up on the other side, one hand clamping on his extended arm to swing him around by the elbow until I'd put him in Ambideaux's favorite hold.

Wrists at his lower back. Knees buckling as I shoved my leg against the back of his thighs.

"Sorry to barge in," I grunted as Foley's detail came at me from the other side. I had a split second to feel guilty for doing what I was about to do but—*fuck it.* I swiveled Quinn to the left, positioning him before me like a shield at the last moment, and *crack!*

Quinn's head whipped to the side from the blow of the pistol connecting with his face.

As I'd been taught growing up, an opportunity gained was never an opportunity wasted—I helped myself to the gun at his hip, and then let his shocked body fall to the floor. Stepped over him and announced, "Not exactly the family reunion most people dream about, but pretty par for the course for me."

Foley's security detail didn't make it two steps before the mayor was barking out, "Everyone, stop!"

The detail froze.

I didn't abide by the mayor's orders and took the seat Quinn had vacated before trying to take me down. One ankle propped up on my opposite knee, I rested the butt of the gun on my thigh, pointing the mouth toward Nat.

"Why don't you take a seat?" I murmured with a motion of a free hand at her empty chair. "We've got some shit to discuss."

Her elegance had long since left the building and she came up spluttering. "I will *not*. Are you out of your mind? Why are you here?"

"Heard you wanted me dead. And I figured what better way to put the shit to bed than to nip it in the bud." Idly, I stroked the polymer frame of Quinn's Glock. At Nat's wide-eyed glance at the gun, I quirked a brow. "You've always thought the worst of me, Nat. I'm not going to *shoot* you."

When the stiff set to her shoulders loosened, I murmured, "Although, trust me, it's tempting as fuck. Between you and your husband, I can't catch a break." A bitter laugh rolled through me like a shard of ice. "To think, at one point I'd considered y'all family."

I'd meant it as a throwaway comment.

There was not a chance in hell I could have predicted the way her red-painted lips twisted in a sneer. The florescent lights caught on the shimmer and glimmer of her gold-sequined dress, making her look like the modern-day equivalent of a disco ball.

"I am *not* your mother," she hissed, chin jutting forward, eyes narrowed into slits. "You were a leech on my marriage, always there, always *existing*. But no matter how much Jason kept you around, you were *never* a son to me."

It wasn't anything I hadn't heard before—Nat had never been good at concealing her feelings for me, and I'd long ago built steel armor to protect myself from her vicious tongue. To be likened to a leech, though? Christ, something had crawled up her ass and died today.

Stroking the Glock, just to keep her off-balance and twitchy, I met her gaze. "I don't know who you're trying to shock right now, Nat. You hate me. That isn't anything I didn't already know—that I haven't known for years." I couldn't help glancing at Foley, just to catch his impression of this showdown, especially since he already found me *disturbing*.

Being this close to him, though . . . fuck, I wished that I had all those testimonies to lock him up for good.

You could have had Avery's.

Maybe. But I'd let my thirst for vengeance and violence override her offer. Even now, I couldn't deny the pulse of anger that sharpened my vision and vibrated just under my skin. It was the anger that pressed the words off my tongue: "And it's not as if I don't have experiences with mothers hating me. I get enough of that shit with my biological one, so I don't need you—"

Jay Foley's deep laugh interrupted me.

I stared at him the way I hadn't done when I'd first walked in—the salt and pepper hair, the dark eyes, the strong jawline. The New Orleans media had once likened him to George Clooney, and I could see it easily. Dressed in a crisp, gray suit, there was an air about him that was deceptively friendly. Easygoing.

It was all too easy to see why all those females had fallen victim to his charms.

As for me, I was too much of a jaded bastard to do anything but stare impassively at him, my thumb coming to rest on the trigger guard. He may have knocked up my mother, but he was as much of a father to me as any other stranger I'd met along the way in my life.

"Care to share what's so funny with the class, Mr. Mayor?"

With his thumb, he swiped at his right eye. "It's heartless of me to laugh, of course."

My grip tightened on the Glock. "There's no press here for you to put on the gentlemanly act. Whatever you've got on your mind, just fucking say it."

His dark eyes swung to Nat, whose brow was once again unpuckered. She smiled, just a little, and there was something in her expression . . . something about the way she turned to me with clear eyes and that smirk . . .

Blood chilling, I growled, "Someone want to get on with the program?"

The mayor shook his head like he was utterly flabbergasted. "How does he not know?" he asked the room, not making eye contact with any one of us. "Jesus, this is rich. How does he *not know*?"

Energy spiked down my spine, and I rose from the chair. I kept Quinn's gun in front of my hips, clasped between my two hands in caution. "What the fuck don't I know?"

"Your mother is *dead*."

Four words from my father's mouth, and I staggered back. Victoria Meriden hadn't loved me, hadn't ever shown me even a smidgeon of affection, but she was still my mother. Still the woman who'd brought me into this world.

Pain slipped over me, needling my skin like the sharp tips of a blade, over and over until I'd been torn open. Gaping wounds. Bleeding profusely.

"How?" I worked out hoarsely, my gaze volleying between Nat and Foley. "When did you find out? Did Jason"—I swallowed, hating the vulnerability in my voice —"tell you?" I looked to Nat. "Is that what happened? He told you?"

Not even a hint of pity lined her features when she stared at me, not saying a word. If I'd wanted to throttle her before, it was nothing compared to the rage that seeped into my marrow now.

"Someone answer me—when did she *die*?" My voice boomed through the room. I spun around to face Quinn, who was now hauled up against the wall, touching a palm to his cheek. Foley's detail was next to him, standing guard.

She couldn't be dead. Yeah, she'd had medical complications over the years. The car accident had robbed so much from her—the use of her legs, her mind, it seemed, which included her memories of me. But Ambideaux had more money than God, and he kept her lifelines steady. That was our deal. Had always been our deal.

I worked for him, and he ensured that my mother—

My legs wavered under my weight. *No*. No, he wouldn't have . . . I was going to be sick. Right here, right now, I was going to lose the contents of my stomach in a way that I'd only ever done three times in my life.

The night I'd committed my first murder and brought the body to the Atchafalaya Basin.

When I'd learned that Avery—Laurel—was dead.

And when I'd driven Tom Townsend out there, just a few weeks ago.

Foley, my father, cleared his throat. "Put the gun down, Sergeant."

I shook my head. The gun wasn't going anywhere.

Firearms weren't capable of betrayal. No, that feat only belonged to humanity.

To people like Nat and Ambideaux and Foley and Hampton.

"When did she die?" I asked again, eyes on my father's face. "*When did she die?*"

He looked at me, and it was the first time that sorrow lined his handsome features. "She's been dead since you were two years old, Lincoln. She died in the car accident."

THREE OF SWORDS
reversed

TWENTY-SIX

Avery

When push came to shove, I'd hailed a cab from Lincoln's townhouse in Bayou St. John and hightailed it straight back to the Sultan's Palace. Katie had kicked me out. She'd vowed that she needed space.

She was my family—my only family—and as I barged up the steps and tried the lock on our apartment door, I prayed that we could get past this.

I needed her.

No matter how I'd entered her life, she'd always been my support system. With Lincoln on a suicide mission, I didn't know where else to go.

The door was locked, and I smashed my fist on the wood in a desperate knock. "Katie! Katie, open the door. Please!"

A second passed.

And then yet another.

And then the door was pulling open wide and my best friend, my roommate, my step-cousin, was standing there looking like a hot mess with rumpled PJ's and hair that looked like it hadn't been brushed in days, even though it'd only been twenty-four hours since I'd walked out.

Her blue eyes blinked back at me.

A half-second later, her arms were around my back and hauling me close. She was taller than me, and my nose ended up in her armpit.

"Katie—"

"Oh, my God, you're back," she whispered, her hand petting the crown of my head like I was her most prized possession. "He said he wouldn't tell you but I'm so glad that he did. I'm so sorry. I'm so fucking sorry, Ave."

I opened my mouth and managed to inhale straight B.O. Coughing, I pushed as much as I could out of her embrace. "I don't even know what you're talking about. *Who* wouldn't tell me what?"

She didn't let me go.

With a palm to my back, she yanked me into place, my nose getting reacquainted with her armpit all over again. "Captain America," she muttered, "he came here looking for you and I said that I was sorry about what happened. And I *am*. I'm so sorry. All the things I said—telling Ambideaux about you. I'm so sorry, Avery. I'm so fucking sorry."

"It's okay." It wasn't okay. Because Katie had only been reacting to my deceit. "I'm the one who needs to apologize," I rushed out, squeezing her back because this was family. *She* was my family, just like I wanted Lincoln to be. "I lied. I lied so many times and you were right to call me out and put me in my place. I left because you were *right*, and what I did . . . it's not excusable, Katie. There are *no* excuses."

Her shoulders sagged. "Friends?"

I nodded into her armpit. "Always."

She released me, and I spent a solid five seconds inhaling fresh air before I stepped into the apartment and fisted my hands on my hips. There was no easy way to phrase what I needed to say, and it didn't escape my notice that for the first time in my life . . . I was asking for help.

Katie sat on the armrest of the sofa, hands folding in her lap as she stared up at me. "What's the matter? You've got a look on your face that I *really* don't like."

I swallowed. Pushed the nerves so far down that I wouldn't choke on them as I spoke. "I need your help." I dove a hand through my hair, still somewhat tangled from sex with Lincoln. "I need . . . I need you to create a distraction."

Katie blinked. "A distraction? Where?"

Here goes nothing. Straightening my spine, I went for broke. "At Ambideaux's party that he invited me to. I need to go, and I need you to go with me."

I couldn't be in multiple places at once, but my gut told me that Lincoln would inevitably show up there. It would either begin with the Basement or with Ambideaux, and I was going for the latter for no other reason than it was a scene I could prepare for. While Katie created a distraction for the guests, I could . . .

Eyes squeezing shut, I tried not to think about what I'd do if needed.

Take a life in order to save Lincoln's.

Sacrifice my own freedom to see that he kept his.

It wasn't what I wanted, and if I had the opportunity to talk some sense into his stubborn head, I would. But if we showed up too late . . . if he'd gone to Ambideaux's first, instead of to the Basement, where I imagined he would go to begin his reign of death, then we were all fucked.

Think positive.

It was hard to do so when the man you were in love with was determined to ruin his life just to prove he was not someone who should be crossed.

Spinning on my heel, I went into the kitchen and climbed up onto the countertop. Resting one hand on the roof of the fridge, I pulled open the cabinet and took out the gun I'd never used.

"Ave? You're freaking me out."

I glanced down at Katie, who'd trailed me into the kitchen. Turning the gun around, I handed her the butt. "Hold this so I can climb down." When her brows arched high, I added, "Please don't shoot me."

"Trust me, of the two of us, I'm pretty sure we're better off with me holding this thing."

I hopped back down to the kitchen tile. "You know how to shoot?" I asked, bewildered at the familiar way she handled the firearm.

The grin she gave me could have lit up a room. "Bonding with my dad meant going to the range. He's an enthusiast."

An . . . enthusiast?

And then I was grinning, too. "You think you can teach me how to use it by the time we make it to the cocktail party?"

Katie didn't even blink. "Hell no. We're going to need more than fifteen minutes."

Refusing to let my confidence waver, I dropped my eyes to the firearm. "You think you can at least help me *look* like I know what the hell I'm doing?"

"Slightly more realistic but if you keep looking at it as though it's a snake, we're going to have some problems."

I didn't know whether to laugh or to feel grateful for having Katie at my side, as we'd always been since meeting a few years back.

In the end, I offered her a shaky smile and muttered, "I *really* need to get a new taser."

MINOR ARCANA
reversed

My finger hovered over the trigger, the palm of my hand slick with sweat against the polymer frame.

"You're lying." Feet rooted to the tile floor, I jerked my gaze from Foley to Nat. "You've seen her," I said, "for years you've *seen her.*"

For fuck's sake, my mother lived with Ambideaux. Sure, she had her own wing in the home, but she wasn't a ghost. She wasn't just a figment of my imagination. Nat had seen her countless times over the years, though my mother hadn't moved out of the hospital and into the house with Jason until some time after he and Nat had divorced.

My throat closed up, and I swear to God my heart iced over as I stood there, waiting for someone to fucking say something that wasn't cryptic. Waited, even longer, for the sensation of being run over by a truck to ease off my worn body and steamroll someone else for a change.

With a nod to his detail, Foley took one of the empty

seats and sat down. Like he was preparing himself for a conversation over tea and baked goods.

Fingers tightening around the gun, I tracked his every movement. "Stop with the bullshit." One step to the left set my back against the wall, giving me the chance to note everyone in the room—as well as the empty doorway. "I know my mother's alive, so if you're hoping to fuck with my head, you're going to need a new intimidation tactic—"

"Jason always was obsessed with your mother." Foley flicked a stray piece of lint off his suit pants. "They were childhood friends. All of us were next-door neighbors. But they were each other's firsts in every capacity of the word."

Nat's expression tightened, and I bit my tongue to keep from saying anything that might encourage Quinn or the security detail to put a bullet through my temple.

He hiked on his pants, pinching the fabric at the knees, and resettled himself in. Foley continued, then, arms loose on the chair as he pinned me in place with an unwavering stare. "And then she had you, her precious boy. You lit up her world. Stole her heart, and there was nothing she wouldn't have done for you."

I couldn't hear my heart pounding—it was buried beneath the blood roaring in my head.

And yet I stood there, back to the wall, hands locked around the gun's grip, my goddamn soul bellowing out for it all to stop.

"She'd died whereas you lived," my father went on, his face completely impassive as he watched me. "But, of course, no one dwelled too long on a death of a girl like Victoria Meriden. Her family were nobodies, but unlike myself or Jason, she never went on to make something of herself. Sweet, beautiful, but a stripper on Bourbon. She was a nobody. *No one cared.*"

I cared.

I cared that Foley was fucking with my head, just to get past my defenses. I cared that he was making shit up—shit that I knew was untrue. I cared so much that I shot forward and, with a hand to the back of his chair, I shoved the frame backward. Foley was big, but I was stronger, and the chair teetered on its hind legs for two interminably long seconds before I gave it another push, and my father and the chair went tumbling down with a crash.

"Is he fucking *insane*?" spat either Quinn or the detail, and I did nothing but glance up, aim my weapon, and shoot at their feet.

Not close enough to get them, but too close for comfort.

"Stay in your lane," I growled, "this shit has nothing to do with you, and the only place I'd ever send your fucking boss is to jail." I shoved my face into Jay's, and his dark eyes stared back, wide but cool. Not even a hint of panic.

Apparently, I'd inherited at least one thing from the bastard: remaining unattached, no matter the situation.

Like Big Hampton had done to me on that damn ride out to the middle of nowhere, I shoved the muzzle up against Jay's jawline. "We're going to try this again." I canted his head, angling the firearm at a sharper slant. Then moved my free hand to my pant leg, where I removed my weapon and positioned that one to face Quinn and the lackey. "You want me to believe that my mother died thirty years ago? Fine, let's play pretend." Breathing heavily, I leaned in. "Jason's version of Victoria, who I've always known . . . who is she?"

A dark chuckle greeted my ears. "Victoria's sister. Your *aunt*."

I would have gone stumbling if I wasn't so determined to maintain the upper hand.

Only, Jay's revelation rocked me. My ears popped and my vision turned red at the periphery, and my weight tipped forward. *No*. "I don't believe you. It's been over thirty years since the accident. She can't walk. The tests, the hospital visits. There's no way he would be able to keep all that going for—"

"You know Jason." My father's mouth twisted angrily, and even though he was flat on his back, his tone remained calm like the politician he was. "You know him better than almost anyone. Do you think he'd risk it all just to get caught? He's a monster. Always has been, even when we were kids."

It was a struggle to pull air into my lungs. If what he said was true . . . "She can't walk," I repeated again, voice fainter than the first go 'round. "The car accident—"

Dark eyes bounced from my hand holding the gun and then to my face, and for the first time, Foley's face turned wary. Nervous. He licked his lips, then grunted when I amped up the pressure of the gun to his jaw. "He gave you those scars on your face, didn't he?" he said at last. "Jason was the kid in the neighborhood popping the heads off of animals. The one our parents never let us spend any time with alone because he wasn't quite right in the head, they said. He did that with her—Samantha—crushed her legs so she couldn't walk. So she fit the part. I knew it. Nat knew it, too."

Behind me, Nat let out a keening sound that rang in my ears and pierced my soul. It was a cry of a wounded animal, and I wasn't sure if she were making fun of the story, adding to the dramatics, or if her own memories were so traumatizing that even the mention of her ex-husband was enough to send her into hysterics.

I thought of my mother—the woman Jason had always claimed to be my mother—and my heart sank, fracturing into a thousand little shards. Just like the antique vase I'd broken at Ambideaux's house. I felt shattered, balanced on the lip of no return, the pieces of my mind unable to fit together what Foley told me now.

It made no sense.

And still it made more sense than anything else ever had.

The way she refused to look at me.

How she'd always rejected me as her son.

He crushed her legs.

The words registered, horrific and horrible, and I fell back onto my ass. "Why?" I demanded, my throat raw. "Why would he do that?"

It wasn't Foley who spoke up, but Nat, and the words she said sent a chill down my spine.

"With her under his care, you couldn't strike back. He manipulated you, Asher, his son—the baby boy I could never give him."

TEN OF SWORDS
reversed

Lincoln

I heard nothing at all.

Not the voices around me.

Not the music echoing from down the hall in the main area of the Basement.

Not the beating of my heart erupting in my chest into a wild staccato that could not be tamed.

Nothing.

If I'd already visited each circle of Dante's hell, I must be in a new one now. Purgatory, maybe. More likely an undiscovered one that was meant only for me—designed and constructed to drown me until the fight left my body and there was nothing left but grief.

This wasn't how it was all supposed to go down.

Foley was meant to be in jail for everything he'd done over the years.

Nat was meant to be so frightened, she'd leave New Orleans for good.

Hampton . . . fuck, I couldn't even think that far right now.

Everything had been a lie. I should have seen it

coming, I should have been able to narrow down why Jason had a hard-on for everyone around him.

"Why?" I rasped to no one and everyone all at once. I blinked, focusing on Foley, the man who'd come to *me* and said he was my father. "Why would you assume that you were my dad?"

What kind of fucked-up, Jerry-Springer shit did I just land myself into?

The mayor of New Orleans rolled over onto his knees from where I'd practically tackled him to the floor. "Jason told me so a few years ago. Who the fuck ever knows why with him?"

The numbness faded, replaced by the familiar sting of fury. Rising onto my feet, I whirled around to face Nat. She'd known. All these years, she'd *known* and had said nothing. I neared her, closing in, both guns clasped in my hands.

She didn't cower. Like Avery, Natalie Lauren never shrank back in fear. Her chin tipped up and she met my gaze as she stared at me over the bridge of her nose. "Furious?" she hissed. "Imagine what it's been like for *me*. Married to a man who became so obsessed with another that when she died, even after cheating on me, he got himself the next best thing—her sister. I've hated you. I have hated you for *years*, and the fact that you will not die . . ."

I should have expected it.

The band of arms that wrapped around my chest and yanked me back. Rough hands that ripped the Glocks from my grip. My heels dragged along the tile as I tightened my core and tried to slow the momentum of being taken off to God-knows-where.

"Stop struggling, asshole," said a deep voice in my ear.

Screw that.

My hands went to his forearms, latching on, holding tight, preparing to send him to Timbuktu when he tightened his grip and grunted, "You want to live? Shut the fuck up and let me do this."

Eyes drifting to the right, I caught sight of Foley yanking on the sleeves of his suit as he traded an inscrutable glance with Nat. Behind him, his detail watched me, eyes narrowed, jaw clenched, gun trained on my face.

The man behind me had to be Quinn. Nat's right-hand man.

And now he was promising to drag me to safety?

I grit my teeth. It was against my innate nature to let him take the wheel. I didn't know him worth a damn—had never seen him before tonight—but there were times when you had to rely on fate.

I let him drag my ass out of that room.

Away from the man who wasn't my father.

Away from the woman who'd wanted me dead for as long as I'd drawn air to breathe.

I struggled in Quinn's hold for the sake of appearances. Spat out vile words and elbowed him in the gut. Let out a quintessential, "Let me go, you fucker!" just before my feet crossed over the threshold of the room.

By the time the door shut, Quinn was heaving like a newbie sprinter. He released me. Then, hand to my back, he corralled me down the hall.

"You need to get out of here," he muttered, giving me no other option than to keep walking forward. "Nat might be playing nice, but she wants your head on a platter."

That stopped me.

Ducking under his arm, I twisted around to face him. He was even in height with me. Older, maybe mid-forties. Gray peppered his dark hair, and he walked with a distinct limp that made me wonder if he'd been shot before.

"I've been in this world too long to know that you aren't just going to let me go because you feel bad." I got in his face, careful to keep enough of a distance that if he held a knife, I was still out of direct reach. "If you're Nat's bitch, then—"

My back slammed against the wall. His fingers grasped my shirt, fisting the fabric as he jerked me in. "I'm nobody's bitch, Sergeant."

I danced my fingers to my back, skimming my waistband to circle the butt of my trench knife. "No?"

"No." His dark eyes narrowed. "No," he repeated, voice low, "I'm the man who kept your girlfriend alive when her stepfather wanted her dead. The one who opened the window downstairs for her to escape and locked her bedroom door so she had the chance to run. That was *me*."

The trench knife dropped to the floor, my grip going loose.

"Yeah, not expecting that, were you?" Quinn's mouth drew up in a dark, sadistic grin. "*I* let her go, and it cost me my right leg."

"You killed her mother."

His hold on my shirt tightened. "She knew it was coming and refused to leave. That was her choice, her decision, and I did what I could. I made sure her daughter got out alive."

Where I'd been sent to kill her.

Because of Ambideaux.

Because of my *father*.

Because Jay Foley had done something so awful that Jason sought nothing but retribution.

"Why did he want her dead?" My gaze cut over to the

left. The hall was empty. Quiet aside from our hushed voices. "Why the hell did Jay want—"

"Because she'd inherited money—her father's living will left everything he owned to her when he was diagnosed with cancer, and he owned most of the city." Quinn squeezed his eyes shut, color cresting on his cheeks. "I wanted her to leave. I *begged* her to leave. She refused, and Jay would have killed her no matter what. He'd so much as told her so."

I'd spent years reading expressions, diagnosing liars, and Quinn . . . Jesus Christ, but he was worse than them all. "You didn't kill her, did you."

Not a question.

He answered anyway, his voice raw, cracking, as the past swarmed over him—looking at his face, it was clear that he might be standing in this hallway, but he wasn't here with me now. Not really.

"She wouldn't leave—her house, her family, the life she knew." Adam's apple dipping, the man swallowed, hard. "I couldn't do it. I'd loved her for years, and I couldn't fucking do it. She pulled the trigger. Ended it all. Wasn't in her right mind and wouldn't listen no matter what I told her. When it came to Laurel . . . she didn't know me, but I knew her from Catherine. I let her go. I don't regret it."

I let her go. I don't regret it.

I'd thought the same thing when I'd left Avery on that front lawn. I couldn't kill her—couldn't do what it was that Ambideaux had asked of me.

Realization hit me square in the gut.

And the words fell from my lips as though they'd been pushed up from my heart: "He was pissed. Holy fuck, Jason was pissed that Foley was about to walk away with the entire city in his pocket."

Quinn's eyes, red with grief, narrowed on me. "What the hell are you talking about?"

"Nothing." I swallowed. "Everything. Shit." I shoved him back with a hand to his chest. "I gotta go. You"—I met his gaze—"you want to make sure Laurel is safe for the rest of her life? Testify."

"*What?*"

Christ, I didn't have time to explain. Dropping to my heels, I grabbed my trench knife off the floor and, snapping it closed, shoved it at his chest. "It's monogramed," I said, kicking my chin toward the knife. "Go to the eighth district station and ask to speak with Lieutenant Stefan Delery. Tell him exactly what you just told me and tell him that Avery—*Laurel Peyton*—will testify too."

When he didn't make a move to grab the knife, I gave it another push at his chest, forcing him to take hold. "If Nat asks where you went, tell her . . . tell her that you brought me out to the Atchafalaya Basin. She'll know what that means, and here's to hoping it gives me enough time to go meet you at the station with Avery ASAP."

She'd been right.

There was a way to end this without total bloodshed—at least when it came to Mayor Jay Foley. Nat would go down, too, there was no denying that. She'd left crumbs throughout the years that made her as much a suspect as the city's beloved mayor.

Ambideaux . . . Skin tightening at the thought of everything I'd learned, I hurried down the steps of the Basement. I wanted to take him down. Wanted to string him up and feed him to the goddamn gators, the way he'd done to me—his own fucking son.

I thought of Quinn, the way he'd been in near tears thinking of Avery's mother. He'd loved her—however that had happened, he'd loved her, and he put her first over his own life. His choice had been to save her.

I chose Avery.

She'd entered my life when I'd least expected it, knocked me on my ass with her wit and her perseverance and the goddamn bravery she radiated like a second skin.

I was a man who'd never known love, but I'd fallen in love with her.

Her safety was priority. Her *life* was priority.

Between me and her, I chose her.

Always.

VIII

THE STRENGTH

MAJOR ARCANA

Avery

"He's not here."

Katie glanced over at me, then locked her arm with mine. "You don't know that. He might be."

He wasn't. I would have sensed his presence or at least spotted his broad frame above all the people milling about.

Lifting my chin, I scoured the room, taking note of all the black cocktail dresses and black suits. It seemed that the whole of New Orleans was packed in the parlor and dining room of Ambideaux's house. No matter which way I turned, I was on the receiving end of an elbow to the side or a splash of a cocktail landing on the silk dress I'd borrowed from Katie.

Worry spliced through me.

He had to be at the Basement, then, going after Nat. *Dammit.* I'd taken a guess and had guessed wrong. By the time we even made it over there . . . I couldn't imagine the sort of damage he might cause.

Or the death.

I understood his anger, had thrived in that anger for

years, but it wasn't worth risking his life. My life. The life we might have together if we managed to get out of this alive.

"We've been here for an hour," I muttered to Katie. "The likelihood that we missed him is slim to none."

She nudged me. "What about the second floor?"

I lifted my gaze to the circular stairwell just beyond the dining room. "I doubt he's up there. He'd be where Ambideaux is, and Ambideaux is . . ." I trailed off, hastily looking for the man of the hour. "He was just there. By the grand piano."

Katie craned her neck. "Bet he went to the bathroom. The man has been tossing back vodka like he's going for a liquor baptism session." Her hands went to her dress and, without even acknowledging that we were surrounded by some of the wealthiest people in the city, shoved her hand down her dress and adjusted her breasts.

My eyes went wide. "What are you doing?"

"Your distraction is here and willing to work." She tugged on the thin straps of her dress, letting them snap against her skin when she released the bands. "I'm going to stalk Mr. Future Mayor by the loo. You go upstairs. Make sure he's not there."

"You do realize you're not British, right?"

Katie winked. "You do realize that you brought me here for a reason, right?"

Dammit, she was right. Leaning back, I checked out the grand piano again, just in case. Nada. Looked like we were going for Plan B, with Katie leading the breast troops over by the loo.

When she stepped back, I circled her arm with my hand, pulling her to a quick stop. "Be safe," I told her, giving her a quick squeeze before letting go.

Her lips pulled up in one of her trademark smiles. "Be

brave, Ave. Go get your man before he does something idiotic and you're forced to visit him in jail for the next fifteen years. You'll be horny for life, and he'll be getting it up the ass from a prison friend. Don't let that be your future."

Well, when she put it that way, there wasn't a shot in hell that I was leaving this house without turning it over first.

We gave each other a little salute, then went off in opposite directions.

My purse slapped my leg as I hustled to the stairwell. It was heavy, my gun tucked inside for safekeeping, and at the sight of the velvet cord hovering above the third step, I climbed over it and hurried up the stairs. They creaked under my weight, no doubt as old as the house was, and I cursed every wooden whine.

Cursed, also, Lincoln's damn stubbornness for not setting aside his need for vengeance.

He wasn't a monster, just a man, and I knew that all men were fallible. But that didn't mean he should go risking his neck just to ensure that he wasn't caught unaware sometime down the line.

The second floor was carpeted, but I stripped off my high heels anyway and hooked the back straps over my finger. Cocked my hip as I walked and gave a little stumble —Katie wasn't the only one good at performing. If someone caught me up here, I'd rather they think I was a drunk wandering than, well, doing what I was *actually* doing.

Ensuring Sergeant Lincoln Asher didn't commit murder and end up somebody's personal friend in prison for the next twenty years.

Peeking into one room, I came up empty and went for the next.

Did the same with the next two rooms, one of which led to a bathroom.

Also empty.

Heart pounding, I neared the end of the hall. There was only one door left. Like the others, it was tugged shut. The ratio factor told me that Lincoln wasn't in there, but I couldn't leave without checking first.

On silent feet, I approached it, hand moving toward the doorknob. Pressed my cheek to the door. Hearing nothing at all, I twisted the handle and glanced inside.

"Who's there?" snapped a feminine voice. "Who is that?"

Don't go in there.

Leave.

Turn around!

I'd never been good at following orders, not even my own.

I stepped inside. Shut the door behind me.

And stared at the woman who couldn't be anyone but Lincoln's mother.

THREE OF WANDS

Lincoln

My townhouse was empty, the front door unlocked but closed shut.

Desperation crawled through me, weighing down my limbs as I stalked down every room, hoping that I was wrong. That she hadn't left. That she hadn't gone looking for me.

"Fuck!"

Fury ricocheted through me, and I twirled around on impact and slammed my fist into the nearest wall. The plaster cracked. My knuckles cracked. My damn heart cracked as I tried to clear my thoughts and assess the situation.

In thirty-four years, I'd always managed to operate with a clear head because I had nothing to lose. *No one* to lose. That wasn't the case now—hadn't been since Avery entered the picture and tossed my life into a blender and flicked the switch to ON.

I couldn't think beyond the stampeding of my heart and the blood thundering in my head.

If she wasn't here, and she hadn't gone to the Basement, then there were only two other options: Big Hampton's or Ambideaux's cocktail party that she'd received an invitation to attend.

Laying a hand on the now-fractured wall, I dropped my chin and inhaled sharply.

If I had more time, I'd go to the Sultan's Palace in the off chance she'd stopped by there to meet with Katie.

But I didn't have time. It wasn't on my side.

Swiping a hand over my face, I pushed away from the wall and beat it to the still-running SUV on the front drive.

I had to take a lucky guess, and my guess was that she'd gone to Jason's.

My father's.

Stomach churning at the thought, I climbed into the SUV and fumbled for my new cell phone. Flicked through the sparse number of contacts until Delery's name was blinking across the screen.

He picked up on the second ring. "What do you want, Ash?"

For the first time in my life, I would try to play by the rules. "I need units at Jason Ambideaux's house."

There was a minute pause. "What the fuck are you talking about?"

It wasn't the first time I'd heard that today.

Palming the steering wheel, I whipped the SUV down along the bayou. "Units, L-T. Police officers. Trust me on this."

Laughter echoed in my ear. "Ash, man, you feeling okay? I'm telling you that—"

"No," I bit out, "I'm telling *you* that unless you want shit about one of your officers being blasted all across the news tomorrow morning, you'll send me some backup so things don't get that far."

"Well, shit."

Yeah, that about summed up my day.

"L-T?"

Delery breathed into the phone. "Please tell me you don't have anything else to say."

Swinging a right, the SUV went airborne when I hit a massive bump crossing the intersection. "Yeah," I grunted, gunning the car once I'd hit the back road that would lead me to Jason's, "I sent someone over to you. About the Foley case. Turn him away and I'll shoot your dick off the next time we see each other."

"That threat's been old since we were in the East."

"Yeah, well, I never said I've gotten more original with age."

Canceling the call, I tossed my phone onto the passenger's seat.

Hold on, sweetheart. I'm coming for you.

QUEEN of SWORDS

MINOR ARCANA
reversed

Avery

She was blindfolded.

Shock skated down my spine as I took in what had to be Lincoln's mother.

Posted up in bed, her wiry arms were crossed over her chest, her legs hidden beneath swaths of comforters and sheets. A TV sat opposite her, on top of a waist-high table. Large murals graced the walls, turning what would have been an ordinary room into something resembling a rainforest. And, to the left of the bed, a wheelchair waited, angled toward the mattress.

"Jason?" she called, her arms jolting into action. Shaky fingers reached up, up, up, searching for the scrap of fabric over her eyes. "Jason, is that you?"

If I said nothing at all, she'd know in three seconds when she whipped the blindfold off and spotted me by the doorway.

I cleared my throat. Swallowed, hard. "No, not Jason."

She stiffened in the bed. "Who are you?"

Seeing her like this, all trussed up in the bed, made pity beat a steady pace in my heart. Handicapped or not, no one deserved the pure isolation of being unable to see—because someone else wanted to remove that ability from you.

Dropping my heels to the plush carpet, I moved to her side and did the honors—sliding the black fabric up and off her face, until she was blinking up at me with eerily familiar-colored eyes.

Haint-blue, the same as Lincoln's.

God, I hurt for them both. Lincoln, who'd been forced, through no fault of his own, to put up with the moods of a woman who was clearly in pain. For his mother, who clearly had been held here like some sort of captive.

Everything was in perfect order. The wheelchair, the TV, the paintings on the wall. But who blindfolded a woman with a condition like hers? *Someone cruel, like Ambideaux.*

"I'm so sorry for intruding," I whispered, my tongue swollen with nerves. "I'm a . . . guest downstairs. Of Jason's."

Her mouth firmed into a thin line. "This is a private room."

There were so many things I wished to say, the most important being: did Lincoln know how she was kept here?

I balled the scrap of fabric in my hand. "Yes, I'm sorry."

What else was there to say? I needed to go. Lincoln's mother wasn't like the strays I picked up or the homeless that I brought food to whenever I could. She wasn't in need of a savior, and she certainly didn't need me—but I couldn't turn away.

"You need to go."

Yes, I thought, *you're completely right.*

My feet wouldn't budge.

"Does Jason treat you well?"

Her thin, dark brows lifted. "That's not your business."

No, it wasn't.

The blindfold tangled in my fingers as I held it up. "Do you like this?" I asked softly. "If so, then there's no concern. None. But I can't help but feel as though you're kept blinded on purpose. You're not . . . are you?"

Her already fragile-like features winced, pinching at her brow and then again in her jawline. Her fingers fluttered in her lap. "He said it would help me to focus when I want to think about something. I have a hard time focusing. Always have, but especially after—"

"Lincoln was born?"

It was the wrong thing to say.

I saw it immediately, the way her gaze shuttered, and her chest heaved with a big, uneven breath. "Get out."

"Ma'am, I'm—"

"*Get out!*"

She shrieked the words at the top of her lungs. I knew it was only my imagination, but it seemed like even the walls shook with the force of her rage. There was no doubt that even the party downstairs had heard her bellow, and I backpedaled, feet tripping over the carpet in my haste to get the hell out of dodge.

"Get out!" Her coloring turned red, the color of the murals on the wall. The color of blood. "Get out! Get *out!*"

Her arm shot out to the left and she smacked something on her bedside table. When her hand came away, I saw that it was a button. A button that was clearly important to her because her palm came down again and again and again on it.

Oh, *shit*.

The straps of my purse swung left as I went right.

Lurching toward the door, I ripped it open to the

chorus of Lincoln's mother losing her shit behind me. Slammed it shut to another verse of "Get out!"

The music downstairs was still playing. Thank God.

Maybe no one had heard her catastrophic shrieking.

Please, let no one have heard her.

Shoeless, my feet padded over the floor. It was time to go. Maybe Lincoln had gone to the Basement or maybe he'd developed a lick of sense and had gone straight to the police station. Maybe—

Footsteps that weren't mine drew my attention up off the floor and to the end of the hallway.

Jason Ambideaux stared back at me, his black hair slicked back, his suit pristine.

Then, his mouth curved in a smile that made me sick. "How wonderful of you to join us, Miss Peyton."

My gaze jerked to the left and to the right—there was nowhere to go.

Nowhere to escape.

Like when I'd heard Momma die, I was stuck. Frozen. Unable to move.

He took a step toward me.

I wouldn't be my mother, dead on the floor with the blood coating my hair.

I spun on my bare heels and ran.

"There's nowhere for you to go, Miss Peyton," Ambideaux said, his voice a pitch above a menacing murmur. "Or should I call you Miss Washington?"

The rooms were prison cells on this floor. There were no fire escapes that I'd seen from the outside when walking up. No big bushes to catch my fall if I leapt out.

Be brave.

Be bold.

My gaze caught on Lincoln's mother's room. She was still shrieking, still yelling at the top of her lungs. There was no other option, and I didn't dare take the time to risk looking back at Ambideaux.

With my shoulder, I burst the door open like a battering ram, which did nothing to calm the woman's shrieking from the bed.

"Get out! Get out! Get out!"

"Sorry, lady," I muttered, turning the lock and stumbling backward, "we're stuck together for the time being."

The doorknob jiggled a second later, and then there was Ambideaux's voice, no longer so smooth or cajoling. "Victoria!" The door visibly shook on its hinges, like he'd thrown his body against it from the other side. "*Victoria!*"

Behind me, Lincoln's mother didn't miss a beat: "Get *out! Get out!*"

The door creaked. And then, beyond it, again: "Victoria!"

My head swirled from the cacophony of noises. Heart thudded against my ribcage. Stomach churned as I clutched the strap of my purse and turned in a slow circle, assessing my surroundings. The closet was an obvious— and dumb—choice, and so I shot toward the window as the next best thing, hoping, praying . . .

Forehead kissing the glass, I glanced down and bit out a curse. No fire escape. No bushes to catch my fall. If I didn't break my neck, I'd be lucky to be the recipient of a bum leg, which would do me no favors when I couldn't flee.

Taking the time to move furniture to the door might work in the movies but wouldn't do me much good. I didn't have the time.

I was a sitting duck.

"Get out! Get out! Get out!"

Gaze snapping to the woman panicking in her bed, I swallowed.

Don't do it.

Don't you dare fucking do it.

The door squealed as a metal hinge whined in protest, then gave way.

Sometimes good people did bad things.

I didn't give myself time to rethink my decision. Popping my purse open, I ignored the flames of guilt and shame in my belly, and then pulled out the Glock Pete had given to me years ago. It was bulky in my hand, so foreign, and with a squaring of my shoulders, I set the mouth of the gun to Lincoln's mother's head.

And then I waited for Ambideaux to come bursting inside.

KING of SWORDS

MINOR ARCANA

Lincoln

T he units weren't at Ambideaux's house when my SUV squealed to a stop in the middle of the street.

Which meant that either Delery hadn't dispatched them or they simply hadn't arrived yet. I was praying for the latter. Hoping for miracles I didn't actually believe in.

The front lawn was packed to the brim with guests all decked out in cocktail attire. Suits for the men; dresses for the women. I shoved past them all, fully cognizant of the fact that this was the first time I'd ever entered the house while a party was taking place.

I'd always been relegated to security. Peering in through the windows.

Today, I didn't stop to appreciate the beauty of the house or the guests.

Avery, where are you?

Bursting inside, I swiveled my head to scan the parlor. Clusters of people were tossing back cocktails and laughing.

"Can you believe it?" said one, her voice tinkling like

chimes in the wind. "I mean, I know that *I'm* excited to see what the city will look like with Mr. Ambideaux in charge. He's just so charming."

"And hot," teased another. "I wish he'd let his hair go gray. Total silver-fox status."

Putting Ambideaux in office would be the equivalent of setting a city ablaze. Jack the Ripper would be a better alternative.

I powered through the groups, moving them aside, constantly scanning the rooms with the hope that I'd spot a familiar dark head. When I found her, I'd kiss her, owning her mouth with mine. And then I'd bend her over my knee and clap my hand down on her ass until she learned—for once—what it meant to fucking obey an order.

"Captain America?"

My heart leapt, and then resettled with disappointment when I realized it wasn't Avery's voice.

Fingers wrapped around my bicep, and I glanced down. It was her roommate.

"Katie," she supplied without missing a beat. She dropped her hand, only to set it to her collarbone. "I'm so, so glad you're here. We've been looking for you—"

"Avery's here?"

"She's been looking for *you*. So, yes, she's here. We're both here. Where have you been?"

All over this fucking city.

I shook my head, my palm glossing over my stubble. "Doesn't matter. We need to get her and head out." I peered over Katie's head, searching the crowd. "Where is she?"

The light in Katie's eyes dimmed. "I saw her thirty minutes ago. Maybe forty." Swallowing, she bit down on her bottom lip. "I figured that she'd found you. I've been watching Ambideaux this whole time—making sure he stayed where I could see him."

The way her brow puckered was not an encouraging sign.

"But?" I pushed, my patience already wearing thin.

"But he took a door I couldn't enter through about fifteen minutes ago. I've been waiting, figuring he'd come back out." Another swallow. "I was going to give it another five minutes before I went searching for her. I was hoping . . ."

There wasn't any time to listen to her hopes, not right now.

"Wait outside," I told her. "I had my lieutenant call units over here. They should be arriving."

Katie's head bobbed. "Sure, yeah. Okay, I can do that." She stepped back, hands going to the skirt of her dress as she went to spin around—but she slammed to a sudden halt, and then peered back at me. "Cap, I'm just going to say this once. She loves you. She might not know how to say it, but I know she does. Keep her safe or I will personally shoot you."

Despite the bad timing, my lips twitched. "10-4, Black Widow, 10-4."

She preened at that.

And, as pathetic as it was, I preened a little myself.

Avery loves me.

Christ, I was a sap.

Until I found her, there wasn't cause for celebration though. I eyed the stairwell. Palmed my one remaining Glock, and then ascended the stairs.

SIX OF SWORDS
reversed

THIRTY-THREE

Avery

My hands shook around the gun.

They shook even more when the woman's gaze jumped to my face. Those familiar blue eyes of hers were startling clear. No fear at the gun pressed to her temple. No quivering lips.

"Do it," the woman rasped.

My stomach dropped. "What?"

When the door squealed again, the woman's hands went in the air, trying to grasp my arm. "Do it," she said again, desperation tingeing her voice, "*do it*. Please, please, please—"

The hinges gave up their fight.

I twisted at the waist, forcing impassivity to my face when all I felt was frantic energy pulsing through my body. "Mr. Ambideaux," I drawled with false bravado, "how wonderful of you to join us."

He stumbled, the momentum of throwing his body at the door making it hard for him to stop. Dark eyes volleyed from me to Lincoln's mother.

"Victoria and I were just having a lovely conversation."

My index finger hovered over the trigger, and I immediately slipped it to the left. Just in case I got jumpy. Although, who was I kidding? I was beyond jumpy already.

My lungs seized the air, and I struggled to appear unaffected.

"Back away from her," Ambideaux barked. "I'm telling you right now, Miss Peyton, if you pull that trigger, I will end you for good. Better yet, I'll hand-deliver you to your stepfather." Mouth tugging in that same awful smile, he added, "Is that how you want this to end? *I would love nothing more.*"

Beside me, Lincoln's mother began a new, softly uttered chant: "Do it, do it do it do it."

I had no idea if she referred to me still or if she was egging Ambideaux on. I re-grasped the gun, hating the sweat pooling in my palms. "I've got no interest in going to see the mayor."

"Then put the gun down."

I forced steel into my tone. "Screw you."

Eyes narrowing into slits, he swept aside the fabric of his suit jacket to reveal a holstered gun at his hip. "Let me tell you what happens to people who cross me, Miss Peyton." He palmed the gun, bringing it up to eye level before turning it to point at me. "I shoot them, but of course, nowhere where they're particularly likely to die . . . not right away. I want them to suffer. I want them to bleed."

His leather shoes slipped over the carpet silently as he approached.

"Only when they're begging me for life do I move on to the next step." The mouth of his pistol went to his cheek, where he drew a line down the length of his profile. Slow. Menacing. I immediately thought of Lincoln, and the *J* he'd been forced to carve into, just to show that he would never be owned by this man. "They're all marked by me in some way. Tattoos on the living. Scars on the almost-dead. And then, of course, they're then brought out west for the gators to feast on."

The image made my stomach hurt.

My heart, too.

Voice releasing on a rasp, I said, "You're insane."

"No, Miss Peyton," he said with an odd little grin on his face, "that is not at all what I am."

"Do it," whispered Lincoln's mother again, "please, please, do it."

Ambideaux's gaze cut to her. "Victoria—"

"Samantha!" she shrieked, startling me. The gun jerked in my hand, accidentally shoving forward on her temple, and the damn woman didn't even flinch. She tilted her head, giving the gun more space to play along her hairline. "I'm not Victoria. I'm not Victoria. I'm not—"

Confusion gripped me, and then a moment later, a gunshot erupted.

The window to my right shattered just as Ambideaux went down, his big body crumpling as something hit him from behind.

A familiar frame bulldozed Ambideaux over, rolling the older man onto his back while he straddled his midsection.

Lincoln.

Oh, God.

I didn't dare make a sound, fear clogging my throat that I'd distract him and he'd end up with a bullet in his head instead of it sailing through a window.

Hands wrapped around my wrist. "Please," the woman —Samantha?—whispered urgently, her eyes fixed on the gun. "Please kill me. I can't"—a sob wracked her body—"I can't do this anymore. He'll never let me go. Please. Do it, do it, do it."

My mouth went dry.

Lincoln had said his mother had never cared about him, but I couldn't kill her. *I can't end someone's life.* The gun had just been a threat. A way to bend Ambideaux to my demands, letting me escape unscathed.

"*Please.*" She yanked on my hand.

Masculine grunting tore my attention from her to land on the men wrestling on the ground. Lincoln nailed Ambideaux in the face, a fist so powerful that it whipped the man's head to the side and no doubt loosened his teeth on impact.

"I should have killed you," Ambideaux growled loud enough for me to hear, his hands scrabbling for purchase around Lincoln's throat, still wielding his gun as his arm slashed through the air. "I had so many damn opportunities over the years and I was too soft."

Lincoln didn't say a word. His face was a mask of concentration as he weaved out of the way of Ambideaux's grasping hands. Leaning forward, Lincoln hooked his legs around the other man's, and then rolled them over until Ambideaux was eating carpet and Lincoln was on his back.

His gun trained on the back of the man's head.

THE FOOL

MAJOR ARCANA

Lincoln

I was aware of Avery's beautiful hazel eyes on me.

Aware of the woman I'd always thought of as my mother making incoherent pleas that didn't register beyond the thundering of my heart in my chest.

Adrenaline pulsing like I'd been injected with Epinephrine, I kept the muzzle steady on the back of my father's head. *My father.* Bitterness joined the adrenaline, and I leveraged my pistol forward, digging the mouth into Jason's skull.

I leaned down, the Glock brushing my unscarred cheek when I hissed, "Not exactly going down as you'd planned it, wouldn't you say? *Dad.*"

His body twitched under mine, and I laughed.

Fuck, I laughed. Long and hard and so damn bitter. "I always wondered why you'd taken a liking to me in foster care. Me over anyone else. And here I'd been thinking that I was special."

I heard Avery's gasp, but I couldn't let myself be distracted.

The sight of Ambideaux pointing a gun at her would

forever be imprinted in my head. It'd twisted my vision, driven me to the brink of insanity, and now here I was, holding my old man up at gunpoint and not regretting a damn thing.

No one touched her. No one threatened her.

I would fucking send them to hell first.

"What?" My palm landed on the man's head, and I roughly forced him to turn his face to the right, so that his left cheek was planted against the carpet. The gun, I dragged over the side of his profile exposed to me. His right side. "Too bad I'm all out of knives," I drawled, voice low, "or else I'd carve your face the same way you did to mine. To *your son*."

His Adam's apple bobbed. "I love your mother. Don't do this in front of her, Lincoln. Don't make her see—"

"She's not my mother!" I bellowed, which prompted more incoherent mumbles from my mom—*Samantha*. Ambideaux's mouth popped open, cheeks hollowing, as I pushed the gun deeper. "I learned a lot today, Jason, but mostly I learned that you are out of your mind."

He wheezed, and I felt his legs thrash as he struggled to flip me over. "I made you," he bit out harshly, "I made you who you are. A killer. A monster. Just like *me*."

The words arrowed into my heart like pinpricks.

"It's not true."

I glanced up, past the brutal scene before me, to stare at Avery. Her arms were down by her sides. Her gaze transfixed on me.

She wet her lips. "It's not true," she said again, louder this time. "You know that it's not true, Lincoln."

"Do it," chanted Samantha in the bed, her arms around her middle, "do it, do it."

Beneath me, Ambideaux thrashed some more. "You will always be what I made of you. A killer, Lincoln."

The endless noise was an assault on my ears, but I couldn't tear my gaze away from Avery. I watched her move, the way her lips formed the words that I couldn't hear over the roaring in my head.

Don't, she mouthed, *you are better than this. So much better.*

It didn't feel that way. It felt like I wanted to sink into my reality and pull the trigger, ending my father's life. One less threat hanging over my head for years to come when I didn't bend over backward to do his bidding.

I'm better than this.

I wasn't, not really.

But I damn sure wanted to be—because of her, Avery.

Unwilling to loosen my grip and have the roles reversed, with Ambideaux riding cowboy on my back, I sent a quick glance over the room, trying to find something I could use as rope. "Ave," I grunted, "get me—"

"Get out!"

I started at the shriek, my hands jerking from the unexpectedness of it.

"Get out! Get out! Get out!"

I looked to my right, dread lifting my chin slowly, and made eye contact with the mayor of New Orleans. His gaze was on Avery, transfixed in much the same way that guests do while watching a fascinating performance on stage.

The gun he held clasped between two hands was trained on her.

Fuck.

"Get out! *Get out!*"

Weeks ago, Avery had pulled the Death card for my future. It'd matched my fears for so long, but I refused to go down. I had a life to live. A woman to love.

My gun left Ambideaux's temple and I rolled out of

the way. Rose up onto one knee at the same moment Foley grimaced and turned to engage with me.

One . . .

Two . . .

Pft! Pft!

"Jesus Christ."

Foley dropped to his knees, hand going to his stomach where I'd hit him. The stomach, with all of its organs and intestines, would lead to a slow, excruciating death—unless he received medical help soon.

Relief sank into my system.

It was short-lived.

Arms locked around my chest, driving me backward onto the floor. *Jason.* My back landed with a thud, my molars cracking together as Ambideaux straddled me. And, just as he had in my townhouse weeks ago, he shoved the mouth of the gun into my forehead so that all I saw was the barrel and all I heard was his harsh breathing and Samantha's chants and Avery's scream.

"I love her," Jason whispered, his hair disheveled, his suit even more so. "I love her more than anything."

Air expelled sharply from my nose as I fought to remain calm. "More so than Nat? Your wife?"

Mouth flatlining, he shook his head. "Nat had it good. I gave her the world. It's because she's a greedy bitch that she couldn't handle you, that she couldn't look at Victoria." A grim mask settled over his face, and he leaned into my chest, giving me his full weight and making it hard to breathe. "No one crosses me, son. No one. It's a point to prove, to keep the fear moving in my favor in this city." His finger slid over the trigger, taking my long-dead heart right along with it. "I'm sorry that this has to happen. But you deserve it, just like they all did before you. You deserve—"

There was a low *thud* that echoed in my ears and

robbed me of air, and then Ambideaux stared down at me, dazed, swaying, before collapsing on top of me.

Avery stood behind him, a gun gripped in her two hands, a look of resigned horror on her face.

I'd once said that my heart was dead. I'd fully believed it. A person couldn't do the things that I had done and still remain human inside—I'd been a monster, just like Ambideaux had raised me to be. But with my father's slumped weight on top of me and Avery standing just a foot away, her eyes as round as saucers, I knew that wasn't true.

If I'd been a monster, there wouldn't be regret and grief seeping into my marrow.

Regret that Avery had had to take this step when she'd made the decision to abstain from taking another's life.

Grief that Jason, the one man I'd leaned on while growing up, had, at some point, lost his mind so that his delusions became his reality . . . and threatened everyone else in his wake.

Avery's tongue swiped along the cushion of her bottom lip. "He's not dead, I don't think. You were right—I don't know how to shoot a gun. I didn't want to risk killing you instead if I aimed wrong. I-I slammed the barrel on his head."

Rolling Jason's body off mine, I pressed a finger to his throat, just beneath the jut of his jaw. His pulse was light but it was there. A strange mixture of relief and disappointment slid through me, and I didn't bother to sort it all out. Not right now.

My gaze went to Samantha, the woman Ambideaux had kept here in captivity. Her smashed legs. She hadn't been intentionally cruel, I saw that now. Like me, she'd been in her own prison of Ambideaux's making, unable to escape.

"I'm sorry," I rasped when her blue eyes, so much like mine, swung my way. "I'm so sorry, Samantha."

Her eyes went wide and her shoulders shook and a distraught cry pulled from her mouth. "Samantha," she whispered, "I've always been Samantha."

A hand landed on my back, comforting in its softness, in its slight pressure. For years, I'd been strong. Unshakable. The man who got things done and didn't ask questions. My chest was littered with dates and numbers of those who I'd put in their graves way too soon.

In this moment, though, I turned to Avery—the woman who saw beneath my hard veneer—and I swallowed her in a hug that lifted her feet off the floor and had her hands jumping around my back to keep her balance.

"I'm okay, Lincoln." She kissed my chest, right over my heart, right over her number. "I'm okay."

My nose nudged her neck as I inhaled her scent. "I didn't ask for a savior." My lips found the pulse at her neck, and I lingered there, gratification filtering through me that she was safe, she was okay. "I didn't ask for a savior, but you found me anyway."

And then my Avery, the bravest girl I knew, kissed my chest again and propped her chin on my pec, lifting her gaze to mine. Her lashes were wet with tears. Her beautiful face open and transparent as she murmured, "You found me in the shadows, Sergeant, when I was afraid, and you brought me back to the world of the living."

We were two untethered souls who'd found each other, and, Christ, holding her felt so good. So right. "You're mi—"

Commotion at the doorway had me lowering Avery to her feet.

Katie was there. Quinn. Delery. And, to my biggest shock of all, Big Hampton stood before them all. He looked from me to Avery. And then, to her, he said, "I've heard that sometimes good people do bad things, Miss Peyton. I'm making an effort to be good all the way around, so I hope you won't mind that I took the liberty to go to the NOPD in your stead and"—he looked down at the mayor of New Orleans, who was clutching his stomach and moaning—"see to it that things were put into place to make things right."

Avery released a strangled cough. "Well, damn."

And if that wasn't a proper slogan for the last month's events, I didn't know what was.

XXI

THE WORLD

MAJOR ARCANA

Avery

SIX HOURS LATER...

"**C**an I sit here with you?"

Since the showdown at Ambideaux's house, and the bloodshed that had followed, Lincoln and I had been shuffled to NOPD Headquarters. The building was a 1960's monolith with stark, uncompromising lines, and a general air of sterility that made my skin run cold.

Or maybe it was just that, after learning everything that I had today about Foley and Momma, and then Lincoln and Jason Ambideaux and his poor Aunt Samantha, I felt chilled to the bone.

"Miss Laurel?"

Throughout the day, I'd had to answer to Laurel and Avery, and my brain had lost track the number of times I'd failed to turn around when spoken to. For a woman who'd adopted too many identities, I'd grown to know one—Avery—and nothing else seemed to fit any longer.

I glanced up at the familiar husky voice—Quinn—he'd introduced himself to me, earlier, when we'd all first found ourselves at headquarters and camped out in uncomfortable seats to wait our turn to speak with the police.

The man who let me live.

The man who didn't kill Momma.

I knew, somehow, that he'd seemed familiar when I'd first stumbled across him at Whiskey Bay.

I nodded jerkily. "Of course. Sure."

His ass hit the seat next to mine, and he immediately hunched over, elbows on his knees. For a moment, he was quiet. And then, "I thought I was seeing ghosts when you walked into Whiskey Bay a few weeks back. My past coming back to haunt me and all that."

I swallowed, then dropped my gaze to my clasped hands. "Not a ghost," I said softly, "just a girl who learned to hide for a very long time."

A dark noise reverberated in his chest, and he shoved one hand through his salt-and-pepper crewcut. "You didn't deserve any of what happened. You were a child and Foley was a greedy son of a gun. She knew what he'd do to her —what he'd done to others—and that he'd never let her get out alive. I've wracked my brain so many times, so many conversations we never got to have. I wouldn't do it, she knew that, and I think she worried about Foley moving to the next person who'd kill her, no questions asked." He shoved a hand through his hair again, tugging on the short strands. "I want to believe she knew what she was doing and that she'd thought everything through, including what might happen to you."

I stared down at my hands. Watched them curl and unfurl in my lap. "She drank a lot. I remember her falling asleep with the bottle tucked to her chest. I remember her crying at all hours of the day, a glass of wine in her hand." She'd been lightness and shadows, when I really looked back on it—laughter and thunderstorms, a troubled combination that probably had crumpled upon learning what Foley intended.

It pained me to think that Momma had been in such a dark place . . . that she probably hadn't been thinking clearly when she'd pulled the trigger. That maybe she'd felt like she had nowhere to go, nowhere to turn.

Just like I had for all these years.

It hurt to swallow, but no more than my heart already hurt, knowing all that I knew now. And what I'd never know. "I know you feel guilty, but I promise that it's okay. From what I understand, you were stuck. She stole the decision from you and you did what you could—you kept me safe."

I didn't want to understand—I wanted to cling to the rage that had fueled me for so long. But at what purpose? You couldn't reverse the actions of the dead, and you couldn't question them after they were gone. If any of that were possible, the world would be a different place. Momma had made her decision that night, and I had to live with that.

Quinn's Adam's apple bobbed as he continued to stare down at his scarred hands, and it hit me then that he and Lincoln were one and the same. Their loyalties had laid with different people, but at the end of the day . . . two killers, two so-called monsters, two allegedly heartless men who lived for the violence and nothing more.

Quinn swiped a thumb under his eye. Cleared his throat. "I met her first, you know. In Jackson Square. She was twenty-four to my nineteen, but goddamn, she was beautiful. All long, blond hair and brilliant hazel eyes, the kind I wanted to lose myself in."

My heart rocketed to a stop. "In Jackson Square?"

His jaw clenched. "She was one of the artists along the gates. Painted the most beautiful scenes of the city that you'd ever see. I didn't have the courage to do more than talk to her that day, and the next time I saw her, she was on Foley's arm. My boss, the girl I couldn't stop thinking about." He laughed, the sound hollow and sad. "She remembered me because I'd made a fool of myself. I remembered her because I'd never seen another soul with so much light. You were six then, I think."

The heartache in his voice broke my own heart, cleaving it in two. Without giving it a second thought, I touched his forearm in sympathy. He looked like he needed it. Like maybe this was the first time since Momma had passed that he'd had the chance to say what he wanted to say.

"I wasn't allowed to be around you," he added a moment later. "You weren't even his child, but there were rules in play. Like Cat, you belonged to him. He was—*is*— a controlling man, but the night he came to me and told me that I needed to be the one to kill her, I refused. Said no."

It was hard to breathe, harder to digest it all. "Lincoln mentioned something about an inheritance? I just don't understand."

Quinn's shoulders lifted. "From what little I know, your mom was cut off from her family when she had you. She made her living down in the square, sometimes bartending here or there, but then Foley swept her off her feet." His feet began to tap the floor, nervous energy radiating from him. "Your grandfather was dying, and I guess there was no one else to leave the money to—so he gave it to your mom with a single stipulation: if something were to happen to her, the money, the countless properties throughout the city, would go to her husband."

"And not to me."

"Not to you," he repeated, his voice cut with an edge.

"I'm sorry that he wasn't progressive or that he didn't see you as—"

"I'm not."

And I wasn't. I'd never met my grandfather. The sparse memories that I had of life before Jay were of me and my mother living in a small apartment over a corner store in the Marigny. There were no cousins to play with or family to smother me with affection, just me and Momma. I'd done fine without the money all these years, and though it balled my fists to think that she was dead on account of a greedy bastard like Jay wanting to own it all, I knew he felt his own form of regret.

He'd called Nat by my mother's name whenever he screwed her.

He'd found women—sometimes teenagers—throughout the city who looked like her, to do the same.

He'd get what was coming to him, but I . . . I just wanted to go home for tonight. Wherever that was.

"Sweetheart."

That voice.

I blinked up at Lincoln, at the hand he offered me, at the harshness of his features, and the beauty of his Haint-blue eyes.

"Harlonne let me know we can take off for the night." He paused, fingers curling when I didn't take his hand fast enough. Doubt flashed like a bolt of lightning across his face. And then, "Come home with me."

We were two broken souls, our lives somehow aligning parallel throughout the years without either of us knowing. My eyes watered, and just before his hand would have dropped back to his side, I caught him by the fingertips. "Yes," I whispered, "please."

At my side, Quinn cleared his throat again. "I'll let you go, then." He stood, clapping Lincoln on the shoulder.

"Thanks for using me as a human body shield today. Much appreciated."

Lincoln barked out a laugh. "Desperate times."

"Don't I know it." He glanced back at me, brow furrowed. "Before I go . . . Nat's already getting out of the city. We all got the alert, so I—well, I thought you should know. You're not going to have to worry." He turned away without another word, head down. His limp was more pronounced than the first time I'd seen him at Whiskey Bay.

"Quinn!" I shouted, and he immediately checked over his shoulder. "Give me your number. Maybe . . . maybe we could get lunch one day? Talk about my momma or the Saints or whatever it is that you want?"

The man's face lit up like a beacon, and I felt the warmth inside my chest, too. "Fuck yeah. I mean, yeah. Yeah, that would be good. If your boyfriend promises not to clobber me over the head, maybe we can invite him too."

Lincoln's smile was all badass charm. "No promises, man. Bad habits are the hardest to break."

And then my own Captain America, my own Thor, was swooping me up in his arms, just like he had outside that shack when I'd wanted to clobber *him* over the head. He pressed a kiss to my cheek, to my forehead, to the crooked slant of my nose, broken from a skateboard accident gone wrong as a kid.

"I'm taking you home," he said in my ear, "and that's an order you're gonna have to obey."

I grinned. "Funny enough, *no* isn't a word in my vocabulary right now. Better take advantage while you can."

"Oh, I plan to, sweetheart. I plan to."

VII

THE CHARIOT

MAJOR ARCANA

Lincoln

I took advantage, as I promised—and Avery didn't have a single complaint as she sank into the steaming bathwater two hours later.

"God," she groaned, her head tipping back as the water lapped at her small breasts, "that feels so damn good."

I snapped open a shampoo bottle. Squeezed a healthy dose into my palm. "Lean forward," I said, my voice pure grit as my cock hardened in my sweats. "Let me take care of you."

She did as I ordered, leaning forward without question, droplets of water clinging to her smooth skin as she pulled away from the side of the tub. Like a lot of old homes in New Orleans, I was the proud owner of a claw-foot tub. Normally, I hated the damn thing. Now, I counted my lucky blessings as I inched my chair closer to the porcelain and set my hands in Avery's dark hair to massage the shampoo into her scalp.

"Will you keep it black?" I asked. I didn't give a shit one way or the other, but with Jay Foley in the hospital—

and then on a one-way ticket to Louisiana's infamous Angola prison—she was free.

Free to be who she wanted.

Free to look however she pleased.

Free to leave me.

If I had it my way, she'd be suctioned to my side for the rest of our lives. My wife, my anchor, the future mother of our children. Fuck, I wanted it so bad. When death had always been my fated future, however I looked at it, it felt surreal to think that I had a chance for something else now.

"Yeah." A moan escaped her lips as I rocked my thumbs into the base of her skull, kneading the muscles at the nape of her neck. "God, yes."

Laughter rumbled in my chest. "Is that a yes to the dark hair or a yes to me making you feel like heaven right now?"

Her head fell forward. "All of it. Particularly the heaven bit."

My hands glided down the expanse of her back, thumbs digging in along either side of her spine. She was perfect under my touch. Beautiful. Expressive. Her arms went to the sides of the tub, and then she arched her back. The mirror on the wall opposite us showed me what my vantage point didn't: her breasts thrusting forward, her eyes open and homed in on me, the slope of her belly rising above the water as she stretched upward gracefully.

Fingers teasing the sides of her ribcage, I blatantly flirted with the outer swells of her breasts. "What do you want, sweetheart? Tell me what you want."

If she heard the urgency in my voice, it only seemed to spur hers on. In the mirror, her hazel eyes rounded. She reached back over her shoulder, seeking my hand. I dunked my hand in the water, rinsing off the shampoo and then tangled our fingers together.

"I want to be wanted," she said, and I didn't miss the slight quiver in her hands. "But more than that, I want to be loved." She swallowed. Squeezed my hand. "By you, though. Only you."

I'd never been particularly sentimental, but as I brought her hand up to my mouth to press a kiss to her knuckles, I realized that I'd never let my guard down long enough to fall either. "Make room for me, Ave." I let her go. Shucked my sweats and my shirt and put all the horrors of my life on display for her to see. "I'm coming in."

The water swirled around her diaphragm as she moved to the opposite end of the tub. Craned her back and rinsed some of the soap from her head. Steam enveloped me as I set one foot into the water, then did the same with the other. And when I lowered myself to sit, the water rose from her diaphragm to her collarbone. It flirted with the lip of the tub, splashing over the side.

I didn't give a fuck.

"C'mere," I growled. "Let me love you."

A small smile played at her lips as she crawled on her hands and knees toward me, the water caressing her bottom lip. She looked like a sea goddess, sent to ruin my piece of mind.

Gorgeous. So fucking gorgeous, and she was all mine.

My hand gripped her waist, spinning her around so that her back was to my chest. She floated up, and I clamped my legs over hers to keep her in place. Bent my legs, so that hers would do the same, driving her open for me down below.

The back of her head fell to my collarbone. "I feel like there's so much to say." Her fingers teased the short hairs on my thighs, dragging her nails down, down, down until they came mighty damn close to grazing my cock. "I want to say everything—how shocked I feel that Momma took her own life, knowing that he would kill her anyway. That I'm trying not to feel disappointed that Jay will probably live or that Ambideaux . . ."

The blow she'd delivered him had shaken his brains, that's for sure. He'd fallen into a coma—maybe I was still that heartless bastard I'd always been because I felt no remorse about hoping he never woke up from it. A tiger couldn't always change his stripes, and I'd done enough changing in the last few weeks. For the better. I may not be a monster, but I'd never be citizen of the year.

I kissed Avery's damp shoulder. "We'll watch and see how it goes with the medics. He might come out of it."

"I wish I felt guiltier, for your sake more than mine. He was your father, but what he did to Samantha all these years . . ."

The way I looked at it, Samantha was the true victim in this situation. The doctors had found both heroin and Methamphetamine in her system—no doubt injected by Jason himself to keep her hooked and sedated. She'd told me over and over again that I wasn't her son, and instead of feeling dejected over it, I should have wondered why. Should have done something more instead of giving Jason more time to buy off the doctors so they told me what he wanted me to hear: her head was scrambled from the accident.

No, her head was scrambled from decades of drug usage that had been forced upon her.

My grip tightened on Avery's waist, and I wrapped an arm around her front like a band. "They'll wean her off," I said into the curve of her shoulder, "and if he survives, he'll rot in jail the way he should have for all these years."

Avery's soft hand, wrinkled from the water, closed over mine. "Look at me, Lincoln."

I met her gaze in the mirror, my chin on her shoulder. Struggled to not let her see the pain that I couldn't shake. "It'll all be fine. All of it."

Her nail bit into my knuckles. "Stop being so strong."

I smiled—and the one that reflected back in the mirror was just as weak as I suspected it was. "Thought I was Captain America. Thor, whatever. I have to be strong."

She shook her head, the strands of her hair brushing my face. "What did you once tell me? I'm a brave girl." Gently, she removed my arm from her middle and turned around. "Sit on the edge of the tub and let me be the one who takes care of you."

I wanted to tell her no. I wanted to be the one who cared for her, who made her feel safe.

Fuck it.

The bathwater surged as I ripped my body from its fold and sat on the edge of the tub, my hands going to the curved lip. Avery licked her lips. Glided closer. Rose onto her knees and circled my cock at the root.

My stomach tightened at the feel of her. I'd had her only hours ago, but, Christ, it felt like ages. Months. Years, even. With her eyes on my face, she brought her mouth to my hard-on. Swiped her tongue along the crown, and I'd be lying if I said that the one touch didn't light me up like an inferno.

"Ave," I grunted, hands still on the lip of the tub. *Don't push her to go faster. Let her set the pace.* It went against my nature to do that, to take the backseat . . . but with her, I'd done a lot of things that weren't very *me*.

Picnics under the moonlight.

Conversations that didn't stick on sex and only sex.

Falling in love.

Her mouth enveloped me. Her wet heat. The water splashing around my knees as she worked my cock until my eyes were crossed and my breathing came in hard pants that sounded choked even to my own ears. Her tongue glided along the base as she sucked me in deep. Her fingers tugged on my balls.

She was pushing me, testing my limits with a playful glint in her hazel eyes whenever she looked up at me, her pink lips opened wide. It was the exact visual I'd had when I met her in Jackson Square.

Avery was the girl who could handle my darkness, who dusted off the glowing embers with a flick of her hand and pulled me from the roots of hell to make love to her under the moon.

She licked the tip of my dick, then challenged me with a saucily delivered, "Give me everything, Sergeant. I can take it."

With a deep-seated groan, I submitted.

My hands went to her head, tangling in her hair. My hips rose off the porcelain as I drove my cock into her mouth, deep enough that I glanced off the back of her throat. My heart thundered with the words I only knew with her: *I love you, Iloveyou, Iloveyou.*

And then I was tearing myself away, watching my cock pop free from her mouth, as I dragged her up from the water and spun her around to stand. With me seated on the edge of the tub and her standing, she was at the perfect height. I nudged her legs together, so that her thighs touched, and then positioned her in front of me.

Her pussy hovering just above the tip of my cock.

"I want you like this," I said, voice low, my hand following the curve of her ass. "You taking your pleasure from me, no barriers between us."

There was a minute pause where I worried that I'd

come too strong, that I'd demanded more than she was willing to give just yet.

Then, her sweet, throaty voice greeted my ears and I almost came right then and there: "Challenge accepted, Cap. Challenge accepted."

The first glide in was a tight fit, and we both groaned.

"Oh, God, you feel big." She sank back, testing the waters by inching down the length of my cock. "You feel so big . . . like this."

I squeezed her ass cheeks and tried not to blow my load. "The hammer doesn't mess around."

A half-laugh fell from her mouth. "You always make jokes at the very worst times." Her fingers dug into my thighs as she slipped down another inch. "First when we're jumping out of windows and now this?"

Glancing down, I watched my cock sink fully into her. Gritting my teeth, I bit out, "Trust me, sweetheart, this isn't a joke."

Arching her back, she rose up, straightening her knees, before coming back down on me again. And then did it again. And again. Her ass moving up, her pussy sucking me in, she controlled the rhythm, the pace, the goddamn way that I breathed.

My skin felt like it was on fire, burning like I'd sat amidst the flames as opposed to the gradually cooling water lapping at our legs. I barely noticed, not when I sat there, letting Avery take me exactly how she wanted me.

Fast. Then slow. Then fast again.

My palm glanced off her ass cheek, punishing her the way that she was punishing me by never keeping the same rhythm for long. The pleasure was addicting. The way she rode me, like I was here to quench her desire alone, was addicting.

Circling her hip, my hand cupped between her legs and her pace jerked to a halt.

"Keep going," I muttered, the pad of my middle finger finding her swollen clit.

On shaky legs, she continued. Her back arched. Her ass bouncing. Her head dropped forward as she let out a moan that rattled my soul. I couldn't see her face in this angle, the mirror too far to the right.

"Are you watching me?" I demanded.

Her only response was a jerk of her hips and a loud, "Oh, my God, *Lincoln*."

My balls tightened, my orgasm creeping in. Fuck, not yet. *Not yet.* I applied more pressure on her clit. Gripped her hip with my other hand, forcing her to take the entire length of my cock with every downward thrust she gave me. "Are you watching me play with you?" I said again, pushing us both to our limits. "One finger or two?"

"Two," she gasped, her pussy squeezing me like a vice when I rubbed her clit with two fingers, just as she wanted. "*Please*, Lincoln."

She felt so damn good.

Air pumped out of my lungs, so uneven with each exhale that it almost hurt. Hurt even more when I managed a guttural, "Please what, sweetheart? *Please what?*"

"Love me. Just love me."

She burst apart in that moment and I jerked her off me just in time for my own orgasm to hit. I came all over her back, wishing that I'd come inside her instead. *Soon. Just not yet.* I wasn't a patient sort of guy—I took, knowing that no one would be waiting on the sidelines to give me what I wanted.

But Avery . . . I wanted her for forever. We'd get there.

Cupping the water in my hands, I washed her back.

Grabbed a loofah and drizzled soap into it, and then soaped her up. I turned her to face me. Swept the loofah up her flat belly to tease at her nipples.

And then I gave her my heart, for whatever it was worth: "I love you, Ave." I swallowed past my nerves—ones I'd never experienced before. "I walked into your world and then dragged you into mine. I've never been a gentleman—one look at my face and you know exactly what I mean. I'm rough around the edges. Dark all the way to my soul. My past is Ruin, as you told me with the cards. But the way you look at me . . . like you know I can be someone better . . . Christ, I want to be that man for you. The good one. The one who you know would do anything for you, no matter what it is." I dropped the loofah. Brought my hands down on her hips. Soaked up her warmth like it was a balm to the ice that had always coated my skin. "You're not looking for a savior, but I fucking hope you might be looking for a guy like me . . . the kind of guy who loves you, even if he knows he'll spend the rest of his life trying to be worthy of a brave girl like you."

My confession wasn't pretty.

It was barely articulate.

And yet, Avery dropped to her knees before me. Water splashed her chest, the underside of her chin. Her hazel eyes were red with unshed tears, and her nails dug into the back of my calves. She could draw blood and I wouldn't give two shits, so long as she—

"I bow to no man," she whispered, her gaze locked on my face. "I tattooed the words on my skin on my momma's ten-year anniversary." She inhaled sharply, and a lone tear fell from her bottom lash to land on her cheek. "I made that vow, knowing what had happened to her. I made that vow, determined to keep my heart safe and my body untouched from those who abuse me. I bowed to no one . . . until you. Until you walked up to me like the king of darkness and forced me to shed the shadows. You pushed me. You baited me. You made me *come alive* when I'd been dead for so damn long."

She kissed my knee, pressing her lips to the skin as her lids fell shut. "I wanted you, even when Big Hampton dropped the bomb that we may or may not be related. I wanted you, even when you showed me your darkness and I matched it with mine. And I love you, knowing that your rough edges will always be outweighed by the size of your hammer and the goodness in your heart."

I blinked. Rewound her words in my head to replay.

Stared down at her when she grinned brilliantly back at me, another tear joining the first on her cheek. "I'm trying to be romantic here and you're cracking jokes."

She nipped my knee. "Like you said before, your hammer is *not* a joke, Sergeant. Although neither was me jumping from a fire escape with no underwear on either. Could this be . . . karma, maybe?"

Reading the intent in my eyes, Avery launched from the bathtub and nearly slipped when her feet hit the tile.

I swiveled around, keeping my ass on the tub and my feet now on the floor. Water dripped from every inch of our skin and I didn't even care.

"You still feel good about following orders?" I asked her when she righted herself and skipped out of the bathroom, her perky ass making me hard all over again.

She glanced at me over her shoulder, her hazel eyes bright. "Catch me and see for yourself."

I caught her. Down the hall, where I then pressed her up against the wall and hiked her leg up, spreading her wide as I thrust into her.

"I love you," she whispered into my chest, kissing my heart.

All my life, I'd been a man resigned to death. But maybe the tarot cards had it wrong. Maybe it wasn't death in the literal sense, but maybe something like a new beginning. A fresh start. I could get down with that, so long as I had Avery at my side.

I slid my arm behind her, then pressed my mouth to her neck, just the way she liked. "I love you, sweetheart. Christ, how I love you."

NINE OF PENTACLES

Epilogue

AVERY

A year and two months later . . .

Jay Foley survived his gunshot wound.

Most days, I tried not to be bitter about it.

But because he didn't die, I sought out to ensure he'd never make it outside of a prison. When I wasn't taking my GED classes or working in the women's shelter I'd helped to found with the help of Lincoln's Aunt Samantha—who'd finally weaned herself off the drugs with the help of her nephew and the good doctors at University Hospital—I tracked down every female Lincoln had ever spoken to about the case against Foley.

I had lived in the shadows of New Orleans for over a decade, and because of that, I knew where to look. Like me in my teenage years, they'd feared men. They'd feared Lincoln, even when he'd assured them he only wanted to help.

In the end, I was the one who convinced them to testify against a man who had ripped families apart because of his greed. I was the one who stood next to them in each court date, my encouraging words the persuasion they needed to come forward.

"Corruption and New Orleans go hand-in-hand, and have since 1718," I told the judge when I began my testimony, using the words Jay once had repeated to me. Mayors in this city weren't immune and they weren't gods. They murdered, they sinned, they embezzled money like every other criminal to sit behind prison walls.

The judge dismissed court with a hammer of his gavel, but we already knew what his judgment would be. The city wanted Foley's head on a platter, and unless the judge wanted to face serious criticism from the public, the former mayor would be sentenced to Angola by the time the day was over.

I glanced back at the row of people who'd come to support me. Lincoln with Aunt Samantha. Pete and Sal were seated beside Katie, who was next to the city's new mayor, Joshua "Big" Hampton. He was an unlikely ally, no doubt driven by guilt for the way he'd manhandled Lincoln and me. Over the last year, though, he'd stood by his word to right his wrongs.

Sometimes good people did bad things—I was willing to overlook his faults for the way he'd turned the city around and led by example.

Quinn was here, somewhere, watching my back as he'd grown to do over the last year. I was a tarot reader in Jackson Square, a twenty-six-year-old woman studying for her GED, and part-owner to a shelter—but to Quinn, I would always be the daughter of the woman he'd loved. I didn't need a bodyguard just like I didn't need a savior, but the men in my life didn't give a damn when it came to seeing me safe.

Foley met my gaze when I stopped before his row. His handsome features were sallow, drawn, with deep, dark circles beneath his eyes. He looked like hell personified . . . and I'd never been more satisfied.

"Laurel." The metal cuffs around his ankles clanged their presence as he climbed to his feet. "I . . . I wanted to say that—"

I didn't shrink into myself, not the way I had outside our dining room all those years ago. Kicking up my chin, I forced out the words I'd rehearsed all morning on the drive in with Katie and Lincoln. "It's Avery."

Those weren't the words I'd rehearsed. Digging into my purse, I pulled out the one tarot card I'd brought with me today. The illustration was dark, composed of greens and blues and grays and drowning fountains. I set the card on the balustrade that separated us.

"What is that?"

"Gluttony." When his eyes narrowed, I added, "I hope that your stay in Angola is a frequent reminder that every step that led you there was on account of your own greed." I nodded toward the card. "I used to think that I wanted death for you, but I think . . . no, I think the sort of lifelong suffering you're in for is so much more appropriate."

Nodding, more to myself than to him, I turned on my heels and started to head over to my people. My family.

"Avery."

That voice, that sickening voice which had been the source of comfort to me as a child. I didn't look back— wouldn't give him that sort of satisfaction.

The silence stretched uncomfortably, and then: "She would be proud of you. Your momma, she would be so proud."

I knew that.

Be brave.

Be bold.

Sometimes being brave meant holding your tongue and

letting someone else drown in their own guilt. I said nothing in return.

After all these years, I'd come face to face with Jay Foley—and I'd ensured, after saying my piece during today's session, that I would never have to do so again.

Vengeance, sometimes, was best served by legal professionals.

THE SUN

MAJOR ARCANA

"Lagniappe" - Because New Orleans Always Gives More Than You Asked For

LINCOLN

Later that night . . .

My wife was exhausted.

The signs were there in the dark thumbprints beneath her hazel eyes and the quiet way she watched a recap of today's court proceedings on the TV opposite our bed. Over the last few months, she'd run herself ragged trying to get everything in line to send Foley to lockup for good.

Hell, she'd done a lot more than I had when Ambideaux's court date had rolled around. I'd shown up, dressed in my Class-B's from work, my new lieutenant patch all shiny on my arm, and did what needed to be done. Jason and I hadn't exchanged a word, but I hadn't expected anything less.

And when news had broken three months ago that he'd been killed in a prison fight, a knife straight to his gut, I'd simply driven to my Aunt Samantha's new place and poured her a glass of her favorite lemonade, and said, "You don't have to worry anymore. The fucker's dead."

She rarely smiled in my direction—too many years, I guessed, from having to put up with a life that wasn't hers —but she'd opened her arms wide and a tremulous smile had graced her thin lips as she said, "Give me a hug, nephew."

Nephew, never son.

But goddamn, had it felt good.

She loved Avery, though, and I'd sensed her seething hatred for Foley as she sat beside me in court today, her fingers digging into the cushioned armrests of her wheelchair.

I'd seethed hatred all day, too. Even now, as Avery lay beside me, her eyes glued to the TV, I seethed. Pushed it down, squashing it into a million little places so I could be the man my wife deserved.

"You did good today," I murmured, coasting my palm up along her arm. "Phenomenal."

She fiddled with the engagement ring I'd purchased for her from a shop in the Quarter. Gold filigree and topped off with a ruby, it'd reminded me of her. Delicate but with a badass outlook on life that turned me on in a way that no one else ever could. The simple gold band nestled along it had been slid onto her finger a month ago in Jackson Square, at the base of the steps of St. Louis Cathedral where we'd met.

"Love you," she said, craning her neck to plant a soft kiss on my neck. "Sorry, today has me all messed up."

I covered her hand with mine, then dragged it up to hold to my scarred cheek. "Don't apologize for doing what you needed to do."

Her fingers curled against my skin, and she swept her thumb over the corner of my mouth. "Don't tell me you weren't thinking about unloading a round in the back of his head the entire time."

With a kiss to her palm, I flashed her a quick grin. "Guilty as charged." I waggled my brows. "Too soon with the legal talk?" I slid on top of her, and her legs immediately separated to make room for my body. "Or maybe just right?"

The pucker between her brows cleared when she gave a light laugh. "Always making jokes when you shouldn't."

Leaning down, I nipped her exposed shoulder. "Haven't made a joke at a funeral yet."

"That's because the opportunity hasn't presented itself to you."

I winked. "Good point."

Dropping my mouth to hers, I sipped at her lips, pulling her out of her shell and back into the light. We'd shared a million different kisses. Soft, hard, challenging. This one, though, was all comfort.

She clasped the back of my head, and I chuckled against her mouth. "There's my brave girl."

Her hips rose off the bed to press against mine. "More than you know."

I rolled away. Ignored the tent in my sweats as I motioned for her to stand. "I'm gonna need you to be brave for me tonight."

Avery sat up, her hair mussed from the pillow. "Lincoln," she drawled, "I'm pretty sure I've slept with you enough times by now that you don't need to give me the *be brave speech* just before you drop your pants."

Laughter climbed my throat as I threw her a skirt from where she'd left the folded laundry earlier this morning. One fault we had? Neither of us enjoyed putting laundry away. We'd get to it, at some point.

Tugging a shirt over my head, I said, "We're going on a little drive. Something to perk you up."

"Oh, really?" She jumped out of the bed, then yanked

her skirt up her legs and settled it around her hips. A second later, she had a top on and was ready to go.

Christ, she could be fast when she wanted to be.

On the drive, she propped her chin on her hand and stared out the front window. "Are we going to our picnic spot?" she mused, reaching forward to turn down the volume of the radio. "Or maybe we're going to satisfy one of your late-night frozen yogurt cravings?"

She knew me way too well. When I wanted to play Mr. Romantic, I brought her to the same spot on the side of the levee with the view of downtown New Orleans. And when I wanted to make her laugh at me for having the same food cravings as a kid, I took her to the frozen-yogurt joint over on Magazine Street, where we could watch the traffic pass us by from the floor to ceiling windows.

Avery Washington Asher wasn't just my wife, she was my favorite person in this world.

I squeezed her thigh, then left my hand there. "Wrong," I said as I took us on the 1-10 and headed east. "Try again, ma'am."

She settled her hand over mine, overlapping our fingers. "All right . . . not a picnic, not frozen yogurt. Are we heading to the Quarter? You know how I feel about going down there on my nights off from the square."

"Are you saying that you *don't* like convincing tourists to give you more money now that you fully believe in the cards?"

"I always believed in the cards."

"That's because I taught you the best way to do it— pick the card you want and then tell everyone around that you're about to make the magic happen."

She snorted, fingers squeezing mine. "Guess it's going to be a surprise then."

Hell yeah it was.

Sliding my hand out from hers, I reached into my pocket and pulled out one of her scarves that she bought every other week from her friends in the French Market. "Put this on."

"Are we going to do something scandalous?" Her tone was playful, but she slipped the scarf around her head anyway, blindfolding herself, trusting me explicitly.

Maybe. Yes. One-hundred-percent.

With her sight blocked, I gunned the gas pedal and brought us into the Bywater. A few minutes later, we were parked, and I was walking around to Avery's side of the SUV. "Don't peek." I wrapped my hands around hers and pulled her from the car, careful to make sure she didn't tumble out. "It'll ruin the fun."

I led her up to the large brick building, ignoring the front entrance and choosing instead the new side door that led club members to the recently renovated second floor. Whiskey Bay wasn't Whiskey Bay anymore, and the Basement was a thing of the past—Nat had fled the state, taking with her my old coworker Josiah Templeton, and a few other folks like Kevan.

Quinn took bets that his old boss was living it up in Vegas.

Avery tossed in her vote for California-dreaming.

And I knew exactly where she was, thanks to Zak Benson trailing her out there and leaving crumbs wherever he went—but some shit was better to just keep to myself. So long as she stayed out of Louisiana, I didn't give a damn where she went.

"Watch your step," I told Ave, my hand on her lower back.

We climbed the steep staircase. Only when we were fully upstairs, the door locked behind us, the club-member key in my pocket, did I pull the scarf off Avery's head. Her delighted gasp was like fireworks in July, and I stepped behind her. Lowered my mouth to her ear, and murmured, "Like what you see?"

The new owner of the building had changed things up.

The old stage lights had been exchanged with fairy lights, strung up to create a romantic glow over the myriad couples that were positioned throughout the room. A four-string quartet—yes, a *quartet*—was seated in the far-left corner, playing a song that made the space less about the kink and more about the romance.

The sex was still the sex.

That would never change, no matter who owned the building.

"I feel like I should say no," Avery said, falling into me.

"Because we're married?" I nuzzled her ear, nipped the lobe. "You like what you like, but if you ever think someone else will touch you . . . that shit's not happening. You're mine, and I don't share."

"You don't even share your frozen yogurt."

"Damn right I don't." Squeezing her hips, I gave her a little push. "Find the stage you want, and I'll meet you there after I buy us cocktails."

She twisted to stare up at me. "How will you find me?"

Another nudge, this one to her ass. "I'll always find you, sweetheart. Always."

And I did.

Stage One wasn't the same—the couple up there weren't fitted with ball-gags—but I'd known she'd come back here out of memory's sake. She'd selected the same position on the sofa, though the furniture was all new. I sat next to her, handing her one of those frozen margaritas she liked so much.

Our cheeks grazed as we both leaned in.

"What's on the lineup?" I asked at the same time she

said, "I don't think he knows what he's doing. I mean, he's slapped her ass so many times I think I'm . . . I can't believe I'm about to say this, but I might be bored."

I glanced up at the couple on the stage with the fairy lights hanging so low that they were almost swimming in the cords. Sure enough, the dude was slap-happy. My brows arched when I counted ten in as many seconds.

"She's not going to be able to sit down for a week," I muttered out of the corner of my mouth.

"I know!" Avery shifted in her seat as if she were experiencing sympathy slaps to her ass. A second later: "My butt hurts just looking at them."

I set my beer on the small table to my left. "Don't worry, Captain America is here to save the day."

Avery snorted with laughter. "Please don't tell me you're about to pull out the hammer and show the poor guy on the stage exactly how it's done. You'll embarrass him while he's on the clock."

My fingers went to her skirt, and I pulled the fabric up, up, up until it was around her waist and she was thrusting her hips forward, no matter the protests that fell from her lips. And, no matter who owned the Basement now, and no matter what name it was called, Stage One would always be just about the same.

I got down on my knees before my wife, the soles of my shoes rubbing up against the stage, the sound of incessant slapping behind me. And for memory's sake, I ripped her underwear straight from her hips and jerked her close, so that my tongue could run along her slit.

"Don't worry," I said, just before I put every other man to shame in this room, "I won't make you jump out of any fire escapes tonight."

And then my mouth was on her clit, my hand clutching

her quivering leg, and all I heard was her gasp and the throaty way she whispered, "God, I love you."

I swallowed my laugh and set about making my wife come so loud she'd have an encore after. I probably would never know what I did to deserve her, but I would never give her up.

I love you, too, sweetheart. So damn much.

The End.

Dear Fabulous Reader

Hi there! I so hope you enjoyed the Blood Duet, and if you are new to my books, welcome to the family!

In the back of all my books, I always love to include a Dear Reader section that talks about what locations from the book can be visited in real life or what sparked my inspiration for a particular plot point.

We'll break it down bullet-point style :)

- The Sultan's Palace where Avery and Katie live is…real! But, much like in *Sworn*, the story is very much spun of tall tales and rumors. As the legend goes, a man arrived at the port of New Orleans around the 1860s and immediately rented out the property at Dauphine and Orleans from a well-to-do gentleman. Some months later, a ship arrived in the port and it took a full *week* for everyone to disembark and make the four-block trek to the house from the docks. Arriving from somewhere in the Middle East, it was a sultan, his harem, and his bodyguards. Once they entered the house, no one was ever seen coming or going until one night, some many months later, when a storm ravaged the city. The next morning, a little boy was running down the street when he caught sight of a trickle of blood leading down the front steps. He rushed to the police precinct, and they all hurried over. Opening the door, what they found turned their stomachs. There was the metallic scent of blood in the air and there were bodies strewn this way and that, all decapitated. They went to the courtyard in search of the sultan, and while the soil was still soggy from the night before, they found him there, his one hand reaching out from the ground, where he'd been buried alive. Who did it? Well, they say it was the first man who'd arrived in the city, perhaps the sultan's brother who'd orchestrated the whole thing, and who was jealous of all the riches his brother had….PHEW. That was dramatic, am I right? And all untrue, but it makes for a great story and I couldn't resist using it as the backdrop for Avery's apartment. It is actually an apartment building today, and thanks to some lovely condo owners who let me in while I was a tour guide, I can say that it's quite beautiful! But, yep, definitely not the stage of a horrific scene as the stories go! If you are keen to learn more, a quick search of "Sultan's Palace New Orleans" will bring it right up for you!

- Mr. Luis and I like to joke around that between the two of us, we have all the shadowy parts of New Orleans covered. Him as a police officer for the city, and me, as a former tour guide for a ghost tour company. When beginning *SWORN*, I became (rather) obsessed with the idea of a book that played in on inner-city politics, quietly hushed events involving our finest men in blue, and the local lore that is so intrinsically *New Orleans* that it can't be separated without causing a loss to the city's culture. New Orleans has been my home for over a decade, and it carries a torch of vitality that anyone who has ever lived here will just say, "Yep, that's New Orleans for you." We are a city of people that loves our history, and here are a few ways I pulled that all in to *SWORN*:

- Tarot readers in Jackson Square—aside from my mother reading Tarot and so having a special place in my heart, I truly wanted to bring this somewhat "otherworldly" feel into *SWORN*. The readers in Jackson Square are staples of the French Quarter, but they've had their rough patches with city ordinances cracking down on them, enforcing permits and times in which they can operate. Moreover, I wanted to show that Tarot isn't an "evil" thing, and like Avery showed us—it's all in the way the cards are read. Poor Lincoln! ;)

- The Atchafalaya Basin, also known as "Whiskey Bay"—the Basin has long since been a spot for, unfortunately, crime. Check online and you'll find article after article about bodies popping up. But what really interested me was the case of Baton Rouge's serial killer [name redacted here but can be found online] dating to the early 2000's. In fact, there were *two* serial killers operating at the same time in the same areas, though they had no known links to each other. Many of the victims were found in their homes, but a few were discovered at the base of the bridge of the Basin. When it came to Ambideaux, it felt important that he teeter the line of respectability—and, more specifically, that everything he did was calculated and methodical. A drive out to Whiskey Bay, and therefore seeming "innocent" of any of the people disappearing from New Orleans, fit his profile. Even so, I had to include the term "Whiskey Bay" somehow, and I hope Nat would approve.

- Sex and New Orleans go hand-in-hand. Home to Gallatin Street, a nineteenth-century strip of seven or so blocks that would make anyone quiver in their boots, it was once said that if you could make it on Gallatin, you could make it anywhere in the world. Fast-forward some forty years, and you'd find yourself smack-dub in the middle of the Storyville era, which was a quarantined section within the French Quarter that allowed all brothels to operate without penalty. Naturally, if you operated *outside* of that area in the Quarter, you'd be shut down immediately. Storyville produced Louis Armstrong—okay, well, he was born there and got his start there—and was the first legalized red light district in the country with some of the madams (i.e. Josie Arlington) making so much money that they mingled with politicians on the regular, owned some of the finest homes in the city, and were take-charge businesswomen, despite the unfortunate business they operated in. The Basement is my little nod to that era in time, which has always fascinated me. And I have to imagine that if Nat had lived at the turn of the century, she would have given any of those ladies a run for their money. Literally!

- I hardly know where to begin! But I suppose I can begin with one of the names from the book… Pershing University, anyone? Some who know New Orleans may have noticed that it is seated on St. Charles Avenue (think: gorgeous, gorgeous mansions) alongside Loyola University. Loyola is my alma mater, and Pershing (in my head) is Tulane University next door. There's always been a longstanding competition between the two schools, so it was fun to play on that! "Pershing," however, comes from General Pershing, the street I lived on once upon a time in the city.

- Flambeaux, the corner store that Pete and Sal own: did you know that "flambeaux" in New Orleans actually refers to the people who hold the lanterns during Mardi Gras parades? In much earlier years/centuries, these "flambeauxs" (as they were called) tended to be inmates who were allowed to come out and help and also earn a coin or two for providing light (and heat) along the route. Nowadays, parades still have "flambeauxs" but they aren't inmates - although tips are still appreciated! Pete's store is my little nod to this little part of New Orleans culture that is so firmly rooted in history.

- Captain America & Thor: Yes, I have an obsession. Yes, Mr. Luis knows. Yes, he also has man-crushes! Therefore, it had to be involved ;)
- The story Nat tells Avery: Do you remember the small anecdote that Nat tells Avery at the Basement? When she mentions the policemen who tried to cover up a murder? Yes, that is a *true* story, dating to the early 2000's. For many years, it was very hush-hush because of the gravity of the crime they committed, but the police involved were eventually caught and sentenced to jail. When I asked Mr. Luis for a story that would rattle our souls and show us just why Avery would have a hard time trusting anyone, that is the one he gave me. It's heartbreaking, terrible, but goes to show the nature of humanity, both the good and the bad.
- Algiers Point: Fun Fact (and get ready to learn how naive I was to Louisiana geography when I moved here a decade ago), Algiers is actually located just across the river from the French Quarter! Yes, I once fully believed that New Orleans was the farthest south you could go. Yes, I was promptly corrected *multiple* times by friends. No, you can't swim across the river, LOL. Since moving to this area of the city, I've found that it's actually one of the most romantic - especially at night when the city glitters across the river - and I couldn't resist staging a moonlight picnic with lots of steam and heat because…why not? LOL.

Although there are many others, I may have rambled long enough! LOL! If you're thinking to yourself, "*Did this happen in real life, Maria?"* Always feel free to reach out. I'm happy to talk New Orleans, and generally speaking, scandalous activities are my favorite discussion topics when it comes to history :)

Xoxo,
Maria

Also by Maria Luis

Nola Heart

Say You'll Be Mine

Take A Chance On Me

Dare You To Love Me

Tempt Me With Forever

Blades Hockey

Power Play

Sin Bin

Hat Trick

Body Check

Blood Duet

Sworn

Defied

Put A Ring On It

Hold Me Today

Kiss Me Tonight

Love Me Tomorrow

Broken Crown

Road To Fire

Sound of Madness

A New King

FREEBIES (AVAILABLE AT WWW.MARIALUIS.ORG)

Breathless (a Love Serial, #1)

Undeniable (a Love Serial, #2)

The First Fix

Black Widow

About the Author

Maria Luis is the author of sexy contemporary romances.

Historian by day and romance novelist by night, Maria lives in New Orleans, and loves bringing the city's cultural flair into her books. When Maria isn't frantically typing with coffee in hand, she can be found binging on reality TV, going on adventures with her other half and two pups, or plotting her next flirty romance.

Stalk Maria in the Wild at the following!
Join Maria's Newsletter:
https://geni.us/MariaLuisSubscribe

Join Maria's Facebook Reader Group:
Book Boyfriends Anonymous

facebook.com/marialuisauthor

instagram.com/marialuisauthor

amazon.com/kindle-dbs/entity/author/B06XRRS5QD

goodreads.com/marialuisauthor

bookbub.com/authors/maria-luis

tiktok.com/@marialuisauthor

Printed in Great Britain
by Amazon